NO MAN'S MERCY...

NO GOD'S

FORGIVENESS

I0658968

Zachary Mannheim – Book 1

John Hayden

Library of Congress Control Number: 2021921586

Names: John Hayden

ISBN: 978-1-7356187-6-0 (paperback)

978-1-7356187-7-0 (Epub)

ACKNOWLEDGMENT

The Military and Intelligence Communities share a constant concern for security. This acknowledgement suffers from being unable to identify officers of both communities, whose advice, concerns and opinions were critical to the development and publication of this story. I am grateful for everything learned in the process.

ALSO BY JOHN HAYDEN

ACT OF GOD

THE GARBAGE GAME

PERCEPTIONS OF DECEPTION

A SCORPION'S REVENGE

FALLING FROM HIGH PLACES

Terrorists aren't ignorant nut-jobs. Americans aren't super-heroes. Greed, lust and power make people stupid and crazy. If you can't live without too much money, sex or clout, there's no God worshipped on earth who'll save you. Don't make policy or grant clemency…that's above your pay grade. Do your job –

Fulton Bennett, Director/National Clandestine Service, Central Intelligence Agency, Langley, Virginia, USA

CHAPTER 1

A short fellow, who could be overlooked with ease, watched as the target ran towards the Bay and its marshland, half inundated by an incoming tide.

"I cannot," he stated in a milquetoast tone, preferring to abandon a clear act of desecration as set forth in the Qur'an.

Built like a gymnast, the second man's words provided reassurance. "This fellow is more sad than dangerous, more wicked than righteous, more pathetic than prideful. He chases his last moments on this earth. You will be strong not hesitant. Slit his throat in one deep cut. Avoid the gush of blood. He will fall of his own accord. Take no joy from his death. Go now before the tide takes him."

***

Frivolous conversation churned behind him where a dozen staffers, most of them little more than children, exhibited no comprehension of the pressure he suffered under. An odor of strong coffee wafted over and around the Honorable Lester Peale Morgan of Florida's 4th Congressional District. Eyebrows screwed into a look of consternation by these real or imagined injuries, he spoke over the chorus of fledglings.

"All due respect to the Subcommittee, but who gives a rat's ass about one dead spy? An emergency session at this ungodly hour, Mr. Chairman? Our limited attendance speaks for itself."

Three members of the House Subcommittee on Terrorism, HUMINT, Analysis, and Counterintelligence watched a smug smile spread across the face of its Chairman, Congressman Rupert Jones Perry of the Great State of Alabama.

After removing a *Roll Tide* mug from view, Perry observed to no one in particular, "Glad we're not recording the proceedings, Mr. Vice Chairman, since the Subcommittee's God-given purpose under the Constitution is bein' concerned with all the rats asses."

Laughter rose and subsided.

Congressman Jedediah Sewell, of the Great State of Maine, nodded discrete agreement; laughter was not conducive to the Subcommittee's sacred purposes.

"Y'all ready to go, Mr. Mannheim...any opening statement?" Perry's conversational tone suggested Subcommittee members could exercise informality, since the usual preening for the media could be dispensed with.

Mannheim, Chief of CIA's Counter Intelligence Center ("CIC") despised informality. "No opening statement, Mr. Chairman."

"Well, then, Zachary..." Congressman Perry's eyes sought concurrence from his Vice Chairman "...let's get to it."

Prepared with ill intent in too short a time, Daniel Santamaria, the Subcommittee's Chief Counsel, examined a list of questions. "Mr. Mannheim, please describe the circumstances of Mr. Probst's death?"

"Gunther Probst, a Field Director who served twenty-two years prior to his death, was shot in Cotuit, Massachusetts, three quarters of a mile as the crow flies from the residence of Ms. Raissa Ribeiro, a retired Field Officer. Mr. Probst teamed with Ms. Ribeiro on numerous assignments, several involving terminations of foreign nationals. Mr. Probst was not on duty at the time of his death. His appearance earlier that day, in Boston, interfered with an NCS surveillance operation involving multiple Agency assets. It's unknown whether Mr. Probst was aware of this error, but someone with his deep well of experience couldn't claim operational ignorance."

Mannheim saw Santamaria set aside the bulk of his questions at the mention of Raissa.

"Was Mr. Probst a security risk?"

"No."

"Was Mr. Probst a known pervert?"

Hushed by the attorney's ill-timed characterization, the room awaited a righteous retort from Zachary Mannheim.

"Mr. Probst was gay. There never was a report of inappropriate conduct."

"Ribeiro's running?"

The idea nauseated Mannheim. "Ms. Ribeiro's location is unknown. House and car are undisturbed. Her licensed weapons are secured in the house. No unusual withdrawals from any of her banks."

"There have been no withdrawals from bank accounts Ms. Ribeiro self-reported to the Agency?"

"Correct."

"Has CIC identified other funds available to a former Officer such as Ms. Ribeiro?"

Tempted to strangle Santamaria, Chairman Perry, believed it best not to return fire until, or unless, provoked in an unreasonable manner.

Mannheim's voice displayed an even temper. "No."

"Ribeiro's behavior warranted CIC's interest once or twice. Is she working as an independent?"

"Unknown."

"Given what we know, what do you recommend Mr. Mannheim? Should CIC be interested again?"

This is the tricky part, Mannheim admonished himself—getting past Santamaria's questions and onto the single item prepared for the Chairman.

"Probst's actions in Boston would've been informed…by what we don't know. The fact he's dead should give rise to a full CIC investigation."

Santamaria believed this mouse well trapped and ready for a lethal injection. "CIC has broad authority when internal Langley security is the subject. Your long history at CIC's helm, Mr. Mannheim, has shown repeated disinterest in this Subcommittee's oversight. Why are you here?"

Chairman Perry scratched an ingrown follicle on his chin. "Zachary, you said Ms. Ribeiro's current location is unknown…has she been interviewed since Probst's murder?"

"Yes, Mr. Chairman. I requested this meeting so the Subcommittee could listen to her recorded statement."

Santamaria rose to his feet. Perry sat him down without a word. "Is the tape probative?"

"The tape is the tip of an iceberg."

Congressman Morgan roused himself from earlier petulance. "Mr. Chairman, can we just get on listenin' to the tape."

Chairman Perry agreed. "Let's hear it, Zachary. Start with the who, what, where, when and why."

"Ms. Ribeiro requested a meeting, which she attended alone. She isn't under suspicion by any law enforcement agency, or by CIC, in Gunther Probst's death. The recording hasn't yet been subjected to detailed analysis. Ms. Ribeiro's voice has been verified. No other voice exists on the tape. The recording the Subcommittee will hear is the unedited original. There are no copies."

Tape begins:

"I stood at the window where a bubbling cauldron of clouds announced the devil's messenger. Wondered whether those clouds or my rotten mood would prove most intransigent. I quit smoking after the fire, but nicotine cravings were strident. Terrible memories clawed at me, not for the first or last time. Pain and loss again proved an unrelenting burden.

"How long ago had it been? Why did she hate me so? Wasn't burning me alive enough? I recognized this tragicomic baggage for what it was: Self-pity stored in a scheming corner of my brain. Drag me down, will you, with endless reminders and useless desires?

"*Goddammit*, I said it out loud as the *Hino Nacional Brasileiro* erupted behind me. Triangulation suggested the prepaid cell cohabited with the crockpot and rice maker. Numbers filled the screen. I scanned them girlishly, long enough for doubt to germinate. Imagine Raissa acting like a teenager. Such a silly response, when more pressing issues surrounded me.

"*Am I safe?*

"*Is he using me?*

"A woman in love, Mr. Mannheim...fathomless naiveté. The room whirled. Answers wouldn't be found in any factual account of Aaron and my lengthy relationship, and, though I attempted to avoid a third question, it persisted. Jesus, Mary and Joseph, I opened drawers, pulled out cereal boxes and looked in canisters for those cigarettes. Sweat oozed from facial pores...how's that sound from a super-model? I petitioned the walls and floors: *Does he still love me?*

From every voice which consoled, pitied or been glad of my misfortune came a grim judgment: *No. He never loved you.*

"Book ciphers, the old fashioned method, are my preference…encryption experts and their super-computers can't be thwarted by using the Bible, a dictionary or the meanderings of Sartre. Perfection comes from a book available only to those communicating via the cipher, though perfection can always be compromised by betrayal. I decided Aaron had a lot of balls to even ask: *Pick me up at eleven/4.* That last bit, the /4, told me his plane would land at Quonset, a State Airport in Rhode Island.

"Time became an issue, because arriving late was unacceptable on so many levels. Not a girl to stand naked too long, Raissa's love affair with fashion, fame, jealousy, drugs, money and death was an old movie which ended in flames. Naked made it easier for the horrid odor of burnt flesh to invade nose and psyche. Stand naked long enough and I couldn't prevent the re-emergence of the face that ignited my ruination. Tan leather pants. Off-white fisherman's knit over a sports bra. The hell with my hair. No jewelry or makeup. What else can they take from me, when everything Raissa once valued is gone?

"The Maranello was an anachronism; it looked like a super-model could own it. My hand absentmindedly scrounged under the driver's seat; the FNP-9 felt cool to the touch.

"No one could miss two security types at the jet's open door. Uncertainty is a bad thing for Raissa, Mr. Mannheim. Uncertainty precedes a bad ending as hesitation in the field precedes death. Aaron emerged carrying a thin, black briefcase in his left hand and a good-sized shopping bag in his right. After putting the bags in the Ferrari, he looked me up and down. 'Bet you still love me.'

"Can't explain it, but I leaned over and kissed him.

"He held the kiss several seconds before pushing me inches away. 'God you taste good. Let me look at you.'

"Like a schoolgirl, I said, 'Where to?'

"His face darkened for less time than it took to notice. Aaron maintains an extensive network of associates, sycophants, informers, and underlings. Ex-lovers don't qualify in any category. 'I brought you skates. I miss watching you skate.'

"'Are you serious, Aaron? You of all people know when I last skated.'

"Please. We can grab lunch after, before I give a speech.'

"My bullshit meter never twitched. 'Seven years is a long time, Aaron?'

"He didn't vacillate. 'Do you remember what you said to me...the last time I came to the hospital?'

"Rhetorical question, of course, issued as salve to the open wound of his absence. Raissa, not Aaron, not Fulton Bennett, not anyone else, declared a no fly zone around her damaged body. I told him with a thousand-watt smile, 'Sounds like fun.'

"In the Boston Skating Club's parking lot, Aaron placed the gift-wrapped box on the Ferrari's rear deck. New skates...my fingers caressed intoxicating white leather and razor-sharp edges.

"'Not enough time to order custom-made,' he said. 'They're nines, half a size larger than you used to wear. For expansion, you know.' Aaron's sense of humor suffered from atrophy. On the ice, my legs shook harder than did non-existent confidence. Music blared from the sound system as a talented teen worked through his competition routine. I heard a chorus of applause and looked up, embarrassed. Adulation now belonged to a boy of fourteen, not a has-been twice the kid's age. Three times I fell on my ass. An athlete's oldest friend and most persistent critic, the competitive Raissa expressed disappointment: *Success requires bearing pain for a minute, an hour or a week...quitting hurts forever.* Half an hour later, panting with exhaustion, I waited for Aaron.

"The boy sprayed a sheet of ice chips. 'Are you really Raissa Ribeiro? You could've been great...I mean...you are great. Would you skate with me?'

"I gave Aaron the skeptical look he deserved. Told the kid, 'You're too nice. My friend paid you, but thanks anyway.' I took the kid's hand.

"Aaron raised his voice. 'Gotta go. You look great out there. I'll get back to the plane in the Bentley.'

"Halfway around the rink something unattractive clicked into place. I searched the arena for paparazzi. Bright lights making me squint, the profile of a heavy-set man with a tripod appeared long enough to be certain: Aaron lied about lunch.

"Pissed-off...I wanted to catch the past and mangle it.

Old realities slapped me silly: Undercover is a place where lies are a convenience, where lies get tangled with other lies, and where lies steal hope and make killing easier.

"Dim, dirty and smelling of things dead or dying, the garage under Boston Common led to a left on Tremont and one of Aaron's favorite haunts.

"Why do this to me? What would he gain?

"A black mood, Mr. Mannheim, lets suspicions grow from their own seeds. I ran to the Aquarium MBTA stop where *Legal Seafoods'* glass façade couldn't be ignored. One scan sucked my lungs dry: Two shadows leaned across a table, close enough so their foreheads touched. Aaron whispered sweet nothings in another woman's ear. Prettier than me? Younger looking? How old do I look, when I'm trying? This whole time I'm staring through the window, breaking every rule of tradecraft, castrating common sense. I couldn't break away. Who will you call, Aaron Frankel, when you're alone and afraid? Who will love you when there's nothing left to love you for?

"Our eyes locked…his other woman and me.

"A man and woman, at the table next to Aaron's, glared at me.

"Jesus, Mr. Mannheim. Spellbound doesn't happen to Raissa. Years of hard-learned lessons screamed: Protect yourself. Frozen in the moment, my mind raced ahead of good sense.

"What's happening? Why is *she* here?

"Could it never have occurred to Aaron? He can't trust her. Not like he trusted me. All those faces should've stayed in the past. I waited for tears that wouldn't come, thoughts running close to a cliff where sanity hung on a knife's edge. Aaron Frankel, a juggler mingling three women in an infantile error, mixed business with pleasure in a daredevil's cocktail. What does that make Raissa: Ex-model, ex-skater and ex-lover?

"Yes to each, Mr. Mannheim, but I'm other things he holds no sway over.

"Careless is an excuse for amateurs; I backed away into the lunchtime crowd.

"More nimble than he appeared, the Paparazzo replaced me at the window, camera's burst-mode storing dozens of photographs of *Legal's* interior.

"Stupidity escalated out of control. My brain fought to assess images frozen in a time warp.

I yanked my hat down and found a rear corner table in the *Marriott's* bar.

"Soon enough Gunther's eyes flashed warnings as his electronic flash blinded me...one last, miserable, straw in a rotten day. Thank God the 9mil was missing from my purse. How would it have looked? Television video and scathing media headlines: *Burned Supermodel Runs Amok Threatening Crowd*. Gunther turned and hurried for the exit. Next second he's coming back at me, herded by a middle-aged man in a suit. Gunther was a complete professional; his act of desperation deserved applause. 'Apparently you got an expectation of privacy today, Raissa. Maybe 'cause you don't look too good. Maybe you still shootin'-up?'

"Down the rabbit hole, everything upside down.

"The man in the suit made the big Paparazzo wince. Bloody spittle erupted from the corner of his mouth: Memory card from the camera appeared, as if from nowhere, in my savior's hand.

"The Paparazzo fled as I pushed tears aside.

"Cursory examination of my savior's face delivered a chilling effect: Broken nose, beginnings of a second-chin, blank eyes, he stunk of Langley. 'Thank you, kind sir,' was the best I could do.

A magician fingering the memory card, he made it disappear without changing expression. 'Work's hard enough. Shouldn't get kicked when you're down.'

"Just some guy in a suit, intervening with a chivalrous tip of his hat...happens all the time. A guy who knows the other Raissa, knows my work history. I wiggled my fingers so he'd see what was expected. The man-in-the-suit let go...memory card floated into my palm without a sound. His face showed how sorry he was to leave without it.

"Once upon a time a tenth of the day's frailty would've seen me dead.

"Hard effort propelled my two-person kayak against a changeling wind. Seemed a good way to work out stress, when we left the dock. I remember telling Agatha: 'All-world stupid, Agatha, that's me.' She nodded with a philosopher's wisdom as the ebb tide sucked us towards Nantucket Sound. I turned out of the channel past a sliver of sandy beach...Agatha dove in, head of black hair bobbing to the surface. I yelled. 'Not the time or place. Come on, Agatha. Really?'

"With a shiver, I slid into chest high saltwater. Three strokes and my legs found purchase in the marsh. A hundred yards later, I stumbled.

"Agatha moaned.

"Adrenaline pumping, my fingers felt her muscular body, anticipating blood. A pathetic yelp escaped as she raised all eighty pounds, lifting her nose to where a fatal odor assaulted us.

"Enveloped in beach grass Gunther's body reminded me of a dead baby whale.

"A quarter mile distant, a car engine revved. I left Agatha with Gunther. After fifty yards of pointless sprint, I dug-in a heel breathing great gulps of air. Two assessments sliced me like a razor across a throat: My aerobic conditioning was non-existent and the killer would be over-hyped, feeling ecstatic and lousy at the same time, and in need of a place to collect his, or her, wits.

"Raissa didn't find it hard to dredge-up the stink of sweat, fear and the metallic taste of a target's blood. Somewhere the assassin kept a place to rest and cleanup before the most important part of the job; there's never been a pre-paid hit, so somewhere there'd be a meeting.

Facts are facts, Mr. Mannheim. Someone wanted Raissa up close and personal with the dead friend I'd trusted without reserve. Worst feeling you can imagine, letting your Field Director down, being responsible for Gunther dying like that, when he'd tried to warn me off. Anger blinded me. I sunk to my knees in the sand. Dead friend, bleeding dog, useless Raissa...perfect day for the opposition, Mr. Mannheim. Couldn't cry at first, then wept for hours."

Tape ends.

Funereal silence descended, her Congressional listeners having eavesdropped on a confessional more than a CIC interview.

Congressman Jedediah Sewell, veteran in-fighter and a politician not to be trifled with, broke the ice. "Must've been tough listening. She came to you because of your close relationship?"

"Never met before," Mannheim responded.

"So...where's Raissa now?"

Chairman Perry interrupted to restore order. "Lots of whys and wherefores, Jedediah. Let's focus on what it is the Chief of CIC wants from the Subcommittee. Proceed Zachary."

"Aaron Frankel, better known as the Terrorist's Banker, is no stranger to this Subcommittee. His recent involvement with Raissa Ribeiro, an old flame and the Agency's deepest cover officer, would be troubling enough. The idea Frankel and/or Raissa was surveilled by Gunther Probst, without authorization, is disturbing. The fact Probst perished trying to reach Raissa's home indicates a Field Director's emergent operational concern for his Agent. What concerns CIC is the disappearance of the memory card. Those images would tell us whose presence, beyond Frankel's, shocked and caught Raissa so off guard. Those photos warrant CIC's serious attention. My appearance before you this morning is FYI."

Congressman Perry, no stranger to Zachary Mannheim's obfuscation and occasional disinformation, responded in kind. "Bullwhistle, Zachary. Why isn't Ms. Ribeiro sitting next to you, telling her own bedtime story?"

"Would it be preferable to detain a private citizen by force, Mr. Chairman?" Farcical in its construction, the question spoke volumes.

"So she's scared shitless?"

Zachary moved his considerable bulk to attention and spoke with admonition and admiration. "Mr. Chairman, if Raissa is, as you say, scared shitless, how agitated should mere mortals be?"

***

Off to one side and apart from Lieutenant Tom Nichols, David Nazarian watched the third act in a sad ballet—the State Police Crime Scene Unit parrying bureaucratic thrusts from local County cops. Initiative would prove tricky. Applied with a trowel, it guaranteed failure. Applied with a Q-tip and a spy-hunter's chance at success evaporated. Either way, Nazarian knew, Mannheim's doghouse awaited the faint of heart.

Nichols seemed a decent sort when, before first light, Nazarian added misery to the Lieutenant's sleepless night. Advised of pending National Security implications, Nichols balked. An unexpected surprise—David arrived with coffee and the cooperative attitude of an old pro—eased the State cop's dismay caused by a wet, lonely overnight spent puzzling over two late-night phone calls. Nichols being wary enough to record the questionable calls was a blessing beyond expectation. A woman's voice, devoid of emotion, struck Nichols as educated and not local.

"Man's been executed...in the reeds near the local buoy where Pinquickset Cove meets the Bay."

All the call's implications proved impossible to grasp. Ambivalent reactions—no cop enjoyed being out of his element—Nichols had all but decided to hand over a contract killing to the local County Sheriff. Then his phone vibrated a second time.

An unrecognizable man's voice spoke six words. "Call Martin Haslett. The body's his."

Yesterday's suit, a wrinkled shirt, dirty underwear and a coffee-stained tie made a sartorial mess, but Nazarian's boots, fresh out of the box from the nearby LL Bean, kept his feet warm and dry. Technology, when treated with respect, was best applied in a similar way to initiative. Multiple phone taps and cameras, ordered contrary to a dozen legal prohibitions, required hours for implementation under ordinary circumstances. Threatened with Mannheim's wrath, Langley's technology crowd had worked all night.

Fingerprints taken by the State Police handheld resided on Nazarian's phone. Gunther Probst, now deceased, resided in Somerville, a hardscrabble pretender lying cheek to jowl with Boston, and worked hard to maintain his cover as a freelance photographer. Massachusetts law enforcement encountered Probst twice, DUIs quashed in both cases. Nothing in the records suggested a conspicuous life—exactly the desired outcome when a Field Director was the subject of inquiries.

Little could be cobbled together to explain the phone calls plaguing Nichols. Unless two plus two equaled seven, a summation not uncommon for Martin Haslett of the FBI. Unless Probst's life and death hinged on one spy's response to a convoluted situation, as David Nazarian could attest with growing regret.

Nazarian's presence at the crime scene could be explained by extrapolation of his position at Langley. Assigned to the National Clandestine Service (NCS), he reported to its Deputy Director, Fulton Bennett. An unofficial and occasional secondment to CIC, rife with potential conflicts of interest as it was, demonstrated David's ability to hurdle or side-step embarrassment and worse. This attribute made him both skillful as well as useful to Fulton Bennett at NCS and Zachary Mannheim at CIC.

No conflict burdened David this day. Both his masters prioritized an explanation of Gunther Probst's execution-style murder.

Nazarian hoped repetition would bring clarity, so queued up Nichols' latest call a fourth time.

"Hello...who're you?"

"Lieutenant Tom Nichols. State Police. Look...I'm standing at a crime scene on the Cape. Male...Gunther Probst. Fifty-three. Five eight or nine. Overweight. Freelance photographer floating in the beach grass with his throat cut and a double-tap in his forehead. Body's about to leave the scene, I'm assuming you care."

"You're an all-star prick, huh? Sat on this till your ass was covered. Where's the body headed?"

"Ask the Chief Medical Examiner's crew."

"Who found him?"

"I did."

"A State Police Lieutenant found the body. You shoot him?"

This sarcastic accusation, David figured, could be a fly in the ointment. Lies led to complications.

"No, I didn't shoot Mr. Probst. You comin' down?" Nichols felt no need to genuflect by addressing Haslett as Agent.

"Can you hold the body?"

"No, I can't."

"Like I said...you're a prick. Wait right where you are. Where can I land a chopper?"

Two miles trudged back to his rental, Nazarian wondered whether the forces at work in Probst's death would ever be understood. Nazarian would report every undisputed fact to Bennett and Mannheim. Anything else would comprise the ritual suicide of David's career; opposite sides of the same coin, oil and water were more compatible than Mannheim and Bennett.

Parked in front of Raissa Ribeiro's home on the bay, fight or flight would've required no debate for a spy in distress: Distance equated to safety. Nazarian couldn't afford that luxury. Yesterday's interaction with Raissa and Probst would, after the investigation ran its course, pass muster; no blowback would materialize. Hard truth was different: Shame was a crutch; woulda, coulda, shoulda a coward's game; and accepting blame the hardest thing in a spy's repertoire.

Fulton Bennett's credo held the single way forward: Do your job.

Nazarian plugged-in an earbud while waiting for Langley's notification that Nichols new phone could be monitored. Voice activated, he listened with no concern for an invasion of privacy.

Haslett. "Tell me again what the guy on the phone said."

Haslett's arrival surely brought Nichols a migraine headache. Six counting Haslett, all wearing business suits and shoes, they would've been none too pleased to find the crime scene underwater.

"Call Martin Haslett. The body's his. Won't make the words any different asking a ninth time"

"Your cell phone…the one you took these calls on, then lost looking for the body? I should believe that?"

"Don't give a shit what you believe."

"First call definitely a woman?"

"Could've been synthesized, but yeah, I'll stick with a woman."

"Didn't identify herself?"

"No."

"Your opinion…caller was Raissa Ribeiro…the old super-model?"

"Raissa's been living here a while. Stays to herself. People see her around…seems nice enough." Nichols resisted reminding Haslett: The old super-model wasn't very old.

"So you concluded she did the deed?" Haslett then asked the last of too many questions. "Why Raissa?"

"Rumors say she used to be a spy."

Tom Nichols' reputation would survive Haslett's skepticism.

Cape Cod could be an insular place and local sympathies would be foursquare behind Raissa. Did Raissa shoot Probst? Tom didn't seem to think so.

Nazarian's conclusion was straightforward: Buying Raissa twelve hours was what Nichols could do, and had done.

CHAPTER 2

Jamie Norris stood on one leg to lean around the doorframe and summon Yusef Schwartz. "Hey, Jew-boy can't jump. Grab your gear. Chop-chop."

Yusef's ears twitched at the absurdity.

In CIA's mailroom, where self-preservation trumped immutable laws of physics, the more clever faces remained impassive. Not strong enough to spawn revolt, nor unusual within a culture which devalued routine drudgery of mailroom employees, the words failed to qualify as abuse. Spewed without forethought or malice, by a man both familiar yet unknown, Norris's disembodied face lingered in the doorway long enough to see his words heeded.

Maury Lipmann felt a familiar sting of resentment. Mail-room Manager, his title held no sway with those who rode the elevator. The man in question rode it like the patrician his title and parentage warranted. Maury wouldn't piss into the wind.

Norris reset his stocky frame, nearly colliding with Fulton Bennett. Almost certainly the team would be late.

Bennett's mind lived in several different time zones, calculating probabilities of success and the implications of failure. "Be just like those jerks to want a forfeit."

Jarrick Ervan Taylor, gym bag in hand, adopted a half-sneer as he addressed Yusef. "I know your secret."

Yusef grabbed for the brown paper bag imprinted with diagonal slashes of maroon. Security and a chain of custody demanded no one meddle in his most important task.

Lipmann and Schwartz collided elbows as they both sought the bag. Irritated, Maury told Schwartz, "I'll get it. You go."

Schwartz ignored both men. With painstaking care each piece of paper was collected, re-inserted and the Burn-bag re-closed.

***

Two black Suburbans hardly constituted a motorcade. In the lead vehicle, which held four men and a woman, the driver felt pressured by Director Bennett. Fifteen feet behind, a second SUV carried three men and two women. The makeup of teams was rigid: No fewer than three women on each squad; no less than one woman on the floor at all times. For each player under twenty-five, a team was required to carry one player over forty-five.

Fulton Bennett, at fifty-seven, reveled in being a hard-nosed prick. This trait amounted to a minimal job requirement for America's Spy-in-Chief.

Sarah Gullickson, former second-team All-American with a Masters in International Relations, and an officer on the rise in covert operations, whispered to Jamie, "Things set up at Frankel's love nest?"

Norris made an obscene gesture. "Guess those Wall Street cocksuckers won't be so keen on Fearsome Frankel, when the blogs go crazy."

Unprofessional language curtailed, Jamie wondered whom Sarah would recruit to screw Aaron Frankel's brains out. An agent operating under non-official cover, inserted next to Frankel, would represent another in a series of complex steps to dismantle the money management side of international terrorism. Controversial, it was a plan with supporters and detractors which continued its Top-Secret classification. Jamie frowned at the thought of failure's ramifications. Sarah was always probing; what she wanted to know counted as different from the literal nature of her question. Street smart, yet willing to push her perky little nose, and likely her perky little whatever, where it didn't belong, made Jamie wonder how far Sarah might push the envelope.

"Careful, Sarah." Jamie stared until her blue eyes turned away. "You better get a clamp on Ayeesha today. She's been on fire lately."

Yusef dozed. Players came and went with Bennett's mercurial

temper and unrelenting ambition. Commonplace among Bennett's Bashers was an impression of Yusef as the polar opposite of Bennett—a man with no temper or ambition

***

"I hate this place." Bennett chewed on a section of orange while pressing an ice bag on his left eye. "Goddam POAC. Goddam piss-poor shot selection. Asshole hit me with his elbow on purpose."

POAC's identity as the Pentagon Officer's Athletic Club, having fallen to egalitarian correctness, now carried the unisex moniker of Pentagon Athletic Center. Available to any employee prepared to hazard the crowds, Bennett's Bashers huddled in a corner waiting for their leader to regain control. Nowhere near the finest of several Pentagon teams, General Cook's crew trailed CIA's best by a mere three points.

Bennett lowered protective goggles. "Push the ball. JET...you and Jamie fill the lanes. Sarah...look for the baseline cutter." Bennett's instructions meant less than nothing as motivation and damned little as basketball wisdom.

One thing concerned Yusef Schwartz: *I know your secret.*

General Cook set a screen which leveled Yusef. Bennett, guarding a taller opponent, got lost in the ensuing switch. An intolerable outcome was reversed as Jarrick Ervan Taylor, former first round draft choice, rose from the floor, blocked a stunned Major's layup and watched the carom turn into an easy bucket for the Bashers.

Bennett thrust his fist in the air.

Yusef re-established a defensive position, his mind refusing to focus. Which of my secrets could Jarrick Taylor know? Never seeing a long pass, the ball clanked off a metal folding chair, bringing Yusef back to earth. Bennett's team had reversed a five-point lead into an identical deficit.

"Bullshit," screamed Bennett.

Yusef's garden-variety life appeared little different from a hermit's existence. To abandon a lifetime of mental discipline would be the emotional equivalent of throwing himself off a bridge. Despite what childhood hardships burned into consciousness, ego's prickliness picked this moment to arise from long-suffering slumber.

Near the top of the circle, Yusef waited for the double-team.

Filled with hubris he lifted from the floor, floated higher, and watched his shot plunge through the net. Seconds before the double-team could react, he stole Cook's entrance pass for an uncontested dunk. Leaped to steal a second inbound attempt by the General, hurling the ball in one continuous motion. Watched Sarah drain an uncontested shot: Eight points for the Bashers in seven seconds.

In the *Book of Proverbs* the Lord detested a proud look, a lying tongue, hands that shed innocent blood, a heart which devised wicked plots, feet that were swift to run into mischief, a deceitful witness that uttered lies, and he that sowed discord among brethren. Seven Deadly Sins weren't the exclusive province of Catholics, Jews or Muslims, although Muslims made no assertion of seven as a magic number. Idols, raised to be worshiped alongside Allah—there was a serious sin for a Muslim. Sins, in Yusef's experience and belief, were both misunderstood and over-rated—if sin existed outside the abstract. Tit for tat platitudes, theology and morality were false gods in the reality of lives lived under the threat of sudden, violent, end.

Product of a love affair between an Israeli and a Palestinian, fluent in Arabic and Hebrew, Yusef had been confused as a boy by the cultures and religions in his life. Two decades after his mother died in a terrorist's bomb blast and his father on a desert battlefield, Yusef preferred the practical nature of God described in *Proverbs*.

Yusef detested pride which revealed him to anyone with eyes to see.

Face dripping sweat into a towel, the game's progression was unchanged with the exception of JET's thousand-watt grin. Maybe you fooled those other fools, the toothy expression announced, but not me: *No run-of-the-mill dickhead can move like that. You, Yusef Schwartz, aren't what you play at.*

***

Darkness hid Yusef running the streets.

Dressed from hoodie to running shoes in black, moving at a pace that would wither all but world-class marathoners, arms pumped with fluidity and legs maintained a monotonic stride. Discipline would be imposed over a rebellious nature.

Dribs and drabs of information would be analyzed.

A parallel circuit in his brain took notice of the bulk of Nationals Park on his left. Later, as the Navy Yard dominated his right side, he turned onto 7th and ran under I-395. No one would see him emerge.

CHAPTER 3

Guilt pressed hard as Andrew Poynter escaped the taxi, shut in on all sides by traffic as it approached Union Station. Horns blasted, one of which emanated from a Langley watcher. Andrew flipped them the bird, pressing through a maze of vehicles and harried travelers.

Two watchers jumped from parked cars. Two more extinguished cigarettes in preparation for entering the train station.

Nasha meant perfume in Arabic—Nazarian googled it.

Her scent clung to Andrew's cheek where thirty minutes ago his wife's tears stained the gray wool of last year's best suit. Hair pulled back in a tight bun, face unadorned by makeup still to be applied, beautiful despite having given birth to their second child four months earlier, his departure—a day before their eleventh wedding anniversary—stung as hard as a hundred hornets.

Indelible now, Poynter would be wishing time could be warped and the moment replayed. Andrew's explanation, tossed at her like dirty boxer shorts for the laundry, suggested a devaluation of intimacy. "Marco's in Munich; he needs me."

Andrew Poynter belonged to the Church of England. Numerous conversations, taped at Nazarian's direction, demonstrated meanderings about religion's possible impediment to long-term marital bliss. An insufferable British father never failed to express more aggressive views. Offered often enough they created disharmony between father and son.

"I don't disapprove because she's a damned Muslim, Andrew, don't you see? Nor do I hold her at fault for having been raised by the Jew banker. I don't disapprove at all. I think you'll disappoint each other and the children you are blessed with."

In the secret world, no tradecraft was needed to determine Andrew viewed his father as unfair: A son's every flaw highlighted, but nary a blemish in a daughter's crown of English roses. In Caroline Poynter Panero, Sir Edward Poynter saw perfection, not whom Caroline was and would forever be.

Video from watcher 3 depicted Andrew in line to grab a doughnut and coffee for the train. He texted Marco: *Nasha will regain the bounce in her step.* After all, his trip was business. Its fruit would feed the family, and his explanation contained little more than a guiltless lie.

Within the station's din, distilled from a thousand conversations conducted in shouts and whispers, David Nazarian discerned the sharp contact of high heels on marble.

Practiced in their cadence, she was long-legged and statuesque in bearing, not in mammary measure. A lengthening line brought her to a sudden stop at Andrew's shoulder, one high-heeled shoe tapping impatience.

Andrew turned.

Come to life in a midnight black suit with a mysterious V-neck, any man's fantasy examined the menu board. Her voice, sweet syrup as she tossed ultra-fine hair over her right shoulder, ordered black coffee. By the gift of her shoes' height, she was taller than Poynter's sixty-eight inches.

Aided by sucking in his stomach and standing tall, Andrew managed not to gape.

Nazarian could only wonder what Marie was doing here.

Amtrak's Northeast Regional was announced. On Nazarian's phone screen, Andrew juggled luggage and a single bagel, clenching a coffee between his teeth. Cut by the plastic, he swore, losing track of high heels now three paces to his rear. Andrew maintained a discrete distance behind a small man carrying an umbrella and wearing a multi-colored knit hat. In Coach number three, one behind the Quiet-Car, Andrew muscled his carry-on into the overhead rack. An Asian businessman sat on Andrew's left by the window.

Nazarian's watcher slid into the isle seat one forward of Poynter, phone angled to show both men.

Andrew nodded at his companion with studied diffidence. With similar lack of enthusiasm, the diminutive Asian in a gray sweater vest acknowledged Andrew with a minor bow.

No conversation appropriate, eye contact between them made one thing clear to David Nazarian: Behind round, dainty lenses the Asian man was afraid. Distress afflicting his seatmate created a vague apprehension in Andrew.

All the signs of a data transfer were present. When the train arrived at BWI or Newark, the Asian would depart, leaving behind a memory stick. Only when the train reached Penn Station in New York would Andrew take possession. So why would the courier be frightened?

Andrew was adroit enough not to stare.

When the train accelerated out of New Carrollton, Andrew evaluated the wisdom of looking for the dark-haired woman in the Café Car. Watched his companion's body grow rigid. Andrew stayed seated and the businessman issued a second nod of recognition. Sixteen minutes passed before the Asian rose with the conductor's announcement of the train's arrival at BWI, departing without word or glance.

Andrew Poynter eyed the empty coffee cup with a hungry look.

***

Shown in high definition by cameras fixed throughout the home, Nasha Gemayel Poynter hurried from the front porch of their Arlington, Virginia home, when screams were heard inside. Bathrobe clutched around her, she found Miriam plastering egg over her brother's fresh onesy. She tilted her head and smiled.

"You wait till Brad gets bigger, little lady. He'll remember who tortured him."

Regret slathered over her choice of words, she kissed Miriam's forehead in silent apology. Torture was never a good analogy, when it came to children—her children in particular.

Lucia Morales let herself in, observing the high chair and its wriggling occupant. "Good morning, Miriam, how are you this beautiful morning?"

Nasha called from the kitchen. "I'm at the sink, washing egg off Lord Bradford. Ask Princess M how it got there. Andrew's away...could you wash her face, please, so school doesn't think me the world's worst mother."

Ten minutes later, in a conservative dress and one-inch heels, wearing a minimum of makeup and absent any jewelry, Nasha backed the minivan down the drive.

Nazarian spoke on a comms-set. "Does Mrs. Poynter have her phone?" As long as she had either her personal or work phone, the watch-team was good-to-go. Hacked by Russia, England, Israel, Langley and likely several others, the Lebanese embassy's intra-office video calling system was a leaky old boat.

A fake British accent responded. "Everything sorted, Guvner."

"Don't be a dick, Tommy."

Nasha sat in her office examining pink message slips with evaporating resolve. Coffee cold, gooey Knafe made a puddle of sweetness in a suddenly too hot office.

"Come in," she said in English, when rapping on the door jolted her.

Colonel Nabil Hanna's blocky build was crowned by a thick scar near a bushy mustache. In Arabic, Hanna inquired with a directness unsuited to their professional relationship.

"Nasha, why are you sad?"

Hanna's interest in the emotional state of embassy staff was often described as non-existent. Chief of Intelligence, if one ignored the oxymoron, Hanna was cunning and a terrorist by inclination.

"Because, my dear Colonel, this draft for the embassy's website is dry and dense. Most of my week will be devoted to fixing it."

"Who wrote the draft?"

Nasha tasted bile in his question. "Not the ambassador. Otherwise, what does it matter?" Her face told Hanna: If the Ambassador thought her words inadequate, then so be it. She wouldn't be belittled by Nabil Hanna.

Dedicated to catching-out those with flexible loyalty, in public Hanna pined to return home to Sidon and his beloved Mediterranean. Though it would pain him to admit, gossip described the aging spy as a troglodyte with a fancy man-cave overlooking the Potomac.

When she held his gaze without blinking, he drew the laptop screen towards him and donned reading glasses. Hanna's disapproval of women in high positions was wrapped in vacuous charm. An unaffordable anachronism in twenty-first century Washington, a false face was a staple of life in the male dominated Arab desert.

Hanna never hid his sexual interest in Nasha. The new Ambassador's weak, Western style of appeasement required he mask his intentions.

Nazarian's familiarity came from witnessing these skirmishes on at least three occasions. Nasha's habitual defense settled into a faux undressing: David's mind's eye saw it CAFB. Rough hands would release his man-girdle. Paunch sagging over a shrunken groin, he pleaded for manual stimulation to achieve arousal. Fantasy always ended in revelation: Nabil Hanna would slit her throat before allowing his sexual failure to be flouted on social media.

Lebanon's long endured suffering, none of which can be considered the fault of its peace-loving people, continues. We share with the United States a sincere belief in the dignity of mankind. We pledge to dedicate our actions to counter the goals of those who would terrorize the citizens of the world. Hanna held a straight face as he lifted his eyes from the screen.

"Where's the fanciful, soaring vision of a perfect world brought about by the partnership of poor, lowly Lebanon with the high moral fiber of the US of A?"

"Mock me as you wish, Colonel. The language should offend no one in Lebanon, states our case to Americans who visit *Lebanon Online*...and the hell with everyone else."

Besides Hanna's inability to bring Nasha to political or sexual heel, Nazarian understood his excellent reasons for critiquing her: Nabil Hanna's dossier on Nasha Gemayel Poynter exposed not a Gemayel, but a Beirut street urchin adopted by a well-to-do family. In a debate about nature versus nurture, not that the Colonel would engage in such absurdity, his opinion favored genes. How else could she have grown to become taller than many Lebanese men, a graduate of the American University of Beirut and Harvard's Kennedy School of Government, a favorite of the new Ambassador and a high order bitch? Among odd associates and personal traits, Nasha's marriage to Brit-the-Twit most rankled the Colonel. Marrying beneath her substantial intelligence suggested a motive besides love or lust.

Hanna left Arabic behind. "How are Andrew and the children? Is my favorite Promise-Man out on the hunt?"

"Really, Colonel, is there Embassy business you wish to conduct today?"

CHAPTER 4

Within minutes of Yusef's absorption by the underpass, a garbage truck groaned as it geared-down. He hurtled down the concrete embankment to flop like a coked-out high jumper into the truck's rear bucket. Plastic tarp forming a barrier between man and waste, he couldn't be distinguished from a cadaver, pulse ticking at forty-two beats per minute.

Concern or curiosity served no purpose as the destination varied each time. Eyes closed, hands clamped across his abdomen, there'd been no communication amongst Yusef and Hassan, his contact. No emissions of radio, infrared or intergalactic waveforms would allow the Great Oppressor to triangulate and target him. Too many combinations of people and events made for too many worries. Life as Hassan lived it proved the value of simplicity, although the true name of an otherwise sincere prophet of global change remained undiscovered.

Time stretched until the machine's bowels vibrated.

Trust or doubt counted for nothing; faith was what a man could rely upon. Materialized from the garbage across from Anacostia Senior High School, he broke into a run in towards Good Hope Road.

Inshallah, in Arabic, had three accepted interpretations: If Allah wills; when Allah wills; or If Allah wishes. A man of singular caution, placing his future in the hands of the almighty counted as a most substantial accomplishment.

All because of Sarah Gullickson's indiscreet conversation.

A cold drizzle spattered the sidewalk. Even given the reduced visibility produced by misting rain, the woman couldn't be identified as Shelly, his prior greeter. Blonde and skinny, in the way of an end-stage drug user, fit a description of Shelly. Not this woman. Seconds separated Yusef from a final decision. Anxiety made for a conflicted few beats of a heart trained for such moments. Closer still, the woman wore a white tube-top over firm breasts and hooker heels; she chewed an acrylic nail extension covered in glitter.

"S'posed to be hurryin' to get fucked. Get on up here."

When Yusef reached the porch, her arms encircled his neck, legs wrapped around his waist. She kissed him violently, while hands worked his upper torso, down his backside and squeezed into his crotch, all in the manner of an overeager lover.

"Take me into the house," she directed as bright green hair buried itself into his neck.

For a watching world, her performance signaled sexual coupling. Left hand opening the front door, her right gave the appearance of slapping his rear. The penlet stung as its contents infiltrated his body. Not yet feeling the drug's full effect, Yusef stumbled in anticipation. In preceding visits to Hassan, nothing like this had been part of the security protocol. Should the expiration of his earthly vessel come next, his soul's eternal journey would be uninterrupted.

"Would you like tea?"

Yusef heard proper English words and judged them sincere.

An imposing man wore a well-fitted, dark suit. Relaxed, his demeanor fit a professional doing a job of work. "Alexis will assist you, otherwise you'll burn yourself." Distinct tonality marked the voice, but Yusef's effort to assess origin or intent failed.

What drug? What might its half-life be?

Yusef drank what the woman offered without resistance. Examined his location and its occupants through eyes beginning to cloud over. His verdict was reached on the drug's short-term nature; a brutal headache would arrive later.

"Please, Mr. Schwartz. Focus your attention on me. It is I whom you came to visit."

This didn't seem right. Through tapered cloudiness, Yusef responded in Arabic. "Is Hassan here?"

"Hassan isn't your concern. Please be still while the leads are attached."

Fear of a polygraph made no sense to a man whose intention was to tell the whole truth. With nothing to hide, why would I lie?

Strong hands ripped running gear over his head.

Yusef wouldn't accept the obvious. To underestimate an opponent was always a mistake, whether in basketball or politics. The big man will start with a preliminary test to gain information for control questions, then follow with a stimulation test where he'll want me to lie. I'll pass, if he judges my physiological responses during probable-lie questions to be larger than those of the baseline.

Good 'ol Boy, standing on the sideline, will shoot me if I don't pass, or if my performance is judged inadequate.

"Mr. Schwartz, what is your heart rate?"

Yusef assessed the examiner as Swiss. "Fifty-five."

"Are you an athlete?"

"Yes." Yusef knew to stick with yes and no responses, when it served his interests.

"Are you an employee of CIA?"

"Yes."

"Are you a covert officer?"

"No." The Swiss knew CIA employed officers not spies.

"Are you an honest man?"

"No."

"Are you a religious man?"

"Yes."

"Are you a practicing Muslim?"

Yusef thought the question poorly worded, but understood its basis. "Yes."

"Are you married?"

"No."

"Would you enjoy sex with Alexis?"

"No."

"Are you a homosexual?"

"No."

"Were you born in Israel?"

"Yes."

"Your father was Israeli?"

"Yes."

"Are you Mossad?'

"No."

"Did you kill Hassan?"

Caught off guard, could Hassan be dead? Physiologically, nothing was altered by this thought process. "No."

"Have you ever thought of killing Hassan?"

"No."

"Have you passed CIA secrets to Hassan?"

There could be cameras. This could be a trap; answering other than with the truth was unthinkable. "Yes."

"Were the secrets valuable to Hassan?"

"Hassan never offered an evaluation, but received my information with deference."

The Swiss never indicated displeasure with the answer's inappropriate length. "Are you afraid of going to prison?"

"No."

"Afraid of death?"

"No."

"Are you overconfident in your ability to continue traitorous behavior?"

This was an attempt to raise Yusef's blood pressure and heart rate. "No."

Accompanied by a hand motion indicating the blonde man, the Swiss asked, "Would you shoot me, if so instructed by Billy Ray?"

"No."

"Are you here to harm the cause?"

"What cause?"

"Hassan's cause."

"No."

The Swiss maintained eye contact with Yusef, addressing neither Alexis nor Billy Ray with specificity. "This man has been truthful."

We are live streaming, Yusef concluded: Audio and video over a private, encrypted, network. He spoke to an ethereal presence with purposeful recalcitrance.

"I have important information specific to Aaron Frankel. I need a meeting with Frankel...no one else. Can you arrange that?"

In clipped English, an educated, disembodied, voice responded.

"Your prior information is low level drivel. You work in CIA's basement, an aging athlete kept on by Bennett too long. You're a malcontent, Mr. Schwartz. You'll tell me what's so important that only an errand boy should be entrusted to convey it. Or you may leave. Speak again without answering and you will die."

With a choice of Hebrew, Yusef answered. "Whoever you are, Sheikh bin Rahman will cut off your balls and feed them to your children for allowing a boil to fester."

The next words Yusef heard imitated his Hebrew. "Kill him. Dump his corpse near the river. Rats need to eat."

Neither Alexis nor Billy Ray moved. The Swiss's smile indicated resignation.

Still in Hebrew, Yusef insisted. "So you're a Jew? I need to talk to Frankel. I don't care if you're the Prime Minister of Israel, or King of Saudi Arabia." Provocative language had been impertinent and a distinct risk, however identifying and assessing those employed by Sheikh bin Rahman defined his mission. Does bin Rahman speak Hebrew? Who would use Hebrew? Why? Who among the listeners understood their exchange?

Clarity could be achieved in a process of elimination—the Swiss was more than a polygraph examiner.

Ego assured Yusef he could identify the detached voice, if heard in a different setting. Though frustrating, second thoughts brought lucidity: The voice could be anyone, including an electronic someone. Could its origin have been female? He began to process syntax looking for a pattern. Only with identification of the voice could he be successful, or safe.

The Swiss's face showed veiled amusement.

"We're done for tonight. Go home, Mr. Schwartz."

***

Panero's file provided basic information: Marco spoke his native Italian, German, French, Chinese and Russian in addition to English. Born in Milan, educated in Britain and the United States, his company was a well-known defense consultant to industries and governments across the globe. Shaped like a duckpin, his bald pate gave rise to good-natured ribbing he suffered with apparent aplomb.

Charlatan was the descriptor applied to Panero by Andrew's father, who believed serving multiple masters qualified a chap as shady. Married to Andrew's sister Caroline, the Panero couple enjoyed homes in London, Washington, Berlin, and Hong Kong.

Andrew's little white lie claimed Marco summoned him for an important opportunity, whereas a high-speed tour in a factory fresh BMW was Marco's true ambition. On its maiden voyage, they'd prepare Andrew for Paris, Cherbourg, and on to Mumbai.

For not the first or last time, Nazarian puzzled over the attention being shown this family of small-time spies and crooks.

"Must I slog out to Cherbourg?" Andrew's voice sounded testy. "Sorry, Marco, my freaking legs are still cramped. Brain must be mucked-up as a result."

David revisited the contradiction Andrew Poynter presented. Is Andrew a pleasant buffoon, or play-acting? Sir Edward, no fool, couldn't be this blind. Caroline, despite an indulgent decade in the glamour industry, didn't lack for cunning or intelligence. Could brilliant genes produce a man organically ordained a jester?

Marco wondered if his brother-in-law would appreciate the irony. "Napoléon transformed a perfect natural harbor into a major transatlantic port...an equestrian statue commemorates his boast that in Cherbourg he recreated the wonders of Egypt...though there are no pyramids nearer than the Louvre. Don't indulge in foreplay with Marcel...he's in it for the money. He'll meet you at the Cité de la Mer...marine life explained in a hands-on sort of way. *Redoubtable* is there. You'll meet Marcel at the sub's boarding area. Looks like an engineer...quite unmistakable."

Poynter asked with realistic curiosity, "How does the money get transferred?"

"Cherbourg possesses a quaint Gallic ambiance. Find a warm café. Relax with a coffee or glass of wine...ferries will be empty and so will Cherbourg. Your job isn't the money. Your job is to smell our French friend's armpits. Marcel will be edgy. Calm him. If you're convinced the two of you have been ignored, give him the e-mail address and password." Marco held out a slip of paper for Andrew to memorize. "If anyone approaches asking directions to Le Havre...leave without another word. Board the fast ferry to Portsmouth and go to your father's house. Clear?"

"What will Marcel give me?"

"Nothing."

Andrew's puzzled face asked the question for him.

David thought Andrew Poynter a cranky fool.

"Come on, lad. My wife's brother can't be found in possession of classified French military secrets."

"So...some kind of electronic exchange?"

"Just so." Marco glanced at the speedometer. "How did things go on the train?"

From his jacket pocket, Andrew withdrew the thumb drive; held it up as evidence. "No difficulty, but the courier was jumpy as hell."

Taking the memory-stick, 64 GB was what Marco had anticipated. Moderate though the French data would be, it barely scratched the surface of what could be offered to the military starved Brazilians.

"Couriers invent things to worry about. Our Malaysian friend suffers an overactive imagination. You know the embarrassment with the KD Tunku Abdul Shahman?"

"Nine hundred million for two Scorpènes...one couldn't submerge upon delivery."

"Let's not ignore allegations of a 540 mm Ringgit commission paid to a close associate of Prime Minister Najib. That's enough to make any law abiding parent of a Royal Malaysian Naval Officer jittery."

Poynter offered Marco an admiring glance.

Even given Nazarian's less than educated technical expertise, tracking and killing submarines relied upon hearing them. So Marco's ultimate goal was to sell unique sound signatures of submarines, from multiple countries including NATO, for use in anti-submarine warfare by Brazil. Success in France would be followed by a similar foray into India.

"Who do I meet in Mumbai?"

"In 2005, India chose the Scorpène design, purchasing six boats for $3 billion. Those submarines are being manufactured at the government-owned Mazagon Docks. India operates fifteen diesel-electrics and two nukes. Fear of the Chinese is the impetus. You'll stay at the Taj Lands End by the Bandra Sea Bridge. Jayant Murtha is our guy...a big cheese at the shipyard. He'll be careful whom and where he meets. You do everything he says and along the line you'll get what we need."

Marco's fixed stare suggested twenty questions would elicit no elaboration.

Andrew's mouth felt full of cotton. "India will be dangerous?"

"You don't acquire state secrets without risk, m'boy."

Andrew sweat bullets at the thought.

Marco tried to lessen his distress. "Truly Andrew, Murtha's extra careful, that's all. Be a tourist...there's the Mahalaxmi Temple, devoted to the Goddess of wealth." Marco slapped Andrew's leg. "We approve of wealth, don't we my boy?"

***

Köln-Bonn Airport provided Nazarian's anticipated migraine headache.

Andrew paid for the VIP Lounge and powered his phone down until his flight to Paris was called.

David rifled through his phone for a local stringer. Considered a call to Marie Truchet, who was a wild card in a den of thieves.

At Charles de Gaulle, Andrew's phone came on-line while transiting customs as a Canadian named Anthony Trout. His blue passport's micro-printing, holographic images, UV visible imaging, watermarks and other security details were authentic.

David wanted dinner, three beers, and sleep, none of which was possible. He waited, contemplating another line of work.

Avenue George Cinq was home to the renovated Hotel Prince de Gaulle. After entering the grand lobby, a teenage girl in a beret, jeans, sloppy sweater and tennis shoes knelt in front of Poynter. Andrew went down in a heap on top of her. Inches from the girls unadorned face, he began to apologize.

Fueled by urgency, she spoke in Andrew's ear, near enough to his phone so David heard, "Don't check in. Find a hotel off the grid. Come to La Fermette Marbeuf at ten o'clock."

"Shit," Nazarian said out loud. "Goddam Marie, I should've bought her off."

Jet-lagged, Andrew's mind fogged. If this pesky girl hadn't waylaid him, if she would—wait, something's out of place.

Her fist punched his shoulder. "I work for Marco. Do what I say." She hurried out through those revolving doors.

Andrew's Amtrak fantasy wasn't an apparition; she was all too real. He walked the short distance to the Champs-Elysée, managing a modicum of dignity.

As Sir Edward Poynter's strapping son, he made a living by introducing salivating executives to government officials of various stripes. But Marco meant to procure and deliver real secrets to Britain's enemies.

After a lengthy delay, Nazarian heard Andrew's final words, perhaps sparked by some ancient British poet. "Where blood and treasure mingle as exotic temptation, perchance a brother may compete with sister sorcerer for father's truest affection."

CHAPTER 5

After a mandatory on-line meeting at Langley, David lingered, hoping for a word with Mannheim. He switched feeds to see Nasha staring out a window at a man halfway down the hill, a pall of nicotine vapor encapsulating his face. No one in the Poynter's neighborhood loitered so close to a school bus stop, vaping.

Did vaping-man belong to Nabil Hanna?

Nasha hurried into running tights and a quarter-zip, stepped into cross-trainers and dashed downstairs checking on the kids as she went. Brad was asleep. Miriam sat on her bed, examining a picture book.

David caught sight of a second man, inside a green pickup truck. "Watcher 4, where are you? Is the green truck guy one of ours?" Nazarian felt things getting away from him.

Guilt laden scenes of injured children and a destroyed home chased Nasha out the back door.

"Someone get on Nasha," David demanded.

Nasha vaulted the railed fence covered with dormant roses, then slowed at the street intersecting her own.

She brought out a lethal folding knife—it reminded her of the Army, of the *Dinnieh Fighting* when Takfir wal-Hijra and the Lebanese Army fought for eight days in the mountains east of Tripoli. Nasha, nineteen at the time, was unwilling to be belittled as a woman who wouldn't serve, while enjoying a life in the US underwritten by the banker who rescued her.

"This is nuts..." Nazarian yelled "...no Islamist tanks are roaming Arlington, Virginia."

Muddled with fear, Nasha watched a light green pickup towing a trailer crammed with leaf blowers. Three workmen—not ragtag rebels—joined the driver. The first blower backfired, belching smoke. Nasha's expression melted into memories of a nightmare.

Her Agency file was a stale repetition of past horrors.

Nasha was seven, South Lebanon occupied by the PLO, Beirut in ruins from the *Karantina Massacre*. The Syrian Army shelled Christian neighborhoods. PLO fighters controlled Sidon and Tyre. Extortion was the price of safe passage through random checkpoints controlled by terrorists and outlaws. Nasha scurried to keep up with her Aunt, unable to differentiate apartment buildings destroyed by Israeli aircraft, Syrian artillery or dozens of factions claiming a righteous destiny to govern.

Auntie only wanted to find meat and cheese for her niece's birthday. Nasha heard Auntie's sobs before she saw two fifty-caliber machine guns mounted on a truck. In hollowed out canyons of Beirut's former splendor, before machine gun shells walked towards them absent interruption or mercy, a little girl heard Cat Stevens's voice from the truck's boom box:

...Out on the edge of darkness, there rides a peace train
...Peace train take this country, come take me home again...

Helpless, Nasha witnessed the explosion of tissue, blood and bone that once formed a loving relative. With her mother's death during childbirth, no one survived to care for her. In shock, tiny Nasha stared at unfazed faces, whose peels of laughter continued until they faded with distance.

Nasha the orphan was too busy surviving the camps to notice Bachir Gemayel's election as President on the 23rd of August that year, or his subsequent assassination on September 14th.

A police siren's chirp interrupted Nasha's whirlwind visit to the past. "Get the goddam police away from her," David yelled at his watchers.

The officer asked with a distinct undertone, "Would you be Mrs. Poynter?"

"Yes, officer, is something wrong?"

"We're responding to a 911 call from your daughter. Something about mommy leaving her alone. This your house?"

Nasha checked the street. No man vaping, no green truck, no danger to her children. She apologized. "Sorry officer. My husband's in Europe on business and I took a quick run. Miriam must not have heard me...that's all I've been gone...a few minutes."

"May we come in with you, ma'am? Just to make certain."

Brad was asleep, Miriam blissfully ignorant of Murphy's Law. Nasha watched strangers with guns inspect her home. Without protest, she listened as they called Child Services.

A caseworker noted Mrs. Poynter's answers to a hundred intrusive questions, but reacted when hearing Nasha worked at the Lebanese Embassy: *You don't look like a Muslim.*

Familiar feelings assailed her. Not the empty despair born in the camps, but the odor of disapproval from the police made her uncertain and hesitant.

Nasha stood at the front door, focused on where a green truck had been parked. Figments of her imagination would never carry the sign, *Coelho Grows Everything.*

***

Settled in her office, Nasha tried to shake feelings of shame, disorientation and unease. Coffee cold, she read a recent report on Lebanon's unending struggle against Israeli spies.

Eyes blurred from no sleep, David pulled the report from Langley archives onto his screen.

In Lebanon large numbers had been arrested, all alleged to be on the Israeli payroll. Alleged, of course, was a word used in civilized briefings with the media. The guilt of those taken into custody wasn't in doubt. Neither was their future.

Taken into custody, a euphemism ill-fitting true circumstances, sounded to Nazarian like most witch-hunts, where witch was defined in the eye of the beholder. Yet Sunnis, Shiites, Christians and Palestinians numbered among those detained, indicative of no political or sectarian bias.

David considered Nabil Hanna.

Nasha's job description wasn't to comment on policy underpinning the government's actions. Nasha Gemayel was a diplomat when serving the needs of the Ambassador and a counter-intelligence analyst at other times—a less powerful yin to Colonel Hanna's over-arching yang. An argument could be made, David believed, that no counterbalance would exist in Lebanon's embassy save for the influence of her adopted father, a powerful international banker.

Her desk phone interrupted. "Hello, this is Nasha Poynter."

"Good morning, Nasha."

"Hi, Souraya. What can I do for the Ambassador?"

"The reception this week...at the British Embassy. You'll have to fill in for Gaelle."

There would be no point in protest. "What type of affair?"

"Long gown. Not too much jewelry, since you're a substitute. Drinks and canapés...six to nine. You can't leave early unless he does."

"Is Colonel Hanna attending?"

"Colonel Hanna has other priorities." Souraya meant this soiree was above Nabil Hanna's pay grade.

Nasha probed. "Cigars, brandy and lechery. Home with my children would be preferable. I'll miss your company."

"Be always prepared, Nasha. Be always faithful."

Semper Paratus. Semper Fidelis. Phrases with multiple meanings, Souraya's admonition seemed prepared in advance.

***

"Tell me again."

Fulton Bennett, a difficult man to surprise, was even harder to bullshit. Jamie Norris's preliminary report lacked intellectual scrutiny, slinging crap to obfuscate failure.

"Sarah's been narrowing the field of candidates."

Bennett held out his hand like a traffic cop. "How many candidates are there...as of yesterday."

"There's the French woman who teaches at Georgetown, the Syrian model in New York, and the Canadian skater."

"Why a team on Frankel?"

Norris would've preferred Gullickson do the answering, but the purpose of this impromptu sit-down precluded witnesses.

"New girlfriend. Needed to assess how we get rid of her...or recruit her."

Honey-traps: Bennett wasn't a fan. Hadn't supported installing a female operative next to Frankel. Bennett gave approval for an exploratory evaluation of the plan without enthusiasm and succumbed to pressure from upstairs with signature reluctance. Given any reasonable opportunity, or excuse, this cockamamie scheme would wither from neglect.

Bennett pursued disbelief. "Out of nowhere...Ribeiro just appeared?"

"Yes."

"How many on each side?"

"Frankel had two. His date was alone. For us, a team of four on each of them." Jamie anticipated the next question. "Frankel left Ribeiro at the skating rink. Sarah decided not to dilute our effort by covering her. We missed Probst. Ribeiro showed up...one of our guys finessed the situation...kept Raissa from further contact with Frankel."

Bennett exhaled. Field Directors weren't easily killed, especially on home ground—and weren't replaceable. What had Gunther known or guessed? More important, did Gunther know something we still don't know? Fuming at a dead man, Bennett failed to keep sarcasm at bay.

"I assume we finessed the After-Action Report on Gunther, a Field Director with twenty years experience, who died on US soil within a mile of a retired Field Officer he formerly ran?"

Jamie showed enough good sense to sit quietly, thoughts going a million miles an hour.

Bennett waved his hand in an eloquent motion. "There's a hitter in the mix...maybe a multiple given Gunther's skill set. Someone's paying for our people to die. Get us where this Frankel Op can succeed or recommend cancellation." Bennett's pallor turned darker.

Norris tucked his tail between his legs.

When Jamie reached the door, Bennett looked up from his computer screen. "Any chance we're still missing something?"

Jamie knew he was gagging on a breakaway layup.

Bennett relented—beating-up Norris wouldn't help. "Where's Raissa?"

Jamie dropped his head to his chest. "Sorry. We...tagging along with Haslett of course...checked her home. Locals are checking family and friends. Right now she's in the wind."

"In the wind, Jamie? Find her before the shooters do."

Jamie pondered Bennett's use of the plural, but maintained the language of the After-action Report. "Shooter might be sorry based on Ribeiro's history."

Bennett's face fell. "That's all in the past."

CHAPTER 6

David reviewed the latest data: Andrew hadn't gone to La Fermette Marbeuf. A salesman at heart, he'd lean on Marco's words—and Marco never mentioned being watched over by a sexual apparition.

Nazarian's review of Marco's words, examining them for hidden, even duplicitous meaning, brought one revelation—who might ask directions to Le Havre? What had seemed a simple exchange became something else, when factoring Andrew's bouillabaisse of stress and misgivings.

Dropped by a taxi at Paris St. Lazarre, Andrew drank coffee, boarded early, and sat near the rear where fellow passengers could be cataloged. At nine-thirty, the train arrived at Carentan, where he jumped off at the last moment. Tradecraft not Andrew's specialty, he at least employed a lengthy delay before renting a car.

Nazarian's watcher peeled away in fear of being blown.

Parked nearby Cherbourg's Hôtel de la Gare, cold from wind whipping off the English Channel, Andrew groused. "Where's the quintessential French charm?"

Redoubtable's formidable shape soon dominated the horizon, an imprisoned sea monster in a stark, concrete sarcophagus. Fifteen Euros lighter, and once again under video surveillance, he hurried through the exhibition hall towards the decommissioned nuclear sub.

Nazarian complained. "Fricking puissant...daddy's little boy plans to sell the acoustic signatures of dozens of submarines to the highest bidder."

Sardonic smile fixed in place, he thought: Andrew Poynter should be nominated for the Nobel Peace Prize.

Other than a forlorn attendant, Andrew stood alone on multi-tiered stairs leading to the submarine's entrance. Where was his contact—a duplicitous bastard who looked like an engineer?

A hand gripped his shoulder. He heard, "I am Marcel. Show me your passport." This strident demand coincided with a hand patting Andrew's body in search of a weapon.

Poynter's face exposed his thoughts: Could this actually be Marcel? Eyeglasses rode low on the engineer's nose. A well worn, begrudging expression substituted for apology, as a hand searched Andrew's groin.

"S'il vous plaît, mon ami. Your passport."

"My name is An..." Andrew choked at a near blunder "...Anthony Trout. I'm not here for little games where you pretend to be dangerous. You're an engineer. You like..."

Nazarian watched the man's index finger go to his lips, demanding silence. Paranoia peaked as they disappeared from the exhibition's CCTV. Somewhere, perhaps in the officers' sitting room, Marcel, if the pudgy fellow was Marcel, planned to test Andrew's authenticity.

Andrew's transmission suffered in the sub's bowels. "God it's cold in here. Let's find a warm café...share a coffee. Yes?"

"You are, perhaps, a madman? Exchange top-secret data in a café? Dieu nous aide."

David's ongoing mental narrative was certain: Changing Marco's script a second time would be two times too many. Andrew wanted this deal, wanted to prove his father wrong. Wanted his share of proceeds promised by Caroline's husband, but not enough to be stupid.

Andrew rose to the occasion. "What exchange?"

"DCNS is overrun with investigators. Everything and anything is being monitored. Assholes from DCRI have demanded access to our personal computers as well as transmissions over the net. Direction de la Surveillance du Territoire is part of the French National Police...like your MI-5. Direction Centrale du Renseignement Intérieur consumed DST. Like America's Homeland Security."

Poynter was off the rails.

"That's not Marcel, Andrew." Unheard, David urged a newbie in the business of buying and selling secrets to run. "Walk away. Catch the fast ferry to England."

David's suspicions peaked, when Andrew inquired, "Are you a suspect, Marcel?"

"Everyone is suspect. Pay me. Take these *clés USB* now or the chance won't come again."

Andrew whispered as if to a co-conspirator. "What rank do you hold in DCRI, Monsieur Piggy?"

Depressed by having no viable option, Nazarian plotted his fastest route to Cherbourg. As blood pressure stabilized, anger faded to practicality. He telephoned Marie Truchet and left no doubt about what he needed and what payment Marie could expect in return.

***

Raissa invented all manner of nasty retributions during months while raw skin transplants settled into gnarled whorls of scar tissue. Endless procedures—how delicate that idiom sounded, glossing over endless agony—allowed her to hone the sophisticated suffering to be inflicted on those who intruded upon her last refuge.

That was then. Gunther's execution was now.

Kayaks hung underneath the porch. Her hand-built wooden sloop floated at its dock, sails wrapped in weathered canvas. The boys at the boatyard took Agatha and her damaged shoulder without hesitation. If winter came early, or Raissa never returned, the big dog would be cared-for with affection. She left the Ferrari unlocked. If someone stole it, so what? A Ferrari wasn't real. Losing your life was real.

There had been years when rage and resentment drove her every thought and action. Back then Raissa's life held no value to speak of, courtesy of a jealous rival. Now she'd revisit those bad old days.

***

Restless, Bennett threw file folders in his briefcase. Flicked latches and spun security cylinders. With a final look around he hesitated, then gave in to the glass globe half full of wrapped chocolates. The globe and its enticements represented an exercise in self-control;

negotiating with himself, he selected three as the phone bleated.

"You're late for dinner, old friend. Anne must be a patient woman."

"You, Jacques, are nothing less than a scoundrel. What secret, or whose soul, is for sale this early morning in Euro-world?"

Laughter of the self-deprecating variety preceded a question. "Will you be attending the get-together the Brits are hosting at their run-down mansion?"

"Classified Intel...need to know and all that, old man." When inclined, Bennett did a passable British accent.

"Will Sir Edward be there?"

"Jacques, are you peddling something of value?"

"Sir Edward's little boy has been taken into custody on a French nuclear submarine. It's unlikely Sir Edward knows. What does that buy me?"

"A great big attaboy and my almost undying gratitude." Bennett hung up, keeping his hand fixed to the handset. After a minute's thought, he hit the speakerphone button.

"Hello, this is Greg Riley."

Like so many in high positions, Bennett disdained introductions.

"Greg, what do we know about the French submarine program...can you find out what we're hearing in the way of chatter and get it to me in the morning?"

"What time?"

"Let's say seven...in my office. Bring whomever you need."

Bennett left the office whistling a naughty sea-chantey describing sailors with a turtle's energy, a fox's slyness, an idiot's brains, a Sea Captain's tales, and Casanova's inventiveness. Door to his pride and joy opened, he tuned its old AM radio, thinking the caricature painted Sir Edward Poynter in bright colors.

***

Marie Truchet employed multiple counter-surveillance techniques, when two DCRI officers brought Andrew Poynter out of *Redoubtable*.

Unrestrained, Poynter walked without resistance, or seeming objection, between professorial Claude Garennier and his attack dog, Philippe Rayner. Had Poynter made some asinine mistake, or had Garennier detained him on general principle?

To Marie's surprise, the panicked expression of a boy about to wet his pants was missing. She spoke into her phone, unaware Nazarian was listening.

"Are they still watching Marcel?

Marie's French hard-man told her, "One sitting at the next table. Three parked out front. Does the professor have your boy?"

Marie made the only possible decision. "Oui, Jonny, but it's still a go. Tell the driver…don't kill them."

In Bar/Pub Le Scuba, a camera mounted high above the bar showed real-Marcel drinking Anisette, while DCRI cops nursed a second beer.

Obvious to Marie, less than a minute would pass before poor Marcel's courage, and bladder, would betray him. Months of planning and scheming would go poof; Marcel would be arrested on suspicion of treason and tortured for the identities of co-conspirators.

Video transmitted from Marie's phone showed the Renault Midlum hurtling through Le Scuba's front wall of glass before Marcel moved. From the dining room to the kitchen, its cargo of live chickens flew in every direction. Stunned but bleeding, DCRI's detachment were very much alive.

Marie aimed the phone at Marcel, who mingled with a crowd of bystanders, then crossed to Hotel Moderna.

Six weeks ago, when visiting the Moderna, Marcel mislaid his laptop bag in the breakfast area. Today only minutes would elapse, during which a password would be received and a terabyte of acoustic data uploaded. Marcel, so corruptible, was minutes from a funds transfer guaranteeing retirement in Tenerife.

***

With the camera switched on, and the required internet-connection codes texted to an untraceable cellphone, Garennier assured himself of a satisfactory evening regardless of the interrogation's outcome. Focused on Andrew, he banged his open palm on the table. Indicated his formidable colleague, whose face marked him a pugilist.

"Phillipe used to be an Olympic boxer, Mr. Anthony Trout. I'm going to tolerate him beating you…in places where it will hurt, but not look so awful."

Andrew sat stone-faced, pretending not to understand. Bits and bobs of his interrogator's rant made sense, but he was unable to join them together to form sentences, or intent

"J'comprend un peut l'francais." Andrew held his hands outstretched, palms up, pleading for an interpreter.

Nazarian concentrated on the screen, cursing Marie for being late. "Protect your face, kid, help's on the way."

Rayner kicked the chair over; stopped short of staving-in Andrew's head with his boot.

Andrew caught sight of a spider scurrying towards the radiator pipe. Wishing he, too, could run away, he was hauled upright and struck several more times, before hard knocks on the exterior door interrupted.

Intercom activated, Rayner uttered an unpleasant warning about seeking entrance at this doorway. Garbled, only the word Avocat was recognizable in the reply. Rayner wondered: Who knew where we took him? Who could've sent a lawyer? He kicked Andrew in the groin.

Pain radiating through every part of his body, Andrew rested his head on the floor and moaned.

Garennier wore an acquired look of resignation.

Marie stood steps to Michel Lecroix's right, out of the fisheye lens' range.

Lecroix made an excellent living as a multilingual Avocat. Very seldom he ventured into murky relations among competing agencies of like-minded governments, which, along with Kruggerands acquired in previous arrangements with David Nazarian, led to his presence at a nondescript building well-known for enhanced interrogations by DCRI.

Even with tin can acoustics, Garennier recognized the voice. He sent Rayner while snipping the end of a cigar.

Marie raised her mobile; its camera click caused Rayner to snarl for the camera.

"Good evening, Philippe. I assume you're trampling the civil rights of some poor devil from Canada?" Lecroix had been an actual Olympic boxer.

Rayner, who once had his bell rung by Lecroix, ogled Marie. "Tout le monde sait déjà que t'es une salope."

Lecroix had had enough. "Come, come, Philippe, be a gentleman. You're holding Mr. Anthony Trout. Somewhere within earshot is the Great Garennier, who speaks in complete sentences."

Marie flipped Phillipe the bird. "I hope Trout isn't too damaged." As Rayner leaned forward to grab the phone, her Beretta's muzzle brought spurts of blood from his nose.

From inside, Garennier signaled Rayner: Release Trout. Extracted his mobile from deep in a coat pocket. Called his superior. It would be at this level that details of the English bastard's release had been fleshed out. Garennier's suspicions notwithstanding, one couldn't defeat the system. Not in Cherbourg.

Andrew heard a voice calling. "Mr. Trout, my name is Lecroix. I'm acting as your solicitor. Let us not linger."

***

The ride to Caen's airport lasted an hour. Ten minutes from the terminal, Marie, without introducing herself, suggested they'd both benefit from a stiff drink.

Exasperated, Andrew would be gladly rid of French Intelligence, an Olympic boxer, and a sexual fantasy in possession of an itinerary prepared by Marco Panero. Distrustful of a triple Scotch with a woman he madly desired less than eighteen hours earlier, Andrew tapped at his phone's keyboard. Remain at a French airport—or drive a rental twelve hundred klicks to Barcelona? Where would be best?

"Thanks for the lift," Andrew told her after the car stopped.

For an instant, Marie contemplated an offer he wouldn't refuse. Honed instinct insisted sex wasn't what Andrew Poynter needed to buck-up, so she chose pablum.

"Travel safe, Andrew. I'll tell Marco you did well."

Before pulling away from the curb, she texted Marco, whose attention would be diverted by the triumphant receipt of every last byte of France's multi-country acoustic data: *Andrew's likely to fall apart...or run home to daddy, crying for a cookie.*

She granted herself a malicious thought: The text to Marco would drive Nazarian mad.

CHAPTER 7

Zachary Mannheim wasn't ambivalent when it came to Phyllis Martell. She'd keep her head down and speak when spoken to: Interviews at CIC bred that reaction. Regarded well by previous supervisors, Martell was in her eighteenth year with the Agency.

Spy-hunters weren't popular and working in Mannheim's closest circle could make Phyllis a pariah. Despite no public spotlight, there had always been counter-intelligence staff focused on traitors acting for friendly or unfriendly foreign governments. Provocateur was the antiquated title of those seeking to penetrate the Agency, and Angleton, Golitsyn, Nosenko, Philby, MacLean, Burgess, Ames, Hanssen and Tretyakov raised the hackles of anyone with an appreciation of past fuckups.

To become the next traitor—bartering America's secrets to enemies—caused Phyllis to live with persistent anxiety. The constancy of this concern was common ground Zachary Mannheim shared with his senior staff. Mannheim would, if cornered by circumstances of professional failure, admit the most capable female officers fell short of an above average male. Martell would have to be better than capable to survive where he planned to send her.

"Did you review the Probst file?"

"Yes, sir." There would be no usage of Zachary.

"What do you think?"

Phyllis opted to stick with what she knew. "Gunther Probst's throat was cut and he was shot twice in the head with a twenty-two caliber handgun, in Cotuit, Massachusetts, three quarters of a mile as the crow flies from the residence of Ms. Raissa Ribeiro, a Field Officer on medical retirement. Mr. Probst served for twenty-two years prior to his death...most of that as a Field Director. Mr. Probst teamed with Ms. Ribeiro numerous times, but wasn't on duty at the time of his death. His appearance earlier that day, in Boston, interfered with a surveillance operation involving multiple Agency assets."

"Subcommittee staff asked me about Probst's security status."

"There's not even a whisper in his file."

"Why ask if Probst was a pervert? Are they unenlightened, or juvenile?"

"Mr. Probst was gay. No operational notes comment further."

"Ribeiro's current location...anything new?"

"No, sir."

"Given what we know, what do you recommend?"

Written plain on her face, Phyllis would climb a mountain and jump off a cliff to avoid an answer.

"Execution of a Field Director is rare. Ms. Ribeiro's emotional audio recording notwithstanding, more than one current operation may be compromised. Assign a senior Field Officer with broad latitude, reporting direct to you, sir. The hell with protocol."

"Whom should we give it to?"

Phyllis saw the tripwire.

Creeping from his eyes to the edges of his mouth, Mannheim's Cheshire Cat grin indicated satisfaction.

"Let Fulton's folks find Ribeiro...if they can. You interview everyone in Ops who Probst worked with. Let it be known...anyone who wishes is welcome to chat. You're well liked over there, Ms. Martell. Play it up. We're looking for an executioner, not a common gun-thug...one who is brazen and unafraid. For the moment, we'll hope Ribeiro's alive and well. What do you think?"

"Can you fix it so Robby Turcott works with me? Alone I could miss areas where I've no familiarity. Robby will play it straight."

"Mr. Turcott is one of Fulton's special lads...is he not?"

Mannheim's neutral inflection masked intent. Bennett broke Agency rules with his athletic fixations. Not significant rules—which would be Bennett's counter argument. Rules, however, served specific purposes.

"Yes sir...I believe that's common knowledge within certain circles."

"Utilize Mr. Turcott for CIC's purposes. Not so you can be one of the boys, Phyllis. Not to look for a better job."

Martell's face reddened at Mannheim's warning and his use of the familiar; a first occurrence, it was unwelcome.

***

Turcott and Martell winnowed their list to two names.

Phyllis' lack of attention, obliquely obvious to David Nazarian, brought palpable discomfort to them both during these rare interactions. Their affair, ended years ago, left scars both visible and invisible. David remained a Field Officer. Phyllis stayed a minion, less even than a cog.

"So you were on the north side of the wharf, when you noticed Ribeiro?"

He observed her observing him, taking note of his inconsequential weight gain. Does it matter? CIC granted no favoritism. Part of the DNA for spy-hunters, the policy occupied the top spot of day-to-day protocol.

"I was covering the Aquarium Station exit. Ribeiro walked right past me, making a beeline for the restaurant. She stared through the front window almost a minute. Wanted to kill Frankel...right there in front of hundreds of tourists."

"So you followed her into the Marriott?" Phyllis could've phrased the question as an accusation—*Why'd you leave your position, endangering your team?*

"We both know I shouldn't have. I saw the photographer going after her...didn't seem fair after what she's been through."

"Have you worked with Ribeiro?" A warning suffused Phyllis' tone.

"No."

"Know her socially?"

Nazarian wanted to ask if Phyllis was pulling his leg. "No."

"Took pity on her?" Nazarian could wonder why Phyllis was jealous, but denying it made no sense.

"Sort of."

"Didn't recognize Gunther Probst?"

"Obviously I'd heard his name, but didn't know him and wouldn't have recognized him in any setting."

"From your point of view, you forced a photographer to give up his work product...photos taken in a public place without breaking any law...to save a former Agency officer embarrassment?"

"That's all I did. Left the hotel not thirty seconds after the photographer and resumed my position."

"What did you say to Ribeiro after the photographer dropped the memory card?"

"Nothing," Nazarian lied, not wanting questionable behavior to be questioned further.

"Why didn't you bring the memory in for analysis?"

"I didn't know Probst. So there was no reason to examine the memory card. Ribeiro being hassled without cause...that's where I focused. The entire episode was over in three minutes."

"Did you notice anyone paying particular attention to Probst, or Ribeiro?"

"Nothing struck me wrong. But a professional hitter doesn't get made before the attempt. Any experienced field operative knows that."

Phyllis noted the rebuke. Realized its truth. She glanced at Robby Turcott, who nodded.

Nazarian felt he'd wind up with a reprimand, if that. Might've gone much worse in different circumstances, if Bennett and Mannheim hadn't put him in the middle of their private war.

***

Raissa stood in the main square of Pamplona, feeling the effects of non-stop travel.

Gunther's death made a public announcement of someone's intentions towards her.

In a place where neither Raissa's name nor history carried import, in a place at once familiar and nowhere near centers of fashion or espionage, well over a million steps in good boots would be required. November's invasive weather, and her need to recover old skills, gave rise to significant obstacles, but less so than the necessity to conquer relentless fear.

Survival, if taken a minute at a time, would maneuver Raissa away from misgivings of a clouded mind and closer to pilgrims who'd walked the Camino de Santiago de Compostela for a thousand years.

Hips took the weight of a rucksack carrying needle and thread for blisters, all-weather trousers, self-wicking shirt, wool socks, underpants, sport bras, sleeping bag, rain gear, aspirin, sunscreen, sunglasses, ultra-light laptop, toilet paper, quick-dry towel, mini-light, knife, battery charger and the Sat phone which guaranteed she'd be fully functional. Euros were stuffed in an outside pocket. No credit card to be traced. Parka tied round her waist, wearing a floppy hat, she trudged towards Puenta La Reina, twenty-three kilometers in the distance.

In Cizur Menor, she stuffed herself with protein and pastries, feeling elated.

The climb up the Alto del Perdon left the Atlantic Basin behind. Barren fields greeted her, and from the top the route became steep and uneven. Raissa fell twice, sedentary life resisting transformation of fat to muscle.

After dark she slid into the sleeping bag by a small stream on the far side of Puenta.

She needed a weapon.

***

Misery was her sole companion on the uphill trek to Villamayor de Monjardin. Sheltered in a grocery, she bought water, cheese and energy bars. Under a dripping awning she phoned Tom Nichols.

"Tom, it's Raissa, please wake up."

"Yuh, I guess I'm sorta...where are you?"

"Who's looking, Tom?"

Nichols glanced at a wife unaccustomed to phone calls at all hours. "Martin Haslett...FBI. Bit of an asshole, but far from the worst. Different guy...David Nazarian...came by today. Langley written all over him. An even less savory type's been hanging round the boatyard, asking questions. Southern accent. Mean and pushy."

November, a month when summer folks had vanished and locals preferred working to talking, meant mean and pushy wouldn't get Mr. Southern Accent much cooperation at the boatyard.

"Doesn't sound like anyone I might expect, but who knows. Gotta go, Tom. Thanks."

Her internal clock issued a twenty second warning; even the best tracking algorithms needed more time.

Headed for Los Arcos, three young men offered the name of an albergue still open in the town ahead. Raissa slowed, watching them disappear.

Who's a threat? When will my innate sense for danger return?

At six hundred fifty meters altitude, she called a dozen years old number. "Erramun, is it you?"

Other than insults and curses, Raissa neither spoke nor understood Basque. Gunther had friends in Bilbao and her phone's notes confirmed Erramun spoke English.

An accented bass answered. "Who wants Erramun?"

"Gunther's strong right arm." The code sequence felt like it came from a dozen centuries in the past.

"The health of Gunther is good?"

"Gunther throat was cut—two bullets in the forehead for emphasis. A few days ago." Aware of seconds counting down towards her cutoff, a thought bounced through her mind: Erramun could be for sale.

Deadline imminent, she heard, "This is so. I'll help you."

"I need a weapon…here in Spain. Can I call tonight?"

***

She ate a meal in Los Arcos, suffering anxiety being inside with strangers. Unsure of the distance to steep ravines in Sansol, she hiked five klicks and again found a sheltered depression within a copse of trees. At eleven she woke to reconnect with Erramun.

His rough voice asked, "Where?"

"Tomorrow night in Navarette…is that possible?"

"In the Church of the Assumption."

"What can you bring?"

"What Gunther would want."

"How will I know you?"

"My youngest son will recognize you…there are many pictures of Raissa."

She slept in rain threatening to become snow.

CHAPTER 8

Nazarian sat quietly in the rear as Bennett entered twenty minutes late.

"Greg...start the introductions."

Greg Riley, closing in on fifty, regularly received more than generous offers from outside the blinkered existence of Science & Technology at Langley. Bennett, however, was a man worthy of admiration. Uncertain whether satisfaction could be replaced by money, time enough existed to postpone a decision.

"My name's Greg Riley. My area is technology." A wary smile substituted for a complete biography. "To my left is Commander James Feeley, US Navy. To his left is Madeleine Finisterre, a NATO specialist in European military capabilities. To Madeleine's left is Joe Steele...Electric Boat Groton. Thanks to Madeleine who flew all night, albeit in great comfort, and Joe, who got up before God to catch our charter."

Bennett nodded—Jamie Norris sat next to Nazarian, sipping hot tea, fragile psyche vibrating at high frequency. Aaron Frankel's disappearance from public view was convenient only for Frankel. Raissa Ribeiro, traced to Montreal, slipped away without a trace. Jamie needed something fresh. Nazarian looked more than half asleep. Don't kill the horse carrying the load, Fulton reminded himself, repeating an oft-quoted homily from his paternal grandfather.

"Down the end there, wearing a grimace, is Jamie Norris, one of my staff. David Nazarian is sitting-in to acquire some background.

Move up, Jamie, you'll hear better. You're good where you are, David."

Not embarrassed or offended, Jamie swapped chairs, confused that submarines were today's topic. What, Norris wondered, could submarines have to do with Aaron Frankel or Sheikh bin Rahman?

David added sugar to a large coffee. Though half starved, he ignored the famous Fulton Bennett baked goods.

Bennett nodded thanks to Riley, then got to the point.

"Commander Feeley...why would a businessman brokering deals in the international marketplace, a man whose background would reveal nothing to do with submarines, be taken into custody on a French nuke?"

Feeley, uncomfortable in a building where lies comprised a key part of the mission, answered with discretion despite his CO's order to be candid. "Can you tell me the submarine's name?"

"Don't know. What could a neophyte gain?"

Feeley smelled a half-truth. "What could your best operative, knowing even a little about a nuclear submarine, gain by being aboard one?"

"I get your point...if you don't know shit, shit's what you'll get. So tell me what's interesting about French submarines."

Madeleine Finisterre, who flew from Brussels in a private Gulfstream, answered as soon as Feeley turned to her.

"Module d'Energie Sous-Marine Autonome...ESMA for short...or AIP, air independent propulsion. DCNS, the French shipyard, builds the Scorpène class with a modified version of their nuclear propulsion system using steam generated by combusting ethanol and oxygen, both stored in the boat, under high pressure. A conventional turbine operates off that steam. Pressure firing allows exhausted carbon dioxide to be ejected at any depth. Damned clever design."

Joe Steele jumped-in, sounding jealous. "On a Scorpène, ESMA requires adding eight meters and three-hundred tons to the sub's hull for oxygen storage and ancillaries. The boat can operate longer than twenty days underwater. ESMA makes a poor man's nuclear sub. Quiet. Potent. They sell."

Attack submarines at a fraction of a nuke's cost—Bennett thought the story made sense. The Poynter kid is selling something to somebody. Exactly what and to whom, nobody knows. Damn Jacques—he'd held onto the best part to sell another day.

"Who buys them?"

Steele parroted a ready answer. "Chile, Malaysia, Spain, India and Brazil are major customers. Spain ordered four...then cancelled that order, replacing it with four standard boats built by Navantia, the Spanish shipbuilder. Made for ugly recriminations among DCNS and Navantia."

Bennett believed he was close to sticking something far up the nose of Sir Bloody Edward Poynter.

Steele finished. "India chose Scorpène...six for three billion US. These boats are being manufactured by the state-owned Mazagon Docks in Mumbai. Brazil purchased four Scorpènes...ten billion US. That deal also requires the French to develop a French/Brazilian nuclear powered boat.

Brazil finished Arsenal de Sepetiba shipyard three hundred miles south of Rio; a new submarine base is adjacent to the yard. Three conventional boats built at Sepetiba are scheduled for commissioning. The nuke will be a variant of the Scorpène."

Feeley continued, "An investigation is ongoing involving a wide range of corruption in these submarine sales. Scorpenes are of particular interest to prosecutors. Sales to Malaysia and Brazil are getting the most attention. If your influence peddler is charged, perhaps French prosecutors are making progress."

Bennett's mind could be seen spinning. Only David Nazarian could interpret Fulton's vacuous grin.

Jamie and David stayed behind, knowing there was more yet to come.

Bennett returned from a cloud of thought, letting his eyes roam Norris's features. The next few minutes might tell a tale, he thought, with no certain expectation.

"Well, Jamie, is your tux pressed for tonight's ball?"

Jamie's heart thumped: Jesus, this isn't good at all. "No, sir."

"Does that mean you weren't invited, or did you decline your dad's polite request?"

Jamie overcame a case of dry-mouth. "Declined, sir. Not a place for someone at my level to be seen."

"Dad isn't happy, huh?"

"In general, my father isn't a happy man."

"Take Sarah, not your wife...get a feel for the room and deliver a message to Sir Edward for me."

No detail needed, Jamie Norris was acquainted with Sir Edward Poynter. "I'm sorry, sir. That won't be possible."

"Consider it an order, if you like. I realize it's not easy."

"I'm not making myself clear, sir. It isn't possible because Sarah's attending with my father."

Bennett swallowed the temptation to accuse Jamie of a social lie. Not so Jamie could see, he was angry enough to draw blood from his tongue. "Well..." Bennett paused, then both men laughed in a strained, off-kilter fashion "...guess a former Director/CIA can commandeer a serving officer any old time."

Bennett would later bay at the moon over the self-indulgent idiocy of Grover Norris, former Director of Central Intelligence, and now Investment Banking legend in his own mind.

"Sarah's over the moon at the chance...Frankel will be there."

Bennett wouldn't acknowledge an inconvenient truth; he didn't know and hadn't been told about Frankel's attendance at the British Embassy party.

"You can escort Madeleine. She's good company."

Head spinning, Jamie realized NATO's expert worked for Bennett. He managed to say, "What message for Sir Edward?"

Nazarian saw Bennett's signal and slipped from the room.

***

A rotating schedule of Nazarian's watchers felt no shame invading a private life.

Nasha's old Singer machine, left behind in departing the refugee camp, had been all that remained of her Aunt. This twin, glowing black with gold lettering, had been a precious gift from her second mother.

Demands such as high fashion creations and their price tags, incurred as part of her Embassy job, challenged the family budget. Nasha could, with a single phone call, enjoy the fussing and fitting of any designer. Could, but never would. Contrasted to the deprivation of war and months in the camps, a small girl built barricades of disbelief to guard against assuming any mansion would be normal or lasting. Forever sharing and giving love to her second parents, the woman she became was wary of money and its complications. The woman she became was an American of Lebanese ancestry, an

American who happened to be Muslim. At work, Nasha tilted in the direction of Mecca. At home she leaned towards jeans.

An old designer gown from Previous Passions, re-designed to disguise its origins, accommodate still swollen breasts and a mildly intransigent waistline, was now strapless. A scalloped top line plunged and gathered above a large, contrasting gold bow set below the cleavage on an empire waist, trailing to the hem in an electric blue fabric that swirled at a different rate than the dress's chiffon. Reversible for practicality, a wrap allowed Nasha to swathe her shoulders, winding the smooth fabric around her arms to cover what the dress exposed. She could be two women, a chaste Muslim or a dazzling American. Aware there would be controversy, her Ambassador would recognize an employee straddling both worlds.

"Bloody Sir Edward, can suck a lemon."

Nasha called to Lucia. "Do you have a minute? Something's not right with this bow." Fidgeting in front of the mirror, she couldn't be still as the clock in her head ticked.

Lucia slapped her on the rump. "Stand still or this needle will...there, all done. Your shoes need to dry; the dye is damp, so wear something else in the car."

The doorbell rang.

A woman carried a metal case by its handle. "Let me look at you. Nice dress...how's a nice Muslim girl get away with showing off her rack? Here to do your hair and makeup. Look at all this thick black hair...wires are finer than your hair. Maybe the scan will miss it."

"The Ambassador will be here in twenty-five minutes. Who the hell are you?"

"Look honey, I'm a contractor. I do all Colonel Hanna's electronic wizardry. Sit. I'll be done in ten."

"Maybe the scan will miss...maybe? Get out." Nasha fumed, spitting the words. "I could kill that man."

***

Raissa entered Logrono over the Bridge of Stone, reckoning it was ten klicks to Navarette. She dawdled, taking time to buy a supply of energy bars. Earlier she drained a huge blister, leaving a length of thread behind to hasten healing.

Navarette was a medieval town which, in summer, made a charming stopover for pilgrims sharing the wines of *La Rioja*. With flakes of snow driven by a sharpening north wind, a matching blister gestating on her left foot and cold biting at her neck's scar tissue, the church's west portal was an oasis of forgiveness. By rote she removed her hat and blessed herself. Gawking at the golden baroque altarpiece, she stood dumbfounded, failing to see the old woman.

"You arc too late."

Raissa stepped backwards, but saw no imminent threat.

"The son of Erramun could not stay. What he delivered is in the sacristy." Her shambling gait exited the church.

Raissa was left deep in shadow to watch and wait. "Patience may be a virtue, dear Lord, but I'm cold and tired." Not much of a prayer, Raissa said it with reverence, aware of her degraded tactical situation and too leg weary to resist.

As promised, a chair held a Z84 folding stock machine gun. Old it was, but the gun showed signs of being cared-for. Four spare magazines weren't much, when firing six hundred rounds per minute.

Insecure, she willed shaky legs to cover nine klicks to *Ventosa*. Telling herself she wasn't hungry, the Z84 remained within reach in its oil-stained horse blanket. Against any enemy at all, Raissa reckoned, she'd have died in the church.

The reemergence of iron will nudge the arrow in her favor while she slept fitfully.

CHAPTER 9

To Nasha, Ambassador Razouk seemed far away. Was it present, past or future he saw?

Offhandedly he offered her a clue. "There'll be a large crowd. Lebanon's presence won't make much of a splash." Offhanded became wistful. "Thank you for your help this evening, Nasha." Further effort led to a strained, yet out of place, compliment. "You look radiant." Turning back to the window, his good words faded.

Help struck her odd. No suggestion of how she would help accompanied Razouk's remark. Window dressing seemed a more fitting description of her role.

A queue of black limousines slowed to a crawl. Razouk addressed the chauffeur. "Can you see the problem?"

"Security is checking everyone at the curb, sir. A new procedure, I think."

Razouk muttered under his breath. "Perhaps there's been a credible threat."

***

Security for the Embassy reception blended ballet's precision steps with tanks maneuvering in the desert. For British staffers, the problem began and ended with parking limousines flying flags either of sovereign nations or multi-national corporations. Guests would exit outside spiked, twelve-foot iron gates assisted by attendants from the embassy's regular contractor. Guests moving into the courtyard passed through discrete metal detectors, received an offer of champagne or orange juice by contracted wait-staff, and were escorted inside by senior officials.

Back at their vehicle, personal security staff would be accompanied to a minibus for transport to a holding area. No request would be made of these security personnel to relinquish their weapons. Chauffeurs would be directed to an assigned, off-site, lot. Practiced movements assured that, as one set of guests and one limousine completed the process, the next would be met by an ever-rotating collection of attendants.

Hired by Specialist Parking Group, which wasn't a selective proposition, proved Yusef's simplest task; a part-time employee for better than six years, he'd proved capable of handling egos at the fanciest of shindigs. Menial jobs—FedEx Field, Nationals Park and Verizon Center—augmented a façade of normalcy. Maury Lipmann approved each part-time gig, as required for even the lowliest of Agency employees.

His immediate problem was juggling the line of limos. He could see four vehicles at a time and there were seven other attendants. Mathematical anomalies, holes into which theories rarely emerged in useable form, tested self-control. Being capable, even brilliant, guaranteed nothing in a quiet world where an unexpected anomaly rained down predictable violence. Yusef computed the probabilities easily enough. Managing those probabilities would be random and tricky—manipulation was an art form which, when well practiced, appeared ordinary and when botched, stood out.

He'd prepared an encrypted note for Aaron Frankel.

Encrypted wasn't technically accurate; the crude convention was designed to evade prying eyes nearby the limo. Frankel's was a brilliant mind—understanding Yusef's meaning would be trivial.

Yusef stood third in line, when the gloom revealed Lebanon's flag flying on a stretch Mercedes. Without hesitation he tapped the wheezing man in front of him, pushed a water bottle into the man's hand and said gently, "Move back, Oscar. Catch your breath. We'll cover it."

Oscar, with bad knees and a three pack a day habit, complied.

Behind Yusef a sarcastic voice protested, "Never cut me no slack, big guy."

Yusef responded while snatching pen and paper from his shirt pocket. This note, unlike one prepared for Frankel, would be more last moment haste than proven algorithm.

"Cause you're a heartless dick, Willy my man."

Willy laughed in momentary camaraderie among working stiffs.

***

Nasha knocked on the bulletproof divider, smiling without a clue at CIA's camera.

"Could I leave my shoes on the front seat?" A glowing smile thanked the chauffeur. She slipped on high heels reserved, according to Miriam, for pretending.

Razouk suggested, "Leave your phone, Nasha, or you'll wait forever when we leave."

"No phones?"

"Not for this event."

Nasha, sitting on the right, would exit first beside black lacquered security bollards. As the door opened, she saw a man wearing the brass-buttoned jacket emblematic of Specialist Parking. Face unnoticed, his hand gave three tight squeezes as she rose. Nasha's wrap came undone; she was falling.

Cat like, the attendant caught her, his left arm supporting her right shoulder. Simultaneously, his right hand brushed against flesh and fabric on her right breast.

Face impassive, his eyes burned white-hot.

To the chauffeur, Nasha's face reddened with what could only be lust. Her face an open invitation, lingering to the point of embarrassment for the chauffeur, she would allow anyone to touch her. The harlot's pretense of awkwardness a cheap charade, Nasha Poynter was a whore. After being stoned and left for vultures, what sinful enticement would she offer?

Two inches down her décolletage, Nasha felt discomfort from the folded paper's creased edges. She looked back for Yusef. Saw the willing face of a Royal Marine, who offered his arm and an approving glance. Within seconds no exposed skin felt the chill. Within a minute she entered the receiving line to refuse a fluted champagne glass. Gas-fired heaters stood in a row like the Assyrian Guard of Sennacherib, warming a composed face.

In the limo, the chauffeur repeated the attendant's name: "Schwartz, Schwartz, Schwartz." He'd proven what Colonel Hanna preached about the pretty woman. A satisfied smile of anticipation displaced the chauffeur's glower.

***

At the far end of an elegant, wood-paneled, room a roaring fire filled a fieldstone fireplace, its warmth magnetic to earlier arrivals. Conversation leaked from other rooms, each of which resounded with echoes of crackling hardwood. A string quartet performed in the largest room. Decorated military dress uniforms were scattered among tuxedos, a rainbow of gowns, jewelry and subdued conversation. Those inside the Embassy abandoned drinks and debate to determine the identity of arriving rivals, allies or non-combatants.

Gilded paintings depicted triumphant Englishmen and their lathered mounts, fresh from conquests of men whose skin was other than pasty white. Trophy heads of magnificent animals removed for the occasion, CCTV transmitted how Nasha felt about their non-presence. In a non-existent family tree, too few branches would require examination before discovering Nasha's relatives in service to these sashed and sword wielding servants of the British realm. As much as the folded paper grated against curiosity, fleeing to a powder room so soon would be a faux pas.

Razouk's arm, intertwined with her own, tensed several times as he took inventory of fellow guests.

Nasha's mind wandered: How different was today from a time when embassies in the Middle East, populated by self-proclaimed elitists, who mastered Arabic as they previously conquered Latin and ancient Greek, then chose to patronize Arabs and the Arab world.

"Treasure the past," was the mantra of her second father, her Papa. "Expect those representing the West to be ignorant of what preceded them. Anticipate basic blunders. Presume America's siege mentality will make things worse. Americans believe their own bullshit and invent solutions bearing no relation to the real world on the ground." Then Papa would smile, admitting he too, as a proud Lebanese American, was often guilty-as-charged.

Sweet and sour recollections presaged the parting of a group to her left: Nasha saw the wheelchair and its occupant. Saw Papa's affectionate tears welling in the eyes of a man who saved her because he could—and loved her because he craved a daughter's love in return. His distress warned her not to approach; she should discharge her obligations. There would be stolen family moments later in the evening. Nasha's second mother, her Momma, stood wrapped in rigid memory at Papa's side.

Nasha turned away.

A hushed moment announced the arrival of Grover Norris, former head of CIA and advisor to US Presidents. On Norris's arm a young blonde, dressed in shimmering silver, drew attention away from her dignified escort. Nasha's disapproval cemented distaste for a known Agency officer. Behind Grover an even taller man made the ever-so-British gesture of grooming his mustache. Alone in the spotlight as he was, Nasha watched Sir Edward Poynter's affectations cascade: He shot his cuffs to expose the family crest; unbuttoned his jacket to show off aging abdominals; and placed an unlit pipe in plain view. The world would see Sir Edward Poynter as a proper English nobleman. Hair-plugs, scattered about an arid scalp, distracted from the desired impression.

A warm hand touched her arm. She turned to be greeted by the infamous financier, Aaron Frankel, who wore a moonstruck expression. "Ambassador Razouk, in ten thousand Arabian nights could there ever have been a Princess to rival this lady? Please, introduce me."

Razouk performed the introduction, excusing himself with ceremonial apology to join ambassadors from Jordan and Syria. A look crossed Nasha's face as her employer walked away, suggesting the introduction and his exit could have been contrived.

"Nasha...such a poetic sound...what does it mean?" Frankel stood transfixed in ostensible adoration.

Without flirting, but with a playful retort, Nasha said, "My name implies sweet aromas, Mr. Frankel, but in this case they're of diaper cream and dishwashing detergent. I'm a wife and a mother...you're a man whose reputation precedes you."

"Nothing will precede me again but my adoration of you, dear lady. Please, have dinner with me later." Turning his head in an obvious search pattern, he challenged her. "Where's your husband? He should be drawn and quartered for leaving your side. Given the opportunity, I'll never treat you with such shame."

Frankel couldn't realize the tender nerve inflamed by a flamboyant attempt to sweep Nasha off her feet. In less than seconds she relived a husband's neglect—no card, no expression of love at all. Then she blinked, saw Frankel interpret her loss of color, and responded in an accusatory tone.

"Could you keep your word, Mr. Frankel? Should I abandon my marriage? Trust my heart to a Jew who funds terrorist attacks on his people?"

"Sticks and stones, Nasha, do not become you…a child of the camps. From your ivory tower in Lebanon's embassy, you should leave room for the world to be more convoluted than epithets."

***

Across a massive Kazvin, Jamie Norris fixed his attention on Frankel and the woman who entered with the Lebanese Ambassador. From time to time he glanced at Grover, who held an audience in thrall, creating heroes from whole cloth without coming nearer a mile of classified intelligence or the truth.

Sarah clung to Grover's synthetic radiance, half a step to the rear of his left shoulder in a spot where she, too, viewed parries and thrusts between Frankel and the Poynter woman. Sarah nodded at Norris the Younger, intending Jamie to move closer, the better to hear their conversation. To Sarah, heat from the twosome radiated sexual explosiveness ideal for her Op's purposes.

Jamie whispered in Madeleine's ear. Upon their arrival within earshot, Nasha broke-off her conversation with Frankel, asking a waiter for directions to the ladies room.

Distracted in the midst of munching a scallop wrapped in bacon, Jamie heard Madeleine hiss. "Stop staring. Don't be like your father."

A guilty shrug providing an answer, Jamie guided Madeleine's elbow in Sarah's direction. Before taking two steps, as his eyes met Sarah's, their thoughts needed no added alignment. The perfect candidate to bell the cat named Aaron Frankel wore a strapless blue dress adorned with a gold bow.

Nasha had almost escaped, when Andrew's father stepped in front of her. "You seemed quite charmed by that chap. I heard him ask you to dinner." Two declarative sentences, if written they'd appear harmless. Spoken by your disapproving father-in-law, they hurt to the degree intended.

"Well then, Edward..." Years earlier, Sir Edward insisted he be addressed in the familiar "...you heard my reply. It's lovely to see you as well."

"Of course I didn't mean..."

"Of course you did, Old Boy. Andrew isn't here so you feel free to unleash the hounds." Nasha bit her tongue, more to stop an escalation than in self-rebuke.

"I won't have you speaking to me like that."

"Will you be coming to visit Miriam and Brad?" Sir Edward Poynter's failure to visit his only grandson festered as an infected wound.

Sir Edward gathered himself: Bradford Poynter was the future of the family. Caroline had given birth to two girls and, against the wishes of her father, decided against more children.

"I'm required at Whitehall. My flight leaves when this affair comes to an end."

"Whom did you come to see?"

"You're in the business, woman. You should know better."

Nasha reminded herself: Diplomats tell you to go to hell so tactfully, you look forward to the trip. Why, then, is Sir Edward Poynter incapable of subtlety?

"Where is your son, Edward? Do you know?"

Sir Edward turned on his heel, wearing a look which could kill. His odd behavior, so not the formal, officious, obnoxious Minister of Her Majesty's Government, left Nasha with a horrible tingling down her spine.

***

Toilet door locked, she used two trembling fingers to fish the square of paper from its lodging. Scrawled in block letters she read: BEN HARPER.

Just as her sewing machine permitted time travel, so did the printing of Yusef Schwartz; the first swept her off to early childhood while the second returned her entire adolescence.

Yusef, Nasha's first friend in the camps, helped her fend for herself, refuse to back down or run away. She stole food with Yusef, shared her one and only book with a boy who couldn't read, and cried on his shoulder when nightmares ruptured sleep. Nasha threw herself at the feet of the man who would save her, begging for Yusef to be her brother as the man would become her father. Tears burrowed tracks in filthy cheeks as crusted nails dug into the man's wrists. Until he relented.

Yusef and Nasha were inseparable.

Yusef was brilliant, excelling at sports, music, and academics. Whatever puzzle Papa put in front of them, Yusef found the key. They played in the school orchestra, shot hoops, swam endless laps and ran till Nasha dropped to watch Yusef go on and on.

On to college in Beirut, where Yusef changed.

She'd put it down to Momma's passing. Papa, too, suffered regular bouts of melancholy during months of mourning. Yusef became incommunicative, absent from her life and from Papa's. After college, after injury blurred athletic dreams, he disappeared. Missed her wedding and the births of both children. Only to resurface tonight of all nights, at the British Embassy, to tuck a note down the front of her dress.

Nasha pushed back tears. Focus on the word-game.

Yusef would remember her affinity for quirky rhythms and a soft guitar. His warning counted on what some called rebellion from the mandates of conservative Islam. Yusef meant her to recall specific lyrics: *You just have to walk away...walk away and head for the door.*

Without warning, the Embassy's fire system klaxon sounded at ear-splitting levels.

CHAPTER 10

Yusef knew evacuation of the building, determination of the alarm's cause and implementation of security protocols would suffer from disorganization and disorder; these moments of maximum confusion would become his ally.

Intelligence officers from a mixed bag of countries, beginning to mitigate potential losses, acted with a single mind: Move senior officials to safety. Seven parking attendants benefitted from near invisibility; their job, by definition, identified them as above suspicion. Limousines would remain unavailable until chauffeurs could be alerted to double-park near the Embassy without interfering with fire apparatus.

At a side entrance, Yusef scanned for a man who didn't belong.

Jean-Louis Michani looked frantically for Nasha; his girl-child, the ultimate wild card for a billionaire with secrets, was an unanticipated presence. The single guest pre-warned of the alarm, he convinced himself Nasha would be safe. His wheelchair, subject to periodic accusations of hypocrisy, drove the financial press to indulge in constant speculation. Jean-Louis rose with unforeseen alacrity in a room where few screams, but a beehive of commotion, greeted Embassy staff raising their voices to command attention.

Yusef saw Frankel follow the swarm towards the main exit. Watched as Jean-Louis, without generating overt commotion, hooked Frankel's arm with his cane.

Father is no fool—this is his moment.

Astounded, Frankel heard the diminutive Michani say, "Hassan's dead. You're next...here...tonight." Michani then commanded while pointing at the wheelchair, "Slump down...chin on your chest."

Frankel stood paralyzed, digesting a revelation that couldn't be true from a messenger who couldn't know. Then he complied, unable to do anything other than what was decreed.

Michani, in counterpoint, thoroughly contemplated the task requested by Yusef. Glimpsed his son standing helpless no more than thirty feet away.

Yusef sensed his father's intention and nodded: Warning Frankel would be insufficient, if assassins were present.

Jean-Louis pushed the wheelchair not towards the embassy's front door, but to a side exit where fewer guests could interfere and Yusef could guide Frankel to safety.

While the wealthy and high-placed focused on removing themselves from danger, Yusef saw Grover Norris scan the room for stragglers. Give him credit, Yusef admitted, Grover's no coward.

When the wheelchair's left wheel snagged on a dragging tablecloth, Grover ran to help.

Yusef ached at Michani's helplessness.

Norris senior reached down to untangle the wheel. White gloves belonging to a tall man in parking attendant's mufti took the wheelchair's load. Yusef said, "Mr. Director, no need to soil your hands."

Behind Yusef, two SAS troopers in full kit helped hoist the chair and occupant over the sill onto the brick path. In a seamless transition, Yusef assisted Michani and Frankel towards the street.

***

The best laid plans, Nasha barked at herself; she should've read the note sooner. *Walk away* meant go now—not after the damnable alarm goes off.

Her initial instinct involved throwing open the bathroom door, finding Papa and Yusef together outside in a safe place. More reasoned logic insisted Yusef wanted her out of harm's way. Harm, however, couldn't include a fire, because no fire existed. Nasha pulled off her heels, hiked the gown, opened the door and turned right down a short hall.

Clipped British accents on a back staircase drew her upward. Nasha stood in an open doorway, shoes in hand. Each male occupant turned in her direction, except the man she addressed.

"Was the fire alarm a drill, Edward? Or a ruse for some brilliant, quixotic, purpose?"

An officer spoke sharply. "Foreign nationals aren't allowed here."

"That will do, Leftenant. Mrs. Poynter is the mother of my grandchildren, and is I assure you, no threat to British security." He paused in deliberation before measuring his next words. "Nasha is counter-intelligence at the Lebanese Embassy. Show her what's been happening...then Foster..." Sir Edward indicated a Trooper who looked twelve "...you'll find transport and take Mrs. Poynter home. She'll have missed the Embassy's limo."

"Yes, Minister." Both Lieutenant and Trooper answered as one.

Sir Edward swept from the room towing his SAS cadre behind him.

In matter-of-fact manner, the console's operator inquired, "Shall I show you what's been happening, Mrs. Poynter?"

"Show me the grand hall, please."

Grover Norris appeared on the screen, fixated on a disappearing wheelchair.

"Could you back it up?"

Papa's helping Aaron Frankel. What's he saying? Drowned out by the klaxon and the din of evacuation, the sound quality on the recording left speech unrecognizable with the exception of *Hassan* and *tonight*. This is lunacy—Papa pushes while Frankel sits. Nasha focused on every detail, every nuance of expression. Until the camera caught Yusef framed in the side exit.

"Freeze it." Father and brother together; unexpected didn't come close to capturing her concerns. "Go forward...to where Director Norris helps with the wheelchair."

Grover, having taken no notice of the parking attendant, or the British soldiers who managed the heavy lifting, could be seen aghast: Michani and Frankel involved together in some unspoken conspiracy. Grover stared too hard and too long, making his self-interest too plain.

Jamie Norris arrived, having witnessed the rescue without identifying all the actors. Embassy microphones captured the entirety of his exchange with Sarah Gullickson.

"What did I miss?" asked Jamie.

Sarah began to move; former Director Grover Norris remained her responsibility until safely ensconced in a CIA SUV. "Our target for one thing...and a situation I don't understand at all."

***

Flee, the voice in Yusef's head ordered. Run faster than the devil chasing. Abandon Frankel and Nasha. He offered a short prayer and took two additional breaths.

"Yo, little dude. Need the phones for Michani, Frankel and Poynter."

Half a dozen prior claimants succeeded with similar requests, now Yusef watched the kid with brain overload sort white stickers on plastic bags.

"Here you go, big man. Ten bucks apiece."

American entrepreneurial spirit, out of place though it might be, focused on profit above all else. Yusef grabbed the wrist holding two bags.

"Where's the third phone, my young friend?"

"No phone for Poynter. Look for yourself, friend." No shortage of moxie, thought Yusef.

"Thanks, then."

"Where's my tip?"

"Don't buy British war bonds, my little man."

Yusef approached Frankel from behind, passing the cell over the investment expert's right shoulder. "CIA intends to plant a woman...recruited to get close to you. She'll be run by the woman in the silver dress...the one with Grover Norris."

Aaron Frankel's world spun upside down. Feted on cable and interviewed in reverential tones by networks, he was accustomed to solicitations and temptations. Tonight had offered access to shadow governments, men on the front lines of diplomacy and espionage unknown to the public. For the opportunity to listen in, ask questions and receive guarded answers, these shadow advisors anticipated commensurate value from a man who made and moved markets. Yet here I am, hiding in plain sight, warned of impending assassination by Jean Louis Michani, one of few men I'd take seriously. Warned by using the name Hassan, a name I've uttered to no one. Warned by informing me of Hassan's death. How can I confirm such a thing and keep myself alive in the bargain?

Frankel twisted in the wheelchair. What person, from what team, had returned his phone and altered the course of his life?

Three blocks from the Embassy and high on adrenaline, Yusef stripped off the attendant's jacket and stuffed it in a fanny pack as he ran.

***

"Can you show me the secondary exits?"

Nasha's intensity spilled-over to the well-dressed man at the video system's controls. On the screen marked Kitchen, a tuxedoed male with thinning, dark hair, whose bearing marked a military background, carried an overcoat. Unobserved, he clearly believed, a kitchen towel was dropped in a garbage can. Before it disappeared into the receptacle, the outline of a suppressed handgun was there for anyone to see.

The operator keyed his comms-set, anticipating Nasha's request.

"Corporal Mathias, gather anything interesting from the slop bucket nearest the kitchen exit. Quick as you please."

One step from exiting the Embassy is safety, the dark haired man removed latex and silicon facial alterations, eased implants from his mouth and peeled off a wig. Walked away a streaked blonde. The operator's face conveyed disappointment.

"Bet you a hundred quid the weapon will be proved property of the British Army."

Corporal Mathias stood in the doorway. "Mr. Gormley, I found a pistol done up with a silencer." The Corporal held up a plastic kitchen bag. "Shall I leave it with you, sir?"

Gormley shot Nasha a conspiratorial look.

"Bastard beat British security to locate a weapon salted-away on the premises. No fool this fellow; an embassy running hot with SAS Troopers and pissed-off firefighters would be a poor place to commit ritual suicide."

***

Trooper Edwin Foster, barely twenty from a farm in Cornwall, oozed nervous energy as Nasha started up the front walk of her home.

Nazarian toggled the front-porch camera—if escorting the mother of the Minister's grandchildren turned into a cockup, this kid soldier will barf his guts out.

"Watcher 3, are you armed?"

"Roger that."

"On your toes. Engage as indicated."

Nasha walked through the front door.

Foster saw two Iraqis in the living room. Déjà vu lowered a sepia cloud over his vision as he dropped to a knee, brought his rifle to bear and shouted. "On the floor. Do it now." Foster's hands twitched on the Enfield L85a1.

Hostility, not jitters, shone in the woman's eyes, her body taut, lips tight and drawn.

"Want these towelheads..." With enough grace to swallow the word in embarrassment, Foster took a step behind her, biting his lip till it bled.

Towel-head. Camel driver. Rag-head. Desert-nigger. Sleeping cobra. Not one was new to Nasha. This British kid hadn't invented military slang. She'd heard worse, when in the army, but not in her home. Nasha looked around for reassurance about the children. Made a rapid calculation which advocated for Nabil Hanna being unprepared to do harm. Miriam and Brad must be upstairs with Lucia.

A moment of abject weakness buckled her knees.

She should ignore the Colonel and his barky dog—tell him to piss off. In a world where two men could describe one women's reality as hallucination, making an unalterable record made sense. In a setting where her security cameras and sound equipment guaranteed the truth of any accusations, the Colonel might make an irretrievable error. Without conscious thought, she tightened the wrap around her shoulders and arms.

"Colonel Hanna, you're unwelcome in my home. My husband is away, as you're all too aware. You and..." She paused, contemplating how to address the Ambassador's chauffeur "...your cockroach should leave."

The chauffeur edged towards Nasha, uttering a guttural slur. "Look at the whore. How many fathers can claim your children? You should be stoned."

Hanna raised his hand, one eye on the Enfield. "Mahbeer believes your public behavior brings shame to us all. Look at you...your breasts exposed."

Hanna's leering examination made Nasha laugh, further enraging Mahbeer. Enough, she thought, of a two-faced reprobate with pretensions.

"Younger Muslims complain about the blanket of Islamic orthodoxy. The weight is being thrown off, faster in America, slower in other places. Change will be a deluge over the Litani River Dam. Your generation, Nabil, clings to religious orthodoxy and sins in secret." She angled her head to address the chauffeur. "As for you, sinning in the seedy back rooms of strip clubs you frequent...you're a puffed-up pretender. Allah knows you." Face to face with the Colonel, she laughed a second time. "You're too far out of touch to influence the future, other than with force...like you enjoy coercing women. Your generation should be cautious when determining who is devout. Girls in Beirut want answers. They'll be uncomfortable trying to understand Islam as a religion of peace, uncomfortable because of you and your trained monkey. If my behavior is so repulsive, if this country is so corrupt, why not return to Beirut? For now, get out of my house."

Colonel Hanna clapped his hands three times in derisive applause.

"Are you a politician after all, Nasha? Perhaps you are an Arab whore serving the British elite? We shall see." Never taking his eyes from the assault rifle, Nabil Hanna pushed Mahbeer out the front door, bowing with rancid scorn. "Your good Muslim children, if they are Muslim, are safe in their beds."

Nasha locked the door and ran upstairs. Brad safe in his crib, Miriam slept beside him on a spare mattress. Lucia sagged in relief between the mattress and crib, holding a long cold baby bottle.

***

Several large monitors occupied a semicircular workspace. Wires snaked in uncontrolled confusion. The arrangement made a reasonable facsimile of a Wall Street trading floor in miniature. Like the parent of a gifted child, whose intellect soared above and beyond a father's capacity to comprehend, Fulton Bennett's role in their collective effort was worn to a nub.

A rolling chair carried its occupant across a wooden floor. Castors and computer fans produced the only sounds. Only a trained eye could make sense of green numbers filling one screen when full color graphs and charts populated others. Frantic to make mathematical sense of trading patterns by the hundreds, the occupant wrote and tested algorithms to mimic buy/sell decisions. Ten fingers alternated between multiple keyboards, replicating trading activity in real time.

Nothing less than complete accuracy was acceptable.

An hour passed, Bennett exhausted by repetitive, soul-sucking failure. In a world of financial manipulation, where brilliance was a prerequisite, this kid filled the bill. Speed, sometimes more important than brilliance, didn't seem an insurmountable hurdle. Alone inside the beast, the ride kept the kid alive, not money, but money mattered more than anything. Money's the scorecard. Without a result, how much longer will this deception hold water? Money let's us suction the air out of terrorist lungs.

Bennett turned away, closing the attic door.

When Fulton Bennett replaced his cell phone on the night table, sleep wasn't a priority. Whether a blessing of psychological training or a side effect of numbing repetition, having operations and agents in a myriad of time zones made phone calls after midnight a recurring norm. Except when the caller, or the topic, brought down walls erected to preserve emotional stability or sanity itself.

Like all those who've had normalcy shattered, his eyes searched for a clock to calculate the time available to balance personal morality against unfulfilled yearning.

CHAPTER 11

Bennett promised himself to listen, to give Jamie adequate rope.

Jamie looked at Sarah with exasperation. "Run it down for us." Norris the Younger had spent the wee hours running it down for himself, but sections of a paint-by-numbers picture kept changing color and perspective.

"OK…here goes. Item: Frankel was introduced to Nasha Poynter by Razouk, the Lebanese Ambassador. Lebanon can't seem to hold onto a real government…never mind Hezbollah, Hamas or whatever terrorist organization holds power today…damn place has been in limbo forever. So does Ambassador Razouk hold any power and, if he does, will he sell his loyalties? Item: Frankel was so hot for the Poynter woman his pants were on fire. So it will be tough to interest him in one of ours, if he wants Nasha. Item: When the fire alarm went off, Frankel wound up in Jean-Louis Michani's wheelchair…completely shaken. Are Frankel and Michani tight? What was the threat to Frankel…because it wasn't us and wouldn't have been the Brits? And it got incredibly interesting…Grover so anxious for Frankel and Michani to get out safely. Item: Sir Edward Poynter had nasty words with his daughter-in-law. Maybe there's a lever there. Item: Sir Edward was nowhere to be seen as we all evacuated. Wasn't he concerned about his daughter-in-law? And by the way, where was Nasha Poynter after the alarm?"

Jamie agreed with most of the hypotheticals and all the questions —could answer almost none of them. Didn't believe Sarah could, either. Instead of staying on point, he snapped at her.

"Did you sleep with Grover?"

"Be like sleeping with James Bond...no upside and not much exclusivity."

Disapproval spread across Bennett's face.

Sarah tried to recover. "No, sir, Jamie. No sex with your father. Never gonna happen."

Jamie's outrage spilled over. "Did he ask?"

"Yes, in his peculiar way."

"All right..." Jamie hesitated, thinking about his father the enigma.

Sarah felt bad for Jamie. Following a legend, when you'd never be one, was a life sentence. "Where do you want to go with all this?"

"Let's take'em one at a time. What are Razouk's politics?"

Sarah offered a non-answer. "We could approach him."

"No. Get some analysis. We're listening, I presume."

"Will do...and, yes, we're listening. Want to try for cameras?"

"No cameras. Turn up the attention...see if we can get inside Razouk's home. Work a full profile on the Poynter woman."

Sarah nodded agreement.

Jamie Norris leaned back, intending to tick-off the balance of a to-do list. An inevitable conclusion brought him up short. "It's all shit until we know more about Nasha Poynter. You can't recruit her in the dark. We can't approach a man like Michani without..." He met Sarah's gaze and held it "...at our level we'll never approach Michani. Director Bennett can't. Maybe not D/CIA. For God's sake, I don't know who influences a billionaire banker with fingers in half the Middle East's pies. Focus on Poynter...focus on her husband...focus on her whole damn family." Jamie tapped his fingers, then stated the obvious. "I'll talk to my father."

Bennett couldn't ignore Jamie's declaration of defeat.

***

Nasha stood at the reception desk in khakis, Andrew's faded rugby sweater, cross-trainers, not an ounce of makeup or a slash of lipstick. Ordinary was the target, not stuck-up bitch connected by marriage to the Minister. Gormley was professional and hospitable during the fire alarm, and responded with pleasant neutrality to her request this morning. Escorted to the Security Operations room, she shook his hand and accepted tea.

"Did it turn out a technical glitch?"

Gormley winked. "You're aware how these high profile things go. The Embassy is at Status: MINTUA."

"Well...at the Lebanese Embassy, we've not achieved that level of enlightenment. SUSFU is a permanent condition." Performed in a stinging imitation of Minister Sir Edward Poynter, it brought a smile.

Gormley held up his tea, toasting bureaucratic idiocy.

"Edward made his flight to England?"

Gormley responded with tact to her conspiratorial expression. "Sir Edward, as you're aware, doesn't make flights. His charter waits for a government Minister."

"Mr. Gormley..."

"We agreed...you'll call me Frank."

"I'm Nasha." Stress and exceptional circumstances dominated last evening. Both appreciated how stress broke a person down. Today we'll need to rely on fragile goodwill. "Will the Embassy make the video from last evening available to attending nations?

"After it's analyzed and vetted. There are no standing orders either way."

Aah, thought Nasha, the diplomatic fib. "Well...I'm hoping, since you and I went through most of the footage before I left...could I see it all again, here in the Embassy of course, at a convenient time?"

"I can't make you a copy. I'm sorry."

"I don't need a copy...not until it's been cleared."

"Foster spoke to me last night, after he took you home."

Nasha returned to stark formality. "I was a soldier, Mr. Gormley, and the limited combat I experienced left a mark. Please tell Trooper Foster that a fellow soldier is grateful for his assistance and company...my Lebanese co-workers and I apologize for our boorish conduct."

"Edwin says the men in your home behaved as oafs...not that his term was so delicate. Are you in danger...would they...?"

This opening wouldn't repeat itself. The incident file from her home security system, copied to the small device in her hand, played the recording of last evening's confrontation.

"Mahbeer is like all bullies. Should he find me alone in the Embassy, at night, he might try to assault me. Should he find me on the street, no, he's too much a coward. In Beirut, in a group of like-minded men...yes. Colonel Hanna is quite different. In his hands, your Embassy video showing my less than elegant exit from the limo would put me at risk."

Gormley was without meaningful words. "I'll leave your name, and your relationship to the Minister, with reception and the night staff. Call the security office during the second shift…that's three to eleven…the video room will be yours and tea will be brought from the kitchen. Lebanon's copy will be hand delivered to you…no one else. Who knows…perhaps Lebanon's copy may suffer from degradation in video quality…you'll understand our failings. Accept our apologies in advance."

***

Jamie knocked. Stood in the open doorway without entering.

Bennett looked up from a phone call, guessing the visit's purpose. Waved Norris in. Jamie couldn't possibly have delivered Bennett's message to Edward Poynter, not with the big commotion at the embassy. Otherwise Bennett's office phone would be flooded by the Minister's indignant complaints and insistent warnings.

Mouthpiece covered, Bennett asked, "What d'you need?"

"I'll come back later."

Bennett insisted. "What's up?"

"Never got a chance to speak with Sir Edward…with the fire alarm and all the confusion afterwards"

"Yeah…whatever."

Jamie crawled out the door.

Bennett accused himself of behaving like a jackass. Hardass was important in the Intelligence business; being a jackass, not so much.

***

Razouk's call caught her leaving the meeting with Gormley.

The Ambassador explained: A charity luncheon for women of Lebanese descent, being held at the Ritz Carlton-Tysons Corner, included himself as keynote speaker. A more pressing engagement created an unfortunate conflict. Colonel Hanna suggested Nasha stand-in, further advocating that Nasha's topic be the ever-changing role of the Muslim-American woman.

Should've let young Foster shoot the son-of-a-bitch, Nasha thought in perfect hindsight. Another dress-up occasion and me looking like a ragamuffin.

***

Bennett pushed the Mustang's small block V-8. It responded, purring past four thousand RPM before he eased the throttle back. He took the exit onto Chain Bridge Road then found the turns for Tysons Blvd. With the rearview clear, an illegal turn delivered him to the Ritz's garage, circling ramps to the roof. Parked, he sat silent and still for several minutes. Intellect and instinct attempted intercession without any sign Bennett would pay heed. He stripped off his suit jacket, replacing it with a nondescript barn coat. A knit hat, pulled down over his ears, would block the wind and hide his features. Thin leather driving gloves encased fingers that reached into the glove box to snag a burner phone and one of a menagerie of untraceable handguns.

Fulton Bennett, not qualified as a Field Officer, accepted how far out of bounds his behavior fell. His head would roll, if this escapade wound up fodder for either ravenous blogs or cannibals in Congress.

Ritz Carlton Tyson's, Room 422, that's what last night's voice instructed. *Arrive later than 12:30, your precious Caroline will be dead on the floor.*

Bennett had the short message analyzed with no useful result. The man might be European, or East Asian adopting European inflection. Similarly, he'd made inquiries through London Station as to Caroline Panero's whereabouts; Caroline hadn't entered England or the US in the last month, not officially.

So where is she?

As he approached, the hallway in both directions was vacant. No maids. No men with guns. The door was different; a plush white hand towel propped it open.

***

Nasha took I-66 to the beltway. Unaware of being surveilled, stop and go traffic and spitting rain became her most pressing concerns.

Her minivan reached the garage behind three other vehicles. Patience tested, when the occupant of a light blue Lexus dropped her ticket, cigarette dangling from bright red lips, the woman leaned out an open door, hand probing the pavement. A horn blared. Out of the Lexus, the woman snatched the ticket and flipped-off the horn blower. On the second level, Nasha watched the Lexus grab a spot near the elevator. No open space presented itself until Nasha approached the roof.

Even with the wet windshield, Nasha had a full-on view of the man closing the Mustang's trunk. When Fulton Bennett checked behind him, she was a suburban housewife in one of Washington's gazillion minivans. Though on the cusp of being late, curiosity bubbled and prodded. Inside the Mustang she saw business attire strewn over the car's interior.

Chased by a peculiar sensation, Nasha moved the van to the opposite side of the roof.

Fathima Laniado clutched an invitation to the luncheon as the heels of her pumps clicked over the garage floor. "Nasha...wait."

Nasha turned and watched the embassy's Cultural Attaché hurry to her side.

Deadpan, Fathima gave nothing away. "I'm excited to hear you speak today. Nabil tells me he got a preview at your home last night."

Was Laniado's false sincerity cold-blooded evil or sickening syrup? Nasha vamped, "Won't this afternoon be such fun."

Fathima enjoyed the anticipation. *Nasha isn't stupid; she believes I'll embarrass her in front of social climbing women with too much money and nothing better to do.*

On the ground floor, Nasha glimpsed the flowing mane, shapely legs and crimson lips of the Lexus owner entering the main bank of hotel elevators. Moments later, as Fathima angled towards the ladies room, Nasha carried understated intensity into the private dining room. Many of the women were greeted as friends. Not in any way did reasoning suggest this get-together as enemy territory.

***

Bennett thought about knocking. Considered calling hotel security. Evaluated several less attractive options, but not once did a rapid departure receive scrutiny.

For years he grappled with the addiction to Caroline. Perhaps a high-toned, teenage fashion model, with pouty lips and razor-sharp tongue, was yesterday's illusion. Perhaps Caroline, socialite princess and daughter of Britain's Intelligence impresario, never offered mindless, extravagant, sex to a married CIA officer. Perhaps Fulton Bennett never turned to jelly in the presence of beauty and brilliance, or been besotted enough to fantasize marriage. Now he resembled a silly old drunk for whom one drink saw him off the cliff, and a barrel wouldn't break his fall.

He pushed open the door with his left hand, the right full of false bravado. Swiveled the gun across a room unoccupied by person or luggage. Adrenaline withdrawal strangling courage, he examined the bathroom before standing, stupidly aware, nerves sizzling, at the foot of the king-sized bed. Flooded with regret, he prepared for a kill team's arrival. Legs quivered and his grasp on life deteriorated in expectation.

"Good afternoon, Mr. Bennett."

Bennett's partial recovery suggested the accent as South African, if not electronic in origin.

"By now, you understand. Your actions, from when you parked your charming antique, changed clothes, checked the magazine of your un-registered weapon and entered Room 422 have been, and are being, recorded. I'm prepared to execute you, Mr. Bennett, and, should you attempt to depart without permission, execute you I will. Shooting an armed intruder is a well-defended right of all Americans…and you no more than a rogue spy intent on mayhem. Please acknowledge that you understand our rapprochement."

"I understand you intend to execute me and make a claim of self defense in what will be seen as murder."

"Only if you attempt to go walk-about."

A hundred things could be nitpicked regarding the voice's claims. None rose to a level worth challenging. Not when winning a verbal sparring match ended with twin bullets in the brain.

Bennett abandoned guilt and disappointment. "What can I do for you?"

"In a few minutes a woman…not the exquisite yet troubled Mrs. Panero…will enter the room using her card key. You'll not speak.

Remove the clip, place your weapon on the dresser and undress for compulsory embarrassing photographs. Full frontal nudity, if you please...copulation optional. Is your role clear? Please...verbalize for the recording."

Certain humiliation versus probable death—not an optimal choice. Bennett believed the voice. Believed its owner as neither dim-witted nor flexible. This is a situation of my own making; like a freaking virgin I walked in wearing no more than a nervous smile carrying a chilled bottle of wine.

"I understand. I'll pose for explicit video."

"Judicious choice, Mr. Bennett. My photographer...another lovely lady...will join you and your paramour shortly. You'll be back in your office in less than an hour. We'll talk again another time."

Bennett watched a long-legged platinum blonde enter the room carrying a sack purse slung across her back. Not some back alley hooker, whoever is stringing me out matched the call girl to what a man with experience, professional standing and a certain means would expect. Long coat dropped to the floor, she pulled an expensive, short knit dress over her head allowing its absence to reveal everything.

Mesmerized by his colossal mistake and her smooth figure, he complied with the voice's demand. Each movement burned more of a lifetime's achievement to the ground. She lay on the bottom sheet, inviting him with open arms and inviting lips. Here stands Fulton Bennett, he thought, at the pinnacle of his career with nowhere to go: A man supervising Agency officers in the manipulation of Aaron Frankel using sex; a man whose career witnessed a dozen qualified Field Officers drawn into liaisons that proved false; a man who lost a wife and family to infantile infidelity.

It would almost be better to escape or die trying.

Bennett became erect as she touched him.

Braced by the cellphone's light, he observed white protective clothing accented by flyaway orange hair—and a gloved hand operating the phone's video function. Identified an odd looking jig holding his gun. Saw and heard a gunshot's explosion.

Bennett lay coupled with a dead woman in a pool of blood, brains, and commingled DNA. Ears ringing, all mental and intellectual systems paralytic, he watched the back of the photographer as she exited.

Bennett would recollect nothing of her presence except shimmering orange against bright white.

Movements governed by an autopilot he'd mostly forgotten, Bennett's emotions were marked by self-loathing. Face the truth. Risk anything. Care no more for the opinions of others. Do the hardest thing on earth for you—advice issued in the early nineteen hundreds had been Bennett's personal Bible. He rolled the dead woman's body onto the floor—stripped the bed sheet, tying it into a sack containing the towel used to clean himself. Spilled the minibar's entire contents into the ice bucket, sprinkling the mixture over everything he could. Repeated the procedure on the corpse's genitals and face. Asked himself—would it be enough to contaminate evidence?

Nineteen minutes after his gun, carrying his fingerprints, shot the escort; twelve minutes after Fairfax dispatch received the call reporting shots fired; three minutes after the police arrived at the Ritz, Bennett plodded the hallway carrying the knotted sheet. In the service elevator he offered a calm nod to a man carrying a toolbox. Paid the parking attendant in cash. Drove away without looking in the direction of police vehicles sitting motionless at the main entrance. Doors askew, their red and blue strobe lights reflected off low clouds.

***

Two British agents heard rumors flooding the hotel. Hearsay regarding murder wouldn't alter their directive vis a vis Nasha Poynter, but increased their attention to detail.

The female agent stepped inside the dining room as if she belonged.

A shooting at Tysons made it a local matter; FBI agents remained focused on Nasha Poynter and those arriving or leaving the Ritz. Aware the shooter might be among that group, they engaged long lens cameras.

***

Lunch hadn't reached dessert, when an unsettling ripple coursed through the dining room. The group's Chairwoman announced the occurrence of a violent incident on the fourth floor. After assuring attendees Police were in the hotel, and the situation was under control, Lebanese women decided to enjoy dessert and coffee while listening to Nasha Poynter's views on the modern, Lebanese-American, Muslim woman.

Nasha wandered the room holding a wireless microphone, making eye contact with each woman as she spoke of what the United States meant to her children, as well as how living as an Arab-American changed her dreams and faith. Much of what she hurled in defiance at Nabil Hanna, regarding Muslim women wedged between the old ways and emerging attitudes, flooded her emotions. Nasha segued to a Q&A. After nine responses, not one about growing up Muslim in a Jewish household, Nasha intended to surrender the microphone.

An elegant woman, silver streaks in cropped dark hair, rose to speak.

"All across the globe women are assuming roles reserved in tradition for males..." The room broke out in supportive murmurs "...be those roles at the lowest or highest echelons of political power. Times are changing...I don't dispute it. Too slow to suit my taste." Half the room laughed. "It's been argued that Lebanon fails itself by having no women in high political posts. My question, dear Nasha...given women are an untapped resource, and we Lebanese suffered in conflict after conflict despite our differing faiths...why hasn't an educated, well spoken, brave and beautiful mother such as Nasha Gemayel taken the mantel of her martyred father?"

Nasha Gemayel never knew her biological father and didn't covet a birthright more wishful thinking than reality—one which couldn't be proven, not without tearing my life to shreds. Her answer shocked Nasha most of all.

"Political and economic stability will be unreachable until women are inseparable from men in the decision-making processes of Lebanon's government, as is the case in other societies. Muslim countries, in addition to suffering women's exclusion from economics and politics, are characterized by circumstances and mores defeating the progress of women in these same areas. What should concern us are the reasons for women's absence. Arguments in favor of women can focus on ideals like equal democracy, constitutional protections, and the rule of law, but they shouldn't suffer flights of fancy."

As the room buzzed with the kind of excitement attending ambush journalism, Nasha turned to the lights, camera and her questioner.

"That Muslim women are allowed to participate in politics is itself a serious misconception. Muslim women haven't attained influence in Lebanon, or other Arab countries, equal to their counterparts in other parts of the world. Women are fifty percent of the world's population, but our political, economic and social powers are abominably lower than men. Lebanon is an Arab country, sixty percent Muslim...forty percent Christian. Lebanon is a democratic state; every religious sect either shares or competes for influence and power. Lebanon has political and social freedom, but political stability isn't our homeland's trademark. Our love of intrigue, sectarian conflict, and high profile assassinations make investors hesitate and children tremble. When will the door to leadership, or the Presidency, be opened by a woman...not by a man? My name may be Nasha Gemayel Poynter...whether Bachir Gemayel is my father cannot be known. I make no claim to his lineage. I'm American, like all of you."

A voice rose from near the entrance doorway. "You're the bastard child of a street whore, who stands in this room with your head covered, while exposing your body and spreading your legs for the infidel as your mother did."

Fathima's words echoed with grotesque impact, bounced off faces aghast and angered at their crudity. Fathima's incendiary stare perforated Nasha; Nabil Hanna's vitriolic response half expected, if unwelcome. Fathima's change of clothes brought an unavoidable conclusion, one requiring investigation and mitigation, though both would come later.

Nasha refocused her eyes: The busboy's white coat turned away almost fast enough to avoid recognition.

To reconnect with her audience, she rotated her gaze to each table. Spoke in a bright tone to prove Fathima's vitriol left no bruises.

"Let me introduce Fathima Laniado, an employee of the Embassy and a citizen of Lebanon residing in Washington as a guest of the United States. Fathima appreciates the rights of free speech we Americans enjoy. What repercussions would she face in many Middle Eastern countries, if Fathima aimed such verbal bile at a man?

"For my blessed mother's sake, this character assassination is despicable…Fathima should be ashamed. My mother's sister, cut to pieces by a machine gun on my seventh birthday, described my mother as sensitive and loving. For myself…I brought virginity to my marriage bed and feel no shame for my life or actions. I'm neither a Lebanese or American politician and won't change my mind. Thank you for having me as your guest."

Nasha replaced the microphone. A different reporter raised her voice. "Nasha…women candidates say bribery and corruption will be less of an issue, if women are voted into parliament. They say women are less susceptible to underhanded behavior. Would you agree?"

"Does it honestly matter, if your hypothesis is true? No claim about women's performance in government can be disproved or discounted unless and until women are given similar opportunity. Indonesia, Pakistan, Bangladesh and India…all elected women as Prime Minister. In the abstract, some aspects of Islam are incompatible with women's rights. Reality can be quite different."

Restlessness filled the room. An experienced reporter grasped the opportunity to inject another question. "The argument goes…men hold power and men, by their nature, are more capable of carrying out the duties of power. Men, so the argument goes, are better suited for the pressures of governing in an anarchical world. What do you think?"

Nasha guffawed. "My experience with men is based on my infant son and British husband. Anarchy is expertly generated by men and only calmed by a woman. Thank you again for inviting the Ambassador and making me welcome in his absence."

No matter Nasha's urgent impulse to pursue the heavyset busboy, decorum prevailed. As she moved through the crowd, shaking hands and expressing the Ambassador's regrets, Fathima reminded one and all of the *Hadith* long used as a sledgehammer to exclude women from politics: "A people who place women in charge of their affairs will never prosper."

Nasha raised her voice upon catching a glimpse of the British agent easing herself towards the door. "Could you wait a moment, please?"

The agent seemed anxious to establish bona fides. "I can offer you a nice package of pictures."

Nasha sat in the closest chair and indicated the agent should join her. "I noticed you, before the police went running by the doors." Nasha observed the agent, whose embarrassment and career concerns dominated good judgment.

"Let's just say you're a photographer, shall we?"

The agent raised her eyebrows. Earlier she might have sworn Nasha Poynter another ambitious politician on the make. Now? Sir Edward's daughter-in-law is focused on something other than playing to the camera.

"Could you show me shots you took, when I arrived? You might leave with more than you bargained for." Nasha watched the agent's wheels spin, trying to calculate peril versus prize. Both viewing the small screen, she scrolled until Nasha pointed at a sharp, full-length shot of herself and Fathima in dresses the color of clotted cream.

Nasha prodded. "See the time stamp?"

Puzzled, contemplative then enlightened, the agent nodded.

Nasha's satisfaction showed in her compliment. "Only a woman would notice."

The agent fast-forwarded, stopping when the small screen displayed a shot of Fathima shouting accusations. "When did Laniado change clothes? Why?" Seconds passed. "You arrived together, but this first one...Laniado went to the loo. You're suggesting she's involved in the shooting." She proceeded to examine each photo of Fathima and Nasha in detail. "Nothing shows Fathima entering the luncheon. Shit, that's easy to miss."

"I'd like to review all the hotel security footage...looking for a woman in a cream colored dress with a brown headscarf...looking for a woman who just might, if someone altered time stamps, be Nasha Gemayel Poynter, daughter-in-law of Minister Sir Edward Poynter." Unflinching sense of humor on display, Nasha added, "Possibly such an accusation would portray the long lost daughter of the former President of Lebanon as a murderer."

"What's Laniado's motive?"

"No offense, but that's a question for higher up the food chain."

"What will you do?"

"I'll be in Mr. Gormley's hidey-hole this evening, after dinner." Nasha offered a knowing look. "Thanks in advance."

The British agent made eye contact with her partner, as she followed the Minister's daughter-in-law at a discrete distance. Any simplistic assessment of Nasha Gemayel Poynter would be subject to substantial revision.

***

A taxi dropped her in front of the Embassy of Finland. Intended to expose cars or people assigned to follow her, a counter-surveillance pattern marked the biggest change since she'd come to the United States.

Tonight she was no longer safe.

A black leather holster pushed against the small of her back. She'd defend herself first; worries about consequences would finish distant second.

Crooked circle almost complete, Nasha rang the bell at the Embassy of Great Britain.

Nasha volunteered her weapon and allowed a pro forma pat down. A Royal Marine escorted her to the security station. Inside, one of several dedicated video stations held a sticky note bearing the name of Sir Edward Poynter. Taking notice of Gormley's snide humor, she arranged a yellow legal pad in her lap, placed the headphones on her ears and pressed *Play*.

CHAPTER 12

Oh momma. Oh daddy. Why can't you hear me cry? I'm lost and so, so lonely, please find me 'fore I die. Bennett was certain he messed-up the lyrics, but a tortured soul couldn't be picky.

Bennett's rational self insisted procedures and protocols should prevail. He listened to directives coming from inside his head: Point the Mustang in Langley's direction; find the D/CIA; get ahead of the shit-storm. When faced with other officers involved in serious fuckups, he'd spouted interchangeable advice, ad nauseam, to those others.

Behind what remained of a high fence constructed of stone rubble, in a restored gatehouse belonging to an estate long since subdivided, Anne Linton heard the Mustang's deep exhaust.

Head down, shoulders hanging low, he approached.

Restoration work no longer relevant, hidden behind shutters in what passed as Fulton's guest bedroom, Anne heard the heavy mahogany entrance door open. Without any attempt to brush sawdust from her hair, face and everywhere else, she descended a half-finished staircase.

Bennett witnessed her sympathy, disoriented and disjointed as he knew it must be. Passed by Anne as if she no longer existed.

***

When Phyllis Martell asked where to find Yusef Schwartz, she spotted alarm bells ringing in Maury Lipmann's head.

With the Mailroom's routine fractured, bile rose in Maury's throat. Worried, yet riveted by Martell's arrival, Maury scoured recent events for some error of omission or commission. He pointed to where Yusef knotted the drawstring on a canvas carryall which contained individual Burn-bags.

Martell wore a pained face. No introduction or prologue prefaced her question. "Mr. Schwartz, when did you become aware Mr. Bennett wouldn't be playing basketball this evening?"

A puzzled look explained Yusef's hesitation. "Right now...when you asked your question."

"Are you certain?"

"Been here my entire shift."

Why did she come to the mailroom, instead of seeking higher-ranking players on Bennett's Bashers? Yusef sniffed rebellious sweat hanging in the air. Two hours later, stress levels in the gym reminded Yusef of the moment when Martell approached him like a guided missile.

Grover Norris—a real-life Washington God—waved his hands at Fred Rasby. All the high-pitched hooey suggested Norris's arguments for postponement fell on deaf ears.

Yusef let himself enjoy the show.

Jamie stood two steps behind his father, saying less than nothing. Along the sideline with Yusef, Sarah dribbled in-place, trying to project an attitude of laissez faire. JET shot jumpers by himself.

Any way Grover counted, four Bashers were present and dressed for the game.

Yusef could tell; Jamie would forfeit before supporting his father as a fifth player.

Yusef sought normalcy in all things. Under these circumstances, normal included an expected dollop of curiosity. "Sarah, some lady came down the basement. Asked me when I found out Bennett wouldn't play tonight. What's up?"

"What lady?"

"She wasn't much for introductions."

Sarah whipped her head around, all of a sudden her interest more than a little tweaked. "Who else did she speak to?"

"Maury Lipmann, Mailroom Manager."

Yusef didn't think Sarah could find the mailroom with a map. "Is Bennett okay?" It seemed acceptable to act concerned as long as an innocent interest didn't blossom into overt attentiveness.

Sarah's eyes grew larger, then collapsed in pained self-adsorption.

Yusef Schwartz observed her body language: Sarah Gullickson would waste no mental energy on a pawn, whose employment by, and largest contribution to the Agency consisted of having grown tall.

Grover headed for the exit like a scalded cat.

Jamie informed his three teammates, "No game. Sorry."

JET slammed a ball hard off the floor. "So whassup? No small shit...your daddy bein' here. Bennett dead? In some Taliban cave? Seventh floor suits got Special Snowflake Syndrome...never even know if the man gone rogue."

Yusef looked-on with suspicious concern. Clear as a bell to the entire gym, Jamie Norris possessed no answers. Bennett's operations and people, leaderless and adrift, would suffer the slings and arrows of Grover's ascension to power. He exchanged glances with JET. Shrugged. Tossed a ball over his shoulder, heard it hit the rim and fall through.

An ugly question brewed in Yusef's mind: To whose tune am I dancing?

***

Zachary Mannheim intended to disagree with the Agency's Director.

D/CIA Theodore Granholm, advanced to the Agency from the military when nominated by the president, accepted his appointment as a political expedience. Not greeted with rave reviews, he led an Agency with values and customs often at odds with the military.

Mannheim wouldn't cross the line into disagreeing disagreeably, and was prepared to understand, if either the Agency's second in command ("DD/CIA") or the Agency's General Counsel, felt otherwise. As for Grover Norris, Mannheim observed an historical precedent; he would walk on eggs.

There would be five, DD/CIA had informed him. No need for Mannheim to bring staff or take notes, the topic being too sensitive.

Baloney, Zachary remembered thinking, the topic would be Fulton Bennett.

The building vibrated with theories; Martell had confirmed Bennett's unusual absence. Spies kept secrets badly, when spies were the subjects.

When Mannheim entered the conference room appended to D/CIA's office, a funereal pall hung over whatever deliberations preceded him. No massive acuity was needed to grasp the purpose of his presence: I'm to be employed as a blunt instrument. After hearing an outline of Fulton's circumstances straight from the horse's ass, Mannheim watched as D/CIA resumed a sphinxlike silence.

General Counsel, abhorring a vacuum, opined that Bennett's actions replicated a swamp, filled with snakes and alligators prepared to bite the Agency and its senior executives on an indelicate body part. "Bennett's the Pope of clandestine operations. For Christ's sake, what's the fucking Pope doing in bed with a dead hooker. The man cannot manage his issues."

Mannheim spoke for the first time.

"History eludes you, Owen. Popes married before becoming Pontiff, enjoyed sex during their pontificate, even fathered a future Pope. John XII, anointed the Caligula of Popes, was deposed by conclave and murdered by a jealous husband. Damian, an eleventh century monk, called priests' sex partners *devil's choice tidbits, virus of minds, sword of soul, poison to companions…the ancient enemy*. It's an old story, Owen…" Mannheim allowed a spare smile to escape "…and none of us in this glass house even a Pope."

DD/CIA scowled in mock disapproval, before informing Mannheim that Grover would, henceforth, act in Bennett's stead. Never verbalized, Norris's approbation from the White House, and the Select Committees on Intelligence of the House and Senate, weighed on Mannheim's expectations.

Norris's words, spoken from the mouth of DD/CIA, spelled-out Mannheim's assignment.

"Interrogate Bennett, Zachary. We need to isolate Bennett from the Agency. Insulate any and all loose ends from prying eyes. Preserve the operational integrity of NCS. Can you do that?"

Purely rhetorical as a legitimate inquiry, Mannheim's opinion of Bennett's situation remained unsolicited. Mannheim believed it possible these four knew less than they let on. Just minutes earlier, D/CIA had danced around the how and from whom came the sparse information now passed to Zachary by the fulsome foursome.

General Counsel's task, in this instance, prioritized protection of D/CIA and the reputation of the Agency, more or less in that order.

Grover Norris's first concern could only be to grandstand, talk to the media on Sunday morning television and, if Granholm went off the rails, find adequate rationale for the President to dump D/CIA on the scrap heap of failed Intelligence.

A clumsy period ensued as Mannheim searched for consensus. Tormented at the ease with which Bennett's support, if not defense, had been abandoned, he elected to enquire.

"Is there room to consider middle ground? Bennett's record is stellar and his reputation, until now, unassailable. The Agency could bury allegations under denunciation...terrorists trying to weaken the Agency with lies and excrement, trying to diminish the field capabilities of an Agency filled with junior officers possessed of little field experience and senior executives with scant history managing covert operations."

Mannheim's veiled indictment should've brought righteous indignation and a warning against contravening direct orders. Indeed, Owen Lattimore would remind them: A direct order was the last thing which would be issued by the seventh floor.

No offense seemingly taken, Granholm turned Mannheim's earlier misgivings around. "Bennett's the one who suggested this course of action, Zach. Bulletproof clearance by CIC keeps him out of prison...nothing less will do."

Mannheim detested phony camaraderie draped over D/CIA's use of *Zach*. We aren't friends. Not even colleagues. In his four-month tenure, Granholm demonstrated faint interest in what went on at CIC.

"Perhaps it would be best...for CIC's investigation, that is...to start at the beginning. What is Fulton Bennett's neck size...for the noose, you know? Or, with apologies in advance, I'd ask what crime he is accused of...aside from being stupid and human."

Grover Norris understood how to use the President's unseen hand. "No cover-ups. Not this time. Not ever again. What did we know? When did we know it? What did we do about it? Perception is reality...Bennett gets no slack."

Lattimore stepped into a breach of political etiquette. "There's no we in this instance, Grover. D/CIA's office is not the subject of CIC's investigation. I've instructed D/CIA Granholm not to answer questions about his short phone conversation with Mr. Bennett."

Bennett's title of Deputy Director/National Clandestine Service, lapsed from usage in this meeting, left no ambiguity surrounding its intentional omission.

Mannheim considered allowing a mild scolding to slide. Then didn't. "Owen, are you suggesting CIC won't be granted access to D/CIA, if warranted, or CIC's investigation will be frustrated by withholding access?" Mannheim chose *frustrated* over *impeded*, but his Germanic tone contributed clarification. Lattimore's warning walked up to the line separating politics from obstruction. Perhaps Owen even took a peek over a demarcation with real consequence.

Mannheim's recorded ability to playback the General Counsel's voice counted as a spy-hunter's advantage.

Lattimore was quick to bite a second time. "You'll get all the access you're entitled to. What you won't get is the unfettered right to interrogate D/CIA, DD/CIA or Mr. Norris about a sketchy phone call, the details of which haven't been vetted. Are you clear on this point?"

Satisfied or not, it was time for Mannheim to give the appearance of substantive cooperation.

"Oh yes, Owen, I'm quite clear on the mandate held by CIC. For the record and because you seem sensitized to D/CIA's involvement with Deputy Director Bennett's issues, whatever they may be, I'll be sending DD/CIA a written summary of today's instructions to CIC. I'd very much appreciate his and your counter-signatures."

Mannheim made eye contact with each man in turn.

"Oh, and Owen, I'd almost forgotten…has Bennett been formally suspended from NCS, or is Mr. Norris the Younger acting under an ad hoc arrangement?"

Lattimore's face convulsed under strain, while his inflection never faltered from agreeable. "Informal as a request from the President of the United States can be."

***

In a room gone quiet, Jamie Norris waited for the reactions of his team. Bennett's team in reality, but nothing could be done about that state of affairs.

Robby Turcott stared at the ceiling, thinking about Phyllis Martell's investigation.

Sarah Gullickson tread water, searching for a chance to say her piece.

David Nazarian wanted nothing to do with this crowd.

Puzzled by the request for his participation, Greg Riley considered the entire discussion a bad joke. How Fulton Bennett found himself down in this ditch no longer mattered. I won't be an Agency employee much longer, if the likes of Jamie Norris replace Fulton Bennett. Unable to keep whimsy from his voice, there was none on his face.

"Grover told you Bennett's in deep shit, but didn't offer more than a non-explanation. Is that where we stand?"

Jamie pushed words out his mouth, expression an empty space between sad and heartbroken. "Yup, all the old sayings fit my old man. Can juggle a hot potato long enough for it to become a cold issue. Will lay your life down for his country."

Riley lowered his opinion of Norris the Younger. "Grover wants you to focus all your team's efforts on Aaron Frankel and grabbing bin Rahman's money?"

Jamie again found himself embarrassed. "I decided to include you, Greg, so all of us, even those with peripheral involvement, know what the team is working to accomplish."

Riley wouldn't reveal the depth of his anger. "Don't read me in. I don't work for you. I don't work for Bennett, if Bennett still works here. I know nothing about Aaron Frankel...with the exception of what's been discussed today, and what anybody who can read already knows. Let's cover my operation for everyone else...then let me get out of your way."

Jamie shook his head. "No, Greg. We're a man down. Bennett respects you. We're in need of a Devil's Advocate...for now that's you."

Nazarian gave Norris a half-ounce of credit; an independent opinion on pending Ops made sense. Jamie's logic didn't, however, factor a hole so obvious, so plainly written on other faces it needn't be rubbed raw, unless David refused a role nowhere in his job description.

Jamie asked Robby, "What are you doing about Martell's investigation of the Probst assassination?"

"Nada. Martell's been unavailable since Bennett went AWOL. Prior to all this chaos, we did a few interviews. Report's on your desk. David's sitting right here...experienced field agent followed his instincts. Didn't recognize Gunther in the hotel bar. Sure, he left his position on Frankel for a few minutes. Got away with it—nothing changed with Frankel's surveillance while he played White Knight to an undercover legend."

Robby's emphasis on *legend* carried equal measures of sympathy and mockery

Sarah jumped in. "Raissa is now, and always has been, drop-dead gorgeous. She was also the very best at her job. If we had someone like her for the Frankel Op, we'd be near the finish line. Give me a decision on Nasha Poynter, Jamie. Op is withering from neglect."

Jamie pulled the pin from an allegorical grenade.

"Nazarian's job is finding Ribeiro. She's either the next target...or could be the hitter, if for some reason she wanted Gunther dead. Bennett wanted Ribeiro found. Seventh floor wants Nazarian given carte blanche. Grover..." Jamie pronounced his father's name with antipathy "...wants Raissa eliminated. Grover believes we'll never find the hitter, never be sure of Ribeiro's innocence. Simpler all around if Raissa's terminated."

David Nazarian wore a sickened expression.

Riley, appalled, fought against open rebellion. "Is that what the great god Bennett would do?"

Nobody laughed. Each of them knew Fulton Bennett would slit Grover Norris's throat rather than see a retired and decorated officer executed for the sake of expedience.

Riley offered more pertinent questions. "Who does Grover think he is? Who authorized such a termination? Grover can't...can he?"

Faced with the ultimate query, the room's awkward silence filled a void. Not a coward, and not naive, Jamie Norris acknowledged what others believed. "Ask a specific question about Grover Norris's authority and watch your career vaporize."

Riley turned to Nazarian. "David...who tasked you with Ribeiro's termination?"

Unwilling to answer, Nazarian shrugged.

Riley mumbled something, then repeated it for all to hear.

"Can't be right."

With a few moments further contemplation, he took a difficult stance. "Nothing I've heard warrants such an action."

Sarah wanted the last word. "Maybe David can't tell us?"

Jamie changed the topic. "Sarah, are you recommending an approach to Nasha Poynter...about Frankel?"

Sarah Gullickson had no difficulty with Jamie's weakness. Grover wielded the President's imprimatur with the deft touch of a neurosurgeon. Saw events at the molecular level. Controlled outcomes leaving behind the fingerprints of DD/CIA, a tool attached to Grover's robotic arm.

Sarah had watched Nasha Poynter's interaction with Aaron Frankel, and observed Frankel's feverish pursuit. What Sarah needed was a way around Jamie's myopia.

"Three women made our shortlist: A French woman teaching at Georgetown; a Syrian model; and a Canadian ice skater. Final vetting gave us problems: The Syrian has acquired a drug habit and the Canadian suffered a torn ACL. Reconstructive surgery eliminates her. The French professor remains viable but lacks real zing. Frankel went gaga over Nasha Poynter at the British Embassy shindig. American/Lebanese background, employed at Lebanon's embassy, she's married to the son of Sir Edward Poynter. Beyond the connection to British Intelligence, she's bright and sexy as hell. Related by marriage to Sir Edward makes her forbidden fruit. On top of that, there's speculation she's the love child of former Lebanese President, Bachir Gemayel. Nasha Poynter is hot...in every possible way. Frankel wants her."

Nazarian considered asking Mannheim for an immediate meeting. Sarah wouldn't soon admit how, back in Grover's suite after the British party, she whispered in Grover's ear while his tongue roamed her nipples. Unauthorized video of the twosome, from a yet unidentified source, burned a hole in David's pocket.

Jamie limited his questions. "Who makes the approach...and when?"

Sarah made her case. "Her husband's overseas, so it's got to be before he gets home. Who? Poynter was orphaned at seven...adopted and brought to Washington by Jean-Louis Michani. Michani and Grover are business rivals. Michani will know Grover's back at the Agency, so it's hard to see him cooperating. Not Bennett...Bennett and Sir Edward hate each other. It's been our Op, Jamie. Now that you're Acting Deputy Director, the Op should be mine."

Riley, still disturbed, could make no sense of what he heard.

"Sir Edward Poynter…Minister in charge of MI-5, MI-6 and all the rest? A little over Bennett's head, wouldn't you say? Who says their relationship's in the shitter…who's the source for that?"

Jamie refused to let the meeting shift into reverse.

"Grover's the source. He goes way back with lots of people. His familiarity with Frankel is a key reason he's back on the seventh floor."

Riley suffered an ugly epiphany: Bennett's sudden interest in French submarines centered on a Washington influence peddler arrested on a French nuclear sub. Riley wondered—could French success have come at British expense? "What's the husband's name?"

Sarah Gullickson glanced at her notes, unhappy with this development. "Andrew…why do you ask?"

Riley didn't answer. "How about other family members…other Poynters besides Sir Edward and Andrew."

Sarah could object or refuse to respond, but Riley's interest sounded innocent enough. "Sir Edward's wife passed away years ago. There's a daughter…Caroline Poynter Panero. Married, lives in London with three kids. Again, Greg…why does it matter?"

Again Riley pursued actionable intelligence. "Is it fair to assume Sir Edward is wealthy…English nobility and such."

"Once upon a time. Sir Edward's wife inherited a fortune…he pissed it away. London home, country estate, a certain style required for a peer of the realm…a Minister's pittance and his wife's cash to pay for it. So, if your wondering whether the Poynter woman might be purchased, you may be right. Money talks and we've got the budget."

Greg Riley's point hadn't been anything like inducing Nasha Poynter to prostitute herself, so he decided to let the meeting run its course.

Nazarian found it difficult to accept the crap this crowd passed-off as intelligence. Jamie is weak. Sarah's an amoral backstabber, without the experience to make it work. Only Riley, a scientist not a spy, is a critical thinker. Absent Bennett's professionalism and leadership, the so-called team barely qualified as spies. David slipped from the room, consumed with the need to find a way forward.

Jamie wanted to wrap things up. "Sarah...let me know when you're ready to make the approach." He looked round the table. "Anything else?"

Riley wanted Jamie's official direction. "Bennett showed strong interest in French submarines and their sale to India, Malaysia and Brazil. Stay on it...or let it go?"

Jamie Norris neglected to mention submarines to his father or the DD/CIA. Where could Bennett have been headed? On the chance Bennett would rise from his grave, he conceded.

"Stay on it, Greg. Your area...your call. E-mail with news."

***

Bennett, asleep when the phone rang, waited to hear the exact excuse Anne would make for him. After chopping wood for hours, he felt no better. A gigantic headache dominated any ability to think or plan.

Anne caught it on the second ring. "Hello."

"Hello, Anne. This is Zachary Mannheim from Langley. Is Fulton available, please?"

Anne Linton's long since adopted routine, for calls such as this one, kicked-in with a pleasant rejection. "I'm sorry, Mr. Mannheim, he's not available. I'll tell him you called."

"Ms. Linton, my call is a courtesy. Fulton should expect my arrival within the hour. Let him know it would be unwise to leave home. Please tell him I'll be unescorted and unarmed."

CHAPTER 13

Nasha watched the monitor for the best part of three hours.

Watcher 3 alerted Nazarian, but the British Embassy's security room turned out to be impenetrable.

Sometimes she could see the complete movements of a partygoer through the rooms and halls of the Embassy. In other cases her target would disappear and reappear at random. With the activities of persons-of-interest catalogued, question marks placed on others needing added research, or elucidation from Gormley, no face had been ignored. Drained from bending her mind around evidence the video showed with clarity, and what it hinted at, being a lip reader would've helped. A mind reader would've solved all her problems.

Lukewarm tea set aside, her hand ran down raw notes with a green highlighter: Green slashes merited a second review. Conclusions supported by actual data informed a valuable mental list: Sir Edward Poynter is more devious than I thought possible; Fouad Razouk's ambition isn't limited to Ambassador; Yusef is a stranger to me, but not to Papa; Papa is tied somehow to Aaron Frankel; Grover Norris isn't retired from the Agency; Frankel is very frightened sitting in Papa's wheelchair; Papa wasn't frightened, he was determined.

A knock on the door interrupted. The female British agent asked, "Got a minute?"

"Come in, please. I'm the guest, not you."

Armed with sandwiches and more tea, the agent offered a smile. "Listen, I'm Grace...didn't mean to be rude at the hotel. How go the movies?"

Nasha queued up Grace's positions on the video: By the curb as a greeter; mingling inside as the party got started; and, after the fire alarm, manning the main entrance routing guests to safety.

Nasha typed a digital address and pointed at the screen. "Seen him before?"

Grace examined the face. "You know...that's anybody and everybody."

"Well-dressed, shoes buffed, a gentleman's manicure...and a forehead that doesn't move a millimeter. Maybe Botox." They shared an unexpected moment of professional camaraderie. Nasha added, "Any luck with security video at the Ritz?"

Grace's face turned serious. "If someone gave it a quick once-over without examining the file frame by frame, the woman who murdered the call-girl could've been you."

"Any chance you suggested where Fairfax cops might look?"

"Not my job...though I mentioned Arab Television would account for every woman at the luncheon."

***

One last time Andrew listened to the audio file. Marco's superimposed commentary enlightened the exchange between French law enforcement officials and their suspect.

"Yes. It appears my office was the portal used by hackers. So what? Hackers could've used any of hundreds of terminals...or none at all. That's why it's called hacking."

"Andrew, my boy, that voice belongs to Rahjput Anwari, brilliant engineer but an absolute tosser. Any talk of hacking the shipyard's network is beneath a man dedicated to pure science and disinterested in corporate finagling. Next voice you hear belongs to Kamal Sharma, Managing Director of Mazagon Docks. Poor bastard won't last a week without a tidy solution, a workable excuse or an accurate listing of data pilfered, copied, or corrupted."

The lead investigator asked the obvious. "All the personnel records are wrecked?"

"Yes."

"Poor Sharma has no clue what hacking means or how it works. Mistresses, bribes and kickbacks—those things he knows from A to Z."

Sharma. "All our internal cost data...is it gone forever?"

Anwari was increasingly disinterested. "The data was copied then corrupted."

"*Reconstruction of Mazagon's accounting records, m'boy, will take months and cost a fortune in gold and humiliation. Hiding the noodle…that's the tricky part.*"

Sharma. "Subcontractor bids?"

Anwari. "The hackers invaded all financial records, accessed subcontractor data…bids and qualifications included."

"*Remember Andrew, Sharma shit his pants until Murtha suggested bringing-on an outside consultant to assess the damage and correct Mazagon's IT vulnerabilities. By now Sharma thinks it's all his idea—making certain the shipyard's list of payees never becomes public is what matters.*"

Seated in the limousine, Andrew examined his cuticles, pushing at them with the top of a cheap ballpoint. His briefcase contained three proposals, each with differing prices and contract conditions—fine evidence for a trial involving bid fixing, bribery, perjury, and fraud. How will Murtha let me know which proposal to submit?

In a crisp voice a middle-aged escort punctured Andrew's composure. "Are you the representative from PaneroGlobal LLC…a Mr. Trout?"

Andrew nodded.

"Please follow me. You're our final interview."

The elevator doors opened. His guide pointed at a glass-walled conference room where nine men and two women gathered. Andrew took the proffered seat at the head of a table whose glass top was tinted to match blue/gray walls. Chrome supports mimicked shear-lines of naval warships pictured in massive stainless steel frames.

Dr. Rahjput Anwari made the introductions.

"Mr. Anthony Trout represents PaneroGlobal LLC as their authorized North American representative. Mr. Trout, I'm pleased to introduce Dr. Sharma, Mazagon's Managing Director; Mr. Murtha, our General Manager…and blah, blah, blah."

That's what Andrew heard—blah, blah, blah. He'd given hundreds of dog and pony shows. Sharma and Murtha mattered. Everyone else was window dressing: Name, rank and serial number.

Anwari smiled with a scientist's disdain. "We look forward to your presentation and to understanding your terms and conditions. You may begin."

Andrew took note of a man and a woman seated at the rear, apart from Mazagon's employees. His pulse shot-up with the dawn of understanding: No cost or contractual information had yet been submitted for Mazagon's review. All three competitors would be asked to reveal their information here, today, in each other's presence. This was crazy; the entire process so easy to discredit. Without the names of competitors, he hit the highlights of PaneroGlobal's experience, personnel and commitment to completion on a fast-track schedule. Twenty minutes in, he concluded with a listing of references.

"PaneroGlobal hopes Mazagon will speak at length with our three references: Sir Edward Poynter, Minister in Her British Majesty's Government; Mr. Grover Norris, former Director of the United States Central Intelligence Agency; and last but not least, Mr. Georges Desmarais, Managing Director of DCNS."

Dr. Anwari invited the two prior competitors to the front of the room, where they joined Andrew in chairs arranged for a presentation of financial proposals. "We will ask each of you, in order, to submit your original and four copies to Mr. Murtha...then fill-in your offer on the whiteboard behind you. Technology Resources LLC, from here in Mumbai, is first."

A glamorous woman deposited her sealed manila envelope, then wrote: €14,230,000; 7 months; €5,000 per day penalty for late delivery.

Dr. Anwari nodded without a smile. "Thank you, Dr. Srivarna. Mr. Trout...PaneroGlobal is second, if you please."

Second—what else can it mean? Andrew spun the dials of his case and withdrew documents from a bright yellow security envelope. Then he wrote: €15,000,000; 5 months; €100,000 per day penalty for late delivery.

A Japanese man bowed before submitting documents tied with a ribbon and sealed in red wax. Then he wrote: €14,750,000; 6 months; €500 per day penalty.

***

Andrew's search turned up a South African Airways flight to Brasilia through Johannesburg and Sao Paolo; twenty-one hours of misery lessened by his purchase of a first-class ticket. For the high bidder, yet winner of a €15,000,000 deal, the stimulation from walking the tightrope, of being high beyond the reach of alcohol or drugs, would last longer than twenty-one hours.

Millions banked before selling a damn thing to the Brazilian navy.

Marco is a genius.

Marco, ecstatic if a little preoccupied upon hearing the news, promised to meet in Brazil. They agreed to speak again when Andrew got settled.

CHAPTER 14

Disconcerted, not worried, applied to alterations in Yusef's plans.

The bike he kept double locked to the stoop's railing held an empty plastic bottle in its wicker basket. In a neighborhood of a thousand bicycles, in a country which discarded billions of used containers each year, the combination of bike and bottle signified nothing. Yusef often left a similar water bottle in the same location, but not this brand.

This brand formed the first element in a message from Hassan.

Its four-cylinder combination lock rotated to all zeros, the first lock was secure. Four zeros translated to: Urgent. Unlatched in a way not easily noticed, the second lock wasn't quite coupled as intended. Translation: Someone's been compromised. Tumblers on the second lock read 0207, map coordinates found on the sole copy of a single map, indicating where to meet later today.

Is Hassan alive? No, he is dead, was the answer Yusef chose to accept as true.

In chaos, what manifested as random proved illusory: A liter bottle of diet soda with the label oriented just so; running shoes strewn on the sofa; a laptop askew on a smudged paper towel; and basic toiletries arranged just so on a dirty bathroom counter. Nowhere, in books other than the Qur'an, resided an item providing insight to Yusef Schwartz's political beliefs, religion or the state of his finances. The apartment and its appurtenances acted as a first line of defense, a place to sleep, shower and pay for take-out meals with cash. One small frame, propped against a cheap lamp on the nightstand, protected a 5x7 black and white of a small boy and a smaller girl. Nothing approximating a weapon was hidden in vents, under floorboards or in the coffee tin. Amid the expected, Yusef detected the faint odor of strong tobacco. He returned to the door, opened it and inspected the landing for a stubbed butt. Bafra, a tobacco grown in north-central Turkey fit the definition of uncommon.

Who smoked Bafra cigarettes?

Minutes passed. Attempts to dredge the answer from memory required more time. Yusef's memory was not eidetic; it simulated eidetic results as a result of persistent training. As a boy, he explained to curious teachers that memory skills resulted from genes, the ability to organize information, learning tactics, and a growing knowledge base. Put off by a cheeky lad, school administrators responded by testing for Autism, Asperger's and other medical, or metaphysical, explanations. Yusef enjoyed the testing; it provided suggestions for improving what he regarded as his finest asset.

A decision settled upon him: Go to the meeting, whether or not death waited.

Yusef, at nine, reached détente with being dead. All round him in the camps, people died. Life continued until it didn't. Corpses rotted in the sun. Those who held tight to power and wealth, who sacrificed the lives of others at the altar of their selfish future, played at life from a disadvantage. Heavy weighed a future measured against the price paid in its purchase.

Heavy weight slowed a man down.

Bin Rahman loved his legend more than truth, although the Sheikh's senior confidant, the Swiss, was no jackal. The Swiss saw reality and would be difficult to manipulate. In preparation, Yusef opened two cans of pasta sauce and set water to boil. Carbohydrates would be needed, if a test of endurance became the price of escape from those who considered *jackal* a term of endearment.

Thirty minutes after boarding the first bus, latent curiosity forced Yusef to walk until the brown house with light colored shutters could be observed from a dark corner. Deserted as it was, he eliminated one variable in a complex equation. He turned left and began a five-mile run to Kenilworth Avenue NE, near a mosque shared with acquaintances of Hassan.

Religious freedom, in this paved-over neighborhood, evidenced itself in the fundamentalist Christian Commandment Church next door to a local chapter of the Church of Jim Beam.

Yusef waited.

Two bearded men, friends of Hassan, emerged.

Four now stood on the rundown porch. Three sucked greedily on cigarettes, feverish fireflies in the wind. Five minutes passed. Long enough to conclude Hassan was inside the house, or truly dead.

Yusef left the tree trunk's protection behind.

The taller of two men from the mosque examined Yusef; glanced at the porch for approval. "Salaam alaikum, Yusef."

"Alaikum salaam, Ahmed." Then in English, Yusef asked, "Is that Fakhir?"

Ahmed's nerves inhabited his voice. "Yes. Come...let's go in out of the cold."

The woman stepped aside to pull the front door open. In a grim procession, Ahmed flicked away a cigarette and entered first. Fakhir went next, followed by Billy Ray, who spit a piece of tobacco over the railing, crucifying Yusef with his glare. Yusef looked for the Swiss, disappointment bathing him in the inevitable. *Am I to be executed?* With passion he spoke in Arabic.

"Allahu akbar. I obey the Sheikh's command. What is required?"

If Sheikh bin Rahman eavesdropped, an ounce of good fortune might see him flattered.

With practiced ease, the woman arranged herself next to Billy Ray. No illusion of intimacy enlightened her purpose. A curl of jet-black hair struggled to free itself from the wig. A one-piece running suit, unzipped halfway to the waist, coordinated with expensive running shoes. Ahmed and Fakhir, reduced in stature by her assumption of command, faded a half step towards the kitchen. Words in English challenged Yusef.

"Something happened today. Tell me."

Yusef selected Arabic. "You sent for me mimicking Hassan's methods. I came out of respect, but you show me none in return. Is the Sheikh listening? I serve Hassan's cause...and Sheikh bin Rahman."

Like a cobra, she tried to strike his cheek with her open palm.

Yusef caught her hand, twisted the wrist to the point of breaking then released his grip. More observant of Billy Ray than Fathima, he said what bin Rahman would believe.

"You deserve no respect. What you think you know, what you test me with…is less than half of what the Sheikh needs to know."

Impassive, Billy Ray stood by. Did the enigmatic southerner understand Arabic? In Yusef's peripheral vision, Fakhir inched to a position behind and to Yusef's right. Fakhir would crave his Janbiya, its double-sided, curved blade sheathed on a leather belt worn around the lower abdomen. Decorated in silver, semi-precious stones and leather as a symbol of status, any Janbiya would be demeaned if used in a back alley murder.

Yusef kept his tone as moderate as the situation allowed. "Are we celebrating Ahmed's marriage, Fakhir? Shall we draw our steel and dance?"

Fakhir ceased movement. For a brief moment the room's oxygen turned brittle. Billy Ray shifted his weight, hand drifting towards what would be nothing if not a weapon. The woman, serenity personified, shifted tactics.

"Salaam alaikum, Yusef, I am Fathima…the Sheikh's representative this evening. Would you like tea?"

"The Sheikh holds my life in your hands, Fathima." Yusef nodded at Ahmed, who moved to the kitchen and its relic of a samovar.

Fakhir stood, a statue of resentment.

Fathima pointed Yusef towards a ratty sofa. "You're not afraid…a rare quality."

Yusef remained uncertain of Billy Ray's cognition. He directed his words at the dirty man with chemically streaked hair, while looking only at Fathima. Quotations from the Qu'ran ran a risk, but reminding three Muslims of the sanctity of life could do no harm.

"Allah sees me…I cannot see him. I worship Allah to purify my soul. In all my duties as a man, I try my best. When Allah wills me to die…I will die. If by your hand, then the burden of murder falls to you. Even a person who happens by the scene will receive a share of the sin for not defending the victim."

Fathima's face assumed a polished veneer of piety. "Inshallah Yusef. Inshallah. We all will perish when called." Ahmed's presence a temporary distraction, she wrapped both hands around a steaming mug of green tea.

Warmed, her breath no longer turned to vapor in the unheated room. "The infidel Bennett is neutralized. Bennett's removal is significant, is it not?" No more than a rhetorical question, the devaluation of Yusef's opinion delivered a message.

Yusef allowed his mug to drive off the chill in his hands.

"Bennett lives a normal existence in his home. There are rumors. There are no facts, not beyond the plain truth he isn't ill or injured. Bennett's removal, as you describe it, may or may not be important. To assess the true circumstances, I need to know the Sheikh's directed strategy."

She ignored his response. "Tell me Yusef...why is my current Intel less than half what Sheikh bin Rahman *should* know?"

Emphasis dipped in poison and coated with contempt, her switch to English intended offense. To Fathima, Yusef resembled sand in a gold miner's pan, laced with but a grain of treasure.

For Yusef this moment would seal his fate. She would assay his Intel with lives, certainly his life, in the balance. "The infidel is like the *Ladon*; Bennett is but one head. Grover Norris is Bennett's replacement, in-place and running Bennett's operations." Grover Norris was an icon among the infidel's crusaders. His name alone could shatter the morale of unsophisticated Mujahideen. Billy Ray represented continuity with the Swiss, and a careful listener who demonstrated comfort with the Arabic of the street.

Forced to acquiesce, Fathima wouldn't admit failure; bravado covered scattered thoughts. "Did Heracles not kill the *Ladon*? Heracles, whose courage and ingenuity made him the greatest of mythological heroes?"

Yusef detected nothing of bin Rahman's electronic presence. Vital for his purposes, if not enviable, he shifted to English to poke the tigress.

"Yusef Schwartz is nothing, the lowest of your informers on the infidel. How could I know of Grover Norris's insertion...and your trusted sources failed the Sheikh?"

"Perhaps you're a blind squirrel."

Back in Arabic, he quoted an Arab proverb. "If patience is bitter then its result is sweet."

Anger flashed. Fathima demanded, "What happened at the British Embassy? Do you deny involvement?"

Denial never crossed Yusef's mind. "Parking cars was my job."

Instinct proven true, tonight would have seen my throat cut, my physical body dined upon by rodents. Only the information about Grover Norris provided reprieve, temporary though it might be.

Fathima would not be seen as weak. "If lying can save your skin, truth may do even better."

"Grover Norris is no lie. Parking cars, selling hotdogs, these are things I do to live. CIA pays mailroom workers nothing."

Billy Ray interjected with rough words wrapped in a homespun drawl. "Cut the bullshit, dude. You talked to Frankel. Can't think why." Billy Ray, who provided an opening, couldn't be ignored.

Yusef once again addressed himself to Fathima. "Billy Ray should remember...I told the Swiss, and the Sheikh's electronic ghost...a message needed to reach Frankel. The fire alarm presented the perfect opportunity...Frankel in a wheelchair. I approached him. No one noticed or cared."

Yusef watched Billy Ray's features contort in an effort to conceal a loss of equilibrium. Cupping hands to his face, lighting the stub end of an extinguished cigarette, pungent Turkish tobacco clouded his face. In that instant, Yusef needed no deductive powers. Frankel is a target; the fire alarm saved him. Billy Ray is less than a committed assassin, who fled in an abundance of caution.

Or in an abundance of something less attractive.

Fluency in Arabic, demonstrated only moments ago, seemed a point in the blonde man's favor. Now a spark of madness blossomed in brown eyes set too close to a scalpel perfect nose, on a face where perfection didn't belong. This interrogation is a case of too much enjoyment and too little detached appraisal. A sociopath might prefer Yusef pass this examination, to the benefit of the Sheikh. A tightly wound nutjob would crave Yusef's failure, allowing release brought only by a kill.

Fathima's face tightened, amused by Yusef's references: the Swiss, the Sheikh's electronic ghost. "What did you tell Frankel?" The question seemed an afterthought; she knew the answer.

Like the lie detector episode all over again, multiple choice didn't apply. Only a form of the truth would do. "Bennett will soon dangle a woman to attract him...CIA's woman."

"Who is this woman?"

"Norris hasn't chosen."

Disbelief dripped from her tongue. "Grover Norris is vetting a group of women?"

"No...Jamie Norris is running the operation."

"Did you acquire the list?"

"No."

"Get it."

"If I can."

"No ifs...just get it. Don't fail me..." Ego exposed, she modified an ill chosen personal reference "...or the cause."

More than desperation, or the Sheikh's potential praise, marked this demand. Fathima seemed to anticipate what names would appear.

Billy Ray, Yusef decided, was best classified as between a high functioning sociopath and a psychopath.

***

Driven by misgivings of being caught from behind, Yusef snatched a quick look over his shoulder. A gesture seen often along the routes of marathons, born as overreaction, full of hope the pavement behind would be empty, it ended with a spike of adrenaline. Rudimentary calculation placed his pursuer a quarter mile to the rear on Easton Street. The image of a penetrating stride stayed with Yusef.

Ahmed Al-Harazi wasn't an athlete. Bafra cigarettes offset Billy Ray's gymnast's body. Fathima wore the right clothes and was lean—but a poseur from start to finish. Fakhir Khaldun was a marathoner and a good one under competitive pressure. Fakhir would catch Yusef.

Why was Fakhir chasing?

A bluegrass riff on a banjo, Yusef increased pace to match the music's demands.

Fakhir was unfamiliar with this type of race. Not a pack of dogs and a bevy of riders set after a scrawny, terrified animal, this test pits one hound against one fox. At the intersection of Quarles, under the spreading arms of a dying oak, Yusef turned hard right onto cracked concrete sidewalk. All the way to 49th Street NE he pumped his arms in concert with the banjo, turning left to eliminate the possibility Fakhir guessed Minnesota Avenue.

Fakhir could maintain a five-minute mile forever, and four-minutes-thirty seconds for five miles over flat ground.

Yusef's best was fifteen seconds per mile slower.

In a world of marked courses lined with cheering crowds, Yusef would be passed in less than three minutes. With no specified route, Fakhir would be faced with a win or lose decision at every intersection. Probability favored an eventual mistake by the Yemeni.

At Roper Jr. High, another left took Yusef to Meade. Past Houston Elementary, a right onto 50th Place headed him towards Sheriff Road NE, where he intended to hop a bus. Halfway there he rotated his head to see nothing but parked cars and broken streetlights.

New Morning Star Baptist Church occupied the corner; its gleaming white paint and matching wrought iron fence suggested Yusef drop a half story to a staircase that hid his tall frame. Seven minutes later, a bus stopped for a tall man breathing in normal rhythm.

More than a foot shorter and fifty pounds lighter, how had Fakhir assessed his chances to kill Yusef on a dark street? Fakhir was a junior executive in a bank—an acolyte of Sheikh bin Rahman in his free time.

Yusef got off on the corner of 48th where the window of a corner market advertised Maverick cigarettes and Budweiser. Bought a bottle of water and a package of Slim Jims with the ten-dollar bill pulled from his sock. A battered clock, mounted on a wall of indeterminate color, suggested he return to the house on Eastern. Too rare to ignore, an opportunity to eavesdrop on Fathima and Billy Ray beckoned.

An empty lot was littered with junked leftovers. Through the moonscape Yusef picked his way to a chain-link boundary where lights shone through greasy windows bereft of paint. Long ago hit by a delivery truck, the fence leaned at a precarious angle. A single step brought Yusef to the side window where Fathima and Billy Ray could be heard without comprehension.

Lights extinguished, the side yard returned to inky black. The front door opened. Yusef flattened himself, feeling something sharp cut his leg. Face stuffed into the filth, dark hair pointed at the street, he dared not move.

A car glided to a stop. Engine running, a door opened and Fathima could be heard saying, "Where can we drop you?"

"Four..." A door slammed shut. A trail of exhaust vapor truncated Billy Ray's response.

Yusef stood—trees blocked any view of the license plate. Focused on the emblem mounted on the bumper, fate provided a scrap of wood to be shaped in the lathe of persistence. On the porch, he sniffed each abandoned butt, concluding it was Billy Ray who visited his apartment.

Nothing but a dumpsite, would his body have been consigned to eternity with others less fortunate.

What aspirations do Fathima and the Swiss hold dear? Yusef stood straight, prayed to Allah and haggled with Death.

***

Today would prove complicated. Sure of that much and little else, the gun dimmed her mood and required an explanation, when Miriam's hug found the Glock's unforgiving plastic and steel shape. Nasha repeated an identical explanation, in adult tones, to Lucia after the children departed in the car pool.

She refused to relinquish the gun, when Embassy security demanded it.

Now the gun sat on the Ambassador's desk, out of his reach. Done with being judged, threatened and diminished by Nabil Hanna and his goons, Fouad Razouk might be her employer, but by courtesy of the British Embassy's security cameras, and an anonymous e-mail, Nasha might prevail in the end.

"A concealed weapon is abnormal, Nasha. Help me understand why our internal security doesn't reassure you."

Patience drained with demonstrable justification, Nasha found herself in unexpected territory. "Do you enjoy any of the small theaters where Muslim comedians perform?"

"Nasha, how is that relevant?"

"There's a young woman who wraps a hijab over her hair, steps onstage...and transforms into a bisexual Muslim punk rocker."

Razouk began to interrupt once again.

"This alter ego is impetuous, flirtatious and delights in questions most young Muslims wouldn't dare put to parents. Why must she and her father stay in separate rooms at a party in the mosque? If a woman must cover her hair in front of men who aren't part of her family, how about a lesbian…must a lesbian wear a hijab in front of all women? In the audience, twenty-somethings avoid their parents, when she performs a song about falling in love despite religious prohibitions against sex before marriage. Eventually the performer wins over parents…or parental laughter does the job for her. Who knew the Muslim community owned a sense of humor? Just because I'm Muslim doesn't mean I can't also be this other thing, even if that thing is *haram*."

Razouk recognized a parable; his desire was to redirect this meeting. "So I'm listening, Nasha. We should speak about the gun."

"You escorted me to the British Embassy. Did you find my dress inappropriate…or was my behavior an embarrassment to you as a man?"

Razouk's cheeks colored. "You're a lovely woman, Nasha. You're an American. You're Lebanese. You're Muslim. No, I found nothing inappropriate about your dress or conduct." Stiff and formal, the Ambassador lived in a goldfish bowl.

"Our Colonel Hanna and the embassy chauffeur disagree. They forced their way into my home while you and I dealt with diplomacy and the fire alarm's aftermath." Nasha voice quivered in anger. "Terrorized my children, were prepared to harm me…and might've done, except my father-in-law sent me home with an armed British soldier." She placed her home security recording on the desktop beside the pistol. "I'm not safe, Ambassador. For the moment, I'll accept the risk that our so-called Intelligence Chief presents. I won't accept being in this building without the means to defend myself. I made a formal complaint to the Arlington police and appended a copy of the memory device sitting on your desk. There'll be no ramifications for Hanna…I know that. Watch the recording, Ambassador, you'll waive the ban as it applies to me."

She reached forward and slid a second memory-stick within his grasp. Watched him pick it up and turn it over. Saw his eyes grow ever larger as he read the note taped to the tiny case.

Razouk needed a moment to think. Needed to speak with his wife. So he changed the subject. "Your publicity from the luncheon makes me jealous, Nasha. All the Arab networks…you're a budding star. My wife says she'll vote for you, if you should run for office."

"And *your* vote, Ambassador. Whom will you vote for? Perhaps you think yourself Presidential material."

Nasha decided not to bring up Fathima Laniado's connection to a shooting at the Ritz-Carlton. Her gun, however, related directly to Fathima. Using the anonymous e-mail to blackmail the Ambassador had been beneath her; she knew this to be true as well.

***

From the moment Zachary Mannheim hung up, Anne believed the cordless house phone more resembled a brick of explosive than a quotidian instrument of communication. She held the receiver with trepidation and the certain knowledge her presence in this house could last no longer.

"Hello...I don't know who I've reached, but this is Greg Riley. Director Bennett, if it's you listening, we need to meet right now."

"This is Anne Linton, Mr. Riley. Fulton can't come to the phone."

"Hello Anne...we've met twice before, if you don't remember."

Riley expected resistance and hoped a gentle reminder would serve notice that Greg Riley was a friend.

"Yes, Mr. Riley, I recall. It's just that so many things are different this time. I'm afraid I must go."

Her response was a thin thread, but shared knowledge fit a pattern used in emergency conversations by field operatives from the old school. No amount of analysis by someone listening would bear fruit, for no code had been employed. Neither Riley nor Anne Linton was a spy, but they had the same one in common. Riley looked around his office until he located his shaving kit, a clean shirt and underwear. Resolute in his decision, he closed his office door and walked away.

CHAPTER 15

Mannheim imagined Anne Linton as a cast-member of a zombie movie.

Face devoid of color, long hair whipping in a wind which billowed a blue, long sleeved blouse, she approached the old Beemer. Cold, she shivered more in trepidation for the man she might've married than falling temperatures. She consulted a photograph to confirm Mannheim's identity; spoke with deference and deliberation.

"Mr. Mannheim, Fulton requested I meet you at your car. I've been Fulton's friend and lover for several years, but will be leaving for good when we finish speaking. My departure, according to Fulton, substantiates my veracity in telling you the following. Wait thirty minutes in your car without electronic transmissions, then enter the house. Go upstairs, pull down the attic hatch, climb the stairs and read the message on the screen to your right. Do as you will with the information you acquire. Ignore anything else you might see, regardless of your incessant curiosity. Do you understand, Mr. Mannheim?"

Mannheim nodded in the affirmative.

Anne followed a route scuffed in the stone drive. At her Volvo wagon, she checked the front seat for her purse, opened the locked door with keys, took note of suitcases Fulton had loaded in the rear and started the engine. With three minutes to spare on the dashboard's digital clock, she drove away never to return.

With admiration for a professional's work, Mannheim evaluated dilemmas and opportunities. In his opinion, and his opinion was the only available criteria at this juncture, Ms. Linton told the truth—to the extent she knew the truth. Her body language elucidated the dangers of exiting the car before an unseen timer ran its course. Thirty minutes was adequate for a tasked satellite to bring real-time photography to Fulton's laptop—depicting surrounding roads and vehicles bringing unwelcome visitors.

Whose satellite would Fulton borrow?

In a lifetime as a global emissary, Fulton would have friends, enemies and allies of convenience. One of those men or women could, and more important to Fulton, would deliver such a satellite feed.

Back at Langley there would be those quick to cry: J'accuse.

In the real world, where few who worked in Intelligence visited, accommodations would be made and, if momentary alliances among spies couldn't be thought of as common, no spy would find them unusual. All the usual suspects could be nominated, satellites no longer exclusive to the wealthy West. Mannheim laid an imaginary wager on an Israeli; Israelis loved to bank future draft choices. One of India's electronic specialists would be a good bet; an Indian spy would rather provide assistance than learn Bennett called a Pakistani. Casual speculation carried no downside, so Zachary bet against Britain, France, Turkey or any NATO country; NATO operatives wouldn't be trusted with Bennett's life. A Russian was a long shot, but not out of the running. China was unlikely; a Chinese wouldn't see the upside of helping a half-dead CIA Deputy Director, but wearing a self-righteous face would attend Bennett's funeral to lay a wreath.

Minutes passed in a reverie of skepticism.

Mannheim ruminated: Could Bennett be justified in his suspicions. Is the Chief of CIC under active surveillance? How close are the hounds? How many cars? How many officers, how many means and methods of tracking? Mannheim closed his eyes, trying to remember his last time under suspicion. For a spy-hunter, being on the opposite side of the microscope took some getting used to.

Bennett's front door opened one minute after the thirty-minute impediment. A teakettle's whistle blared its shrill warning in the kitchen.

Stairs led upwards; Zachary took them two at a time with accelerated excitement.

"Slow down..." he cautioned himself "...stay alive."

At the top of the stairs three bedroom doors stood as crenellated bastions against entry. Light switches, when flicked up or down, brought failure; semi darkness would remain. Zachary was defenseless. Bennett wanted Mannheim to feel the weight of uncertainty and fear which bad decisions deposited on an exposed spy's shoulders.

Claustrophobia screamed: Any door could open, if Bennett has collaborators.

A bead of perspiration formed and rolled from his hairline onto overheated skin by his ear. He inspected the attic door less than two feet above his head. A contact switch was a simple device; nothing more elaborate was needed. Would he hear the explosion? Like a thousand men before him, in this moment he was reminded of how nations and governments abandoned their spies to the vagaries of fate.

Mannheim reached for the rope handle and pulled hard.

Full of the artificial glow from multiple computer monitors, all blank with the exception of the biggest, a forty-eight-point font spread words across its screen. *Don't bother with these machines. Once you were young and innocent. Where did you go for solace?*

Mannheim almost cried from laughing.

Lost in scar tissue grown during intervening years, 1982 had marked Zachary's year of innocence lost. Marta, his wife, melted into East Germany without warning or so much as a mea culpa. Where he'd gone for solace was the easy part; to whom he'd turned was known by three people.

Outside once more, the illusion of danger from real explosives or Bennett's macabre sense of humor subsided. Mannheim walked to the rear of the house; Bennett's Mustang squatted on fat tires, forlorn under its cover. Concealed in Anne's wagon the entire time, examining my demeanor and deciding my fate, did Fulton's strategy involve more deception or less, more gimmicks or fewer.

Consoled by his assignment of this interrogation, or whatever name a lynching was known by these days, Mannheim threw off his suit coat, selected a Wagner CD and checked the gas gauge.

A four hour drive in the best of times, the hounds would be loosed when news of Bennett bolting for Connecticut hit Langley's seventh floor.

***

The message arrived with no fanfare.

Not the author of the request to NSA, David Nazarian's name was featured near the top of the distribution list. Reports of electronic transmissions in the vicinity of Los Altos and Bilbao, Spain—in which *Gunther* and *weapon* appeared—suggested Raissa's interest in staying current had been dulled by retirement. In the optimism of ignorance, she believed a Sat phone safe. In all likelihood, she'd use it again.

What Nazarian needed would be buried in Probst's After-Action Reports, or in Gunther's dead and buried brain. Either way he'd have to dig-out names from somewhere to find who Raissa called. Among a number of oddities attached to this assignment, it preyed on his mind that she might have a source of weapons.

He phoned Phyllis Martell on the assumption she'd be the gatekeeper of all things Probst.

***

Greg Riley foraged for an address and came up empty.

Located in the Capital Hill district, Anne's skills made the difference to a charity reclaiming abandoned buildings. Green, gray and cream, her home came into view; not much else had survived urban renewal or gentrification, if one was inclined to be snide. Parked a block away, he watched the house for fifteen minutes. Weight shifted back and forth, Greg Riley feigned composure. Turned his back to the door, when no voice blurted from the intercom. Looked up and down the street. Lost for a next move, a fluted aluminum mailbox caught his eye. Under its hinged cover, he found a scrap of cardboard with a partial shipping label.

Greg scurried across the street, having made his first pickup at a dead-drop. He was a spy after all.

***

Anton Leuzinger, raised in Geneva, acquired a rounded worldview along with an appreciation of fine art as a private banker in his native city. Language skills led to years in proximity to the Princes of middle-east oil empires, becoming an independent businessman as an almost inevitable result.

Leuzinger couldn't, and wouldn't, build a terrorist bomb. Leuzinger was himself an infidel, having been brought up in the Roman Catholic Church.

He'd traveled from London to evaluate Yusef Schwartz, Hassan's sole asset within the American intelligence community. Hassan's disappearance proved a mild surprise. The idea of Hassan's death came into focus more by a process of elimination than by specific revelation. Hassan never attracted interest from law enforcement—no illicit drugs or gambling—and lived a life of moderation. It fell to Leuzinger to look beyond the immediate for longer-term ramifications. Hassan's purpose in the bin Rahman firmament was defensive: Probing weaknesses in the financial structure; listening for the earliest signs of discord in markets; evaluating the safety of the democratic system that protected Sheikh bin Rahman's assets.

Could it be possible Hassan was in hiding? Dead or alive, either outcome would be troubling, but not fatal to the continued employment of Aaron Frankel's financial wizardry. Either possibility raised questions from which time would winnow sensible rejoinders.

Leuzinger found Yusef Schwartz intelligent and honest. Within the man, Leuzinger gleaned something else, something cold and immutable; Anton wondered if it was genius. Genius could explain the man's ability to exist deep in the bowels of the Sheikh's worst nightmare without being discovered. Genius could also herald disaster. Scrutiny of Schwartz led to what, in banker's vernacular, was referred to as a stress test. Soon enough, results would arrive from Fathima and Billy Ray Balfour. Balfour, an experiment in contrasting personality traits, bothered Leuzinger. Seen from a restricted point-of-view, Balfour was an ill-trained attack dog, who displayed bursts of intelligence and charm.

Absent Hassan's detail-oriented intellect, better personnel were needed on the ground in the United States. Yusef Schwartz could represent an upgrade, though Leuzinger's opinion would remain his own until something closer to certainty was achieved.

Inside Belga Café on 8th Street SE, Leuzinger watched with indifference as Greg Riley crossed the street. Leuzinger, insulated by never having met an employee of CIA or FBI, traveled as he wished, absent concern for No-Fly Lists. Not a criminal, no law enforcement agency sought to detain him. Private Swiss banks valued discretion in equal parts with conservative investments. In this specific way their modus operandi differed from Intelligence organizations. More than once, though denial would be his first line of defense, Leuzinger splintered Swiss Banking Laws to assist certain of those labyrinthine Intelligence organizations.

After a lunch of Belga's famous mussels, he met representatives of the Central Bank of Lebanon.

***

Raissa Ribeiro was in Spain, Nazarian told Phyllis Martell, located by NSA's vast network of *Five Eyes* computers which intruded on fiber optic, satellite, Internet, microwave, ultra shortwave and every form of communication in between. An unexpected high priority, assigned to discovering Ribeiro's location, was a mild surprise given Mannheim's moderate concern. Where the high priority originated wasn't Phyllis' first concern.

Three things flashed through Phyllis' mind, when David requested Probst's files: CIC gave information to no Agency officer without Mannheim's approval; Martell held no such files in her possession; and, lastly, she wouldn't allow herself to be used.

She refused with a stinging tone.

David reacted with indifference. He'd been looking for a shortcut, some way to find Raissa faster, to keep her from Probst's fate. He apologized for suggesting Phyllis break the rules, and as a peace offering suggested dinner, after he returned from an urgent assignment.

His peace offering stunk like deceased shellfish: David Nazarian was married. Which mightn't have made a difference to Phyllis, if he was less transparent. Too soon old, too late smart, Phyllis wished for a do-over.

***

A restaurant's ability to provide a cheeseburger, fries and a chocolate shake, together with a familiar face in a rear booth, awarded it two Michelin stars in Greg Riley's book.

Coffee sat in front of Anne Linton.

He kissed her cheek in a pro-forma sort of way. They were both uncomfortable.

Anne struggled for an exhausted smile. "So you connected the dots?"

"Remembered where I first met you. Note in the mailbox said I-95 N, 4th Exit 13. I'm a smart guy. Here I am."

She felt a pang of sorrow for Greg; Fulton compartmentalized everyone in his life, with an emphasis on friends. Anne sipped her coffee while Greg ate.

"Let's get a cone on our way out."

Greg didn't want ice cream, but ordered a large mint chocolate chip. Paid the tab for them both and followed. At her car, she kissed him gently on the mouth.

"Goodnight, Greg. See you around."

He stood in the night air watching her taillights recede. Back in his car, in the dark, he reached into the back seat with his right hand—the one holding the cone.

"This's your flavor, right Fulton?"

"North on the Post Road. Make your first left on West Norwalk...see who might be behind us...then left on Powder Horn."

Parked in the driveway of an older home on a cul de sac, Greg decided he should state his case. "I don't know what's happened to you. Not certain I should know. Your guy, Jamie Norris, called a meeting earlier today. What was discussed stuck-out like a pedophile in kindergarten, so I asked to be excluded. Norris told me to stay...as Devil's Advocate. Never had all this in mind...whatever this is."

"Ice cream's good."

"This is how it goes now...you can't recognize your friends?"

Bennett's tone softened. "Tell me, Greg. You came a long way."

"Your team doesn't know shit about your troubles. Grover Norris is pinch-hitting...no one's thrilled. Some guy named Nazarian is being sent to kill Raissa Ribeiro, wherever she might be. Grover gave the order with nothing written for the file.

Don't know whether DD/CIA or D/CIA know or care, but it won't hold up, Fulton. At least one of your guys will leak…they all want to. Figured you'd want to know."

"Not to be too cynical, my friend, but what else? Surely there's something else."

"Condemning one of your best not enough? Well Sarah, the blonde…she plans to recruit Sir Edward Poynter's daughter-in-law for the sting against Frankel. They talked about it like I was cleared. It was nuts, Fulton. Sir Edward Fucking Poynter…British Intelligence. Her husband's name is Andrew by the way. Any chance he's still under arrest on a French submarine?"

Despite cramps in his legs, Bennett appreciated the irony—the opposition screws Fulton Bennett while Sir Edward Poynter takes credit for bringing down the terrorist cash machine. He could hear the Brits gloating.

"So you're angry I didn't tell you, that it?"

"Not angry. Jesus, Fulton…must be a hundred different ways this scheme turns to shit. You're certifiable."

"You'd conclude I'm worse than certifiable, if I told you everything I've done."

"Don't"

"Won't."

Seconds stretched a friendship.

"Listen, I'm gonna get out of the Agency. Next week, the week after, I'll put in my papers. I'll help if I can."

Greg felt a hand grip his shoulder and heard the back door close.

Ships in the night, Zachary Mannheim and Greg Riley passed each other on I-95.

***

Mannheim pulled into Nadine Bennett Walsh's driveway, his sympathy for Fulton Bennett in tatters. Melodrama, like the episode with Anne Linton, wasn't productive. Lone wolves do not end well: Anyone in clandestine ops longer than five minutes knew that much.

Why was Bennett running?

Musing over the past, he allowed how this usurpation of her driveway was unexpected.

Nadine had been barely legal voting age, when Marta defected. Mannheim tried to recall all the reasons he'd turned to the diminutive wife of a brash, unlikable, co-worker. In the half shadow of a front porch light, he saw Fulton sitting on the steps, cocksure smirk on a no longer young face. Zachary tried to count the years as Bennett's professional colleague.

Counting years of friendship took no time at all.

Hand reaching into the backseat, he took hold of his overcoat. Not one to ignore creature comforts, being invited into Nadine's home wasn't likely after all these years.

Nadine was younger than Bennett by six or seven years, which made her fifty-ish. The debt Mannheim owed Nadine had never been extinguished, but left fallow awaiting a seed. In a reality which comes to men nearing sixty and feeling suddenly vulnerable, he despised Bennett for reminding him of Marta, for reconstituting the pain.

Bennett, of course, did it with a purpose.

Mannheim stood over Bennett and sighed. "I brought my coat assuming you'd want to walk."

Once they established a comfortable stride, Bennett said, "Wasn't positive you'd be their choice. Wasn't sure you'd come, if told to. Was Grover his usual charming self?"

"So you heard. May I ask from whom?"

"Jamie took pains to be certain...Grover likes being in command."

"This isn't about Grover."

"For Jamie it is."

"Some friction there, eh?"

Bennett stopped and turned to Mannheim. "Am I under arrest?"

"Am I a policeman?"

"Am I suspended?"

"No. Were you to arrive at work, you'd embarrass me."

Again they ambled. Mannheim reached in the pocket of his overcoat. Handed two items to Bennett.

"Although I give you the choice, Fulton, my preference is always making a formal record."

Bennett flipped the tiny recorder to record. Took a healthy swig from the silver flask. "Bet the boys didn't want any recording made."

"I was instructed to make no notes of my meeting with the boys as you call them. There were no instructions about how I carry out my assignment."

"Want me to tell you...or have you got a list?"

"Questions and answers will provide a better sense of organization. Are you ready?"

"Not ready...but willing."

Mannheim established the timeframe and location of the interview, as well as specific details relating to the incident at the Ritz Carlton.

"Well...we've made a start...I comprehend the broad strokes. Now I think we should take on the hard bits. Who is the Caroline referenced by the anonymous voice on the phone?"

"Caroline Poynter Panero."

"Why would a threat against Mrs. Panero's life be meaningful to you, Deputy Director Bennett?"

"Been in love with Caroline much of my adult life."

"Aah. So you ran into a burning building to save a damsel in distress?"

"Don't be a prick, Zachary."

"No. That would be your realm Mr. Deputy Director, would it not? Do you wish to close this interview?"

"No."

"How long have you known Caroline Poynter Panero?"

"Forever. Not at all."

"Were you married, when you met her?"

Bennett glared. Turned to look at Nadine's current life, a life he could've shared.

"Yes. I was married with babies. I didn't care. Caroline was twenty and magnetic...been on magazine covers since puberty. I was thirty-five...socially underdeveloped is how they diagnose it today. Caroline's mother was dying. Her father was a wreck...or so he professed to those who cared enough to inquire. It didn't last...nothing lasted for Caroline with the exception of drugs and radical politics. For me, it didn't go away."

"So the affair is ongoing?"

"Caroline's settled in her marriage; I'm the one with the addiction. More than four years passed since our last get-together, when the call came."

Mannheim ignored the rationalization of *get-together* and made a special mental note of *settled in her marriage*. "You suspected something nefarious?"

"I suspected everything. I suspected they were using Caroline to turn me around. Nothing mattered. My people didn't find her. Not in Europe. Not in Asia. Not in Washington. I believed the voice on the phone; credible threats are my job."

"Couldn't you have sent others? Your appearance, unsupported by a fully prepped team, was an egregious error."

"Yes, it was. Do it again tomorrow."

"The woman shot in the bed with you…not Caroline Panero?"

"No. I didn't know her."

"She was an escort…an expensive escort. Do you utilize the services of escorts, Mr. Deputy Director?"

"No. I've been in a relationship with Anne Linton for some time."

"Not a committed relationship, however, is that an appropriate characterization?"

"Haven't had sex with anyone since Anne moved in."

Mannheim suspected this answer. The whole truth lay beyond his ken.

"Would you have enjoyed sex with Caroline Panero that afternoon at the Ritz…in other circumstances?"

"Yes."

"When did you last speak to Caroline Poynter Panero?"

"I call her sometimes. She doesn't call back."

"Would you answer for the record, please…your last conversation with Caroline, in person or on the telephone?"

"Seven…perhaps eight years ago. For Christ sakes Zachary…a long time ago. On the phone."

Mannheim paused to attempt a correlation of time and events without immediate success.

"A bit touchy about ancient history, would you say?" Bennett elected not to make a response. "From an emotional standpoint, we can conclude you're unreliable. Would you agree, Mr. Deputy Director?"

"No."

"I'll take that as a yes. The woman using the clever rig to shoot the escort…with your weapon…were you able to identify her?"

"No. She wore a clean-suit and an orange wig. There were a few strands of dark hair sticking out from the wig…all I noticed."

"Was the shooter attractive? Tall? White? Did you notice nothing of importance...a man of your experience should have, wouldn't you agree?"

Those same questions filled Bennett's every waking minute. Would, in his opinion, fill all the minutes left in his miserable existence.

"Nothing helpful. Shorter rather than taller. Not European. Not black."

"Asian then?"

"Maybe. Maybe Middle Eastern."

"Slavic? Chechen?"

"Yes. Maybe."

"You're not much help, Mr. Deputy Director. How about the disembodied voice? Very poetic characterization by the way. Electronic or human?"

"Electronics are very good these days, but no...human...a linguist in my opinion."

"All of a sudden Fulton, you're entitled to opinions. So a male linguist...a Middle Eastern or Chechen woman shooter, and Caroline Poynter Panero...who may, or may not, have been part of this farce. Right so far?"

"Yup. Put me down for gross negligence, stupidity or whatever."

"Best you let me invent both the cartoons and characterizations, Mr. Deputy Director. I may be even less kind." A baseball aficionado, Mannheim thought it time to throw his first breaking ball.

"Were you a suspicious man, Fulton, would you think Caroline involved, innocent victim, or tempting ruse?"

"Perspective is everything, Zachary. You know this is eating me...nobody likes playing the fool. The name Poynter is involved on the periphery of a high profile operation. Caroline is a Poynter by birth. Her sister-in-law is a recruitment target to bring Aaron Frankel into the fold...to grab bin Rahman's investment fortune. I found out today. Might've made a difference if I'd known on the day of the shooting."

"The day of the murder, you meant."

"Yes."

"How could Fulton Bennett, self proclaimed intuitive genius...not be aware of a key decision on an Op watched by anyone who's someone in our government hierarchy? You aren't in denial, are you

Mr. Deputy Director? You do appreciate what's happened?"

Mannheim refused to let go of this critical point.

"When today did you find out about a Poynter being recruited? Who informed you?"

"I can't tell you. Operational security." A lie sounded hollow to them both.

"Strike one, Mr. Deputy Director. Don't find yourself in a pitcher's count."

"Won't tell you. You like that better?"

"It is, at least, not a blatant untruth. It does force me to ask myself...what is true?"

"I found out less than two hours ago. Right on this street. In person. That's what I can tell you."

"From a member of NCS?"

"No."

This answer brought Mannheim to a halt. Disturbed, he asked, "Someone from the seventh floor?" If Zachary Mannheim were being used by D/CIA, outside the bounds of CIC's mandate, the situation would have escalated from daunting to devastating.

Bennett put his hands on his hips in a gesture of defiance.

Mannheim moved on. "Is British Intelligence aware of this recruitment?"

"No."

"Should they be?"

"No."

"Why?"

"Edward Poynter is a dick."

"A dick who remembers his twenty year old daughter seduced by a much older man, not long before her mother died...your kind of dick?"

"He'll screw it up, if he finds out."

Mannheim detected something out of whack in the tone of Bennett's answer.

"You don't think this Frankel Op well founded, do you?"

"High risk. Low probability of success. One dead...not counting the high class hooker in bed with an idiot."

Mannheim's voice was comforting for the first time. "Now we're getting somewhere, Fulton. Who besides the gorgeous blonde in your bed is dead, please? Tell me it isn't another woman."

"Gunther Probst was shot dead on Cape Cod. You goddam know that much from David Nazarian. David, who, let's be clear, I'm kind enough to loan-out, when a spy-hunter has proven inadequate. You didn't know Gunther...old pro. Field Director for Raissa Ribeiro, former girlfriend of Aaron Frankel. None of this would be happening, if she hadn't burned-up in her bed. Which itself was no accident in my book...or in hers. I'm very suspicious of Gunther's death...even more so since Grover ordered Raissa terminated this morning."

Ribeiro's burns, the simple fact she'd been burned, were no secret. Officially and unofficially the incident was filed as an accident. Mannheim knew nothing about them resulting from an Agency operation. It was quite more than remarkable—a fictional story, floated for consumption, was now fact. What would turn out true, when the growing spider's web encircling the Frankel operation collapsed of its own weight.

He showed Bennett the recorder being switched off.

"What was the computer setup in the attic used for?" Mannheim's mind sought to close an important loop with this question.

"Part of a very, very black Op. I can't and won't talk about it."

"Nonsense, Mr. Deputy Director. You're running a parallel but unofficial operation from your home...parallel to the official operation now charged to the care of Jamie Norris. Please confirm my supposition."

Bennett took the advice of President Teddy Roosevelt. "When you reach the end of your rope, all you can do is hold on tight. Am I under house arrest?"

"You are and you aren't. From here you will go straight home without using Agency resources. You don't make policy or grant clemency. Do your job."

Mannheim would need hours of reflection and research to do his job. Hundreds of threads hung loose from a careful cat's ball of twine. Pull at the wrong one? Well, there would be no satisfactory excuse. He couldn't afford to be wrong.

CHAPTER 16

Nasha found several messages on her embassy voicemail. Three reporters wanted in depth interviews—two Arab outlets and an Arlington weekly.

Nasha returned one call. The reporter said she was a mother and a neighbor. When asked for fifteen minutes, Nasha agreed to meet for coffee at four-thirty.

Embassy security recorded a message expressing strong disapproval, but ratified the Ambassador's approval: Her Glock could be worn concealed within the Embassy and its grounds.

Aaron Frankel's voice contained no hint of mischief as it invited her to the Bolshoi at the Kennedy Center. Andrew, not the kind of man to be interested in ballet, laughed at the idea of dancing as an athletic achievement. Stuck in between opposing forces, she pondered whether another opportunity at the Bolshoi would come along.

Papa sounded tired as his voice-mail tirade ended. "My child doesn't ask. You come home to me whenever you like."

She called immediately. "Now, Papa, are you too busy right now?"

Arrangement with Lucia settled, Nasha promised to be home no later than ten-thirty.

Purse, keys and gun gathered to leave, November squeezed daylight in its grip. Great Falls Park behind her, a minute would bring the single lane entrance to Papa's gates into view. A final glance at the rearview camera showed all three watchers lined up like ducklings.

Oncoming tires screeched. Out of control and sliding sideways towards her, a light brown sedan held three men. Nasha stomped the brake pedal, flinging the wheel to the right. The driver and his passengers threw up their hands, shielding their faces from the inevitable. Nasha did the same, praying brakes, airbags or Allah would save her. Inches and the smell of burning rubber separated her minivan from the four-door.

Two passengers sat stunned while the driver approached Nasha, ski mask pulled down over his head and face.

Additional skidding sounds intruded from Nasha's left and rear. Voices screamed in Arabic and English. In Nasha's hand the Glock never wavered. Centered on the masked man, her voice held glacial resolve. "There'll be no rape, Mahbeer. No stoning. Open that door and I'll shoot you dead."

Over before it could start, Mahbeer's hand froze on the door handle, face pleading for compassion both undeserved and unavailable.

To Nasha's left, Grace's weapon pointed at Mahbeer's two accomplices, who knelt under her insistent demand. FBI agents Rainey and Madison swiveled weapons and badges against the potential arrival of additional attackers.

A pickup truck bearing the logo of Papa's bank pivoted broadside to the gated entrance. A fit-looking man of fifty emerged from the cab as two others, in Kevlar vests carrying automatic rifles, took strategic positions. Gavriel Rabin looked askance at Nasha's position; if the masked man nearest her fired a weapon, how would he explain to Jean-Louis? He leveled a Jericho Desert Eagle; its laser beam settled inches below the man's hip.

"This is private property. Guns on the ground. Then we'll sort this out."

One assault rifle covered Grace, the green laser of the second soldier marked two men in the brown sedan.

Grace complied.

Badge held higher, Agent Lawrence Rainey screamed. "FBI, you jackass." Both agents bent over and placed their guns on the pavement.

The pressure of the confrontation began to ease.

Gavriel asked Grace, "Which team do you play for, young lady?"

"British Embassy, Office of Tourism."

"Nice to have MI-6 with us." Without altering his field of fire, Gavriel issued orders. "Ben, restrain the fellows in the masks, then call local police. Avrel, make certain our video remains in operation, and call Mr. Michani. Tell him Nasha will be along shortly." Devoid of inflection, when addressing himself to the FBI, he said, "Feel free to use your cell phones, gentlemen."

Invectives muttered at the ground, Rainey turned away to speak into his phone.

Left for last, Gavriel addressed himself to Nasha. "Please Mrs. Poynter, would you join us inside the gates? Your father is anxious."

"Gavriel, turn off the cameras. We can settle this, if you do."

Rabin was a practical man. More than twenty years Gavriel had guarded the Michani family, jousting with Nasha at every turn. He lowered his gun, waving them all towards the gate.

Nasha spoke before Gainey could. "You're the agents I saw at the Ritz-Carlton. CIA Deputy Director Fulton Bennett was at the Ritz during the shooting, so I assume your surveillance is on Langley's behalf. Mr. Rabin is an Israeli citizen employed by the Israeli Embassy."

She offered a look of sympathy to pissed-off agents.

"My father is a Deputy Ambassador at the Lebanese Embassy…the property inside these gates is an Embassy annex…sovereign Israeli soil. The man who tried to attack me, besides being a would-be rapist, is an Embassy chauffeur. In an hour we'll be inundated by lawyers from all sides…let's not embarrass ourselves. Gavriel…send the heavy weapons home…give the agents your statement. Mahbeer isn't armed, although I admit those masks don't look good for him or his accomplices. Our Embassy won't squawk, when they're prosecuted. We, meaning the Lebanese Embassy, will issue a statement of appreciation to the FBI, whose presence foreclosed what would have been a life-threatening situation. My father will say nothing…by which I mean he won't telephone the FBI Director, and every other muckety-muck he can think of, to maximize grief for all of us. This attack…on an American Muslim woman by this Lebanese Muslim man…was anticipated. I would have shot him, if he opened the door. None of us were harmed…can we leave it there?"

Concede the inevitable, Agent Rainey told his partner via a sharp look. Concession didn't prevent him dissecting how a Jewish banker had a Muslim daughter protected by a Mossad hard-man. Rainey shot a warning look at Gavriel Rabin. "Is Mrs. Poynter's arrangement agreeable?"

"Indeed, sir. I know when I'm outflanked and outnumbered." Gavriel proffered a handshake as a peace offering.

***

Papa was an open book. His first instinct was to wrap a small girl in his arms within the sturdiest fortress his fortune could construct. Blinded to the here and now, eyes like daggers, Papa let loose his exasperation at the black leather holster.

"Put that damn thing where I can't see it. My treasured girl-child, you could've been killed. What were you thinking...you're not some hooligan?"

"You look well, Papa. Whatever you're up to with Yusef must be making you feel younger. Imagine Aaron Frankel...the stronger, younger of two bankers sitting in the wheelchair...and you, Papa, doing the pushing. Aaron's taking me to the Bolshoi tomorrow night, by the way. Did he mention that?"

Nasha had planned something less controversial to break the ice over Papa and Yusef's goings-on. Blurted vexation would carry no weight with Papa, so she sat in demure fashion letting a superior smile respond to his distressed appearance.

"Yusef asked for my help. He received my assistance...no more no less. My sweet girl, if you asked more often, your Papa would be overjoyed. If you're here to have me break faith with Yusef, you'll not succeed...anymore than I'd break a confidence between you and I, to Yusef."

Jean-Louis stuck out his jaw, a familiar movement from her years in puberty. There'd be no movement in, or re-assessment of, his position.

"Do you know what's behind the cooperation you provided...what Yusef is trying to accomplish? This can't be treated like a family secret. Aaron Frankel enables terrorism. My job is counter-terrorism. Tell me something useful. Nasha, your loving daughter, begs for your help."

Michani closed his eyes to remember similar engagements with his wife, battles lost to a superior and unrelenting force. No more talk of

Yusef, he would employ a credible diversion and claim victory.

Papa's jaw moved like a man chewing his words. Stubborn as an old goat. "Elie Bowab believes you can be elected President of Lebanon. Are you aware Ambassador Razouk claimed an imagined scheduling conflict, so Nasha Gemayel Poynter would benefit from such fabulous television coverage? These are things your Papa knows. Perhaps we should talk about those things. What is Yusef doing? I know nothing."

"You could guess, isn't that right Papa? Would you guess for me? Please."

Jean-Louis changed the subject to one with less tar pits to fall into. "Who was this animal in the mask?"

"One of the chauffeurs." Not willing to capitulate on the matter of Yusef, she asked one more time. "Where can I find Yusef, Papa? What's his phone number? He and I should talk."

"Why would a chauffeur wish to hurt you?" Finished discussing Yusef, complicated family dynamics often eluded explanation.

"Do you remember my dress, Papa?"

Jean-Louis' lips separated into a half-smile. "Mama would have slapped me for looking at such a beauty."

"The chauffeur thought I was dressed like a whore. Saw Yusef push a note down my boo…down the front of that dress and concluded I was a street-whore. He and another man forced their way into the house before I got home. They made it clear I should, and would be punished for impurity."

"What note?" Papa zoomed-in on the crux of the matter.

"Yusef had no way of anticipating my arrival. Didn't want me around, when the alarm went off…he arranged for the alarm to go off…so he warned me. Distracted and a bit out of sorts, I didn't get the message."

"Why were you at the Embassy?"

"Razouk's wife begged off…all some kind of deception as you were kind enough, just now, to tell me. He asked me…instructed me to substitute on short notice."

"When did he tell you?"

"A day, more or less."

Michani became thoughtful, then offered no off-handed opinion. "He has too much ambition, that one. Divided loyalties are dangerous to everyone."

Nasha prompted Papa. "He talked to the Syrians about positions in a Hezbollah government...that same night."

Michani challenged, "How do you know this, my little Nasha?"

"Nothing said at the British Embassy is confidential, no matter where it's said or how careful the participants may be. Our Lebanese Embassy is no different, Papa. CIA bugs. Russian bugs. Maybe the Israelis, too. I should ask Gavriel." Again she gave him her most practiced smile. "Perhaps they all share the same wireless feed."

Papa was skeptical. "Edward Poynter allows you regular access to what the British record?"

"This once."

Papa's exact question—why did Edward allow her to access British security footage—returned again and again for Nasha's examination. No single conclusion emerged as more likely than any other. Looking a gift-horse in the mouth would have been dumb; no one in my position would have turned the horse down.

"Why would he do that, I wonder?" Papa sounded like the question was of serious interest. She let the fallout persist in silence.

Rubbing his hands in a gesture of appetite, Papa said, "Let's talk more over dinner. I'll make you something special."

Papa made himself heavy as she pulled him from the armchair. On purpose, she thought, as assistance turned into a prolonged hug. Arm in arm, they walked to his private kitchen. Over Papa's famous crab cakes and home fries, he interrupted conversation about grandchildren with palpable interest about his counterpart.

"Did Edward visit Prince Bradford?"

"No. He left for London later that night."

"Did he now?"

Nasha was too familiar with raised eyebrows and an aporetic tenor. "You know different, do you?"

"He called several days earlier to ask for an appointment. So damned stuffy, I find it intolerable. We share grandchildren for goodness sake."

Nasha was sure the two had never met in private before. Civil enough at the wedding, Papa knew Edward's opinion of the marriage's future. She bit her tongue and waited, heart racing to hear whether the conversation centered on Andrew.

"Are there money problems?" Jean Louis's meaning was vague on purpose.

"Money problems for Andrew and I?"

"Well no, that wasn't what I meant. Are there?" Incredulity marked his words. Papa was always trying to give her money to make life easier.

"Nothing more than the ordinary, Papa, I promise. Do you mean Edward has money trouble?"

"He never got around to describing the exact need. Our meeting centered on fraudulent stock trading. I got the impression Edward might've been a victim. He was circumspect, of course…a man in a delicate position. I asked him outright whether the bank could provide a bridge loan, or some other convenience."

Papa went to the side-by-side. Held-up a vat of hand churned strawberry ice cream. "My unconquered weakness," he said under a disingenuous smirk.

She shook her head no, only to watch him fill two bowls.

He continued after sliding a spoon across the counter. "Edward admitted a bridge loan might become necessary. How much do you think?" Papa's deadpan gave nothing away.

She picked a ridiculous sum. "Twenty-five million."

"Euros or dollars?"

"Don't be silly…tell me how much."

"Forty million Euros."

"Forty million Euros ought to come with bells and bows. What's the money for?"

"Something about the estate…renovations and such. It was drivel…not the real reason."

"Are you going to do it?"

"Do what?" Papa acted as if he hadn't heard.

"Will you make the loan?"

The question hung in the air until Papa spoke again. "Have you heard from Andrew?"

"How did you know he was traveling?"

"Edward mentioned Andrew was in France…headed for India on business."

"That's not right. Andrew's in Germany with Marco. Boys and their toys…Marco picked up a new Beemer at the factory. Andrew thought I couldn't see through him. I got an e-mail saying he planned to visit Caroline and Edward in London before coming home."

"Well…I must have it wrong."

"Papa, what collateral did Edward offer for the loan?"

"Certain kinds of men won't dirty their hands with details, Nasha. Perhaps it belittles them in their own estimation. Let me assure you, sweetheart, Government Ministers have paid their debts with the same currency for three thousand years."

Nasha's phone rang: I'm late for coffee with the local reporter. "Hey...I'm sorry to leave you hanging. How about early tomorrow morning?" She listened to the reporter suggest eight-thirty. "Why don't you come by my house around seven."

Papa's opinion was accompanied by a crafty half-smile. "You even sound like a politician...manipulating the Press. I may reconsider funding Bowab's efforts on your behalf."

***

In the circular drive Nasha found the minivan and Gavriel Rabin. She recognized disapproval seen hundreds of times as a teenager. Gavriel is here to chew me out about the gun.

Rabin tried and failed to sound even-handed. "Your father would lock you in the attic...if he thought an attic would contain you. Why Frankel, Nasha? The man lives in an unpredictable, treacherous, world."

Unable to help herself, she laughed at the too serious Israeli. "To be precise I accepted for the reasons you gave, Gavriel. Because Papa and Yusef are involved with him. Papa won't tell me where Yusef lives. You, Gavriel, won't tell me either. Do you even know?"

His stunned expression was itself a response.

Gavriel's transparency invited deflation. "You're an accomplished thespian, my old guardian. If you don't know what Papa's doing, keep him alive for the sake of his grandchildren. Tell Yusef I miss him."

Gavriel led a double-life which included Mossad...how about Yusef? Was her brother Mossad? Hezbollah? Terrorist?

Inescapable was a truth proven through the ages: Balancing acts which involved multiple lives, lived in secret, ended in regret. How did this come to be—bother and sister on opposite sides?

Families inured to calamities—in the Middle East they seemed a permanent tragedy.

Gavriel took hold of her arm. "Your father is a stubborn mule…you know this. Sometimes he convinces himself being powerful makes him immune to evil. Believe me, Nasha, Yusef is beyond my protection, beyond your father's vast influence. If Jean-Louis is helping Yusef…" Without completing the sentence, Gavriel's meaning was clear. "Frankel will have a box for the ballet. My two young associates, as it happens, will be sharing the ballet with young ladies tomorrow night. They'll be in your father's box, should you need them. Be careful in all things, Nasha."

She reevaluated—things are worse than they appeared. Yusef isn't just Mossad, he's undercover so deep neither Gavriel nor Papa can find, let alone help him. Or perhaps Gavriel doesn't want to find him.

Nasha felt a sudden chill.

"Why would Edward Poynter need forty million Euro, Gavriel? Needing that much money makes him so very vulnerable."

Gavriel gave her the answer he always chose, when appearing inscrutable. "How many angels can dance on the head of a pin?"

CHAPTER 17

Yesterday, for the first time, she saw glimpses of who Raissa used to be. Two steep climbs and descents, halfway from Rabe de las Calzadas, would have broken her five days earlier outside Pamplona. Muscular atrophy and functional instability, twin opponents of fitness, were being transformed. Not yet camera ready, fresh sinew was apparent to the eye. Raissa was encouraged by the results.

Easy, undulating paths across the high plain let her increase the pace to a forced march. At Fromista, she chose the easier of two routes, beginning to value time over spiritual gain. Seventy klicks under her belt, sweat-soaked through all her layers, Raissa threw down her pack in Sahagún, at twenty seven hundred feet above sea level. Sahagún was the middle of nowhere; Jardin de la Huerta, where she paid a hundred bucks for not much of a room, was eight klicks further along the trail.

***

"Come to reception, Señora, por favor."

Selected because the lodging had a pool, flowers and a ground floor room, the clerk's request was unreasonable. While the sun lingered below the horizon as less than a vague promise, and his words carried more than suggestion, such a call would always be disturbing.

Old habits stood her in good stead; she slept in her clothes and needed only boots to be ready. On dew stained grass, she crept past the pool, cloaking herself in bushes where the drive and grounds were always visible.

A battered truck spewed exhaust. A minor army showed determination. Raissa used the Sat phone to dial; a phone rang in the truck's cab. Disconnected without speaking, she took a deep breath and strode forward without excess movement or the appearance of rushing. Swinging at her side, muzzle pointed at the ground, the Z84 threatened no one. At the driver's door, having counted nine armed men, four of whom looked like brothers, Raissa was composed.

"Erramun, what trouble brings you and all your sons to Raissa?"

The second Great War left more than one vacuum in its wake. Franco repressed every minority, including the Basques. Flooding Basque country with internal migration, he diluted their precious regional personality.

A new political movement, Euskadi Ta Askatasuna, known by ETA, turned to violent protest in 1968. ETA resisted not only Franco's grand plan, but also the inertia of Basque nationalists organized as the PNV. For many including Erramun, schisms formed during the turmoil provided fertile soil for espionage. He augmented his income for decades as the *Statute of Autonomy* devolved or dissolved, depending on one's point of view.

"Not all my sons are with me." Distracted and distraught, Erramun's face contorted in rather too much discontent.

Raissa sought to calm Erramun. "I'm sorry to cause you pain. Can I help?"

Independent with a pragmatic streak described Erramun's politics and inclinations. For him, Raissa's presence was a relic of the past as much as a remnant of an unfinished garment. Erramun complied with her plea for a weapon not out of duty, but to honor a friendship and a business relationship with Gunther. This same relationship had purchased his house and educated his children.

"Blood on my doorway forces me to grow young again…full of hate.

From Gunther's notes, Raissa understood his family—three generations within walls built thick with love—was everything to Erramun.

Looking away, he told her, "Leave now. With us."

As the truck rumbled back towards Sahagún, Raissa asked, "What can you tell me?"

"Someone hired people to find Raissa. These intruders came with knowledge possessed only by neighbors or friends. My eldest...beaten while Erramun drank wine and talked the way grandparents talk to other grandparents. My granddaughter Zaballa, cuffed about, threatened with being taken hostage, curled into a fetal ball. It makes me weep. The intruder wearing shiny hunting boots said, 'Zaballa will make wonderful insurance.'" My youngest, the lad who delivered the Z84 to Raissa...my sweet boy...told them about Navarette."

For Raissa, Erramun's countenance was an open book: Those who paid to discover Raissa's location came from far away, unconcerned with a girl of eleven. Intent on Raissa's death, PNV sympathizers had been recruited to harm Erramun's loved ones. Then the phone had rung, bringing complexity laced with opportunity.

As if from his coffin, Gunther whispered secrets to Erramun, stories horrible yet true and, by knowing them, verified the voice's owner with dreadful certainty. The promise of a hefty payment complicated a bad situation, making it untenable.

A story with too many cooks in the kitchen, all wanting Raissa as meat in their stew—each a brigand, one worse than the other, though not very different from Erramun. "Your son didn't speak soon enough. He owed Raissa nothing. I'm very sorry."

Action had provoked reaction. One brigand offset by another had been a favorite tactic of Gunther Probst.

Raissa watched the Basque tally the odds. "Erramun, there are many ways a man could die adulterating betrayal with money."

Eyes filled with sorrow, for whom Raissa couldn't tell, Erramun told her, "My son will live without one eye. Those who took that eye will hurt no others, nor will their wives and children. Because you are Raissa, we came to conclude our obligation."

Erramun's use of *conclude* stuck out. English was a challenge for Erramun; *conclude our obligation* was another man's phrase.

"Where will you take me?"

"León is closest."

"Is León best?"

A bone-weary grin emerged. "Gunther always say...Raissa is feral cat, cool and smart. We could take you north, through the mountains to Santander. From there it would be best to hire a boat."

Every damned word out of Erramun's mouth…complete bullshit.

Erramun had never offered choices; his extraction plan should have left no room for debate. False bravado worse than the truth, Raissa felt cold to the core. Zaballa will live a long life; Erramun wouldn't have used her name, if he believed otherwise. Erramun's honor will suffer, not his wallet or grandchild.

I'm going to die today.

Mind spinning, Raissa's next words could not provoke Erramun. Wracked with guilt already, any imagined affront would serve as absolution for human sacrifice.

"Erramun's decision favors Zaballa…she has many years to live. What of Raissa's grandfather? Will Erramun grant one chance to enjoy my grandfather's love? It needn't endanger your little one."

"Best to shoot a feral cat from a distance…where it cannot scratch."

Freaking Basque homilies, piety didn't suit Erramun. "If that is so, the cat will die. But you, Erramun, figured out who took Zaballa. By now his wife, mother or sister…or all of them…know the terror to come. This coward…young, not cautious or careful enough…he listened to Erramun tell how this coward's family will be disemboweled, how he'll be roasted on a spit like the swine he is. Erramun has taken these steps to protect Zaballa. Who is the foreigner, Erramun? Only foreigners can buy everyone. Can you guess?"

"It is Raissa who guesses."

"I'm not wrong. Erramun would move heaven and hell to keep Zaballa safe. Will you deny me one chance to cheat death?"

"Death in Biscay is so often about Guernica."

In April 1937, during the Spanish Civil War, Franco conspired with the Luftwaffe to destroy the Basque town, including every man, woman and child.

"So he's German?"

"So it is said."

"Professional?"

"If Raissa dies, does it matter?"

She thought Erramun might be softening.

"If he's professional, he'll need a photograph…proof of death. He'll come close. Or send the PNV coward, whose identity will reveal a Basque policeman. Only PNV would dare take Zaballa. Give me one attempt…I'll kill this policeman-coward. I'll make him suffer more than Erramun possibly could."

Erramun licked his lips.

She could tell he agreed; the PNV pig would come very close to a famous beauty.

"Raissa has experience with such scum. This German, after my son spat on a coward's shiny boots, shoved an icepick in my boy's eye.

Raissa kept up quiet pressure, sensing the argument was turning a delicate corner.

"Not the German…I'd never be able to kill the German. So I must pray it's the PNV policeman-coward. I feel blood flowing from him, soaking the ground. Dictate terms…you're Erramun, not some ordinary man. Zaballa…the policeman should deliver her to the church in Navarette at a specified time. In exchange, at the same moment, you leave me tied to a tree, naked, by the Sansol ravines near the stream. Erramun drives home…your debt to Gunther washed away."

Raissa witnessed the veneer of fabrication drop away. Zaballa faced no imminent danger. Erramun sold me without barter.

"I leave you naked and drive away. What chance is this for you?

She knew better than to tell him. "My backpack…put it out of sight in the nearest ravine. I'll need to dress after leaving the policeman's entrails for the animals."

"We will see." Erramun dialed his phone, greed and shame woven into duplicitous grooves across his forehead.

***

Whatever arrangements Erramun made with the faux kidnapper would forever stay a mystery. Desperation continued as the only available mother of Raissa's optimism—every operation had ups and downs.

She was naked.

Naked had been her choice and, while the day warmed to the low fifties and few clouds blocked the sun, exposure would sap her strength. A single cold night without water would finish her, if no deal was struck. If a bargain prevailed, her position facing the ravines prevented a long distance kill.

Thrown into the closest crevice, her backpack no longer held the Sat phone or her knife, but its presence among craggy rocks reassured Raissa.

Well secured to the tree, Erramun wouldn't be seen breaking his word.

Circulation intact, no rags were stuffed her mouth. If the PNV policeman, or the German, came soon enough there would be one, slim opening. Despite the circumstances, two perfect words caused cracked lips to form a contorted sneer.

Erramun, morose and unable to suffer shame or remorse any longer, would soon depart. His claim—Erramun couldn't live as a profiteering reprobate—was absurd. Self interest demanded Raissa's indulgence; play to his pride, play to his self-denial so Erramun might answer.

"Who pays the German, Erramun?"

"You shouldn't have betrayed Gunther."

Unable to breathe, she sagged. Hope sliced to a litany, when Erramun's truck might drive away mattered not one iota. Langley bought the German. Langley bought Erramun as belt and suspenders. Humanity is unknown at Langley. She'd known about their inhumanity from the beginning.

Who was Raissa's Judas?

***

Seconds were a useful measure at the beginning, after the truck drove away. Then minutes. Hours soon followed the sun's arc, proving a challenge to her emotions. Raissa relied on the tree's shadow, rarely twisting her neck to bask in what little warmth remained.

Her face would fire the first salvo, if he came. Super-models learned early how to transmit sexuality. Her face would form much more than a promise: Why kill Raissa without having her first? What a tale a big strong man could tell: I fucked Raissa, then slit her throat. Her body, though bound, would writhe in motions which would make him erect and hungry. Experience taught exacting lessons; not every woman would do these things.

High as a November sun would rise, it shone now in the opposite direction from the morning. A shooter on high ground, across the road, would face blinding reflections. Leg muscles weary from restraint, hatred assisted hope in its struggle to remain alive.

A motorcycle's roar peaked, then ceased. One pair of feet approached.

Adrenaline pumped through her body.

Hands on thin hips, dark glasses hiding eyes above an arrogant mug, this PNV policeman was handsome enough to think himself God's-gift to women. Perfection for my purposes, sex radiated from Raissa's pores.

"So this is where the famous Raissa waits to receive her death sentence? Frightened like a common slut."

English—he even speaks English.

She thrust her breasts towards him, straining to be touched. Saw the bulge in his crotch.

He circled her, eyes roaming over high cheekbones, a sculptured neck where scars on her right side began, unmarked and luxurious breasts, and fibrous tracks of reconstructive surgeries encircling her midsection. Between her legs was where greedy eyeballs ceased their examination.

Two steps closer his movements became edgier and involuntary.

Like a schoolboy with a first porno, a flight of imagination enveloped him. Temptation would win out.

"Your photographs decorate my bedroom walls."

Foolish bastard believes we have a relationship.

Inhibition dropped away as he loosened his pants. There was no visible gun. Either a knife, or the cloth belt to strangle her, would be his intention.

"Wait till you see what I've got for Raissa. You'll remember how good I was. For eternity."

Driven by his urges, pants around his knees, snorting at his joke, he shuffled closer; pushed his erection at her, fingered her nipples. What he wanted was plain enough.

On high ground across the road, the German felt irritation born of errors and the lost opportunity for their correction. Hired at the last minute, the crude PNZ tough-boy was a dodgy decision. From this position, this angle and range, both he and his custom-crafted rifle were impotent. Self-rebuke shaken-off, a solution was as clear as it was undesirable—interrupt the forced rape about to take place under the trees.

Not to rescue the damsel-in-distress would he intercede; she was his client's target. To maintain discretion was his purpose, for the American insisted on tidiness, and this moronic Basque intended to contradict those instructions.

When everyone he hired was dead, when he was across the border in France, the American would complete payment and this job could be put out of sight, out of mind.

With every element of expression, Raissa told the PNZ policeman the geometry was impossible; she needed to lower herself, to kneel in front of his magnificence. Let me please you, those incredible blue eyes insisted.

He fingered the knots of her ropes with affection—her death would be by strangulation.

This pig-in-heat is a neophyte at the business of killing. She didn't know the German, but thanked him for hiring an infantile, pompous, ass.

Raissa's look of pleasure evolved into a huge smile, telling the Basque an explosion of pleasure would send him to heaven. Freed from her bonds, Raissa fell to her knees and played with him until his every fiber vibrated. Then released him.

Devastation and frustration swept over him, until he saw her point at the tampon's white string.

His telescopic scope allowed the German to watch Raissa massage his hireling with her left hand, while squatting in the dirt like a sow. Mesmerized, unwilling arousal imminent, magnification revealed her bewitching smile and let him observe the Polizei's eyes close in rapture. Focused on her right hand, she fingered the tampon. Born in a twisted childhood, his mother's Teutonic disgust rose in his throat; sex with a menstruating woman was barbaric. Fashion models were no better than harlots with their drugs, sex-parties and un-Godly debauchery. Repressed, the German was transfixed as she pulled the Polizei down while she reclined on her back.

Anticipation flooded the Basque, ecstasy moments from fruition. He leaned over to kiss her as she guided him to her.

Something struck the German peculiar: The tampon was clean. Disturbed, his attempt to reconcile an erotic scene with a discordant fact was delayed.

On the verge of orgasm, the Basque was beyond rational thought or action.

Far from cursing his own failure, the German ran downhill, bellowing an unheard warning.

His CIA client bore the brunt of puerile outrage.

A truncated section of straight razor emerged from the tampon's fibrous protection. Raissa forced both arms to relax. She was his lover: He must continue to be deceived. Without the advantage of a first strike, all would end in failure.

Supported on his elbows, he jammed his tongue into her mouth while she guided him into her.

Firm grip established on stainless steel salvation, divorced from where Raissa's flesh ended and a PNV killer's pounding thrusts began, she caressed his neck with two trailing fingers. Returned his kisses. Pressed hard and sliced where his pulse was strongest.

His primal scream deafened her.

Frenzied, she gashed again and again.

He collapsed on her, hands groping for and encasing her neck.

Pinned by his body, Raissa rolled to free her hands. Pummeled him with her left while lacerating anything and everything she could with the blade in her right. Blood spurted, its sticky, slippery ooze coating their connected skin. She struggled to breathe against the bruising strength of his grip, feeling him spasm in pain, anger and desperation to destroy what attacked him.

Their primal struggle continued until neither moved.

Had it been seconds or most of a lifetime, when Raissa saw polished tan boots and heard a sanctimonious laugh? Shit. Her stinking, bleeding lover-corpse brought a friend. The German would show no pity.

With an attempt at irony, he insulted her. "Gott hat deine fotze gesegnet. Du dumme fotze."

Detached and defeated, having crawled from under the dead policeman, she watched as the German's toe nudged a bloodied bit of fresh carcass. A slight frown descended from his brow, as the owner of custom made boots reached inside his leather jacket for a pistol.

No suppressor. Her death would be deafening, but unnoticed. Rolled into the ravine to be eaten by animals and insects, it would be an inglorious end for a once-upon-a-time cover girl.

***

Stay out of sight as long as necessary: Erramun's insistence disallowed thoughts of compromise. Our family's promise can be broken for one reason alone—if you see those shiny boots, kill the one who wears them. Don't leave Raissa any chance at you.

More than once temptation sung to him, while waiting in the ravine. Now, with a valuable lesson learned, he would return a hero, heir apparent to Erramun. With great care, he sighted his target, the range less than a hundred yards.

No pain accompanied the rifle shot's echoes. Raissa raised herself to see an apparition emerge from the ravine, speaking in a bewildered tongue.

Head shaking in disbelief, the youngest son of Erramun seemed on the verge of being ill. "It didn't seem possible you could kill him the way you did. I recognized his boots from when he blinded my brother and kidnapped my niece." Breath coming fast, her improbable savior moved with random, disordered, steps. "My father kept his word to you and faith with Gunther…this is his last message for Raissa."

She listened as the youngest son of Erramun closed the gap between them. Soon shock would wear off. Soon he would kill for the second time in his life. At eighty yards, he relaxed. Raissa didn't like her shot.

Raissa stoked his anger. "No one took Zaballa. Your father pimped me to the German and sold me outright to someone at CIA. Erramun is *putasumea*."

Son of Erramun, he couldn't afford to be aggrieved and infuriated. His brain told him to desist. His legs began to run at Raissa. Five yards subtracted from her range, his rifle's barrel swung upwards.

Raissa rolled hard to her right, hand finding the German's pistol. She aimed and fired three times. For what seemed forever, she lay shaking in the tree's shadow.

Amongst unwritten rules of tradecraft, she knew there existed a recognized hierarchy. Mathematicians presented such a pecking order in terms of immutable laws, theorems and corollaries. *Assume nothing* was number one on every list—a universal law of the spy's universe. Erramun's son was guilty of assuming everything. *Never go against your gut* was a favorite of many, in particular when connected to its corollary: *Technology will always let you down.* In Raissa's gut she'd believed Erramun's son a virgin in the art and science of killing.

She stood over the boy, who bled from his lung and stomach, dead in all but his mind.

"You'll die for the worst of reasons...a sacrifice at the altar of avarice. You should've run away, should never have listened to me insult your father." Raissa saw him stop breathing and offered her limited Basque wisdom to his eternal soul. "Burla minena, egia dioena." The most painful insult is the one that's true.

***

Something was rotten at Langley.

Langley, starting with Gunther floating among the reeds, was more silent than her friend's fresh grave. Gunther's death, and this attempt on her life, connected dissimilar events.

Where was Fulton Bennett, her mentor?

Her stomach tied in knots, it warned of another overused spy's bromide: *Everyone can be under opposition control.* To solve the equation confronting her demanded the use of a well-known principle of physics: To every action there is an equal and opposite reaction.

***

Where the stream overflowed into the ravine, she washed away an ocean of blood never removing its stain. Dressed from the recovered backpack, she resumed a different pilgrimage after dragging three dead men to the fate they callously plotted for Raissa.

In the driver's seat of the German's BMW, she phoned Erramun with his son's cell. A father and mother shouldn't be prevented from burying their child, no matter the circumstances. Her voice delivered the message.

Erramun lapsed into the silence of everlasting pain.

Raissa granted no relief. "Blame yourself old man. Tell me who paid Erramun. It's he who killed Gunther and your boy." Whether a complete or partial truth was unimportant to this intimate conversation. "Your boy's killer will pay for his dance."

"I'll hunt you."

"No, Erramun. You tell yourself...if I hurry, Raissa could die by my hand. You tell yourself what all fools tell themselves, when despair fills their heart. Like all old men, you sent another in the place meant for Erramun. You sent your flesh and blood. If only you kept faith with Gunther...but Erramun chose another way."

Tortured, Erramun wept with the words. "He knew things only Gunther would have known. Knowing what he knew meant he walked at Gunther's side through those years. He knew everything."

He knew everything ground a small list to three: The then and current Deputy Director of NCS, Fulton Bennett; the then and current DD/CIA; and the then D/CIA, Grover Norris.

Vultures all.

***

Brittany Ferries carried Raissa from Santander to Portsmouth, England in the relative comfort of an outside cabin. In Portsmouth, with the German's handgun and her laptop submerged at sea, she re-arranged everything she wore or carried, relegating all things hiking to a variety of dustbins.

A pay-as you-go mobile put her in touch with the world. Two other mobiles would take the place of the first as the risks of exposure dictated.

A carabiner carried a thumb drive attached to a belt loop.

Nothing of new clothes related to high fashion. Her ruined hair was trimmed and self-colored a mousey brown. She wore ordinary glasses chosen to alter the shape of her face. Expert in makeup, those skills were employed to let Raissa, to whose face and figure the world once paid homage, blend-in without scrutiny.

Who most wanted her dead?

The German, without attention to detail or respect for his target, wasn't the best selection to assassinate a retired assassin. Nothing about the German suggested the person who killed Gunther. Why wasn't Gunther's killer sent to Spain? Were two different killers employed by two different paymasters?

In a quiet street she found an Internet café. First on a list was Tom Nichols wedding announcement in the Cape Cod Times. With his wife's maiden name came her cell phone number. No amount of searching located Fulton Bennett's home phone.

By far the bulk of the hour was used to bring her up to date with Aaron Frankel's social life. Concentrate on the women, the voice in her head insisted. She built a file utilizing every scrap of downloaded data, until faces etched themselves in organic memory.

It was mid-morning on Cape Cod. Raissa remembered days leading up to Thanksgiving: A wood fire; new apples; late corn; and the last charity dog-wash before bitter winds swept down from Canada. Melissa Nichols would enjoy morning coffee with a husband she loved, a quiet walk on the beach, lazy sex before Tom watched the Patriots—these pleasures marked a normal life for a normal wife. Her call to Melissa Nichols went to voicemail.

Wide River Boatyard would be peaceful, the hard labor of hauling and winterizing boats complete. One or two of the young guys would be sitting around, maybe playing with Agatha. A boatyard phone would be a good candidate for remote monitoring, if Martin Haslett still had a bug up his ass about Gunther's murder.

Deciding to take the chance, in a bright voice Raissa said, "Hi Teddy, it's Agatha's mom. Could you ask Jonathan to call...it's a new number." Not a controversial word to provoke listeners.

"Sure...but he's not here." Raissa heard Teddy's wheels turning. "Tom's out fishing...how about I give him the number?"

"Perfect Teddy. You treating Agatha right?"

"Yes, ma'am."

***

Without disturbing an inch of dangling ash, Jonathan's hand ran through a shock of white hair and stopped in a sign of contemplation.

"What you thinkin' she's gonna do?"

Tom wasn't troubled by Teddy transmitting the request to phone Raissa. After the hubbub of the initial days, there'd been no new developments related to Gunther Probst's murder. Haslett went home to Boston like a swimming swan; under the surface, the little prick was paddling like hell.

"Well Jonny, I'm with you...she wants help with something."

"So you gonna call, or not. You should help that little slip of a girl. She didn't kill nobody."

"I keep telling you...little slip of a girl could kill all four of us before dinner, without so much as spilling her beer."

"Nope. No reason CIA be screwin' with us."

"You take care, Jonny. I'll make sure to tell you what happens."

"When its over and we read it inna paper, Tommy...thas when you tell us poor, innocent, dickheads."

Nichols drove his cruiser to South Cape Beach. What did he owe a new bride in caution? What did he owe a woman not much more than an acquaintance? Balanced against what he might discover, the little he knew could be weighed against a cop's instinct. Decision finalized, he dialed the number Teddy gave him.

CHAPTER 18

Miriam yelled upstairs, "Mom...there's a lady at the door."

Nasha came to the top of the stairs. "Stay in the kitchen with your brother, sweetheart. I'll be right down."

Downstairs, a quick glance into Brad's den of iniquity showed unexpected tranquility. Her son's cheeks puffed busily, surveying the room from his third, wobbly, attempt in the highchair.

"Miriam, did Brad swallow the last of his cereal?" With the last syllable, her precious son spewed in every direction, including mom's fuchsia blouse.

Wet dishcloth in hand, Nasha hurried to the front door, scrubbing off splatter and deciding she, not Brad, needed a bib emblazoned with multi-colored fish.

"Come on in...be careful, there's cereal all over."

Sarah Gullickson made her way down the hall to stand by the kitchen island, awaiting further instructions. She found nothing about family life appealing.

Back turned to Sarah while kneeling to clean the mess, Nasha cut to the chase. "No need for the neighborhood newswoman thing. I know who you are, Sarah. What can I do for you?"

Sarah winced. "Maybe we could talk somewhere quieter." Diplomacy a better choice, she aimed her next words at Nasha's daughter. "My name is Sarah, what's yours?"

"Miriam. It's Hebrew. In the Bible she hid her baby brother from the Pharaoh."

Sarah misinterpreted the girl's level of interest. "In the Hebrew

Bible and the Qu'ran, Sarah is the wife of Abraham and the mother of Isaac."

Miriam stared back. "I go to pre-school now, but next year I'll be in Kindergarten."

Nasha suggested, "Don't try so hard. Miriam's five...the Bible's only interesting as long as it's about her."

"I don't spend much time with children. She's lovely."

"Thanks, but she pretty much knows how cute works to her advantage...a quality you share."

Unprepared for the change from chatty to cutting, the implied threat blew Sarah's recruitment of Nasha out of the water. Heated response quelled, she responded.

"I think all women know what works in different situations."

"What situation brought you to my kitchen?"

Nasha held out a large mug as a peace offering, at the same moment deciding not to show Sarah the photo. It would be more effective later, if the need became pressing.

The blouse might be ruined. Her hair was streaked with Gerber's, the kids running amok and dishes piled in the sink, but Sarah admitted Nasha Poynter was a number of steps ahead. Nasha had known, or guessed what Sarah and the Agency wanted from her. There was no point in ladling bullshit.

"Help...is what we'd like from you."

"Who's listening, Sarah: Grover Norris, Bennett, Norris the Younger? Who?" Nasha made no physical search for wireless devices. Seconds passed. "Look Sarah, if you're a big girl get rid of the comms-set, lose the transmitter and its backup...talk to me about what kind of help."

Sarah's face reflected a kaleidoscope of emotion as she listened to instructions in her earpiece. Hands moving quickly and efficiently, she followed Nasha's orders.

"Aaron Frankel is our target. Get close enough to access the accounts where Frankel keeps bin Rahman's money...names of banks, account numbers and access codes. That's what kind of help we want."

Doorbell chimes interrupted. Miriam screamed, "Where's my backpack?"

"Sarah, give me a moment."

Comms reattached, Sarah's whispered demand wasted no words. "Jamie, you there? What now?"

Grover Norris's voice invaded her ear. "Find out what she wants. It's a dance...they always want more than they'll get. Take your time. She hasn't thrown you out."

Nasha brought Brad and her tea to the table. Seated, she squeezed lemon in the Denby mug and, looking directly at Sarah, said, "Why?"

"Why are we targeting Frankel...or why recruit you?"

"Neither. Why would I agree?"

"Tell me what you want."

"Is it wrong to think I'm the best candidate? You didn't come without established parameters...what are you offering?"

This isn't good. The Poynter woman might work for a second rate intelligence organization, but she's skillful. When she spoke, Sarah's inexperience led to a serious mistake. "Well, well, now we know what Nasha Poynter is...you'll turn a trick. All that's left is the price." In an instant, satisfaction turned to vinegar on Sarah's tongue.

Unmoved, Nasha cleaved Sarah's neck. "Tonight, as it happens, I'll be Aaron's guest at the Bolshoi. If I receive confirmation of an untraceable donation...one million dollars to Caritas Lebanon...before his limo picks me up, we can meet again. If not don't worry, I won't tell him what you've got in mind."

Sarah Gullickson's composure fell to the floor. "Quite the queen-bitch, aren't you? You're supposed to be an American."

"My employer sent a man to rape me yesterday, Miss Gullickson. Want to insult me? Make a better effort."

Nasha closed the front door and climbed the stairs to Brad's room. Turned off the recorder set next to the nursery's monitoring device. The sending unit sat on the kitchen floor, a plastic walkie-talkie like fifteen other of Brad's toys, all made in China.

***

Intrigued on an irregular basis by the computers in Bennett's attic, Mannheim's primary interest this morning was the report from the tech team dispatched to Bennett's Connecticut home.

The lead technician had bitten the nail on his left thumb to the quick. Juvenile behavior, he accused himself, prompted by a useless summary of useless data. "We spent over an hour starting with the attic. There's nothing to tell. Monitors, high-speed connections, backup storage capability and six new computers, but no drives. Nothing in local memory or cache…on any of the machines. Whatever was there, isn't there any longer."

Mannheim brought his fingertips to his chin, giving the impression of a child praying. "With all your magic?"

"Correct. Without the drives, there's no data to analyze."

"No hidden bytes or mystical bits?"

"I can tell you what's on the inventory: Three sets of fingerprints, two sets of toiletries, one locked weapons safe, no evidence of foreign Intel, zero paper files belonging to the Agency, tax records going back a dozen years for Bennett. Other than that, nothing but normal stuff…all listed on the second tab."

"Let me guess…the third set of prints belong to Vladimir Putin?"

"One set is Bennett. Second is his lady friend, Linton. Third is unknown."

"Edward Poynter?"

"No."

"Caroline Poynter?"

"No."

"Andrew or Nasha Poynter?"

"No. I said the third set is unknown."

"How can that be? Can't you lads access every print in the civilized world?"

"That leaves quite a few unknowns. Sir."

Distressed, Mannheim moved on. "Where is Ms. Linton this freezing, gray morning?"

"I don't know."

"Please locate her. Try her mother's home, wherever that might be. Ms. Linton isn't happy at the moment. Unhappy women most often go home to their mothers."

**

Jacques Desmarais dialed Bennett's number and found a confounding response. Not Bennett, not voicemail, but an actual person came on the line and asked Jacques to identify himself. He refused by instantly disconnecting. In an abundance of caution he removed the SIM, tossed the phone's carcass in the trash and boarded the flight from Charles de Gaulle to Dubai. Prior excitement tempered by jangled nerves, he decided to order a double brandy after takeoff.

Six rows in front of Desmarais, Marie Truchet wondered as she faded into sleep's oblivion: What is important enough about Jacques Desmarais to leave Andrew Poynter half the globe away, unsupervised?

***

Aaron Frankel felt the crush of the inevitable. History taught indelible lessons: Presidents, Popes, Prime Ministers, cheating husbands, deadbeat gamblers, and voracious moneylenders—anyone could be killed.

To continue doing what I do, to challenge and defeat the odds, is to mock fate and spit in the eyes of the Gods. For an inveterate gambler there was one cause for optimism: Not all assassinations succeeded; not all targets were defenseless.

He lifted his eyebrows and pursed his lips.

Second cappuccino in hand, he awaited Anton Leuzinger's call. While a half spoonful of sugar slid through foamed milk, his mind flipped to Nasha Poynter. His inner voyeur undressed her. Startled by the transposition of Raissa's face on Nasha's naked curves, Frankel stared a moment towards Governor's Island and Lady Liberty before picking up the encrypted phone.

"Good morning, Anton. Thanks for returning my call."

Like normal businessmen, they exchanged niceties, as if their mutual client wasn't a man who dealt, albeit indirectly, in the brutal demise of thousands. This existence, Aaron told himself, is madness.

Framed by a halo of static, which indicated the operational nature of the electronics keeping their conversation private, Leuzinger's booming bass sounded normal.

"How are the markets today, Aaron?"

"In the crapper, Anton. Ain't easy making an honest living these days." Black humor formed the best catalyst in taking the Swiss banker's temperature.

"Perhaps you should raise a pirate's flag over the building, yes?"

"Anton...can we meet in person?"

"With the client?"

"No, just us banker types." Frankel fought to make a face-to-face sound ordinary.

"We could talk now, Aaron, I've got time. Or videoconference later. But no, I don't think what you suggest…us meeting together…is wise."

Cold perspiration broke out across Leuzinger's face. Ten out of ten things which resulted from such a meeting would impose dire consequences. Me—Anton Leuzinger—face down, shot in the head, isn't the worst possibility. What is Frankel thinking, or planning?

Real fear drove the Swiss to open his bag and methodically pack his belongings. Occupational hazard as it was, being prepared to run for one's life was a daily reality.

"Aaron…are you still there?"

Frankel's voice recovered its normal pitch. "You're right. Lousy idea. Besides, I'm going to the Bolshoi tonight with a beautiful woman. Let's talk again in a couple of days."

Unnerved by Frankel's offhanded remark, Leuzinger asked himself the obvious: Am I overreacting? Or does Aaron, somehow, know Sheik bin Rahman is concerned for the security of all his investments, not just monetary ones?

Inconsistent with waiting for the airlines, his early warning system pushed for immediate action. Within ten minutes he'd arranged a private charter to London, on to Dubai.

***

Yusef Schwartz, unaware of doubts plaguing Aaron Frankel, was familiar with the stress which fostered them. He'd embarrassed Fathima in front of men who looked to her for leadership. Saved himself only by providing information that none in bin Rahman's group of wannabe terrorists could've known. And in saving himself, made his plight worse. Fathima, proven less informed than a half-Jew who labored in CIA's basement, would wait in the weeds.

More Intel could raise his profile enough to survive.

What a time for the flow of information at Langley to dry up. Yusef examined the pile of Burn Bags and processed them without incident.

Maury Lippman saw JET observing Yusef with too much interest. Not for the first time, it troubled Maury.

***

Fulton Bennett, imprisoned within an I-95 rest area in suburban Maryland along with several hundred others, waited with admirable patience. In the presence of bickering spouses, squawking teens, and dozens of cell phone conversations, a perfect backdrop for solemnity spread out before him. Coffee held in both hands, he took comfort from its heat.

Do your job. He'd screamed at, cajoled and threatened generations of CIA officers with those three elemental words.

Who would've thought Zachary Mannheim, of all people, would be the one to throw them back in my face. Zachary, whose career included not a scintilla of field experience with his life at risk. Zachary, who'd never crossed into East Berlin in the trunk of a Trabant. Who never told himself a joke to keep from soiling his underwear. What's the best feature of a Trabant? There's a heater at the back to warm your hands, when you're pushing it.

How can I do my job under house arrest?

***

Joe Steele's fingers tingled.

Submarines held a unique fascination for those who designed, fabricated, and sold them. Far darker, deep currents of gossip surrounded a submarine's capabilities, crew and the manner in which it might be destroyed. Ruminations of sycophants, enthralled with the suffering of men and women in the milliseconds of a hull's implosion, were despicable.

On his screen a convoluted e-mail created hypothetical dialogue between crew members of a sub doomed by its own existence; sailors bewitched by the sounds of their own breathing. Details tossed with abandon into the public domain led to an exact sub: HMS Astute.

Pure fiction? Am I paranoid? Joe pushed enter.

***

Enveloped in smoke from a chain of cigarettes, Fathima waited impatiently for interruptions to cease, enlightenment to arrive and management to remove its over-sized thumb from its collective anus.

She agreed to this FBI interview, in the matter of Mahbeer's attempt on the Poynter woman, with great reluctance. She stood in the cold, reasoning discomfort would shrink time taken by FBI automatons and deny those who listened the ability to record her lies. Plus she could smoke; nicotine allowed a clear head.

The taller Agent Madison lit up in conspiratorial relief. "Why not inside?"

"Don't ask silly questions?"

Veiled hostility marked the shorter of the two, Agent Rainey. "Sorry to offend Ms. Laniado...what's your position at the Embassy?"

"Deputy Cultural Attaché."

Rainey couldn't restrain a chuckle. "Lebanon is not legendary for its modern culture. So don't give silly answers...we won't ask silly questions. Is Mr. Saadia an employee of the Embassy?"

"He's employed as a chauffeur."

"Only drives...no other duties?"

"He drives."

"Does he drive you?"

"Yes, he drives many of the senior staff."

"In the Embassy's black Cadillac limousine?"

"The limousine is a Mercedes."

"Does he drive Mrs. Poynter as well?"

"She isn't senior staff."

"So he doesn't drive Mrs. Poynter?"

"Look, I don't care if Mahbeer drives her. What else do you want?"

"Why would Mr. Saadia wear a mask, run Mrs. Poynter off the road and threaten her life?"

"Why would any sane person do such a thing?"

Agent Madison. "Ms. Laniado, you seem to bear considerable ill will towards Mrs. Poynter. Did you instruct Mr. Saadia to threaten Nasha Poynter?"

In a nice rhythm, Fathima rejected each and every implication. "Nasha and I are close colleagues. Plus, I'm sane."

"Whole lot of folks heard you on television ripping Mrs. Poynter." Madison read from his notes. "...*but you expose your body and spread your legs for the infidel as your mother did.* Is that how close colleagues in the Embassy treat one another?"

Snapped back to the moment, Fathima considered where the bland, uninteresting man might be going with these questions. "Nasha is safe. Mahbeer truly lost his mind. It's a tragedy."

Tag-teaming her, Rainey changed course. "Your comments about Mrs. Poynter at the luncheon...did you make them near the end, after those attending heard about the shooting?"

"No idea about any shooting."

He handed her a blown-up photo, then pursued his point. "This is you leaving the *Ritz*. Could you tell us...who's driving the vehicle?"

Poor quality, taken through rain sprinkled glass, she could deny the image was Mahbeer. "As I told you, Mahbeer drives senior staff."

After listening to the back and forth, the taller agent wondered aloud. "Isn't it unusual...Mr. Saadia driving you in a beat-up Toyota?"

Fathima spit smoke at the ground, flicked the barely lit cigarette into a bush. "What he drives is no concern of mine."

"Not even if the car was stolen?"

"Mr. Saadia's behavior is not my responsibility. Everything he's done suggests mental incompetence." Laniado wheeled, walking away without waiting for either agent's response.

Rainey said to Madison, "There's a lot going on with that babe. Why don't we get together with our new British girlfriend?"

CHAPTER 19

Minutes remained before the doorbell would ring.

Sweatshirt and jeans tossed on the bed, her evening outfit went on: Wide legged wool pants covered by a long, embroidered tunic with a high neck—all in black. No jewelry. Black flats embroidered to match. Light in weight, a chiffon hijab, trimmed in shiny, coordinated edging, matched the tunic. Nasha chose a silver under-scarf to emphasize the black of the hijab and her nude lips. Tonight there would be no discussion of modesty.

Three formidable men emerged from the limousine. Two remained with the vehicle. The third rang Nasha's bell.

Nasha's earliest memories of Gavriel Rabin resembled these men, whose justifiable paranoia and a complex profession could involve sacrificing your existence for that of another. For a moment she shivered in the warm isolation of the armored Mercedes.

What am I doing?

A laughing man behind a machine gun watched little Nasha shrink from the explosions and the gore.

Goose bumps marched down her spine. She very nearly shouted to be taken home.

***

The terraces of the Kennedy Center drew Nasha's eyes upward. Whether the East, West or River Terrace, each was exposed to the skill of a sniper.

Nasha put on her game face as a small tribe of media approached.

"Nasha...is it true you're dating Aaron Frankel?"

"Sorry to disappoint...I'm happily married. But the Bolshoi is hard to turn down."

Another voice. "Aaron Frankel is a terrorist's banker...why be seen with him if you harbor political ambitions?"

Nasha looked into the TV camera. "Aaron Frankel may be what you claim, but understanding is the product of dialogue. Ballet is a language that crosses borders of ideology, economics and political strategy."

"Are you pandering to the Arab Street with the way you're dressed?"

"Is that what you'll write...a practicing Muslim gets criticized for wearing conservative clothes and a hijab?" A broad smile preceded a challenging suggestion. "Each of you are Arab women in the media...come stand next to me...let the cameras decide who might be pandering." A good-natured finger pointed at her questioner, she added, "Your bikini is famous. Tell me how to lose the last five pounds of baby fat."

A more serious voice interjected. "Your job at the Embassy is counter-intelligence...would a Lebanese government employee act as a contract killer for the Agency?"

"Can't you tell? Nasha Poynter is secretly employed to do away with Kennedy Center's bartenders for watering drinks. While I'm not authorized to speak for the Lebanese government, it's hard to imagine Hezbollah or Phalange, or any Lebanese faction, risking political suicide as a puppet of the United States. It's difficult to believe the US would cause the death of a prominent citizen without due process. By the way, I'm a Cultural Attaché at the Embassy and no one's contract killer."

The serious voice wouldn't be put off. "Rumors claim Frankel is a target. Would you approve of a Western government doing away with Mr. Frankel...the way terrorists are commonly killed by a drone strike?"

"No, I don't approve of governments killing indiscriminately or without due process. As an American, it's my right to disapprove. I disapprove of terrorism in any form and reject any hand employing it."

Two serious questions answered, she decided on one facetious admission. "I would doubt the sanity of any spook contemplating a drone attack on the Kennedy Center."

Laughter cascaded through broken tension.

"Mrs. Poynter...there are reports of a million dollar contribution, received by Caritas Lebanon, made in your name. Did you make such a contribution?"

"No...but isn't it wonderful someone did."

"Why would your name be..."

"Sorry to interrupt...I can't give you an answer. My family budget doesn't give me leeway to make such a contribution. No one asked permission to list my name; I didn't approve my name being listed. Whoever donated the funds should be applauded.

An American journalist on the fringes of Arab media yelled, "Even if it's Frankel...or his terrorist pals?"

"Yes, as long as what funds remain to support terrorism are depleted. I'm not sorry if this opinion makes me politically naïve, but Caritas Lebanon isn't the World Bank. They need the money."

Even louder, the American demanded, "Did Michani make the contribution? Are you just another cynical, pretty face...using money to get elected?"

"Jean-Louis Michani is my adopted father. I love him very much. My husband and I don't accept money from family. We work hard and take care of ourselves. If there's proof my Papa made the contribution, I won't be shocked; I'm a living example of his dedication to altruism." The security man pointed at his wrist. She waved at the gathering. "Sorry...the Bolshoi won't wait."

Robby Turcott began to speak into his phone.

Phyllis Martell stood by Robby's side in contemplation, barely arriving on time after the round trip to the Maryland rest area.

***

Often praised, the Kennedy Center Opera House was configured with twenty three hundred seats. Designed for ballet, opera and musical theater, its signature red and gold silk curtain, and Lobmeyr chandelier, produced a stunning effect.

In the brilliantly lit foyer, Nasha looked inquisitively at her chief guardian.

"We're clear, Mrs. Poynter. Mr. Frankel just reached the box. This way, please."

On any evening, the Kennedy Center attracted its share of dignitaries. For the Bolshoi, even those jaded by money and accomplishment felt excitement. Tickets close to priceless, lobbyists squirreled away the best seats for the best events year after year. In a gathering that included a sitting Vice President, a smattering of visiting Royalty, Ambassadors of several nations, Senators, Members of the House, three Governors, and more billionaires than could be counted, any tactic to gain Aaron Frankel's trust appeared absurd. In a peaceful corridor leading to private boxes, her planned approach would be tell the truth and beg Frankel's reciprocation.

When the door opened, Frankel stood at the railing examining the crowd. He bestowed a look of radiant happiness upon her. "I'm so pleased you decided to come."

"Shall I raise my arms for a search."

"That would be rude, Nasha. You wouldn't think of wearing a wire. And a weapon? You're bright as well as very beautiful...a weapon diminishes intelligence."

"So your team scanned me." She gave a respectful look at the man from the limo. "I never noticed."

"Nasha...you hurt my feelings. I don't scan the women in my life. How petty would that be?"

For a passing instant, Nasha inclined towards trust. She took his hand and allowed him to usher her to a seat. Thrilled at the opportunity to people watch, she put names to famous faces.

Frankel leaned close. "You're not the only one rubber-necking. Those people looking up into the boxes...they're asking each other...who's the babe with that bastard, Aaron Frankel?"

Amused, she showed him a playful expression. "Do you think they're being kind...bastard is a compliment, when you're you."

"Will you torment me all night? You're a guest and I cannot sell a guest to slavers in the souq."

"When have you ever been in a souq?"

"Just this afternoon...at souq.com."

Not strained or fake, they both laughed. Nasha felt a vibe of sincerity for the second time. Take two aspirin and go to bed with Miriam, if you want sincerity. There'll be none here tonight.

"So what are you thinking, Mrs. Andrew Poynter?" Sharpened, these words meant to bring an answer.

"Where are you taking a girl to eat afterwards?"

For the benefit of any directional microphones aimed in their direction, Frankel leered and said seriously, "You mean we're not going to savor wild and crazy sex in the limo?"

Amazed they occupied the same wavelength, she answered like an expectant lover might. "Well, if that happens, we still need pizza afterwards."

***

Do your job.

How can Mannheim expect me to do my job without resources, then foist Phyllis Martell on me as a covert liaison? Covert liaison—a puerile joke typical of Zachary.

Bennett sat in his living room without a single tool of his trade. He half expected an Agency goon squad to confiscate the burner phone. Trust Zachary Mannheim? Mannheim would have several agendas beyond doling out enough rope so, if Bennett tied the wrong knot, it would be him swinging, not the fucking man with a South African accent.

Bennett phoned Greg Riley.

When Riley hung up, he re-read the e-mail from Joe Steele.

***

"Let's review, shall we?" For Mannheim, something was off—a nit to pick at.

Any sense of collegial analysis out the window, Phyllis made a second try at pleasing the boss.

"First, Bennett wanted an update on the recruitment of Nasha Poynter. I promised to speak with Robby Turcott, who refused to brief me. When I informed Robby the Bennett matter has risen to a formal CIC investigation, he complied. Sarah Gullickson approached Poynter, controlled by Grover Norris. A payment of one million dollars to a Lebanese charity was authorized as an ante to the game; the Poynter woman required payment as a pre-condition. Poynter and Frankel are at the Kennedy Center as we speak…quite the couple apparently. I watched her with the Arab Press. She's good."

Mannheim's interest didn't run to media magpies. He held a tight grip on the scope granted by D/CIA. Integrity of the Agency—where all his efforts would be focused.

"Gullickson made the approach in Mrs. Poynter's home, correct?"

"Yes."

"Don't be defensive, Ms. Martell. Be accurate." Mannheim perused his notes for several minutes, leaving Phyllis biting her lip. "Is Mrs. Poynter decked-out with electronic marvels this evening?"

Martell bit down hard. Tasted the metallic sharpness of blood. "I have no information concerning audio or video."

"So…are we to presume Ms. Gullickson concluded no arrangement?"

"I don't make presumptions, sir."

There it was—a sign of submission. Ms. Martell has decided to divulge the whole truth as she knows it.

"So, is Mrs. Nasha Poynter, an American citizen being recruited to NOC status, read-in on the Agency's intended operation? If so, how can she wander around Washington this evening absent a commitment to cooperate?"

"Was your question rhetorical?"

Deadpan expression in place, Mannheim was satisfied with her refusal to respond to a verbal trap. "Tell me again how you learned the status of Ms. Ribeiro's termination?" Mannheim looked prepared to take Phyllis into custody.

How could it have come to this? Career repercussions no longer the issue, Phyllis Martell's options dwindled to one: Return to the officer she once was.

"On two occasions David Nazarian telephoned me. Once before he left on his assignment. A second call came earlier today." From pages in a notebook, she read times and dates. "Nazarian told me the Agency's contractor failed to check-in. The Op's been suspended until the target can be reacquired."

"Why would Nazarian tell a member of CIC anything about such things?"

"Years ago we were together. Sometimes we talk."

Mannheim made no attempt to speak, mind taking up the slack. How sad: Sometimes we talk about a termination which officially, unofficially, or in a fantasy or wet dream can be said to exist.

Whether Nazarian expected Martell to spill the beans seemed the best among bad alternatives. No one, certainly not Mannheim, questioned David's capabilities. How devious could Nazarian be? The intentions of a spy ran counter to instinct and sobriety.

"Who else in the Agency knows Nazarian's current status?"

She squirmed before answering. "I've told no one, sir."

Liar's unease or straightforward embarrassment, knowing which was critical. And as lying was an advanced art, Mannheim believed Phyllis Martell a paint-by-numbers pseudo-Warhol.

"I ask you once more, Ms. Martell. Who else did you inform about the calls from David Nazarian? Before you reply, understand you stand at the precipice. Make a good decision."

Before sound emerged from her mouth, the answer lit her face. "Nazarian asked me to inform Deputy Director Bennett...Ribeiro is still alive. When you sent me to Maryland, I conveyed the message. I'm certain David anticipated this meeting with you, sir. I apologize for having lied, sir."

Time to intubate the un-breathing creature, Mannheim would throw her a lifeline.

"You're assigned to the investigation of Deputy Director Bennett. In that capacity, you did nothing untoward in conveying Nazarian's message. Direct Nazarian to me, when he contacts you next. From this moment forward, he's to speak with me and no one else at the Agency. You will find a succinct way to convey the importance of my orders to Mr. Nazarian. Understood?"

Zachary expected nothing from David Nazarian. Tossed to the wolves by Grover Norris, Langley would hear a sanitized version of conversations between old lovers. What took place at some godforsaken rathole in Spain would be as Nazarian, and Nazarian alone, concocted. Sentiment and sugar water couldn't be more sweet.

***

Parked in the cell phone lot at Reagan National, Aaron Frankel and Nasha Poynter were, finally, alone. Separate security vehicles cordoned them off from intrusion.

With no change in easygoing charm, Frankel said, "Well Nasha...you succeeded where so many others failed. We're alone. What do you want? Whose emissary are you?"

"No more interest in wild and crazy limo sex?"

"Sex is a lovely diversion. Thousands of bobble-heads cast their net for a man in my position. You're not a diversion...what do you want? Who sent you? Tick-tock."

"The British Embassy party...you switched places with my father during the evacuation. Tell me...what's your relationship with Jean-Louis and what made you sit in his wheelchair?"

Disbelief, smeared on Frankel's reply, dripped metaphorically on her shoe. "Why not ask the old buzzard...your father, that is?"

"I did. He won't tell me."

"Like a spoiled brat, you think I'll tell you. Good God, you're a disappointment. We're done." He started to knock on the bulletproof window glass.

"I think Jean-Louis saved your life."

Frankel spun back to her. Exasperated, he raised his voice. "So you knew. Why ask...what the hell do you want?"

"Why would Papa help you?"

"I haven't the first or faintest idea."

"I can show you pictures. How the gun got into the Embassy and who was supposed to use it."

Interested but wary, Frankel probed. "You work for old man Poynter and the British, do you? Should've seen that coming."

"No, I told you the truth. I work for the Lebanese government. Edward Poynter disapproves of me. This matter...being here tonight...this is quite personal."

"Personal how?"

"Personal means it's my business, not yours. Would you like to know...very specifically...who is going to shoot you dead?"

"There are the quite obvious candidates, beginning with my close buddy the Sheikh of all Sheikhs, and ending with a third of the population of so-called developed society. At the risk of seeming crass, at what price would you sell this information?"

"The exact question Sarah Gullickson put to me in my kitchen this morning."

"Sarah Gullickson is...?"

"Young blonde on Grover Norris's arm at the Embassy. You're familiar with the type: Pushy, ambitious, not a bobble-head but not quite who she thinks she is."

"She screwing Grover?" Amused, he carped, "He's not quite who he thinks he is, either."

"Never had the pleasure."

"And you told Sarah to send a million dollars to a Lebanese charity."

"Yes. Everyone seems to know."

"Where should I send my million? Or are my thirty pieces of silver to be paid in a different currency?"

"I told you what I want...what involvement does my Papa have with terrorists?" Nasha regretted slipping into the language of family.

Frankel felt his world click four degrees further off its axis. "Absolutely no freaking connection I know of." He held up his hand like taking an oath. "Scout's honor. Keep your bargain."

Nasha handed him one of two Bolshoi remembrance programs; one he bought for her, the second she'd purchased in advance. "Now please ask your men to take me home."

Program held upside down, Frankel rifled the pages. Looked at her, eyebrows raised.

"I'm an old fashioned girl, Aaron, and Lebanon is a backward country. Everyone says so. You're surely conversant with microdots?"

Smug, he feigned ignorance. "I don't use LSD. It's so last week."

"How do I reach you...since soon I'll be working for Grover Norris?"

"Let me look at your pretty pictures. I'm the sexual predator, I'll pursue you."

Frankel's thoughts rebounded like colliding atomic particles: Over my dead body I'll pursue you; what a surprise, learning something useful at the ballet; telling Nasha the truth wasn't important; Grover Norris is second rate at both his jobs. There remained only one truth which mattered; playtime is over, its time to get out.

***

A full Beaver Moon played peek-a-boo with a roiled ocean as Tom Nichols pounded his way south on Vineyard Sound at a steady twenty-two knots. Jonathan's old Blackfin protested this bitter cold night, but new motors purred without complaint. Wind out of the northwest, he figured an hour to Cuttyhunk, a tiny island at the southern tip of the Elizabeth Chain, which sat, mostly ignored, between the south coast of Massachusetts and Martha's Vineyard.

Though she never said, he figured Raissa to be outbound from New Bedford. Cash would buy a hard-up fishing vessel and a skipper's silence.

Canapitsit Channel, the least friendly entrance from Vineyard Sound to Cuttyhunk Harbor, was unmarked. No lighted buoy, plenty of rocks and a swift running current wouldn't bother Jonathan. Tom, a fair weather sailor better suited to summer days and calm seas, didn't yet regret this rendezvous, but his mind was open to change.

With the salt-crusted sport-fisherman idling through Cuttyhunk's long, narrow entrance, he peered towards the Harbormaster's shanty alongside the ferry dock. Worried his skill wouldn't match the task, he heard the hull collide with barnacled pilings and two feet thud onto the deck.

When Tom's State Police cruiser pulled in beside Raissa's cottage, she ran under the deck and returned with a brightly varnished oar. Said nothing until they basked in the warmth of the boatyard's workshop, oar mounted in a vise.

Raissa's examination penetrated Tom's pretended diffidence. "Ever get so relaxed your brain stops working? Not stops working a little, but shuts down all the way?"

Tom took the query at face value. "Sounds like you enjoyed living here. Maybe you can come back some day."

Just seconds and the drill cut out a neatly crafted plug. Several items emptied from the hollowed-out core. Tom watched her hands and face—an unusual woman, who so loved tools, and who very recently took one hell of a beating. Tonight Raissa wasn't beautiful or delicate. Not a fashionista princess. Nor much to ogle, if he was so inclined. She didn't need advice, just a bath. This woman was a stout tree who could weather a storm.

Without nicking the finish, Raissa reinserted the plug. "Ought to hit it with some two-twenty grit...feather on a new coat of varnish." Wistful, she picked up the oar. Almost inaudible, heartache made her voice quaver. "Later, maybe."

Back at her cottage, oar returned to storage, she let her hand drift across the Ferrari's hood before throwing herself into the cruiser.

Twenty minutes down the road, they crossed the Bourne Bridge and pulled into the commuter lot, where the bus to Boston would make its first run in less than three hours.

"Tom, I'm grateful. Better call Haslett or there'll be hell to pay."

"Screw Haslett."

Her face told him to think again.

"Tell him what?"

"Nothing but the truth. I called and asked to meet. You gave me a ride to the bus. When he asks why I needed to meet, tell him this: Gunther Probst saw something…what he saw relates directly to terrorism…what he saw has everything to do with Raissa Ribeiro. Tell Haslett…go see Fulton Bennett at Langley. Ask him to tell Bennett…someone's contractor tried and failed to kill Raissa. Tell Bennett he'll hear from me when I'm good and ready. Tom, make sure Haslett understands…if he talks to anyone other than Bennett, he'll screw the pooch."

Raissa asked Tom to repeat the message.

Tom wanted to clear up a few items of his own. "When do I call Haslett?"

"As soon as you're back on the road."

"What if Haslett asks whether you're armed and dangerous?"

"Tell him Raissa's cold and afraid."

"How about what you took from the oar?"

"Tell him whatever you like. You don't know what I took. For the sake of your health and the future happiness of your bride, I won't tell you."

"That bad?"

"If anyone but Haslett asks to meet you, find a dozen cops and shoot first."

"Seriously?"

Raissa unwrapped the scarf from her neck. Wide purple bruises in the shape of fingers and thumbs made lethal reminders.

"Tom, I'm un-retired…couldn't think of anyone else to ask for help. Do not get lazy. Until you hear I'm dead, or unless we're having a beer with Melissa on my porch, don't trust anyone from off-Cape."

Raissa slammed the door.

The last time Tom saw Raissa, jeans glued to concrete curbing, shrunken against the breeze waiting for the bus, every ounce of her hundred pounds confirmed how she'd described herself: Cold and afraid. A scarf encircled those gruesome bruises on her neck. Printed with the British Union Jack, loose ends pushed against her cheek with both hands, a single contradictory opinion filled Tom's head—the closer she is to down for the count, bet everything you own on a tough-as-nails lady.

***

Slightly before four in the morning, Martin Haslett answered his phone.

"As I live and breathe...it's the all-star prick of the Massachusetts State Police. To what do I owe the pleasure?"

"I just dropped Raissa Ribeiro at the Sagamore Bridge. She's waiting for the bus."

"You really are an asshole, Nichols. Whaddya want?"

"You get five seconds before I go back home to a warm bed."

Haslett realized—there's no joke. "Why didn't you hold her?"

"Because she and I made a deal. She gave me messages which are only for you and only in person. Want'em...get on your helicopter. I'll be at the Bourne Barracks."

CHAPTER 20

At an altitude of three thousand feet and descending, Dubai equaled Shangri-La, a glittering monument to Arab enterprise and western capitalism.

Marco Panero fought the urge to laugh out loud.

With its ultramodern skyline, Dubai's history as a small town of Bedouin traders could be forgotten. Dubai World Central and Al Maktoum International Airport extended the Disneyland sensation intended by Dubai's designers.

Panero's trip, a command performance set in motion by his wife, served her profit and pleasure—and the needs of Sheikh Khalid bin Rahman, her current dance partner. Caroline's too terse e-mail—Marco never expected a love note from Caroline—provided a location: *Meet at Al Maha Desert Resort, Dubai Desert Conservation Reserve, Al Ain Road, Al Maha Murqquab, Dubai.*

Marco let out a full belly laugh in contemplation of his relationship to the Sheikh. On his way to baggage claim, his hatred of the desert was front and center among other concerns. If desalinated seawater, more expensive than petrol, ceased restraining the desert, Dubai's history of subservience to the desert wind would repeat itself.

Pearl divers and scorpions were most of Dubai's population before fortune hunters from Persia, the Indian subcontinent, and other Arab countries found a barren location with great promise. Tourism and a thriving Urgent Care business followed. Named after a local locust, the Daba, the town was seized by British gunships, who held it by the throat as late as 1971.

The Sir Edward Poynters of the world scurried home as oil discoveries erupted. Dubai allied with six surrounding states and formed the United Arab Emirates. Sheikhs, illiterate nomads who once drove camels through the desert, now owned the game and the gold.

Sheikh Maktoum of Dubai made the desert boom, building a center of tourism and financial services by sucking up cash and talent from across the globe. Tax-free, foreigners came in droves. Dubai seemed the result of a magic wand, fast-forwarded from the 18th century to the 21st in a stroke of genius—as long as one focused relentlessly on high fashion, fast living and gold. As with high wire walkers, *don't look down* formed excellent advice.

Dubai, forced to look down by crushing debt, accepted financial subservience to Abu Dhabi's Sheikh Khalifa, who possessed oil, not sterile sand. Khalifa became ruled where the desert did not.

PaneroGlobal LLC, several years earlier, employed a baker's dozen here. Today one ex-employee stood waiting, faithful and impoverished, for his employer.

Unlike Saudi Arabia, Islamic dress was infrequently enforced; Panero wore a lightweight summer suit. Group Captain Geoffrey Hedley, Royal Air Force (Ret.), sported a stained, slept-in Dishdash—as the ankle length Kandura was called by expatriates.

Sheepish, Marco stuck out his hand. "Jesus, Geoffrey...wish there was more I could do."

Hedley's reputation as a radar expert had led to recruitment by PaneroGlobal. Geoffrey worked four-day shifts in Saudi Arabia; life was good and the couple's prospects better. Fast-forwarded, he resided in a well-worn Range Rover, the last stop in a free-fall encounter with Dubai's underbelly. Bankrupt, excluding good-hearted Bangladeshi who hired Hedley to park cars when they heard of Molly's predicament, his first-rate technical skills persisted.

Molly and Geoffrey, country mice out of their element, began a whirlwind of parties, golf, boats and investments characterized as sure things. When their bubble burst, as all bubbles do, they assumed Dubai law would be modeled on its British equivalent. Nobody told them: Bankruptcy law was non-existent. Get in debt—don't pay—go to prison.

Molly called Geoffrey in Saudi to warn him: Bank accounts and credit cards were frozen. Forbidden to leave, then arrested, her descent into nightmare continued when, for daring to fend off her attorney's sexual assault, a charge of prostitution increased her legal exposure. Tried and sentenced in a courtroom, where strict use of Arabic left her ignorant of the proceedings, Molly remained in prison two and a half years later.

Stuck on a Saudi Airbase, Geoffrey Hedley could do nothing.

Marco was determined to help, until informed by Caroline that assistance would cost PaneroGlobal hard won contracts in the Kingdom. Devastated by his weakness, Marco took to telling horror stories to a coterie of sycophants at his London club.

"Dubai…it's a mirage. Like riding a camel down the frigging yellow brick road. The allure seems real enough, but hiding in the cupboard is a medieval despot." Told with a half-smile riddled with Marco's miasmic worship of his bride and Achilles Heel, Caroline was an indulgence he couldn't resist.

Without apology Hedley told Panero, "We'll need a cab. No petrol at the moment."

Qamardeen Hotel sat in the Old Town, minutes from the world's largest Dubai Mall, the world's tallest Burj Khalifa, the racecourse where camels ran during the day and horses in the cooler evening, and, of course, the Metro which existed to connect stopovers in fantasyland.

Over an hour would be required to reach camps where immigrant laborers lived in concrete silos and steel shipping containers amongst their own filth.

Panero ignored questioning glances garnered by his dirty, non-Emirati, non-Asian companion. In Panero's hotel room Hedley showered, trimmed his scraggly growth and changed into attire from Marco's single suitcase. In the transformation's wake, two businessmen sat opposite each other in comfortable club chairs. Marco handed Geoffrey a manila envelope.

Hedley inquired. "Why show up today, Marco? It's only weeks until Molly gets out of prison. Where were you when it mattered? What do you want from me?" Hedley's remonstrations didn't prevent him tearing the envelope's flap to estimate the total of its contents.

Marco was insistent. "Won't necessarily leave this hellhole passport in hand, will she? You'll both need clothes, plane tickets home to England, and walking-around money. Or these rotters will suck you back in...maybe Molly winds-up a prossy after all."

"You're a shit, Marco."

"But a shit who's told the truth, mate. After prison, she's not British anymore...not in Dubai or anywhere in the Middle East. Just another piece of garbage to be hidden from the tourists. Take the money. Help me. Go home and try to forget. Don't let Molly wind up one of the suicides buried who knows where."

"I can't help myself. What can I do for you?"

"Become a bit of a spy, I hear. Poor man's MI-6."

"That's nonsense, Marco. Table scraps, photographs for journalists are my specialty: Slave labor camps; sewage dumped in the dunes; the odd introduction to a nanny who's been raped by the husband or beaten by the wife. Mostly for a hot meal."

"Exactly what we need. Let's get you fed." Marco watched the gaunt face come alive in anticipation, then go blank. "What's the trouble then?"

"If I'm recognized...?"

Panero stood and patted Hedley on the shoulder. "I barely recognized you, Geoffrey. Let's order room service...steak for four."

***

Sonapur, where a rubble-strewn patchwork of concrete buildings stretched to the horizon, held hundreds of thousands of men, lives crashed in a place forgotten by everyone's God. In the first camp, Hedley stopped beside men huddled and eager to tell someone, anyone, of their plight.

Hedley translated for Panero. "To get you here, they tell you Dubai is heaven. Then you arrive and realize it's altogether different. Agents of the Sheikh go to villages in Southern Bangladesh and tell of a place where men earn forty thousand Takka (£400) a month working nine-to-five with hotel rooms, good food, and excellent working conditions. Pay an up-front fee of two hundred twenty thousand Takka (£2,300) for a work visa, a fee they're told can be paid off in six months, and presto...a ticket to heaven. Here in Sonapur the water isn't desalinated; it makes them sick. They could grow food in Bangladesh. In Dubai, nothing grows but more oil and new buildings."

As night fell, Hedley offered cheap bottles of local rotgut. Away in the distance, the glistening Dubai skyline stood in stark contrast.

Hedley whispered. "These pitiful souls will do anything...if we make simpler promises than the Sheikh's agents. They can never be Emirati, only slaves. They want to go home, but will never earn the money to get there. It's the grand design here in Dubai. You'd be hard pressed to find an Emirati who doesn't support the Sheikh. In Dubai, Islamism is sold as the great threat...the same threat sold by politicians in Britain and the US. Follow your leaders. Don't make waves. All will be well. Sound familiar, Marco? The government appoints every Imam. Every sermon is edited. They built a beach with cooling pipes running below the sand. Tourists flock to swim with dolphins. Wander into a mountain-sized freezer where a ski slope with real snow is an everyday attraction. This is the desert? This is the most water-stressed place on the planet. How can this be happening?"

"How much for insurrection, Geoffrey, it's all I give two shits about."

Hedley leaned closer to the fire. In a pidgin mixture of English, Arabic, and four other East Asian languages, he made the proposal and handed out two hundred Euros per man as a down payment. Waved Panero's mammoth roll of Euros, promising each slave eighteen hundred Euros apiece when their job concluded.

"Two thousand Euros will get each man home...and buy you the appearance of a first-class riot." With a sly look, he added, "If they don't drink themselves to death first."

Astounded at the fool Panero had become, an air of competence and inevitable success must've arrived unannounced for, good God, he's promised hundreds, when pennies would suffice. What's happened to Marco, the savvy businessman?

***

Al Maha Desert Resort & Spa, built sixty klicks outside Dubai, nestled within a verdant oasis. Designed to resemble an ancient Bedouin encampment, tents superimposed over modern structures, this hideaway touted personal and seductive experiences of the region's history and hospitality in absolute comfort.

On the bar terrace overlooking endless sand, flaming torches fired the imagination, and Marco found Caroline holding a drink, staring at a billion stars in splendid isolation. He wrapped his arms around a wasp waist.

"It's a never ending vista. We could be the only two people on earth."

She shrugged her shoulders to loosen his grip. "Jesus Marco, did you get your spiel from the hotel pamphlet? Leave me alone. Better yet, get me another one of these." She held out her glass.

He slid his hands over her breasts, squeezed and pleaded. "Please, Caroline, could we be at least friends, if not lovers."

Her body tightened in what he recognized as revulsion. In an unexpected movement, she slithered round to face him. The woman he despaired of kissed him, offered her tongue and massaged his genitals through his pants.

Temptation. Frustration. If only this wasn't intended to reduce a man to compliant cuckold. If only she wanted him as badly as he wanted her. Marco began to cry.

Caroline walked away, words encased in boredom. "Later, I promise, we'll let the desert wash over us by the pool. I'll make you happy."

With Caroline, later was always the promise. Unless the topic was money. Considerably older, Marco loved her and gave her everything she needed or wanted.

First he learned to pretend, then to look the other way when she cheated. Which produced an arrangement filled with discretion and the benefits of weeklong adventures in makeup sex. Until her mother's extended disease and death wreaked havoc on the Poynter family. Her father proved a pestilence on the wealth mommy left behind. Only when poverty came knocking at the drawbridge, was Marco allowed to view the extent of his bride's dissolution from Britain's titled social caste.

As distance grew between them, so did his yearning. Unrequited, his need for her blended sickness and devotion. He thought Caroline an enchantress. Poor Marco, he would acknowledge, in moments before sleep took him: No different from all her others

***

"*Lagavulin* is my personal favorite, as long as it's the 1979 rotation." Grover Norris's air of entitlement settled like a depressurized balloon, offering confirmation to every man's suspicion, acting as if DD/CIA wasn't sitting right beside him.

Mannheim entered, having been beckoned by a crisply worded e-mail. Pomposity by itself was no guarantor of incompetence. Mannheim's bathroom mirror, were it not inanimate, would testify to an uncomfortable truth. Insufferable was a direct byproduct of pomposity. Grover Norris couldn't differentiate among any Scotch whiskey costing more than a hundred bucks a bottle, let alone the thousand he'd spent for this one.

"A wee bit early in the day, Grover. Thank you, though."

Grover sipped from his glass, eyes launching daggers at Mannheim. Poured an inch on top of what remained in DD/CIA's Waterford crystal. "Your loss. What've you dug up?"

"Is Owen joining us?"

"Lawyers aren't any good at nuance, Zach."

Without the Agency's General Counsel, Grover's search for a fall guy would proceed unimpeded. "CIC has interviewed Deputy Director Bennett."

"Whoa there, Zach. This's your baby, not the bastard child of the whole CIC organization chart. Who interviewed Bennett?"

DD/CIA cringed at Norris's hubris.

Mannheim maintained a modicum of courtesy.

"I interviewed Bennett myself. Members of CIC conducted peripheral interviews and forensic examinations. CIC personnel are in the field looking to expand or contract our investigation's scope. The task given me is, by definition, tasked to CIC as a whole. I believe this approach is still the way it works."

Norris, stymied but not toothless, elected a stern warning. "Of course that's right, Zach. Until your successor is named, CIC is under your command."

Bombast, or not, on the part of Grover Norris, Mannheim would proceed undeterred.

"Based on CIC's interview of Deputy Director Bennett, we believe there's reason for serious concern. There's strong indication

Gunther Probst's murder is linked to the group who committed the murder at the *Ritz*. Beyond the involvement of terrorist entities in the murder at the *Ritz*, there's every reason to conclude bringing Bennett under suspicion, having his duties fall to subordinates or to relief pitchers like you, Grover, was the underlying purpose. Outside CIC's interview of Bennett, we learned the incident involves British Intelligence. CIC also determined the termination of retired officer Raissa Ribeiro is in limbo, after a failed attempt in Spain…and Ms. Ribeiro may possess information critical to resolving this matter. CIC's investigations are ongoing. That's where we stand as of this evening."

DD/CIA appeared stunned.

Grover hoped to exact more detail, though cynicism dripped from his words. "Who are the sources for what you *think* you've unearthed?"

Mannheim submerged himself in the separation of CIC activities from the rest of the Agency. "It's not appropriate to discuss details at this moment."

Grover took Mannheim's answer to mean guesswork, innuendo, lies, unreliable vermin and imaginary fairies couldn't be described, or named, for fear of CIC's work being ridiculed. He couldn't overturn Mannheim's position without owning any subsequent operational abortion. Nazarian's disaster was enough shit to clean up without adding more.

***

Group Captain Geoffrey Hedley wasn't weary of the world, when Dubai police first tossed his wife in prison.

Attempts to generate funds for their basic survival were met with disapproval and disdain. As indignity piled upon misery, he longed to see some of those responsible for his downfall suffer similar slings and arrows. Marco's return, and the man's insistence on jousting at windmills, at last had provided opportunity.

Hedley, a member of the Church of England, cared little for morality, and less for methods employed to gain his ends. For some who paid him, he represented a safety net, a clouded lens into Dubai's downtrodden masses where rebellion fomented. For others, poor Geoff represented a bit of a charity case—a *there but for the grace of God* kind of fellow. For all who put hard currency in his palm he resembled a leper, suitable to exploit but unhealthy to touch.

Priority one was making a secure call to Saudi Arabia. A lesser weight was assigned to reaching-out to local police.

Digital switching equipment, reached via a number at *King Abdulaziz Air Base,* co-located with the *Dharahan International Airport* in Saudi Arabia, transferred callers to a single handset on a desk within *RAF Waddington,* Lincolnshire, England. *RAF Waddington,* the home of British pilots who controlled hunter/killer drones, simmered with unseen activity.

"Colonel Jack Frost, please." A required precursor, stated in an accurate and sequential manner, the operator would connect him when he made a subsequent appeal.

"There's no Colonel Frost in the base directory." Always the operator's response, Hedley was free to make his follow-on request.

"Let me leave a voicemail on Extension 88172268876."

Although the number provided contained the virtual country code and specific number of Hedley's satellite phone, it lacked one specific item—an authenticator.

"Punch in your ID, please."

Hedley entered the nine-digit, revolving, authentication sequence. When his call was returned, he'd identify himself, provide bin Rahman's GPS co-ordinates and request the time of attack be texted to his phone—allowing safe withdrawal from *Al Maha*. Then and only then would the Dubai Police Chief be presented with *Hobson's Choice*.

Hedley sheltered the remainder of Panero's forty thousand Euros in a welded cubby of the Range Rover's undercarriage. Dropped the air pressure in his tires to accommodate desert sand. More than adequate time existed to co-ordinate the protest he promised Marco; no protest would occur, because Hedley wouldn't sacrifice lives to Marco Panero's pretensions and vainglory.

Oh how Hedley would enjoy watching from Al Maha's majestic dunes as fire and death rained from the sky. Every explosion would bring a satisfied smile, every burning body the taste of revenge and, when only coals outlined ruined buildings, a measure of Dubai's humbled pride would hang in the smoke. Then, in less than a fortnight, a husband and wife would be rejoined in England.

Even as he schemed how each move in a life and death game of chess would lead to counter-moves, the truth of the end game sat in an ignored corner of consciousness. How else might a beggar construct a castle-in-the-air?

***

Marie Truchet converted her ever-stylish mode to an abaya, the black over-garment most Emirati women wore. Paired with a niqab, a face veil covering all but the eyes, Truchet added long black gloves. There would be built-in advantages to this ready-made disguise, and a dangerous flip side. Al Maha may have been created as another exercise in Dubai hedonism, but blasphemy and Intelligence gathering would, if discovered, garner the harshest of treatment.

By acquiring PaneroGlobal as a client, Truchet vaulted herself into the upper echelon of contract specialists. As Private Military Companies assumed roles the armed forces couldn't or wouldn't perform, so too the Private Intelligence Company prospered. Truchet's job entailed breaking rules and providing results without regard to social or ethical niceties. Corporations and intelligence agencies of a dozen countries numbered among her clients. Conflicts of interest, an accepted fact of life, demanded good faith efforts to minimize their effects. When that proved impossible, she left deniable suspicions behind her.

Unarmed, moving between Al Maha's suites as an Arab female required tranquility, never haste. Deference headed a short list of plausible excuses.

Marco looked much the worse for wear, drinking alone in the opulent cradle of a society whose ambiguities required citizens to hold a liquor license, while forbidding tourists from acquiring one. Liquor was available in hotels and restaurants, but woe to an impudent foreigner incurring the police's wrath stinking of booze.

Panero tilted the bottle until the last drops ran down his chin mixed with spittle and tears.

Marie stood in the doorway, considering the advice of Mao Tse-Tung: *The enemy advances, we retreat; the enemy camps, we harass; the enemy tires, we attack; the enemy retreats, we pursue.*

"Marco, what have you brought me half way round the world to accomplish?"

Panero looked up, squinting against smoke curling from an untended cigar. Unruly hair brushed from his forehead with the back of his hand, he heard the voice of Truchet emerge from a black clad Arab ninja.

"Say what, dearie?"

Clean-up services, an often-rendered service, generally related to client errors. On the rarest of occasions it applied to physical cleanup. Here in the freaking desert with damned few rational options, she prodded Panero into the shower and turned the temperature to warm. When he flailed, she hit him a single time and watched as he slid down the tiled wall into a puddle of corpulence. Shower turned full cold, she stood guard to assure he didn't drown.

"So you did come after all." Panero's head lolled back and forth.

Truchet knew Marco to be a reliable purveyor of advice and training in matters of military hardware and software. Selection of wives notwithstanding, he could be counted on as reliable, clever and sane. Only this last characteristic made doing business with him possible.

"I left Andrew on his own...you know he's not toilet-trained. Why are you in the desert, pissed out of your mind? Or is the answer obvious?"

Words slurred, what Marco tried to say emerged as unintelligible. He opened his mouth and let the cold shower irrigate his throat. "Get Caroline away from here." With a massive effort, he made the reason sound dire. "There'll be a riot tonight...any minute I should think. He'll abandon her."

She allocated three guesses, needing only one. "Bin Rahman's here...tonight?"

Bin Rahman was many things; a public person he was not. All the classic myths attended him: Doppelgangers made his public appearances; no photographer got within a mile and left alive; never slept in the same location successive nights; and, he suffered from an exotic disease.

Panero sat motionless, neither denying nor confirming what Truchet asked.

She shut off the water, leaving Marco to marinate. Traded the suite for solemnity under the night sky. Does the next call represent more risk than reason? Unable to conclude she wasn't biased, greed fought discretion to a draw. If she traded bin Rahman to the British, she'd reap years of return favors. Truchet would reach-out to a different organization than Geoffrey Hedley had done.

A nondescript voice answered. Truchet enunciated to facilitate voice recognition. "EIP74T1840. Pass me on, please."

Another voice, this time female, asked Truchet her business. "Inform the Duty Officer, Target 7 is nearby my coordinates."

"Probability assessment."

Marie tried to work through a puzzle: Did Panero know, or suspect, she possessed contacts which opposed his business interests. Based on his level of desperation, Marco doesn't give a toss who dies tonight, as long as it isn't his prized Caroline. Poor sod, he'd like as not trade his life for hers, straight up.

"Very high. Repeat...very high."

"Confirm fifty-nine kilometers outside Dubai City." A series of GPS numbers fixed Truchet's position.

"Confirmed."

Inside Panero's suite, Marie knelt again at Panero's side. "Why is Caroline here?" Drunken despair might grant her insight into Marco's depth of participation.

Smile banal, eyebrows lifted as if in self-interrogation, Marie heard a profound pronunciation. "Great gobs of Reals."

Money—not sex or love. Cold hard cash. Truchet spoke, not for Marco's consumption. "Putain de merde. Caroline has pimped PaneroGlobal to bin Rahman?" Tears wouldn't be the only bodily fluids spilled in the sand tonight.

For the smallest moment Marco's eyes blazed in defiance, then returned to a glazed, half-sighted stare.

Marie struggled to digest the reason. "Why, Marco? Why?"

Without waiting for an answer which would never substitute for an explanation, Truchet tightened the thigh strap around her phone and began a search for Sheikh bin Rahman's suite. The mission, if the Brits could find their testicles, would require approval extending up to Ten Downing Street and on to the White House, if CIA drones were to be employed—British drones not within range. Truchet held superficial knowledge of targeting systems, so by her calculus an hour could see the resort consumed in flames.

Marie, determined to be among the survivors, left Marco where he lay.

***

A large presence at Langley, the Chief of the Counter Terrorism Center ("CTC") was a covert officer renowned as a loud-mouthed chain smoker and fierce Agency loyalist. Beyond those attributes, or liabilities as the third generation Mexican-American admitted they could be, years of internecine battles fought alongside Bennett provided a deep appreciation of the man's skill and determination. How Bennett allowed himself to get embroiled—well, it didn't warrant deep thought.

As several hundred people began the second shift, Freddy Medina grabbed his car keys before some real or faux emergency held him back. He wanted a beer, or six, but understood it wouldn't happen this evening or for a much longer stretch, if the long-knives made another appearance at the Agency he loved.

Settled in his car, he took a final precaution. Hated that it was necessary. Hated even more the internal and external adversaries who made it necessary. Settled in his mind, he pulled the plug on each Agency device in his possession.

CHAPTER 21

Not even an FBI agent from the Boston Field Office could obtain the home address of a CIA Deputy Director without straining inter-Agency protocol. Martin Haslett spent the entire morning trying to pry the information from the Agency and most of the afternoon explaining the barrage of complaints made to FBI HQ by Zachary Mannheim.

The result of this Sturm und Drang was official détente and an unofficial escort.

Phyllis Martell, ordered to go nowhere near Bennett's residence just days ago, witnessed those restrictions rescinded without an ounce of explanation or a gram of reasoning. Haslett, an unlikely candidate for the brightest bulb, stood mute while they waited for the doorbell to be answered. Led through a center hallway, whose early colonial wallpaper completed a meticulous and mellifluous arrival, Haslett followed into a kitchen where extensive renovations were ongoing.

Although he arrived prepared to be forceful and, if need be, unpleasant, Haslett said, "Director Bennett...thanks for agreeing to see me."

Bennett chopped words like wood under a sharpened axe. "Gunther Probst did more for this country than most. Though I won't hold my breath, arresting the hitter would be a deserving outcome."

Bennett began a wary assessment of why Mannheim wanted FBI involved. Often a visceral reaction to another's motives heightened his own level of awareness.

Haslett began tentatively. "Director...

"Drop the formality...Fulton's fine."

"Martin's good with me. D'you have relationships in the Massachusetts State Police?"

"I almost never pay speeding tickets...though that's true everywhere, not just Massachusetts."

"Lt. Tom Nichols...any chance you know him?"

"No."

Severe concerns about Ribeiro's near-death withdrawal to an insular backwater like Cape Cod, Bennett had made it a point to profile her neighbors and new friends.

Haslett. "Nichols found Probst's body."

"Saw him mentioned in the report." Bennett's lips curled into something short of a grin.

"Seems off. Nichols finds the body. Drags his feet until Ribeiro disappears. Days later, calls to say she's been home to visit...and out of nowhere a State cop gives me messages for CIA's Fulton Bennett...who isn't in his office these days. Seems abnormal to me...how about you, Fulton?"

When delivered by a two by four to the head, irony lost intrinsic value: Haslett's a jerk and I don't like him. Funny how it works, being a jerk myself. "Do your job, Martin."

Haslett observed Bennett's exercise in restraint. Concluded his irritation of Bennett was bearing fruit, but saw another something harder to identify. "By which you mean?"

"Solve Probst's murder. If you're here, you've decided it's in the FBI's interest to deliver Ribeiro's messages. So do your job."

Haslett turned to Martell. "Is he always like this?"

Phyllis never changed expression. Didn't answer.

Haslett pressed, "Out of curiosity, Fulton, what if I don't?"

"Finish my coffee...then give Nichols a ringy-dingy. Prefer to hear them from you, because Raissa Ribeiro's as good as they come. And she'll have a reason to want you involved." Bennett sipped, made a face and put his coffee in the microwave. "Could be she's lost her touch."

Haslett's instincts satisfied, Bennett's logic matched his own. Although try as he might, no rationale for the FBI's involvement fit the situation. More important, Bennett focused on outcomes, not institutional scorecards. Maybe he's trying to help.

"Gunther Probst saw something he shouldn't have. What he saw has everything to do with terrorism. What he saw has everything to do with Raissa Ribeiro. Someone's contractor tried and failed to kill Raissa. Bennett will hear from me when I'm good and ready. Those are the messages for you, Fulton. She also said something Nichols repeated three times: *Tom...make sure Haslett understands...if he talks to anyone other than Bennett, he'll screw the pooch.* What does that mean?"

Bennett sat straighter while composing an appropriate response. "Aaron Frankel and Raissa were together a long time. Then not together for a long time. Not long ago, Frankel had lunch with a new girlfriend at Legal Seafood...downtown on the wharf. Probst was there in his occasional cover as a photojournalist. Raissa too...as spurned lover. Or maybe in the guise of a wiser woman acting on impulses she couldn't suppress. She's asking you to find out what Gunther's pictures show, or who they show. Wants you to give that information to me and no one else."

FBI agents, if any good, prepared themselves for shocks like this one: Shocks that alter a case and de-clutter the mind; shocks which carry import beyond the petty, or the grinding effort required to solve intricate puzzles.

"Can you interpret the rest of the message?"

"Can I? Or will I?"

"Both. Please."

Bennett took a step in Phyllis' direction and held out his hand. "CIC's recording what we say. In your pocket, maybe? Or do the walls have new ears?"

Phyllis' instructions covered this circumstance. She held out a mini-recorder. "Mr. Mannheim says the house is safe. For now."

"Turn it off a moment, Phyllis. It'll be for the best."

She met Bennett's gaze and shot him a look that said: All of a sudden I'm Phyllis and not some plastic figurine here without purpose. She placed the recorder on the island next to a bag of stale cookies.

Bennett would give Haslett his opinions, mixed as they were with history, regret and hope. It was an emotional concoction, one Bennett would've preferred not to imbibe.

"Frankel's a tough bird. Lives in New York. Travels the world on his jet. Richer than Croesus by all accounts. Got rich being smarter than most. Got richer when an unknown Arab trusted the boy genius with his money. Unknown Arab became well known pretty quick. Money, destruction...dead bodies. Lots of frustration for folks like me...folks like Raissa. There were consequences. Can't begin to understand what it'd be like...to be burned alive. Can you, Agent Martin Haslett?"

Haslett's head shook a 'no', replacing the inadequacy of words.

"When you find out who, or what, Gunther photographed, we'll be much closer to turning off the money tap to Sheikh bin Rahman's terrorist buddies. Maybe we'll be able to identify who, or whom, burned a fine woman in her own bed. By far the worst of her message is this: Someone at CIA wants Raissa dead, but the first try failed...spook-speak meaning Raissa's not a person to trifle with. There'll be a second try. And a third. Because, I think, Probst's killer will keep trying—even if the Agency relents, which it won't unless you catch Probst's killer and prove Raissa uninvolved in Gunther's death. Last on the list, she's gone to ground in Brazil and will surface when Haslett, Bennett or someone else gives her reason to believe the odds are no worse than 30/70 against her."

"Why would she..."

"Because you're the FBI. Because you're a well-known prick...which is, I assume, the only thing you and I share in this work-a-day life. Because she's taken time to find out about you. And because there's no one else working the case who might give a shit...pardon my language."

"I'm not able to...I'm sorry, that's not what I meant. I won't circumvent the Bureau's reporting requirements. If I establish the identities of those in the restaurant, up the channel it goes. You've got the contacts and juice to get the Intel elsewhere. Just not from me."

Bennett reached out and slid the record button into position. Back on the record, he opted for a plea based on an uncommon motivation: The truth.

"I'm more or less under house arrest, Martin. What I'll tell you now will, more or less, guarantee my career never resumes. About which you don't care very much, and I don't blame you for that. My little group..." Bennett stopped speaking, peered at the floor hoping to find inspiration, or courage to tell a better lie "...has been working to bring Khalid bin Rahman's financial empire to ruination. We're so, so, close to accomplishing our goal. There aren't thirty people on earth who know this, and not one of them works for the Justice Department. What you do, or don't find, may not hasten the demise of the son-of-a-bitch, but putting your findings in a report will keep bin Rahman in business a lot longer. I could threaten you. Maybe get you detained just for hearing what I've told you. But I'm straight out asking you to honor Raissa's request. What you find, bring here to this house. Bring Phyllis with you, but no one else. And, please, hurry."

***

Sex with Caroline allowed for the disruption of everything he pretended to hold sacred. With her, and no one else, he shed the chains of hypocrisy. Even now, early in the evening, a time when sex would be off the menu, she could rip her clothes off and insist on being fulfilled. She never ceased to amaze, not only sensually demanding but able to give physical, emotional and intellectual pleasure. Caroline was the opposing argument to every tenet of organized religion, cultural mores and political ethics.

Sex with Caroline gave the lie to the proscription against adultery preached by every major religion. He was married, with children. She was married, with children. When they came together, they improved themselves and so improved their contributions to spouses and offspring. He understood how imams, priests, rabbis or clerics of any stripe would prattle, would ridicule his logic as self-indulgent, counter-intuitive and blasphemous. Religions, after all, spent centuries, and would spend epochs into the future building walls of ignorance to enslave the sheep while shepherds ate lamb. Popes kept mistresses. Priests their secret boys. Imams stoned women. Rabbis were Imams with less authority. Born Again Christians wanted a chance to be like all the others, to slurp at the trough of ultimate authority.

All religion shared one common need: Revenue.

Much the same could be said of governments. Sheer the sheep for the benefit of the ruling class. All in all, he favored government by religion and for religion; it saved time and effort in transferring apparent power to true power. Corporations could be the new religion; God and devil rolled into one. Muhammad had been the ideal Chairman of the Board. Would that Jesus and Muhammad could have negotiated a merger.

See, he laughed, you're finally, actually and irrevocably a revolutionary. If your thoughts were made public, Muslims would behead you, Catholics would condemn you to Jesuit inquisition, Jews would nail you to a cross as a currency hedge and the Church of England would ransom you in order to crown you King.

Thank goodness for Caroline, who needed millions to succor a minor English title, and to fuck whenever it crossed her mind. With reluctance he forgave her fucking others, like Frankel. Even when it was he who insisted on her participation.

She stirred, further evidence of a shared wavelength.

Without revenue there was nothing. In this regard there was mutual agreement among Presidents, Prime Ministers, Ayatollahs, Kings, Queens, Jesters, Potentates and Dictators. The Arab desert showed signs of peril with regard to revenue.

He slapped her bare rump. Reflection ceased, when she rolled to him he entered her a second time.

***

Freddy Medina passed Martin Haslett and Phyllis Martell, their connection in minds prone to cosmic dysphoria limited to blinking turn signals.

Contrary to superstitions of Latin heritage and paternal predilection, Medina knew he was being watched. Medina supported the idea of a spotlight shining upon a man who sent invisible machines to rain biblical reckoning on the guilty and innocent alike. He would, however, limit the opportunities offered his adversaries with every resource at his command. Trained as an engineer, he made no pretense of understanding Greg Riley's illicit trinket which countered electronic emissions from his car, phone and other Agency issued devices. Nevertheless, he appreciated the moments of anonymity it afforded him.

Walk straight through the door, he told himself, the feeling of attending a funeral curious and painful. While everyone observing from the outside claimed spying was a young man's game, mental midgets showed themselves uninformed and ill intentioned in the long run. Losing Bennett would hurt CIA—had already hurt from what Freddy heard.

"Yo, Fulty, where your lily-white ass at?"

"Kitchen...cleaning up for Your Counter-Terrorist Eminence."

Freddy sauntered into the kitchen holding his nose.

"Shithole would be a compliment, Chuntarito. Where's the woman?" Knowing the answer was no substitute for asking; commiseration began and ended with questions.

"Gone. Painless and quick...a lot like having your throat cut."

"She took the pussycat, huh?"

"No, I wrung the cat's neck. Little bugger deserved it...and the alternative was trying to wring my own." Bennett pantomimed the difficulty.

Appreciative of the irony, they clinked long-necked bottles when Bennett's landline trilled.

"Jesus, Mary and Joseph..." Freddy muttered "...there's no fucking rest for the wicked." He didn't apologize. Didn't have to. Phone passed from Bennett to Freddy's ear, all he said to whomever was, "Go." Medina listened five minutes without saying a word or making a sound, then disconnected.

Bennett said, "So..."

"British have a source...claims to be sitting on bin Rahman in the Emirates...sixty klicks outside Dubai." Whereas protocol should've sent Medina running for his vehicle, he sat still as a tomb. "Everybody's got their tits in a wringer...speaking of cats, tits and events involving wringing. CTC is waiting on a decision from the seventh floor...where they're all hiding under a desk waiting for Grover to come back from a White House powwow. They'll say yes...despite three years invested in your other option. Politicians can't help themselves...drones are so clinical, so glitzy and stealthy. Drones piss the Arabs off and everybody loves to piss'em off." Medina sighed, the sound not passing judgment either way. Whatever might happen, good or bad, would be undertaken for the worst of reasons.

Bennett was skeptical. "How long ago?"

"At least an hour. Source hasn't been heard from after the first call. She gave the correct codes and her location checked down to a gnat's ass. Suggested she was less than twenty meters from the target's suite...some pseudo-tent with all the perks."

"Who is she?"

"Brits won't say."

"Who called?"

"Some Brigadier who couldn't locate his higher-ups."

"Want some advice? Don't have to take it." Bennett's voice emphasized the truth of what he'd stated.

"Fire away."

"Get your best people to find Caroline Poynter Panero and Andrew Poynter; brother and sister. Find'em fast Freddy."

"You expect a big surprise?"

"Nope. But if we kill one of Sir Edward's children, and bin Rahman's sipping tea in Jeddah, there'll be scorched careers from here to hell and back."

"C'mon man...gimme more than a back rub."

"You've heard the rumors...I got a distress call from Caroline Panero, at the Ritz. Wound up in bed with a pretty escort who was killed with my weapon."

Bennett waved his hand at an old friend: Don't tell me how stupid this all is.

"Last I heard of Andrew, he was in French custody...something to do with nuclear subs. No idea on Caroline; don't know whether she's innocent or guilty. That's it, Freddy. Not the mother lode, but not nothing. Bin Rahman took me out of the game. He knows things he shouldn't, which doesn't mean the Brits are trying to do us in. Paranoid of me, I know. Unreliable...what Grover says about me. Just do it Freddy."

Medina moved to the dead cold coffee. Nuked a cup and swallowed it like medicine. Beer on his breath and in his system was sub-optimal. "Anything else?"

Bennett handed his former protégé the cell phone and car keys from his pocket. "Mannheim is listening to the land line. Haven't got any other phones. Get the techies scanning for outgoing calls in this area. If this bin Rahman thing in Dubai goes off the rails, I'm the perfect scapegoat. Stick up for me, if you can."

Medina sat very still before firing the car's engine. Tried to remember some words of wisdom from his long dead Grannie, whose sense of things sustained him through many of life's less grandiose moments. After sifting through debris from those lessons, he was saddened by his eventual conclusion: Grannie wouldn't have approved of any of this. As the heater strained to transfer what little entropy remained in its gizzards, Medina plugged himself back into the electronic grid. Put the car in gear and hit speed dial.

There'd be righteous protests about his location over the last hour. It was the way of things in the high tension of crisis mode. He'd prevail, perhaps long enough for reason and temperance to put in their occasional, sought after, appearance. Killing bin Rahman would be welcome, but should we put all of our chips on the table to kill him tonight? With a facial expression which never changed, Freddy howled like a hyena where no one could see.

***

Geoffrey Hedley wore no timepiece, but was aware of seconds ticking away.

Bureaucrats in Whitehall and MOD would break each other's neck for the opportunity to brief the PM. It would be a cluster-fuck worthy of repetition to the Tabloids.

Since telephoning Saudi Arabia and being ignored, he'd left messages with reporters he knew by name at several fountainheads of journalistic integrity. One of them, corrupted by American ownership's dollars, would pass bin Rahman's location to CIA spies in their cushy London apartments.

Uncertain of the overkill needed, a local call reached a squirrelly man whose appearance fooled no one. Tariq al Mahin, despite protestations to the contrary, was a Jew in the employ of Mossad.

With all seeds planted and watered, Geoffrey believed the time for reimbursement was at hand. In Dubai, as elsewhere, status could be determined by the phone numbers a person possessed. Hedley dialed the Chief of Police's personal cellphone.

"Your Excellency, this is Group Captain Hedley with information which will fix your future in Heaven."

"Sheikh Mohammed bin Rashid Al Maktoum is my future, Hedley. And Heaven is talk for another day. What do you want...besides issuing another tiresome request to release your wife."

"Your Excellency is all-knowing. Molly's release is what I want...plus her passport, a sealed safe-passage from Dubai signed by you...and fifty thousand Euros cash in her handbag. Within forty minutes."

Dismissive, the Police Chief tried deprecation. "Why not a limousine and police escort to a chartered jet flying to England? The likelihood of my agreement would be the same."

Hedley heard the laughter. Waited, then laid the cheeky bastard low. "Fifty-five minutes from now, Sheikh Khalid bin Rahman will be french-fried courtesy of a Hellfire missile, on its way from the Seychelles via Reaper. You don't know where bin Rahman is located, who provided CIA the Intel or where I'm located. Newspapers all over Europe have the story, including your unwillingness to pay tribute for the Sheikh's survival. So, yes, a limousine, police escort and a jet will be a lovely addition to Molly's departure plans."

"It would be very easy to make this foolishness up, Mr. Hedley."

"A little bird told me just this morning…you don't intend to give Molly her passport when you let her out of prison. So bollocks whether you enjoy fairytales or bin Rahman dies in a fireball. Sand in the hourglass, Your Excellency."

The Police Chief might renege, if the chance came up, but not now, not when the risk of being beheaded was intuitive.

"Where…"

"At the airport. Call this cell with the proper gate, when you arrive. Drag the British Ambassador from his bed. Bring your son…the nice looking, lanky, footballer. If I don't see your son and Molly…dressed for travel…handcuffed wrist to wrist at the bottom steps of the plane, I won't come out of hiding. No storm troopers."

"These things never end well, Hedley. This is Dubai. Homeless, demented, British men commit suicide in our beloved country, shame though it may be. Be sensible."

CHAPTER 22

Showered and dressed in pure white, bin Rahman looked every inch a Sheikh.

Caroline, waiting for the others, told him so with great flourish. Khalid appreciated Caroline's uncanny ability to seize a moment and squeeze it dry. In many ways this trait was her strongest. Her weakness was a disinclination to see a thing in its concrete reality, to scrutinize and demystify other peoples' emotions. Caroline was not cut from a CEO's cloth.

A CEO must discern the slant of wind before feeling it on the cheek, comprehend the difference between, and the cost of, dignity and restraint while applying brutal and single-purposed logic to the problem at hand. Oil was such a wind. Oil was saint and sinner. England's deep-thinkers could wax poetic about literary parallels, philosophic attributes and economic forecasts related to oil, but refused to watch cultural markers shift as the wind strengthened.

Governments were blind. America. The Euro zone. Now China. Blind as bats with detuned sonar.

It would be nice—he rolled the simplicity of *nice* around his tongue—if more leaders returned problems from abstract clouds and stared at their pointed context. Sometimes circumstances compelled raising taxes, or drilling in sensitive ecosystems. Sometimes circumstances demanded taxes be cut or drills go silent. Sometimes government can promote innovation; in most cases government cannot.

Khalid bin Rahman saw himself through a clear lens, not the optics used by sovereign nations. His was the glass of multi-national corporations, whose loyalty (he hated the word), and fealty (old-fashioned but meaningful), was dedicated to healthy returns on shareholder investments.

Oil in Saudi Arabia, Iran, the Emirates, Kuwait, Iraq, Libya and Qatar, would grow ever more petrified and politicized. His microscope focused on newer, growing revenues and the paranoia attendant to new oil's glimmering, untapped earnings per share. Bin Rahman wasn't *Exxon-Mobil*, nor *British Petroleum* nor a Russian oligarch. He wasn't a Chinese emperor or a Brazilian sun god.

But he recognized China and Brazil as prime targets of future revenue.

***

Khalid bin Rahman and Caroline watched as their American confidants entered the suite in single file—mongrels and misfits, veterans of battles fought willingly, marching towards the next skirmish. He failed to attach *loyal* as a qualifier to these veterans. For within the ranks there were the seeds of destruction from within, its avoidance possible only through constant vigilance, monitoring and tests.

Tonight would be such a test.

Anton Leuzinger, summoned for his dispassionate reasoning, presented himself in subtle shades of color. Outside his zone of comfort, which Khalid assured himself was restricted to the jaded interior of a bank, Anton could flush out a perfect forgery from a suitcase of minted currency or a group of men or women. Leuzinger stood to the side as a sign of respect, nodding affirmation first to the Sheikh and second to Caroline.

"Good evening, Anton. Did you travel well?"

Another gracious nod of the Swiss's head.

Bin Rahman looked behind Leuzinger, delighted to see Jacques Desmarais ignore the stodgy order of rank. Desmarais's collected history included several postings within Direction Générale de la Sécurité Extérieure ("DSGE"), NATO, CIA and INTERPOL. Beside his official position within DSGE, the others were a product of fertile imagination and global badinage with thieves and spies alike.

Jacques was more important than a gadfly. Less than a mole. No one could fault Jacques when it came to accurate, withering gossip and who, among those standing in the Sheikh's way, were best to purchase and whom most susceptible to bullying. Desmarais took his place at the end of a massive leather divan.

"Welcome to Al Maha, Jacques. Wait until you experience sunrise."

"Salaam alaikum, Your Highness. A moment in private?"

Khalid examined Jacques as he would a dubiously fast racehorse.

When they'd gained a few meters of separation, Desmarais whispered. "The British hounds have the scent, Your Excellency. Maybe in hours, without question in days they'll know acoustic data from *Astute*, and her sister ships, has been compromised."

Fathima Laniado gaped at Desmarais' gall as she entered behind him. Second in the chain of command in the US, her place in the Sheikh's constellation should never be disregarded as the Frenchman was doing.

Desmarais bowed in respect to the Sheikh.

Khalid watched Fathima's anger anneal wounded pride. Wondered how many days in a year she wore the abaya and niqab, as she did tonight, to indulge the Arab male.

"Good evening my Daughter of the Prophet. Are you enjoying Washington?"

"Yes, Excellency." Fathima's voice emerged firm and strong.

Khalid had heard much of Billy Ray Balfour, a man of many faces who blended with his surroundings and gave high devotion to his paymaster—as men paid to end the lives of others were wont to do. Billy Ray's legend suggested his origination in America's deep south. Khalid doubted such a claim, for Billy Ray stood a step inside the room and could've arrived direct from Monaco's Baccarat tables. Flawless tuxedo. Jet-black hair swept back and curled at the nape of his neck. Fingernails manicured and buffed to gloss. Shoes worthy of a mirror's reflection. Clasped hands behind his back, he stood at attention lacking only a rifle and dress uniform to complete the image of an elite among elites.

Khalid ignored Billy Ray. He'd arrived unarmed or been made so by Sheikh bin Rahman's security force.

"Sit, all of you, please."

All complied, with the exception of Billy Ray, who remained motionless yet attentive, as if exempt from social mores. Bin Rahman warmed to a man who would rather stand with fellow professionals than insert himself as an equal to his employer.

"Jacques...would you brief us on the political situation in Brazil?"

"Brazil's developing nuclear program demonstrates increasing global prominence and a sort of maniacal hubris. Either explanation forms a suitable backdrop for your intended sale to its government. Brazil's National Defense Strategy, a document which I procured for your purposes..." Desmarais leaned forward and offered a folder to his benefactor "...provides little military justification for the nuclear-powered submarine project. The document stresses Brazil's peaceful traditions, paucity of problems with its neighbors and acknowledges it has been difficult to construct a convincing rationale for armies, navies or budgeting for the country's defense. Brazil hasn't, prior to this effort, enunciated any national strategy, so why nuclear submarines? The answer is oil...and national pride. Estimates of oil reserves in an undersea salt formation range as high as one hundred fifty billion barrels; ten time the country's previous proven reserves. Given the difficulties of extracting oil two hundred miles offshore, Brazil will never be able to recover all the oil. But it's well worth political infighting within Brazil's States...and equally worth protecting from international poaching by constructing a real navy."

Bin Rahman pursed his lips, pointing a finger in the general direction of the fluttering tent's ceiling. "Allahu akbar. Remind me, Jacques, who ranks ahead of Brazil in proven reserves?"

Desmarais wasn't a fool. "Well, of course, our hosts here in the Emirates have reserves of similar size..."

"No, no, my friend, there's no need to soften the blow." The Sheikh waved his hand, a gesture saying: *Tell my associates the truth.*

"Saudi Arabia and Canada have larger proven reserves. Claims exist that Venezuela's reserves exceed one hundred seventy five billion barrels...but the Venezuelans have been known to be excitable in this area of scientific endeavor. Iran's reserves may be competitive. But Brazil's discovery has jumped them from feeble cousin to grand patriarch."

"And where does your beloved France rank?"

"We measure our reserves by red or white; Bordeaux or Champagne."

The room enjoyed a laugh.

"And the Great Satan?" Playfulness, not ideology, marked bin Rahman's interest.

"The US is, maybe, fifteenth on the list."

"Britain?"

"Thirtieth, or thereabouts."

"Continue, Jacques, please."

"Brazil's national-defense concept lays out three maritime goals...denial of sea access, control of designated maritime areas, and projection of power beyond Brazilian waters. Brazil will have a nuclear submarine because it is a necessity for a country which has the maritime coast...but also the petroleum riches discovered in the sea. Brazil hopes to gain a permanent seat on the U.N. Security Council. Euphoria is the only description for what's happened since the offshore discoveries of oil and gas...euphoria which carries over to military purchases. Submarines are their weapons of choice."

Khalid glanced at Caroline. Some sense of agreement passed unseen between them, for the Sheikh became serious. "At the end of the day, how would you assess their sophistication and depth of experience, if you'll pardon my pun."

Khalid bin Rahman spent much of his early childhood in the United States, then was educated in England and Switzerland where he studied languages and economics assiduously. A small pun required no pardon from Jacques Desmarais.

Again the diminutive Frenchman made a respectful head movement before answering.

"Brazil has no Anti-Submarine Warfare ("ASW") capability. Forward presence and expeditionary warfare are the lynchpin of potent navies...Brazil won't be able to dream of exercising such a stratagem for two decades. Potential threats to their sea-lanes are an unacceptable risk and a manageable menace. Effective ASW capabilities will be the equalizer for Brazil's success in future crises and conflicts. This is no less true in the immediate future for Brazil than it was for the West and the Soviets during the Cold War. Brazil must invest or, to coin a phrase, be a Paper Tiger."

Bin Rahman spoke softly. "You're aware of what PaneroGlobal can offer. What does your research suggest Brazil can afford...and of more importance to greedy capitalists, as we all are in this room...what will they pay."

"ASW remains a complex challenge with neither simple nor elegant solutions. Since the end of the Cold War, the challenge has become more severe. Brazil starts at zero. What PaneroGlobal offers should, and will, command in excess of five hundred million Euros. In my humble opinion, of course."

"You've prepared a list of suggested introductions?"

"The names, contact information, background research and any...shall we say special...information is included in your folder."

Bin Rahman surveyed the faces of his US team. With the exception of Leuzinger, they'd heard 'Brazil' for the first time less than a few minutes ago. They wouldn't hear a similar discussion of China, where the potential market could exceed a billion Euros.

"Fathima, you must have questions. What are they, please?"

"Only one...how can we in the US assist?"

"By keeping our interests secure. Are those interests secure...in light of Hassan's untimely death?" Age old attempts to answer such a question were a failure, because the question was unfair as well as unanswerable.

"Each day we try our best to meet your expectations."

A good answer, though unsatisfying. Sometimes unsatisfying was acceptable. Sometimes not. Khalid persisted, in this case seeking a split opinion.

"Mr. Balfour, how long have you been in our employ?"

"Just over a year, sir."

Bin Rahman avoided sounding snide. "Are you happy in your work?"

"I haven't been asked to perform any true work, as yet."

"Aah. You are referring, no doubt, to the permanent elimination of meddlesome competitors or employees."

"Yes."

"You speak well for a Southerner, Mr. Balfour. Where has your southern accent disappeared to, I wonder." Bin Rahman addressed this question in Pashtu, the language of neighboring portions of Afghanistan and Pakistan.

Billy Ray answered in the same language. "Billy Ray Balfour is from Jackson, Mississippi. Today my name is Earnest Rautenbach, from South Africa, whose southern accent would be as poor as your Pashtu."

Wickedly, bin Rahman grinned with pleasure. The man combined moxie with respect. "So...Afrikaans, English, Pashtu...an impressive accomplishment...is it fair to assume there are others?" This time Arabic had been selected for the first portion—and Hebrew for the last.

"Yes, sir, both. Acquired in my line of work."

"What languages don't you speak, Mr. Rautenbach?"

Straight from the Mississippi Delta came an alligator drawl. "Many, sir. Of course, you're welcome to call me Billy Ray...as Rautenbach isn't my real name, either."

"Who employed you before Hassan asked you to join our firm?"

"I was, and am, self-employed, sir. Before starting on my own, I served at Her British Majesty's pleasure in a military unit without formal identification, sir." Billy Ray answered in the King's English.

"Mississippi, England, Iraq, Afghanistan, Pakistan...where else my good man?"

"I'd prefer not to say."

"Fathima tells me your repertoire relies often on changing appearance. Why?"

"It's part of a business model, sir. Similar to your business model for Brazil. Sometimes the only way to reach my objective is from a close vantage point."

"We pay you rather a lot, wouldn't you say?"

"Too much. You should use my services only as-needed."

"What would you do, if ten of my security team arrived to slit your throat tonight?"

Cockney humor emerged with exquisite timing. "I'd rather expect to perish with a slit throat, sir."

Again the room erupted. Even the guards on Billy Ray's left and right let smiles crease their faces.

"Where do you call home today, Mr. Balfour?"

"A small farm outside Quebec, sir."

"Why Canada?"

"One shouldn't work where one lives...and there are none in Canada worth killing. Sir."

Bin Rahman didn't smile. Billy Ray hadn't meant the statement to be humorous.

"Is our American operation secure?"

"In my opinion, no. I'm at great disadvantage, not being availed of the entire data set Fathima or Leuzinger possess…let alone what you and Mrs. Panero know in addition…but there are loose ends and little being done to tuck them away."

"As an example…?"

Bin Rahman glanced at Fathima. Would her infamous temper gain the upper hand? His purpose might've been ham-handed, as a Mississippian might say, but Billy Ray's answer would demand exploration.

"Who killed Hassan? Do you know, sir? Is Hassan's killer dead, or somehow untouchable? It seems a fair question…Hassan was your man."

"Another…if you please." Khalid let nothing of his thoughts escape. Hassan had, indeed, been my man. And how he died would be a significant security concern, if I didn't already know.

"The CIA man…Probst…killing him was justified, but became a liability when the camera's memory wasn't recovered. Ribeiro has, without question, seen the photographs. It's a serious complication. The FBI seems to be nowhere, but experience says the situation may change when it least benefits your businesses. And Ahmed…" A look of confusion on bin Rahman's face required elucidation "…the boy from the mosque who shot Probst. He's an unraveling loose end. It was his first kill and could've been his last. Probst almost grabbed poor Ahmed, who wouldn't have held out long under interrogation."

Bin Rahman appeared non-plussed. "These details…Ahmed has chosen to talk to you about his difficulties…are you his father confessor?"

Billy Ray explained. "I'm the man who shoved a steel rod up Ahmed's ass so he'd kill, so he'd chase Probst into salt grass and slit his throat…shoot and shoot again without puking to leave DNA everywhere. I drove Ahmed there and carried him out. I'm the one he begged for help, after Fathima told him to go kill an experienced spy."

"Are there still more loose ends, Mr. Balfour?"

"Nasha Poynter…sister-in-law of Caroline Poynter Panero…her husband Andrew's in Brazil on your business, sir. Why, then, is Nasha allowed to draw such attention? Fathima sent an underling to attack her. She's being romanced by Aaron Frankel and has appeared on television doing a convincing impression of a politician. Such a high profile…seems bad for your business. Sir."

***

Molly Hedley was past caring where the guards would take her.

Bitter harvests would forever fill her basket of memories. Touched, prodded, attacked, starved, and deprived of sleep—and other indignities—were well known to Dubai's prison population. When shown into the limousine and handed a cheap, plastic, suitcase, no shock or other emotion registered on her face. Neither the British nor Emirati face made an impression, other than that they, too, were uncertain and afraid.

Molly curled into the Mercedes's leather upholstery like a beaten dog.

Geoffrey Hedley manned a garbage truck, carting wastes away from the terminal in large bins. Among low expectations, Molly dead on the tarmac featured in a position of prominence. If the Police Chief sent his son, which he wouldn't, Hedley doubted he could shoot the young man, though armed with a semi-automatic. At best, he'd see Molly one last time. What was the worst case? There wasn't one, not any longer.

As a Gulfstream arrived at the gate, Geoffrey's heart rate soared. Would there be a miracle? Less than a minute later, a sleek, black limo disgorged Molly, a young man wearing football paraphernalia and a well-dressed man with thin, graying hair. A flashlight shone on each face, in turn, then extinguished. These three climbed the jet's self-contained stairs.

Hedley's phone vibrated against his leg. "You've not kept your word, Your Excellency."

"There was no time. He *is* my only son."

Hedley maintained a firm voice. "The Ambassador is not aboard the plane. You gave your word."

"Is there still time?"

"Who can say."

"The plane will be allowed to takeoff. Will that be enough?"

"Planes can return."

"Be merciful, I beg you."

Hedley was pleased. Turned upside down on his head, the Police Chief felt the true pain of loss.

He could be forgiven for begging. All men beg for what hope has forsaken.

The Emirati begged further. "Please. She'll be given a phone to speak with you."

"Let the plane go. Then we'll see."

Geoffrey watched the beautiful silhouette climb towards the rising moon. He walked away, and when a taxi delivered him to his vehicular residence, he let twenty minutes pass. Then called and said six words into the Police Chief's ear. "Allahu akbar. Al Maha. Shukran jazeelan."

The next sound transmitted through the phone came from Geoffrey Hedley firing his weapon.

Poor bastard—taking his own life showed cold calculation, a life for a life. Dubai's Police Chief texted the pilot: *Deliver the woman to London Biggin Hill airport.*

***

Caroline and Fathima seemed eager to differ with Billy Ray, when Suhaym, head of the Sheikh's security, bent over and whispered in bin Rahman's ear.

Dark clouds scudded across his face. Khalid returned to Billy Ray with the gimlet eye of a Vatican lawyer and asked his final question of this night.

"Does Fathima do anything you admire, Mr. Whomever-you-might-truly-be?"

Fathima hoped Billy Ray would feel Suhaym's blade.

Anton Leuzinger believed the interruption could've been orchestrated.

Jacques Desmarais had completed his task. Queasiness suggested this was an unfortunate moment to be redundant.

Billy Ray answered, sensing a need to hurry, yet understanding speed would not serve his interests.

"The ploy used against Bennett…nothing short of a master stroke…Fathima should be commended. I admired its every aspect." Billy Ray long ago deduced the plan came from elsewhere, not Fathima Laniado.

Bin Rahman was angry. There was no need for those around him to employ complex interpretations of his mood.

Caroline swept out of the suite. Twice before she'd seen the same look on her lover's face. Each occasion had demanded an abrupt change in venue.

Bin Rahman said, "Pay attention everyone. We're adjourned. Each of you will be escorted to safety by one of Suhaym's associates. Please cooperate."

CHAPTER 23

U.S. government drones were authorized to carryout lethal attacks in at least seven countries: Afghanistan, Iraq, Syria, Libya, Pakistan, Somalia and Yemen. Attacks were launched from bases in the Republic of Seychelles, offshore Somalia in the Indian Ocean, or the Republic of Djibouti, across from Yemen at the confluence of the Gulf of Aden and the Red Sea.

CTC maintained separate regional units known as: the Pakistan-Afghanistan Department, internally called PAD, and the Yemen-Somalia Department, known as YES. In a burrow of cubicles and offices, among walls and tables spread with maps marking locations of CIA bases and assets, whiteboards listed pending operations annotated with code names of operatives.

On a U.S. Air Force base outside Las Vegas, Intel required to guide drone pilots was sifted, evaluated and assimilated before a final decision by Medina and his deputies. CTC was free to instigate and conclude any mission, except Dubai was out of bounds.

Gathered around a claustrophobic conference table, Langley's seventh floor honchos pulsated with normal nerves and uncommon disputes. D/CIA Granholm wanted to know whether recent developments counted as a practical joke.

"Get goddam Sir Lancelot on the goddam phone."

Freddy Medina spoke to the ceiling, addressing no one and everyone. "Lancelot was French. Wouldn't Gawain be better?" Out of line, Freddy anticipated the middle finger. "Did you ask the Brits where their source was located?"

"Sure I did." Annoyed, Granholm couldn't understand why he'd stoop to the level of some idiot newspaper editor in London. "Should D/CIA ask some schmuck why his source has the same Intel as Langley? You want blood from me, Freddy? Go kill motherfucking bin Rahman."

Medina's response was almost inaudible. "When you give me proper authorization."

Grover Norris arrived late. "You got the President's authority twenty minutes ago. Why do we give a fuck about a British newspaper?"

DD/CIA spoke up. "British newspapers have the story, *before* the drone's in the air. You put a missile in that hotel suite...like as not we'll incinerate American businessmen or tourists. Commander in Chief will love the headlines...film at eleven. We're being baited, Grover. Worse, Mossad's poking around hoping to find a couple of dead CIA bodies."

Grover slumped in his chair, wishing he'd left this mess in Jamie's lap, or let them bring Fulton Bennett in from cold storage.

Ring-tone chiming, Grover checked his screen and mouthed: *Sir Gawain.* "Is it still a good evening, Sir Edward...or a rotten morning?"

"Hell of a ruckus you've got us in, Grover. You old fart...should let Jamie run his own show." Minister at Large, Sir Edward Poynter, refused to show his hand, which held nothing more than a pair of threes. There'd be no conciliatory gesture to the British love-hate relationship with CIA. Sir Edward chased bigger fish with miles to go before he'd sleep.

Grover. "Your source is reliable?"

"Yes, she is. Don't ask again for her identity."

"Who have the newspaper people been talking to?"

"A retired RAF Group Captain, whose wife is imprisoned in Dubai." Poynter's declarative statement intended to indict the American side.

"Not reliable under the circumstances?" Grover preferred to lay any operational cancellation at British feet, and would do so unless the tape of this conversation contradicted his intention. The President of the United States was waiting for an update.

"I wouldn't say either way. This decision is down to you, Grover, all those sitting with you, and to your esteemed President. Group Captain Hedley may be confirming the original source...he's helped us on several occasions. I must say…he accessed an authorized level of communication not used on prior occasions. Of course the Press makes a jolly good way to get everyone's attention. Anything else, old boy? Good luck, Grover. Give my best to Jamie…and that smashing young Sarah of yours."

Norris swore under his breath. "Randy old bastard."

DD/CIA held up his phone. "Got the *Post* on the line, vouching for one of the Brits. Says the guy wouldn't jerk our chain. Anyone wanna talk?"

There were no takers.

They all heard Granholm address the White House Chief of Staff.

"No, I wouldn't schedule photo ops, or anything else, till we nail this down. No…I don't know when target film will be available, or if it will be. This thing isn't a lock and may be a hoax."

To the White House an operation characterized by the word hoax ended any possibility of approval.

***

Marie Truchet watched three different SUVs roar out of *Al Maha* over a period of fifteen minutes. Her obligation complete, making further calls would mark her an amateur, or a crybaby. She left the dunes to discover whether Caroline Panero took her husband with her.

Marie thought not.

***

Billy Ray Balfour sat in the rear. While the driver focused on their high-speed exit, his two colleagues were positioned to converse with, or kill, Billy Ray.

Billy Ray compelled himself to sleep.

***

A small caravan of camels was driven to the west at their best possible speed.

Khalid bin Rahman refused to look backwards at *Al Maha*, his mind taken with other matters. In a matter of hours, they'd be met outside Abu Dhabi and the immediacy of business would intrude. For now, he was content to be in rhythm with the beast beneath him, allowing solutions to well up from composed analysis.

There always would be the first question: *Who divulged my location?*

Anyone could've betrayed him, if their motive was strong enough. Motive and opportunity were critical. Means mattered little in a world where prince and pauper owned a similar ability to communicate. None of his departed associates seemed possessed of guilty knowledge. None had done other than obey, when told to follow Suhaym. Based on appearances, they'd have marched to Buchenwald's gas showers without question or protest.

The traitor was beyond reach.

Could my back-stabber be Marco, the pathetic cuckold? Caroline vouched for poor Marco and how his pitiable devotion might manifest itself in fantasy, but never on a telephone to MI-6. "Marco hasn't the stomach to watch me blown to pieces."

Had some random satellite photo array proven my presence? Such an occurrence couldn't be disproved.

No less fascinating was a different question: Who saved me? Thanks be to Allah and the Chief of Police, but the origin of the Chief's information was layered in bothersome uncertainty. An angel of mercy shouldn't stand in shadow.

Jacques' intelligence regarding *Astute* mandated a change in timing. Marco would be dispatched to Brazil to buttress the wining and dining conducted by Caroline's surprising brother. Andrew had completed his tasks in France and India as called for by Marco's script. Time it was to seal the Brazil deal, before the fox entered the hen house. Then an offer to the Chinese would be unassailable.

Caroline's father would be distraught, after hearing of a possible drone attack. Sir Edward's guilt made him the ally Caroline relied upon as an article of faith. Guilt in Caroline's heart, in the case of Sir Edward, resulted from multiple failings: Allowing Caroline's mother to pass away; frittering away the fortune left behind; rejecting Fulton Bennett as a suitor; forcing an arranged marriage to Panero; and loving Andrew more than herself. Caroline could spout a litany of favoritism and abuse at will. Did so whenever the need to manipulate her father was greatest.

The Probst matter was most troublesome. No resolution fit the scale of the problem: An ill conceived murder, assigned to a neophyte, botched at every level, and, worst of all, exhibited a complete breakdown relative to its purpose. In every scenario Khalid in Rahman examined, exposure was inevitable.

One conclusion stood out: Implement wholesale change.

Leuzinger would devise an alternative to Aaron Frankel and his Wall Street tower.

Public signs of distress or duress would have to be averted. Weakness shown in public would wreak havoc.

Fathima Laniado was a disappointment. Let her make plans for paper airplanes which would never fly. He considered whether Fathima was disloyal? Closed the issue in the opinion disloyal did not apply.

Months ago bin Rahman embarked upon an internal review of US operations. Where a traitor could've been excised like in-situ cancer, mismanagement exemplified the metastasized form of the disease. Only in the United States was it so difficult to find skillful leaders. He let his eyes drift to the heavens in memory of the proverb: *If wishes were horses, then beggars would ride.*

One final thought struck home before he prodded the spitting, urinating animal to a gallop: Incompetence will kill us all.

***

Zachary Mannheim sat erect in CIC's conference room.

His actions this evening would strain his authority, and indeed his career, to the breaking point. What he saw in his mind's eye was a dance floor lit by strobe lights under the effects of a bad LSD trip. A distorted caricature appeared in the corner of his vision. A healthy pink face faded to blue then purple; fragments of what was familiar distorted a wild animal with large teeth. Mannheim rubbed his eyes to shake off disorientation. He needed to abandon loyalties and preconceptions in favor of harsher stuff.

"So Mr. Medina...you had a short, but enjoyable, visit this evening with the esteemed Fulton Bennett?"

Jerked out of CTC within minutes of aborting the drone flight to *Al Maha*, Freddy's adrenaline from the evening's ups and downs produced a less inhibited version of his uninhibited self.

"Up your ass. I've got a report to file...a bunch of good folks to explain things to. Whaddya want?"

"For you not to answer a question with a question."

"For God's sake, someone was listening every minute I spent with Fulton. Ask them what went on. Listen to the tape yourself."

"Does the tape tell the whole truth and nothing but the truth, Freddy?"

"Yuh, it does. Can I go back to work?" Medina planned to leave, despite what Mannheim said next.

"Are the winds of testosterone and mission failure blowing acid rain in the direction of Deputy Director Bennett?" Paramount in Mannheim's consciousness was keeping this meeting connected to Bennett, the only senior Agency executive CIC was directed to investigate.

"The President wanted certainty. Grover thought we could give him certainty. Turned out different. So we scrubbed the mission. In a day or two, we'll know whether we made the right call. Bennett had nothing to do with anything."

"And no one sitting in CTC, or the White House, accused Bennett of causing the mission to abort...either by direct statement, implication or in an attempt at locker-room humor?"

"There might've been a suggestion or two, implying Fulton would be pleased bin Rahman could sleep well, undisturbed by a missile up his ass."

"Who made such an observation?"

"Hmm. Not real sure." Medina's obfuscation included a rueful grin. "Whoever it was...they had less to say when I showed Fulty's electronic gear in my pocket."

"Director Bennett suggested you locate Andrew Poynter and Caroline Panero before making the call to abort. Did you act on his behalf?"

"Staff tried to put coordinates on those individuals, but were unsuccessful prior to the abort."

"Were they located in some subsequent analysis?"

This was much the trickier line of questioning. Quicksand awaited his inability to connect bin Rahman to Bennett.

"Only Andrew Poynter, who's in Rio de Janeiro...a long fucking way from the Dubai desert."

"And Caroline Panero?"

"Nada. No known location for the moment."

"Have you reported the results to Director Bennett?"

"No...there's been no time."

"Please don't continue with these half-truths, Freddy...for your own sake."

Blood in the water, to a shark, would be similar to the warning Mannheim gave Freddy Medina. Without doubt Freddy transmitted the search's results to Fulton, which was the point of Mannheim's subterfuge.

***

In the bar at the *Westin Crystal City*, Greg Riley fit right in: Suit and tie, tired eyes, briefcase open, nursing coffee and a sandwich.

Block letters formed words inscribed clockwise on a paperback's crimped page, in ballpoint, around the page's printed text. Selected from the works of a specific author, it made a crude book cipher.

Brazil—Bennett was asking Riley to travel there to discover what Andrew Poynter was selling the Brazilian Navy. Included were names of people to avoid, and a single ten-digit number. No part of the hidden message provided comfort to a scientist devoid of experience in the realities of espionage.

***

David Nazarian, at the conclusion of conversations with DD/CIA and Zachary Mannheim, could identify nothing satisfying about either.

DD/CIA sounded reluctant, but confirmed Nazarian's earlier kill order without the addition or subtraction of data related to the mission: No input related to the target's current location; no inquiry as to events in Spain. The conversation, if ever acknowledged, lasted less than two minutes and consisted, for the most part, of pregnant silence.

Not so with Mannheim, who made it clear their call was being recorded and asked questions soliciting minute details: How Nazarian planned the Op; contacted the foreign contractor; paid for the contract; how and why the contract failed; what role Phyllis Martell played; from whom was authorization received; and whether said authorization was verbal or written. Nazarian's responses ranged from factual to evasive, and an occasional refusal to respond.

Creative fictions caused Mannheim to threaten repercussions.

Nazarian, in response to a hostile interrogation, hung up and would, if cross-examined further, evade answering at all.

Boiled down to its nub, nothing about Mannheim's view of the botched assignment was altered beyond two critical facts: Nazarian knew about Ribeiro's presence in Brazil; no one else at Langley did.

As Nazarian sat on the first of two flights taking him to Rio de Janeiro, via Amsterdam, one original goal endured. No grand scheme illuminated his purpose. No intention to rebel against Agency policy or leadership existed. Just one man's obstinate opinion: Raissa served her country, paid a severe price and ought to be left in peace.

David Nazarian expected to pay full fare for his autonomy.

***

Nasha bolted upright on Andrew's side of the bed, expecting his reassuring touch. A hollow chill, monitored by a programmable thermostat, was no comfort. She shivered as the dream flashed staccato scenes of misery. Right from wrong, fiction from truth—deciphering the difference no easier than separating a dream from the dawn.

Where are you, Andrew, my husband?

Where are you, Yusef, my brother?

Why hadn't Edward Poynter visited the infant who would sustain his family name?

Why had Nasha been invited into the Embassy security room after the false alarm, and allowed to return to that same room to watch for endless hours.

It all started with her surprise arrival at the Embassy party. No one other than Fouad Razouk had known she was attending. No, that wasn't at all correct. Razouk's staff knew. Lucia knew. Nabil Hanna knew, and, if he knew, so did Fathima Laniado. Nasha didn't count Mahbeer, who knew first-hand.

Sir Edward's shock was too real; he must have been frightened. Not frightened for his daughter-in-law, who was little more than Bradford's caretaker, but for his grandson. Edward had been angry for the best of reasons, not wanting his grandson to grow up without a mother. What were the odds of staying alive—me standing next to Frankel as the man in the tuxedo carried out his assassination?

In the melee of British soldiers seeking and engaging the assassin, fate would've been tempted too far.

Nasha permitted thoughts to tumble in free association: Edward Poynter disapproved of Nasha socializing with Aaron Frankel; disapproved enough to make a scene; Edward himself left the pistol in the library desk; the man in the tuxedo found the gun where he expected it. Ergo, the man in the tuxedo was Edward's creature.

Papa hadn't known; his surprise at seeing his daughter was *not* improvised to suit nefarious purposes. But he'd warned her against an approach, so was complicit to some degree. Even more than Papa's unspoken warning, Yusef tried to make certain I'd be out of the Embassy before chaos erupted.

Yusef saved Aaron Frankel from an assassin's bullet. Either Yusef was Mossad, with some perverted reason to align himself with the terrorist's banker—or Yusef was a terrorist working with, or for, Aaron Frankel—or worse yet working with, or for, Khalid bin Rahman.

Grover Norris assisted Papa with the wheelchair, Jamie Norris and Sarah Gullickson close on Grover's heels.

Nasha rewound the scenes and played them another time. A gaggle of Chatty Cathies, are they all complicit? All singing bin Rahman's tune.

No, it simply wasn't possible.

***

Through alcohol-fogged vision, Marco observed Marie selecting clothes from his travel bag. Dressed, he wobbled after Truchet as she lugged his suitcase to her vehicle. Marie planned a return to a Dubai hotel: Two rooms, discrete access through the service entrance, scrambled eggs, toast and two carafes of hot coffee.

Panero mumbled. "What time is it?"

"Half ten."

"There's a KLM flight at 1:20 tomorrow morning...non-stop to Rio. You bitched about leaving Andrew with no babysitter."

CHAPTER 24

Boston wasn't New York, particularly in the proliferation of CCTV as a response to terrorist threats. Haslett begged and borrowed resources from within FBI and Boston PD. Local business cameras, traffic-cams and MBTA station-cams were canvassed with mixed results. No video from inside Legal Seafood was recovered.

Firsthand evidence of Frankel's luncheon, documented by time-stamped, unaltered, video, remained illusory. Every frame from every video of the surrounding area, taken within two hours either side of the date/time on Frankel's credit card charge, was examined. Facial recognition software was at work identifying thousands of faces.

At CIA, the package of videos was received in the mailroom, logged-in and distributed to Jamie Norris, recently elevated to Acting Deputy Director. Jamie re-routed the information to Greg Riley marked: FYI—analyze as priorities allow.

Haslett flew to Washington and met Phyllis Martell in the terminal at Reagan National.

**

Greg Riley's skills weren't suited to what Bennett asked of him. Riley understood an inescapable fact.

When Riley entered Bennett's office, seeing Jamie behind the desk brought on a prescient shudder. Where unkempt files and journals once prevailed, balled-up foil nestled among pristine wrapped chocolates were the lone signs of use.

"Hey Greg. Whassup?"

"Sorry, Jamie…won't take a couple of minutes."

Jamie Norris's imitation of a harried spymaster could work to Riley's benefit.

"Remember the question of French submarines? You wanted to be kept current."

"E-mail's fine, Greg, or is something hot?"

"Something for sure…either very hot or a false alarm. I'm asking you to authorize my inquiry on behalf of NCS." Whether Jamie's signature arrived without protest, or after a long, detailed technical justification, made no difference.

"Give me the five-cent tour."

" We…the Navy not the Agency…detect submarines via satellite and lasers, infrared, synthetic aperture radar and other modalities. Chinese submarines, as they leave Qingdao and Ningbo headed for deeper water, can't spot our satellites. A much tougher place to operate undetected is the East China Sea, where depths vary from thirty to sixty fathoms…pretty damn shallow if you're a sub skipper…and the Chinese fleet is noisy."

Jamie followed with less concentration than appearance suggested. "Where's this going, Greg? What authorization do you want?"

"The Chinese are begging, buying and stealing their way towards catching us. Today or tomorrow…their fleet wouldn't last a week in a serious conflict. What would be the quickest way for them to accelerate equality?" Riley gained Norris's full attention. "Kill our boats first."

"How…?"

"Noise emission profiles of the latest British nuclear sub class…the *Astute*…have gone walkabout. If the Chinese buy a library of acoustic profiles, and the software to improve their sonar, they'll pull even with our ASW. I want you to authorize an effort to screw-up their plans."

"A field effort?"

"Digital for the primary investigation, but yes, there'll be field work as well."

"You want people, money…or both?"

"I want your support in keeping this off the grid. Any leak and we'll be forced to pack up our effort and call it a day."

"What will *our effort* include?"

"I propose to sell acoustic profiles of US subs, and every foreign sub we've tracked and recorded, to third parties who, in turn, will sell them to the Chinese and their allies."

Norris was paying attention. "So the Agency has acquired these profiles?"

"Not yet."

"Who'll provide them?"

"Assign Madeleine to the Op. Together we'll get what we need."

"Gonna involve the Brits?"

"If we run across their *Astute* data out there in cyber-world, we'll contaminate it, render it useless, then tell the Brits we saved their ass."

Jamie signed the authorization, then said with a sense of ennui, "Madeleine has history with my father. You'll need to assure yourself on that score."

***

Raissa stood naked as a newborn: No clothes, makeup, nail or toe polish, legs unshaven and untended hair. Bruises around her neck, though receding, remained pronounced and discolored. Arms over her head, too much rib cage showed underneath stretched skin. Her skin's color would be classified as pasty or wind burned. Breasts no longer belonged to Raissa in her teens, but they weren't all bad. No hint of sag in her butt, or ragged dimpling on her thighs, leg muscles were well defined.

Thinking of herself in the abstract, she spoke to the mirror. "No joke girl, you'll need great lighting."

Unlike multiple mirrors populating fashion houses, this poor excuse was yellowed, cracked and mounted on a dirty plaster wall with great gobs of ancient glue. The wall separated a one-bedroom apartment in Favela Providencia, Rio de Janeiro, from the identical apartment next-door. On the third floor of a steep hillside building, the apartment would have enjoyed a stunning view of Rio's charms, if only it faced downhill.

Across a gap of two meters, where the sun never penetrated, a mongrel dog owned by a family of seven surveyed Raissa's every movement.

What mattered wasn't dilapidated ambience or the lack of creature comforts. Not the heart-stopping views, the famous beaches of Ipanema, imposing Sugar Loaf Mountain or the white capped, blue, Atlantic. Where outsiders and tourists saw one of Rio's notorious favelas, Raissa found safety in being home amongst extended family.

While Rio might believe itself reinvented by the faded memory of the 2016 Olympics, and entrepreneurs continued to meander through these bastions of poverty, violence and *empáfia* in search of opportunity, such intrusions were transient and tenuous.

Favelas had come to embody the divide between the wretched and the affluent in one of the world's most inequitable societies. Half-assed electricians stole power from the electrical grid with purloined cables. Gasoline was sold on the street in plastic jugs. Murders were committed at an equal rate by police and gangs.

Her appraisal needed to be harsh; Paolo Zabban's critical eye would be unforgiving. His excitement at seeing Raissa would be tempered by whether the camera still loved her. Black and white would be the medium; color claimed no place among those who would hunt each other devoid of remorse or mercy. Her flaws would draw clamoring hordes: Nothing sold to the rapacious world of celebrity and fashion like raw pain. Paolo would be drawn to her scars like a moth to flame. What a coup, if his artistry transformed the injured duckling. For a short time she'd be the other Raissa once more. Spotlights would follow her, if she allowed such intrusions, which she couldn't, not and expect to survive.

For those who killed Gunther, who hired the German and paid Erramun, would chase a fatal attraction.

CHAPTER 25

When the cell phone rang in the pocket of his suit jacket, Nabil Hanna debated letting it go to voicemail. On the third ring, his conscience pushed him out of a high-backed swivel chair. Originated in Beirut, the call was a literal answer to prayer. For forty minutes he listened more than spoke, jotting random notes on the back of an envelope.

Hanna left his office in a hurry after the man in Beirut ended the call.

Not religious, he felt compelled to make the Dhuhr, the noon prayer of the Fard Salat, at his mosque. Although performing the Fard in jama'ah (congregation) was a male obligation when possible, Hanna manipulated the definition to suit his wants and needs. Prayers were obligatory for every Muslim past the age of puberty. Exceptions for mental illness, physical illness making prayer impossible, as well as menstruation or post-partum bleeding, were routine. For a man who served Allah by serving Hezbollah, Hanna believed a special exemption existed. After joyous news, being seen at prayer, being seen as devout, would bring its own blessings.

Years of struggle and political stalemate were now settled in favor the coalition led by Hezbollah. Political groups influenced by Syria and Iran would at long last have their chance to diminish US influence in the region, as change swept across the Middle East. Hanna saw only one cloud on his international horizon: Turmoil in Damascus would always shake the ground in Lebanon.

On the Washington DC horizon, opportunities abounded.

***

Her husband hadn't been much on her mind in Dubai, but here in Washington, as she sat paralyzed by the bank officer's insistence, Marco's absence was a proper inconvenience.

"I'm Vice Chair of PaneroGlobal LLC, Mr. Stevens. Our Corporate Resolution of Authority grants me full rights to establish banking relationships in my discretion. How is it you demand our Chairman's signature?" Caroline Panero possessed the full range of priggishness associated with British aristocracy, however arcane her title.

"I wouldn't care to bother Mr. Michani…our families are related by marriage as you'll be aware, but if you won't arrange an account which will shortly receive a half billion dollars…" She left the sentence to hang, in contemplation of the officious Mr. Stevens hung out the third floor window by his bollocks.

"Perhaps Mr. Panero's signature could be faxed on PaneroGlobal letterhead? The requirement for two signatures is bank policy. I'll gladly reach-out to Mr. Michani's staff, if you'd prefer. We're pleased to be favored with your company's confidence."

Caroline bestowed vestigial approval with a dismissive hand gesture. "Yes, I'll arrange a facsimile. You do have all the incoming and outgoing wire instructions?"

"Certainly Mrs. Panero. Your coded instructions will be part of our systems by tomorrow morning. Access is available continuously via any of your devices."

***

In Favela Rocinha there were no tourists. There was abject poverty and a police helicopter engaged in a geometric search pattern over sloping streets where, among houses crammed together in monolithic destitution, squads of heavily armed police tried to eradicate a powerful gang.

Rocinha, Rio's largest favela, overlooked the city center one klick from a beach where David Nazarian stoked the ego of a gang chieftain.

Preoccupied with the chopper's searchlight, a burst of tracer shells lit the hillside, shattering its sedate ambiance. Tiago sucked hard on his Brazilia Robusto, snorting smoke into soft evening air.

"When the first rounds are fired, the police run away. We could attack the Mayor's house and more than half would flee before they'd fight us." Tiago spit a portion of the cigar's end in the direction of Nazarian's shoe. "Call Edson. Put him on speakerphone and we'll ask if you are who you say you are."

"This time of the morning in London...a few minutes after five..." Nazarian checked his phone for the exact time "...Edson will barely be done partying."

Tiago's interest in verbal sparring evaporated. "Call."

Bullets in the feet—on a beach—the preferred disposal method of Tiago the Lunatic, as the man sitting opposite Nazarian was cravenly known, were his gang's Mark of Cain. With bullets in the feet, a man couldn't walk—at half-tide, crawling meant drowning.

David pressed the cell's speaker icon and dialed.

Edson expressed displeasure with a stream of expletives.

Tiago responded. "An American who gives me a false name, but your name as assurance...do you know him, Edson?"

Nazarian interjected. "CIA bastard number three speaking, Edson. I need help with your cousin Tiago."

A rowdy laugh and the squeal of a woman preceded a half cockney, half Portuguese response. "Take his money, Tiago. Give him what he wants. Be polite, or CIA bastard number three will blind you using your cigar."

Nazarian repeated his request. "A fool is who I need, Senhor Tiago. Someone who thinks too little and drinks too much. Someone who uses a blade, not a gun."

"Who does CIA want to die, bastard number 3?"

"A woman."

"What woman?"

"A woman I want dead."

"You should rent a policeman. They are all women...and they like knives or guns. For a little extra they'll throw her out the chopper door."

"I need a professional."

"Who thinks too little and drinks too much? Then you want an older man, maybe one as old as you." Tiago was less than thirty.

Nazarian remained stationary. It was entirely possible Tiago the Lunatic would demonstrate his nom de guerre.

Tiago was equally wary. "Michael da Silva is perfect. He has a reputation with both gun and blade, but couldn't hit a statue with a truck. When you slit his throat, Rio won't miss him"

"Michael's phone number?"

"No, bastard number 3, give me your number. I'll call tomorrow."

"But you'd prefer CIA's money now."

Negotiations were concluded. Nazarian wouldn't pay on a beach, not when ever-present crabs made his stomach crawl.

"Why not?"

"Because there's no money here; there's only CIA bastard number 3. Tomorrow, at noon, I'll stand outside the US Consulate with ten thousand dollars in an envelope."

Tiago snapped Nazarian's picture with his phone. "She'll look very young, the one I send. But very smart. Goodbye Senhor Bastard."

Two men with automatic rifles rose from a dune halfway to the street. They waited for Tiago the Lunatic, who struck David Nazarian as a capable ally and no crazier than those who supposed themselves sane.

***

Sheikh Khalid bin Rahman re-read Leuzinger's progress summary and recommendations, finding no fault with either the concepts or the planned execution. He chuckled at his double entendre, made a list and began typing instructions to various operatives worldwide.

From his discretionary account held at a bank in Riyadh, he wired twenty million Euros to Caroline's personal account at HSBC Bank in London.

From the same account he wired fifty million dollars to an investment account at Grover Norris's investment bank, an account owned by a corporation organized under the laws of the Cayman Islands.

From a Swiss account, held openly in his name at a correspondent bank owned by Jean-Louis Michani, he wired forty million Euros to the personal account of Sir Edward Poynter.

From an e-mail account to be used once, and impossible to identify, he sent a coded message to Fathima Laniado.

In an identical manner, a message was sent to Caroline.

Neither woman was copied with his missive to the other.

Finally, he spoke with one of his assistants and directed the preparation of a flight plan taking the Sheikh to Toronto on a chartered jet, then, with a change of airport, aircraft and crew, to Atlantic City, New Jersey. It was a vital risk, traveling to the US; one he would not duplicate.

CHAPTER 26

Yusef began the workday with anticipation.

Concentration wasn't required, not really, as today's workload varied in a meager way from other days of other years. His mind concentrated on a null set: What events hadn't happened; what messages hadn't he received; and what actions had yet to be initiated.

Maury Lipmann made morning rounds, giving pep talks where attention was lacking and slurping coffee from a monstrous mug shaped as a Washington Football Team's helmet. He bantered with Yusef about the Bashers' recent decline, utilizing the opportunity to scrutinize Burn-bags still to be processed. A specific grouping of bags drew particular attention; he made certain Yusef's attention matched his own.

Yusef growled. "Lay off the Bashers, Maury. So we've lost some games. So what."

"Don't be so touchy, Bennett's never coming back."

Louder, Yusef warned, "Back off, Maury." Adding a shove to Lipmann's shoulder for emphasis, Yusef turned away.

Coffee rained over Lipmann's shoulder, the floor, and the conveyor where Burn-bags traveled for load-out. Lipmann hopped around the floor in obvious discomfort.

"Look what you've done…dammit Yusef." All eyes centered on their boss.

Paper towels in hand, Yusef's cleanup began on hands and knees where Burn-bags absorbed the hot coffee. Several appeared ready to dissolve.

Grimace in place, Lipmann pointed. "Re-bag those."

Yusef concentrated on a bag with a dark stain which wasn't caused by spilled coffee.

Across the large room, JET paid more than casual notice.

***

Souraya's call was a harbinger, given the undisguised satisfaction dripping from her voice. "The Ambassador wants you in his office. Now."

Aren't Souraya and I supposed to be friends?

Surveillance had dwindled to a single car from the British Embassy. As traffic worsened, Nasha thought back to her last confrontation with Fouad Razouk: Razouk's daughter shouldn't be a helpless pawn. Nasha's lack of clear judgment left a painful conclusion: Pressure makes hypocrites of us all. Nasha Poynter didn't like herself very much as the minivan crept along its route downtown.

In the Ambassador's expansive inner sanctum, two divans covered in a subdued Arab silk mosaic, were arranged by the windows. A pair of armchairs were covered in complimentary leather. A coffee table supported a tall floral arrangement spread within a wide Baccarat vase.

Nabil Hanna was the sole occupant of one divan. To his right sat Agent Lawrence Gainey, a cat expecting the canary to be delectable. Wearing a face absent goodwill was Agent Ralph Madison.

Nasha's immediate reaction—Razouk was gone—required her highest level of concentration. She stopped behind the unoccupied chair, examining each male who awaited her words with hostile eyes.

"Good morning Ambassador Hanna...congratulations on your appointment. Good morning Agents. Hello Nadia."

She elected not to sit, but exhibited no defiance. Discomfort was a burden she could bear. Nasha emulated her Momma's insistent teaching: Stand tall, Nasha; Stand your ground proudly, but without pride.

Hanna's eyebrows lowered, annoyed to have been denied Nasha's shock and awe. "This is unfortunate, summoning you here under such circumstances on my first day as Acting Ambassador. However unpleasant, Lebanon will provide full cooperation to law enforcement agencies of our esteemed host country, the United States."

Nabil delighted in using Nasha as a practice dummy for the lies and spin Hezbollah would require.

Nadia spoke, making her expanded authority evident. "Do sit down Nasha."

Nabil Hanna was a functionary, sentenced to chafe under the imagined yoke of lesser men. His chance to bleat like a neutered goat wouldn't be ignored or rejected.

"Fouad Razouk and his family have been recalled. Your report, Nasha...in particular the outrageous sexual escapades of his daughter...won the day over the former Ambassador's efforts to curry support with certain parties in Syria. Our Prime Minister surely, one day, will remember your contribution."

Hanna, comically vying to be a 21st Century Mephistopheles, was cold-hearted, cynical and given to wit more satirical than satanical. This new Nabil was the invention of the Faustian leaders of Hezbollah.

Nasha sat, maintaining posture and silence.

Nabil fumed.

For Agent Madison the animosity between the two generated enough voltage to light the room—more than enough to spark Mahbeer Saadia's aggression.

Nadia turned to Agent Gainey, suggesting he begin Nasha's interrogation.

Gainey's first tactic was provocation, employed because there was a chance of it being effective, but more for the amusement it would bring him.

"Nasha...you don't mind being called Nasha do you? Were you adopted in Lebanon, as a young girl, by Jean-Louis Michani?"

Two could play, if playing was the objective. "Is this interview being recorded, Agent Gainey? And if not, why not?"

Gainey threw up his hands to dramatic effect. "No need to be belligerent, Nasha. You're a loyal American asked to cooperate with an FBI investigation, nothing more."

"Are you or Ambassador Hanna recording this meeting?"

"Neither Agent Madison nor I are recording anything."

"So the recording devices active in this room are those operated or shared by US, Russian, British and Israeli Intelligence Agencies?"

Gainey ignored her sham question.

Ambassador Hanna's lips thinned into the pretense of a smile.

Nasha finished her preamble with a final question. "Am I either under arrest or a suspect in any criminal investigation?"

Madison knew Gainey's lip would bleed before telling Mrs. Poynter she could leave at any time. "No."

"Then my answer to your first question is yes."

Gainey caught her arrogance. "Well, excuse me for bad grammar, Mrs. Poynter. Would you care to answer my second question?"

"I am Mr. Michani's adopted daughter."

"Jean-Louis Michani is a practicing, devout, Jew…is that correct?"

"America guarantees religious freedom. Ask Mr. Michani about his religious beliefs or practices."

"Are you, Mrs. Poynter, a practicing, devout, Muslim?"

"Yes."

"Are you bound by Sharia Law?"

"Your question is improper, Agent Gainey."

Gainey's face reddened. "Because I'm not Muslim?"

"Because, Agent Gainey, there is Islamic Law and the larger, more encompassing, concept of Sharia…a concept subject to varying interpretation by Muslim scholars of all sects, as well as by modernists, traditionalists and revisionists. Sharia Law, in the way you used the term, doesn't exist. Not being Muslim may put you at a disadvantage in asking me questions about my religion. Perhaps you should allow Ambassador Hanna or Nadia to ask on your behalf."

Gainey began to comprehend the roadblocks she could erect. This entire line of interrogation, a Lutheran trying to sound fluent in Muslim teachings, was bound for frustration. He quoted her the date and time of the women's luncheon at the Ritz-Carlton—showed her a photograph. "Is this you, Mrs. Poynter, arriving at the luncheon?"

Nasha wondered: Who took this photo? Grace hadn't mentioned seeing any like this one. But today it made no difference. "On the right or left, Agent Gainey?"

Gainey consulted his copy which identified Fathima Laniado, on Nasha's left, in red grease pencil. "Either one, Mrs. Poynter. Are you either of the women pictured?"

"I can't be certain from the rear, but it could be Fathima Laniado on the left and myself on the right, arriving at the luncheon."

Gainey placed a series of photos on the coffee table.

Hanna and Nadia hunched over them with great interest.

Nasha watched Nabil with greater attention, but never moved to examine what the pictures demonstrated.

"I'd like you to look carefully, Mrs. Poynter." Gainey sensed something he could not identify.

Madison had guessed a minute earlier.

"Why?" Nasha made the question sound sincere, when it was duplicitous.

"The woman in the fourth floor hallway appears to be you, Mrs. Poynter. Would you care to comment, or make an admission?" What he'd intended to be a moment of triumph, or redemption, faded into wishful thinking.

Only then did Nasha realize—Gainey and Madison hadn't examined the television footage shot by Al Jazeera. She inquired with increasing confidence. "Has Quantico performed a detailed analysis of all footage shot at the hotel?"

Madison intervened to rescue his partner. "Is there something we should know, Mrs. Poynter?"

"Agent Gainey inferred the image in the first picture is me. I'm wondering what the basis for such an inference might be."

Gainey's temper rose, like on Georgetown Pike in front of Papa's gate. "I think you shot the woman at the Ritz. Your billionaire daddy and his Mossad kill-team helped you." Gainey never meant his vitriol to come out quite the way it did, but going back wasn't an option.

Nabil leaned back into the divan's soft cushions. This FBI fool's accusation against Nasha could be enough, he thought, to build a case of his own; a case not subject to proof beyond a reasonable doubt or a jury of her American peers.

Madison sounded anxious when he asked, "And if there's no more basis than the pictures on the table?"

"Then I suggest you speak with the Fairfax detectives, who, I believe, reviewed the entirety of the television video. Video uninterrupted during the timeframe established for the murder."

Madison looked at Gainey, imploring his colleague to focus on the murder. When Gainey couldn't speak, Madison turned the interrogation into a quest for collaboration. "Ambassador Hanna…would Ms. Laniado have had reason to be on the hotel's fourth floor? Or to change her clothes before returning to the luncheon?"

Cautious by definition, Acting Ambassadors conducted their duties under a microscope—and blunders paved the surest path to a short tenure. Besides, there was the small matter of not knowing the answer to Madison's question. Hanna hoped Gainey's interpretation of the evidence was solid, but never acquired a strong belief in Nasha's guilt. Not because she wasn't capable of killing. He of all people knew better, but killing a prostitute made no sense. Which presented an identical dilemma in regards to Fathima. Why would Fathima kill a call girl?

Let events unfold, he told himself.

"No reason I know of. Rest assured, we at the Embassy will continue to cooperate in whatever course of action the FBI feels is appropriate."

***

Paolo Zabban was a man of large appetites. At sixty-three, any woman alive would, and a little less often did, mistake him for forty-five. His tall frame vacillated no more than five pounds in either direction from his weight at twenty. Drugs were a thing of the past. Drink was an accompaniment for food. Sex was more fiction than he would, with good grace, admit. Dark hair streaked with unembellished silver cascaded from his scalp as he bent over the viewfinder to examine deep lines, carved by time, in an old woman's brow.

The woman sitting on a stool wrapped in a shawl was truly beautiful; she was eighty, give or take a few great grandchildren and a memory shattered by life in the favelas.

Focused, there came the smallest moment when he thought he'd died and found heaven—for the old woman's face transformed to a familiar angel. Zabban fought for words which would do justice to his emotions and the vision in front of him. Without moving away from the camera's lens, he found them.

"Your face is lopsided, Raissa. You've let someone hit your nose with his fist."

Smile stretched wide, he waited to enfold his favorite subject in a grasp which threatened her ability to breathe. He released her, straightening strong arms to examine her in minute detail.

"Come and talk with me, little one. Your soul is locked away."

They walked uphill to Zabban's home. On the roof, Rio spread out below in watercolor pastels. His icebox yielded cheese and fruit to accompany a white wine from the Serra Gaúcha. When he spoke, it was an odd mixture of artist, businessman and father confessor.

"You were smarter than the others. You didn't throw away your money in the casinos, fry your brains on the latest drug concoction or give away your body to any man with a fast car or the promise of a Vogue cover. When I read about the fire, never seeing a paparazzo's picture, taken to satisfy the freaks, was a tragedy's saving grace. When you stopped being news, I rejoiced. Our Raissa was free of their Raissa at last. And now…here you are…for money, love or revenge?"

"Survival."

Raissa couldn't tell Paolo what she'd been, when employed by the Agency. So she told him what he'd understand.

"A friend, an occasional news photographer, took pictures which got him killed. I have them now. Only here can I lure the killers and hope to survive."

"Every gang veteran in the favelas hung posters of young Raissa on their walls. Will fondness for the past be enough…what will make the gangs help you?"

"You will, Paolo. We'll turn the fashion world on its ear with photographs…and use the Internet to make short videos go viral. We'll lay a slick of chum in the water and wait for the sharks to feed. Some sharks will die. Others we'll milk. You'll get very rich in the process."

"Will I die in the process?"

"Only if you see me die first."

"How rich?"

"You keep all the money, Paolo. I want nothing but to go home and live a simple life."

"So Raissa still has her wits about her."

"Oh yes, my old friend."

"What happens first?"

"Your vault holds every shot…even the ones we denied. We begin by finding your favorites. Then you discretely gather your best lighting, makeup, hair and computer artists to the studio. Tell them anything. Tell them you've got a fresh, hot discovery. Swear them to secrecy. Then we go to work making today's Raissa look like yesterday."

Zabban's eyes widened. Excitement lifted him out of the low-slung beach chair. "Except the scars. You're going to let me prove to the world scars don't define beauty. Oh you wonderful, courageous girl. Every magazine, all the television people, newspapers...they'll line up like lemmings."

"As long as I stay alive. There'll always be something to keep you on edge."

***

Khalid bin Rahman's charter operator utilized experience and skill in transporting him to Montreal's Pierre Elliott Trudeau Airport. From there, as a Canadian citizen with a valid passport, he hired a taxi to drive, without interference by US law enforcement, across the Canada/US border to the airport in Clinton County, New York. A single engine air taxi completed the trip to Atlantic City. No bribery or complicated trickery was involved.

Aaron Frankel watched the small, innocuous plane approach his jet. Full marks for chutzpah were mentally awarded Khalid, who, among the most wanted and feared men on the planet, walked across twenty yards of airport tarmac alone and unguarded.

Bin Rahman wore a nondescript suit, adopted a suitable haircut and shaved his mustache. Altogether he looked a shadow of the fierce, warlike terrorist the western press made him out to be. He chose a seat immediately opposite Frankel. Offered his hand while studiously ignoring men with guns sitting less than five feet behind.

Not friends, not in any conformed definition of the term, these two were products of shared experience. From different cultures, they were unconcerned with what made them dissimilar.

Bound by the purity of risk and reward, they each held a unique view of the other's accomplishments. Vocal anaesthesia wasn't employed when they discussed business. "Greetings Aaron. You've no doubt prepared for this day."

"From the day a client grants me the privilege of investing his money, the half-life of the relationship begins its measure. Your accounts await any instructions you've prepared."

Nothing less than written, executed and witnessed instructions would carry weight. No verbal direction, e-mail or Fax would suffice. They'd agreed as much on day one.

"Are you curious, Aaron?"

Frankel was much more than curious. He fought the urge to scream out his response, while keeping silent for several moments before saying, "No more than *you* should be, for dissolution of our venture is mutually warranted."

"Well then, for my part a drone targeted me in the desert outside Dubai." Bin Rahman changed tone from serious to amused. "It made quite a hit in the British tabloids. I can't tell you where things have gone wrong, but cutting off the snakes' heads is my answer. In a week, there'll be no one left in the US acting on my behalf."

Frankel made an instantaneous election; he wouldn't hand a certain buff-colored envelope to the Sheikh. Questions would evolve into a lengthy discussion, full of pitfalls: Where did the photos come from; how had they been acquired; how long had they been in his possession? Outside the fiduciary responsibility for the management of Khalid's assets, Aaron Frankel held no obligation. *In a week, there'll be no one left*—those were the operative words. *No one* was all-inclusive. So Aaron Frankel didn't show the photos of Billy Ray Balfour, in a tuxedo, picking up a gun left in the British Embassy library by Sir Edward Poynter.

Instead he said, "Would you like to review your accounts? The plane is equipped with wireless and I can give you a précis of the most significant of recent trades made on your behalf."

"I'll review everything over the next few days, but thank you for offering."

Bin Rahman handed Frankel a delicately wrapped box which, when opened, revealed a gold bracelet. On the inside were a series of engravings in Arabic.

Frankel's response was straightforward. "It's a lovely token. I'll treasure it. Could you tell me what the inscription says?"

"Give bread dough to the baker even if he eats half." Two men laughed and shared tea.

Khalid bin Rahman returned to the Cessna.

Aaron Frankel shivered in the jet's warmth.

CHAPTER 27

Caroline Poynter Panero stood on Fulton Bennett's front doorstep suffering a cold sober case of butterflies. Every contradictory thing she wanted to say banged inside her head. Pithy ripostes they were, prepared over years as Fulton popped-up in imagination at the most ungraceful of times: Her mother's funeral; her wedding day; and during the birth of her first child. Or on any of the days she'd have preferred to be dead than without him.

She'd prepared for this moment.

Our love was an altar, and I the one sacrificed. Our love was about his needs and my desires. Needs and desires were far from the same thing. I've suffered. *Sticks and stones may break your bones, but words can never hurt you*—wasn't true. The entire malarkey people force-fed you about being better off without someone—was a fabrication. I never doubted where I belonged—in your arms.

Did you doubt? Or were you purchased? Why would you go away quietly? Why not fight for me?

All these years I locked you away deep inside of me. Were you comfort or cancer? I've been lonely. Afraid. I've given the best of me for so little in return. Tomorrow I'll be sad and blue. But I shan't forget to say to you what you forgot to say to me: I love you, Fulton.

When he opened the door, her mind an unruly mess, she said none of those things.

Bennett stood unmoving, hands at his side, dumbstruck for the first time in memory. Eyes clouded, the best he could muster was, "Hello Caroline." Suspicious eyes darted beyond her to the driveway.

Satisfied, they returned to her, adoration no longer present.

Caroline found bits of a Lewis Carroll poem, a favorite in times of childhood tribulation. "The time has come, the Walrus said, to talk of many things…of shoes and ships and sealing-wax…and why the sea is boiling hot and whether Pigs have wings."

He held the door aside and dredged-up enough composure to say, "Come in, please."

As they walked through the foyer into the living room, Caroline admired dozens of details restored by hundreds of hours of hand labor. This was a side of Fulton she'd never known. Or were wallpapers, color-schemes, sconces, moldings and hardware the product of another woman?

"It looks like you're nearing the finish line, Fulton."

"No, I'll work another ten years."

Her face expressed confusion.

As realization struck, he made amends. "You mean the house, of course. It's been a marathon, but I'm pleased."

He offered her the cushy sofa and took its twin loveseat, both pieces returned from an upholsterer who took two months salary as ransom. The last of sunset's reflection shone through trees without leaves, and fell with elegance on the mantel and brass of the fireplace.

"Can I get you tea, Caroline? I have Harrods."

"I'd prefer whiskey."

There was no door to the kitchen. She heard him ask, "Ice?"

"Straight up, thank you. Where's your woman friend this evening?"

Glasses in hand, he answered, "There's no woman, Caroline. There's Anne, who's an expensive forensic restoration artist. Thank you for the compliment, though. I'll mention it to Anne when she comes back for the photography session. Not quite what you're doing with the family castle." Bennett smiled warmly to reassure her.

"Every project is meaningful in its own way. The result is lovely." Caroline thought of dainty lady's teas and meaningless drivel exchanged in pretend conversations. Of couples waltzing without romance. She didn't want drivel, not today. Just the romance.

"How close did you come to killing me with your drones?"

He could protest. Tell her of his house arrest. But she knew already, didn't she?

"There was no launch."

"Was it you who saved me?"

"No, I wouldn't have. Couldn't have." His voice dropped lower. "I think you know how it works."

Real pain ripped through her. For she did know how it worked. "You would have, if you could've?"

Bennett tasted the truth and spewed it back. "Yes, damn this whole mess." Neither needed further discussion of *this whole mess*.

"Grover called it off?"

Bennett raised his eyebrows in a movement which said: *The President called it off.* Presidents make every decision regarding the fate of men like bin Rahman.

"Grover likes playing every position on the Pitch, Fulton. Be careful of him."

Grover Norris wasn't worthy of words. "How are your children?"

"I'm a shitty mother. We needn't sugar coat a true flaw." She tossed the rest of her drink down in a single gulp. "Are you civil with Nadine?"

"No." Better to leave that door closed.

"Would you have been sad...if the drone launched?"

No answer forthcoming, none of this was why she'd come.

Tired of the games, she said, "I never stopped loving you. All the mistakes I've made with men, since you left, I never stopped. I'm going home, Fulton. I'm going home to find peace, to be a mother, to take care of my father. All the things I've never done." She went to him, curled up on his lap and said, "I just needed to tell you."

He wanted to believe, so stroked her hair.

They began to talk in the way lovers do, when separated too long

***

No residual doubt lingered in Nasha's mind: Fulton Bennett was the likeliest, missing, piece to talk about events at the *Ritz*. I'm almost one of his employees, after all.

Rush hour over, poise falling as fast as a faulty soufflé, GPS showed the address a mile on the right.

***

Could we vanish like magicians, put our devils and a deep blue sea behind us? Would the devils look? What would they find?

Fulton's hand lingered on her breast. Soon enough they'd find their way upstairs to a world where love would be forever, where they could lie motionless in its flame, where the past wouldn't haunt them, where what might've been might still be possible.

She purred.

Within the house he rebuilt, all ordinary sounds of expansion and contraction, of central heating and the wind's intrusion, of hopes and dreams, all those things retreated leaving a man and a woman content with what they'd regained.

When contentment shattered, Fulton Bennett died.

In one terrible, swift, motion, the garrote's wire encircled Bennett's neck. Connected to two wooden handles, the military style ligature pulled tight in a continuous motion. Knees braced against the back of the loveseat, the attacker threw his full weight backwards to add force to a brutal assault.

Caroline screamed. Rolled onto the floor. Disbelief in control, she watched for a fragment of a moment, screamed again and ran for the front door.

The assassin pulled tighter and tighter until he felt the thin wire cut through the windpipe. Wooden handles released from gloved hands, he returned to the rear door in no apparent hurry.

Upon hearing screams Langley's duty officer, monitoring Bennett's home for CIC, ordered a security team to the residence. Half an hour was an optimistic estimate of their ETA.

Nasha pulled into Bennett's driveway in time to hear Caroline's second scream. Headlights pointed at the front door, she reached for the Glock and circled behind her car and to its right. Crouched low, she knelt as Caroline appeared barefoot, blouse unbuttoned to the waist, in the full flight of panic.

More sounds of skidding tires and more lights settled at a skewed angle to Nasha's vehicle. Grace Crowell yelled, "Caroline Poynter…over here…British Security Service. Caroline…run to my voice."

Caroline began to comply, when she realized who it was aiming a semi-automatic pistol at her. Frozen, Caroline stopped to ask Nasha an absurdity.

"Why are *you* here?"

***

Billy Ray Balfour, born Ian McAlister on the west coast of Scotland, maneuvered into position less than five minutes after Caroline's arrival.

Much of his background, as told to Khalid bin Rahman, was accurate. Out of uniform, and out of Britain almost ten years, he crossed the line between lawful and outlaw so many times its existence became theoretical and pointless.

One did what was ordered, or didn't.

One lived or died according to a personal code matching his government's needs incidentally, not as an article of faith.

Priority one was the safety of Minister Sir Edward Poynter's daughter, Caroline. Priority two was maintaining a position near the center of bin Rahman's US operation to feed unique intelligence to Her Majesty's Secret Services.

Billy Ray fixated on extracting Caroline, crazy diva that she was. By his standards, Caroline's brand of hedonism deserved what it deserved. In his fixation, he hadn't the slightest knowledge who entered the rear of Bennett's home and, if he told the truth, no concern whether Fulton Bennett was alive or dead. Cold calculation prevailed: Entering the house in the aftermath was pure, distilled, stupidity.

Billy Ray was aware of Nasha Poynter thirty yards to his right. Heard Grace's car stop and her voice entreat Caroline to keep running. With so many variables to process, a fourth vehicle entered the driveway unnoticed. He couldn't have hoped to be aware of the black clad figure seventy-five yards to the rear of the house.

The fog of war thickened.

Dozens of times salvation was a byproduct of a heightened sixth-sense. More a feeling than hearing the man behind him, a tenth of a second's warning was the difference between an arm pressuring the carotid artery and a knife threatening his abdomen. Kill or die, Billy Ray reacted with sufficient vehemence to avoid becoming a victim.

***

Yusef was deeply resentful of a turncoat: Data in Jamie Norris's burn bag made such an accusation irrefutable. The episode with Lippman and the spilled coffee had proved worth its risk. With hindsight, Yusef was certain Billy Ray killed Hassan and disposed of his unconsecrated body, a crime equal to the murder itself.

No Sheikh was needed to order Billy Ray's death.

Yusef was unaware the entirety of the Sheikh's US operations were being withdrawn—with the singular exception of Yusef, himself. He sought any opportunity to balance the scales, even one which lacked the benefits of pre-planning. When Fathima asked him to accompany Fakhir, as a test of Yusef's commitment to Hassan's cause, he'd agreed without hesitation.

None of bin Rahman's operatives knew Yusef's true role.

Neither Fathima nor the Swiss nor any of them understood he penetrated their cell looking for the double agent now revealed as Billy Ray. Yusef's compulsion to take Billy Ray's life for Hassan's life dominated conscious thought.

***

From where their stolen car was abandoned, the two hiked several miles on back roads and through multi-acre properties of the wealthy. Fakhir's backpack proved no burden for a marathon runner. When asked what it contained, Fakhir became dismissive.

"You're a needless parasite, whose height will make us memorable."

By mid-afternoon they were hidden in place. Tea emerged from a thermos in Fakhir's backpack. Bread and cheese as well. They observed the arrival of Billy Ray and how he made himself disappear in the wooded area off the driveway. Observed Caroline's hesitation at the front door. Waited with patience and prayer. Fakhir moved with silent ease as he began an approach to the rear of the house. His last words established their rendezvous point, where they'd gather afterwards to return to DC.

***

Now Yusef began a wide circle which would end at Billy Ray's position. Janbiya in hand, years of discipline struggled to retard petulant actions. His approach thwarted, Yusef's left arm and shoulder throttled not the throat of his enemy but his chin and head. Grunts of pain were no sign of hypoxia.

Blade blunted by body armor, Billy Ray's right hand held Yusef's wrist in a relentless grip. Both men struggled. Neither gained advantage. In attrition, Yusef's leverage would lose to Billy Ray's strength.

Through clenched teeth, a Highland Scots accent whispered. "You're a strapping lad, and Bennett must think you a proper wonder, but you've not the stomach for this kind of killing."

Reserves of power applied, Billy Ray bent Yusef's wrist so the curved dagger fell away. He yelled to Grace. "MI-6 here...shoot this bastard."

Confusion enveloped all those present. Any re-telling would never present a coherent picture.

Caroline crouched, hidden in Grace's backseat.

Grace heard the shorter man, of the two vying for control of a knife, plead for assistance in a Scottish accent. His claim of being MI-6 taken at face value, she raised her weapon and fired twice at the taller man.

Anguished by Yusef's actions—could the tall, angular man be anyone but her brother—Nasha aimed at the shorter man and fired three times in what she believed to be a tight group. Then stood upright in silent anguish.

Automatic weapons fire began before Nasha fired a second time. Rounds struck Nasha's minivan, Grace's car and rained destruction against the FBI vehicle. Battlefield sounds produced the women's first conscious understanding: Nasha and Grace were no longer in control or on the offensive.

Gainey and Madison called for backup as the struggle between Billy Ray and Yusef tumbled out of the woods onto a grassy slope lit by secondary glare from six headlamps. Their pistol rounds were no threat to the heavier automatic weapon. Seconds after the automatic weapon ceased firing, neither Yusef nor Billy Ray was visible from the driveway.

With a chance to breathe, Madison heard the *whumpf, whumpf, whumpf* of helicopter blades thrashing cold air. Saw Gainey on the ground, blood pooling beneath. Within a minute, a searchlight scanned the scene and an amplified voice instructed everyone on the ground to cease and desist from hostilities. Two machine guns, manned by helmeted and armored men, emphasized the demand.

Nasha walked twenty paces to where Grace shielded her eyes from the spotlight's brilliance. Grace's voice was hoarse. "What the hell just happened?"

***

Mannheim was the Agency's lead on-scene executive in the aftermath, though dozens of Agency officers occupied the grounds, if not Bennett's home.

Summarily told to wait in the mobile command center established by Fairfax County police, Fulton Bennett's body was on its way to the Virginia's Medical Examiner in Manassas before Detective Arthur Scolen got around to Zachary Mannheim.

"So...Mr. Mannheim." Scolen bit into a stale club sandwich left for him by his partner. "Why don't you tell me who Fulton Bennett was, and why someone nearly sliced his head off with a wire ligature."

Mannheim took a deep breath and exhaled. "After you update me on where we stand, Detective."

Scolen didn't take the retort as a good sign.

"Fairfax County officers, in trying to sort who did what to whom, found themselves hip deep in a shit-storm...ergo good old boy Arthur Scolen drawing the short straw. I can list some things we've learned in no particular order. FBI Agent Madison described an unidentified woman, who left the scene together with an MI-6 agent and unidentified male number one. Unidentified male one had been in a serious altercation with unidentified male 2, who may have been wounded and whose whereabouts remain unknown. FBI agent Gainey, suffering a GSW to the upper right chest, leads the list of bodily damage. Mrs. Caroline Panero, a British citizen, was eventually identified by Mrs. Nasha Poynter, her sister-in-law. Mrs. Poynter, an American citizen working for the Lebanese Embassy, stated she was on the premises in an attempt to meet with Mr. Bennett about a diplomatic matter. Mrs. Poynter further stated she fired three shots in an attempt to prevent either unidentified male from killing the other. Mrs. Poynter's weapon was taken into evidence by my cops, who also noted extensive damage to all three vehicles; dozens of shell casings were found in the rear yard, littering the ground where unknown male 3 fired on everyone in the front yard."

Mannheim closed his eyes and gathered himself. "Thank you, Detective. Bennett served the Central Intelligence Agency as Deputy Director of the National Clandestine Service. As to why he was killed, I refer you to his position in the Agency."

Un-fucking believable. It was Scolen's turn to exhibit signs of incredulity. "You're telling me..."

"Yes, detective. In the vernacular, Mr. Bennett would be referred to as this country's top spy."

"With respect...who are you?"

"I work in counter-intelligence, Detective Scolen. That's all I'll be able to share."

Scolen leaned back and observed a guy who wasn't the physical reincarnation of a super-spy. "You're important?"

"It rather depends on whom you ask. But for your purposes, yes, I'm a big cheese."

"You could send me to Gitmo?" As a form of surrender, the question was nicely played.

"Oh, for a man of your background we'd find somewhere less mindful of beaches and umbrella drinks."

"Would you like to make a recommendation on this shit?"

"Mr. Bennett's favorite aphorism was *Do your job*. You'll be best served by exhibiting considerable patience. Things will work themselves out, but not anytime soon."

Scolen, bright and hard working, needed and wanted more than vague patty cake. "Maybe you could tell me a couple of things to do...and not to do. You know...so I can do my job."

"Well, let's see. Focus on the assassin's automatic weapon. We'd all be well served by his apprehension. Leave everyone else till you catch the killer...their presence was peripheral, I assure you."

Scolen had fox terrier in his personality, so he decided to bite Mannheim's hand then hang on for dear life. "This Caroline Poynter Panero...and Nasha Gemayel Poynter...is it a coincidence they share the name Poynter?"

Mannheim's accent leapt from his words. "I'll save you the *Google* search, Detective. One is the daughter, and the other is the daughter-in-law of Sir Edward Poynter, who is the titular head of all Britain's Security Services."

Head spinning, Scolen gripped the simplest explanation which leapt to mind. "So maybe Princess Caroline's having a bit of slap and tickle with your head spy. Maybe the Arab woman comes to save the family from shame...or Sir Muckety Muck doesn't like any of it and sends James Bond to break it up permanent like. Miles off the mark, or what?"

Mannheim showered Scolen with his finest look of appreciation. "Not miles, Detective. Not miles at all. But not close either. If all the answers were in hand, neither of us would need speculation. I'll admit, your brand of speculation may be useful within the narrow focus of your investigation. But any appearance of it in the media would be counterproductive. This is, after all, the first time in the Agency's history a serving officer of this rank has been assassinated within the United States. Could we agree as a guiding principle...leaks would be unfortunate?"

"Got a business card, Mr. Mannheim?"

"No, Detective Scolen, but the Agency's phone is listed on its web site."

***

Everything Yusef believed about a man's ability to control his actions was tested. He'd no memory of how many shots were fired or who'd fired them, but one round went through-and-through his lower right shoulder. Hurled backwards by the impact, he never hesitated before stumbling in the direction of the meeting point.

Once there, Fakhir told him, "Keep up or I'll leave you."

Yusef never debated the small marathoner's willingness to keep his promise; he employed agony to maintain his stride. Each time loss of consciousness threatened, Yusef accelerated. Although the temperature dropped through the low forties, he stripped off his shirt to crudely wrap both sides of the wound. Maintained a one-yard gap despite Fakhir's punishing pace.

Time lost its meaning.

When lights of a strip mall came into focus, Fakhir sprinted towards a waiting limousine.

Yusef was alone, bleeding seriously from efforts expended to escape. He'd managed to find his janbiya after being shot, but now dropped it in a public trash receptacle; its loss would forever serve as a lesson. Comforted by a seldom-carried phone, he called Gavriel Rabin, gave him GPS coordinates and requested a bag with necessary items be dropped behind the restaurant.

Conflict existent in Gavriel's voice, Yusef felt the hurt in unstated questions and said nothing through the hush of the older man's disappointment.

Crouched behind a dumpster, Yusef observed a dark pickup truck brake to a crawl. A door opened. An arm placed a gym bag on the pavement. Without slowing further, the truck continued until its lights faded.

Stripped to underwear, Yusef soaked both sides of the wound with disinfectant and wrapped gauze over, around and across his front and back until mummified. Added multiple rolls of tape to secure his amateurish handiwork. Dressed in a tracksuit from high school, he stuffed the delivery bag with blood soaked clothes. Added shoes, and the phone absent its SIM. Emptied a bottle of disinfectant into the bag and tossed it in the dumpster to join decaying restaurant waste.

With the new phone he called a cab. Three hundred in twenties allowed him to use two cabs and two buses to make it home, where he passed out after forcing himself to drink a quart of Papaya juice.

***

Ian McAlister recognized the pain and shortness of breath; more than two and possibly three or four ribs were broken.

Nasha's first shot missed into the trees, but the second and third, separated by less than eight inches, slammed into his vest. He'd hobbled to Grace's car and collapsed in the front passenger seat.

"Who are you?" Grace asked without tolerance.

Every irregular bit of pavement on the poorly maintained County road brought misery. McAlister's reply took serious effort. "Best if you concentrate on getting us to the Embassy."

Grace's face bled from flying glass; her sympathy level emerged in a raised voice. "You'd better turn out to be the fucking Archbishop of Whitehall…not some tosser."

"Don't talk gobshite, missy…I'm the slapper's official babysitter." He pointed into the backseat.

Caroline Panero stared into oblivion and wouldn't speak.

***

The question issued from D/CIA Granholm and was aimed at Grover Norris, DD/CIA, Zachary Mannheim and Jamie Norris. Forty minutes of discussion preceded the question, but the elephant in the room neither moved or offered an opinion: Had Edward Poynter authorized Fulton Bennett's execution?

"Why don't we call the son-of-a-bitch and ask him? Plain and simple. Right now."

Grover answered with a groan. "Because, if you whip your dick out in public, someone's liable to bite it off."

DD/CIA chimed in without humor. "Speaking from past experience, eh?"

Jamie thought the big-boys were jumping the rails. "Don't do it, sir." He addressed D/CIA, not his father. "There's not a single piece of intelligence suggesting motive. We should accept what anyone with a digital device knows: Khalid bin Rahman ordered Bennett's assassination as retribution for the aborted drone attack. Tough to admit the Agency could be victimized…but it happened. We should provide extra security to each of you."

DD/CIA offered what he considered the strongest argument. "Does anyone here think Edward would put his flesh and blood in the middle of such a thing? On purpose? Pretty amazing Caroline Panero's not in the morgue."

Jamie preferred not to amplify the guesses and theories, but this was his chance to add value to career ambitions. "Caroline Poynter has a lengthy list of lovers in her past, including Aaron Frankel. There've been rumors linking her with bin Rahman. Maybe bin Rahman is cleaning house. Maybe Caroline should have been victim number two."

Grover said facetiously, "Maybe she was the principle target of her pissed-off husband."

CHAPTER 28

A green-screen dominated a low ceilinged studio where reality was transformed into Surreality. Assistants scurried every which way to serve their artist masters.

Unappeased, Raissa raised her voice.

"Don't you see, Paolo, if I could tell you which one killed Gunther, I'd have hung him or her by their thumbs...until it suited me to skin him or her alive."

Paolo scowled in front of a storyboard where his mangled creation was a shadow of its former glory. Raissa's crusade, if allowed to bulldoze creative license, would have no less than a battalion of demons. He ripped down the sketches and turned to her in frustration.

"There are too many. All the oomph flies out the window with so many villains. You will lose your audience, my sweet, dear, girl. And if you lose the audience, need I remind you..."

Raissa squirmed under the makeup artist's attention. Her evil mood wasn't improved under hot lights designed to improve even a heavenly appearance.

Paolo threw an empty plastic bottle in her direction. "So ill-tempered Raissa should guess. I promise you, Ms. Stubborn Cow, Paolo will have no more than four demons in his video."

In a darkened corner of the room, enveloped by computer monitors racked one upon the other, an older Director stood behind a young savant, whose fingers flew across a keyboard. In ten minutes the teen turned to his father for approval.

The Director's drooping mustache raised into a grin, he squeezed the boy's shoulder in agreement.

Plunged into darkness, where the green-screen had seemed out-of-place an eight-foot high Raissa-at-eighteen emerged. From Paolo's vault came images lovingly created and repeatedly denied. Platinum blonde hair, high cheekbones in no need of enhancement, dark eyebrows in solitary contrast, eyes on fire and lips apart in amazement, she stood with arms stretched high, barefoot on tiptoes—a goddess imitating a ballerina, an alabaster sculpture in the flesh, who pirouetted in slow motion and offered the observer a shy, girlish smile. As the screen was subsumed by glowing, consumptive coals, four hooded demons, faces clear and identifiable, contorted in twisted pleasure. From the fire's embers Raissa rose anew, an older vision in the same form, adorned by bright red lips, nails and toes. She turned more slowly so scars of lost innocence stood out, yet, somehow, failed to subtract from her appeal. She rotated twice before words erupted in haunting script: *Raissa Resurrected - I Will Destroy My Demons.*

Paolo spoke with a master's emphasis. "Bravo Arturo. Bravo Javier. When music is added, it will be more than perfect...as long as we do something about those sagging boobs."

Twenty people in the studio clapped and laughed. From his position behind Javier, Arturo the Director asked, "So Raissa, can you live with four demons? Three would be perfect."

"Bring them up one by one, please, Javier."

Paolo would have none of this. "Later, Javier. Her makeup will melt under the lights and I need to shoot stills. Raissa...poses, if you please...poses to make the world adore you."

Raissa Ribeiro threw off the sheet. Walked to the other side of the studio where clothes, shoes and additional trappings of a commercial venture awaited.

***

Andrew Poynter could see the pot of gold at rainbow's end.

Marco's technical presentation was a last run-up to the interactive simulation prepared by PaneroGlobal. An exchange of views related to ASW was under way.

A Capitão-de-mar-e-guerra (Captain of Sea and War) advocated for a comprehensive approach.

"Senhor Panero, isn't it true the best advantage comes from satellite-enabled links between space-based sensors and detection systems mounted on surrounding ships, subs, UUVs, aircraft, helicopters and UAVs? No single sensor platform provides all the answers. Each has its limitations, do they not?"

"Thank you, Captain Saldanha, for making my next point. PaneroGlobal believes current ASW thinking is stuck in the Cold War. American capabilities, for example, remain those deployed to prevail over the Soviets in a global, deep-water conflict. Newer concerns...like asymmetric diesel and advanced Air-Independent-Propulsion boats contribute to uncertainties which Brazilian submariners face today. Your naval proficiency declined in the last decade, merely by standing still. With new boats and new oil discoveries, you must reassess requirements and capabilities to meet an uncertain but still-dangerous threat. Let me repeat three fundamental ASW truths. First, ASW is a critical element of Brazil's strategies of sea control, power projection, and direct support of oil production. Second, ASW requires diverse capabilities...exactly as you say Captain...no single ASW system will produce acceptable results. You need undersea, surface, airborne, and space-based systems to ensure satisfactory performance. Third and most important today...ASW is expensive and requires years to build capability. I'm about to show you the most cost-effective way to be ready when your ocean-based oil reserves reach peak production."

Applause rang out.

"PaneroGlobal's software uses a vast database and proprietary algorithms to create computer-generated visualizations of underwater sound fields and propagation phenomena to develop operator intuition and greater understanding of sonar conditions and sensor effectiveness. All these systems are compatible with existing fixed, towed or drifting acoustic arrays as well as advanced sonar."

***

The aftermath of Fulton Bennett's execution was felt most in the underbelly of Intelligence agencies worldwide. On most days, leaked information was the lifeblood of capitol cities like Washington,

London, and Berlin. Not in this case. Leaks about Fulton Bennett's blatant execution would make the leaker radioactive.

"All prospective operations in Britain, the Middle-East, Africa and the entire Western Hemisphere are on hold until further notice. No exceptions. Make it work, people."

Jamie Norris hadn't agreed with Director Granholm's decision, but his objections carried minor weight against his father's full-throated support. As he ended his conference call with every NCS Station affected, he could see objections building at Langley. Over the next several hours, across half a dozen time zones, Jamie issued exemptions which would never be acknowledged and for which no record would be made.

***

"Sorry, Greg, you're to stand down. I've turned Madeleine around…don't want her on US soil right now. China is off limits. French submarines are off-limits. Acoustic profiles of submarines are off-limits. You don't see me winking or giving you any leeway to ignore this order. Got it?"

***

Zachary Mannheim turned out the lights and locked his office door.

Contemplation of the sort he wished for wasn't suited to light. He held the small recorder in his hand and repeatedly played one portion of his Connecticut meeting with Fulton Bennett. Rewound and played it again until the entirety of the recording was chewed into small bites and digested. Then he meticulously transcribed the recording onto a legal pad with his favorite fountain pen, loaded with a custom color ink between plum and black.

Mannheim doodled a perspective of six boxes, nested together next to the first notation: *I haven't had sex with anyone since Anne moved in.* Bennett made this claim in response to a question he resented—a question about Caroline Poynter Panero. Bennett answered for posterity, at least as posterity was represented by CIC. He told the whole truth while lying through his teeth, no mean feat. It lent credence to what Fulton told Caroline before he was killed: *There's no woman, Caroline.* Artwork expanded as Mannheim drew each box of the first three with their lids open: *Raissa Ribeiro...former girlfriend of Aaron Frankel. None of this would be happening, if she hadn't burned alive in her bed. Which itself is no accident in my book, especially since Grover ordered Raissa terminated.* Under broad strokes of Mannheim's fountain pen, a running figure fell, impaled by a spear.

Zachary arrived at an uncharitable conclusion: I'm a man who should've listened more carefully and worried less about—well, about everything a man worries about, when the inmates have assumed control over the asylum.

Unwelcome banging on the door forced Mannheim to cease his deliberations. "Go away." Mannheim returned to his recriminations.

No voice responded, but banging turned to pounding.

"I'll shoot you."

"Open the damn door, will you please." Greg Riley was out of sorts and out of options.

Door open, Mannheim remained an obstacle to entrance. Feet fixed to the floor, he said, "I opened the door as you requested. I'm busy. Go away."

"I'm selling secrets to the Chinese. I want to confess."

"You may well be a boor, Mr. Riley...excuse me, Dr. Riley...but not a very interesting one. Come in, if you must."

With his hands holding up his chin, and his elbows supporting his hands, Mannheim acted the part of an interested listener.

Greg got the message, but refused to be amused. "You're investigating Bennett's murder, correct?"

"CIC investigates what needs investigation, Dr. Riley. We're quite a lot like scientists in our mealy-mouthed fashion."

"So you know about Edward Poynter's son being arrested aboard a French nuclear sub."

Raised eyebrows notwithstanding, Mannheim lied. "Certainly."

"Needless to say, you know there's been a theft of acoustic signatures associated with the latest British nuclear subs."

"Doesn't everyone who owns a super-spy signet ring, know such things?"

"How about Andrew Poynter selling those acoustic signatures to Brazil?"

Mannheim relented, wearing a fresh-minted frown.

"There seem far too many Poynters lurking in Fulton's lurid past.

Would you agree, Dr. Riley?"

"Too many women in general, Mr. Chief Inquisitor."

"Which ones in particular?"

"Anne Linton for one. Raissa Ribeiro for another." Greg Riley was tired of the nonsense. "Listen...Fulton asked me to help. But now what can I do...he's dead and I'm a nerd."

"What kind of help did he ask for?"

"Go to Brazil and screw up whatever Andrew Poynter is doing...I think."

"You think?"

"Message was in book code...not much detail." Riley felt he should be cautious about revealing who Bennett suggested might help and who fit in the opposite category.

"Book code, indeed, Dr. Riley. How does a scientist know about book code?"

"My interests are eclectic." Riley wasn't about to review his Agency career with anyone from CIC.

"Well then, Olá Rio, when do you leave?"

"All Ops are holding...no travel. Haven't you heard?"

***

Nasha was suspended in stasis.

Work held no allure, if she was still employed under Nabil Hanna's regime. As if she would work under the auspices of a terrorist whose facial veil was in tatters.

Andrew was MIA, as her phone calls to England confirmed.

She was without a husband, could be a suspect in the Ritz-Carlton shooting and was embroiled in the investigation of Fulton Bennett's demise. She'd hidden Yusef's presence at the scene and told a transparent lie as to why she aimed three shots at a serving officer in MI-6. I'm a law abiding American, Nasha told herself, who has reason to suspect Yusef of terrible things.

She began to cry.

Miriam padded into the bedroom and sat on the floor. "Why are you crying? Are you sad?" A small girl began to rub the big girl's leg in a role reversal which broke her mother's heart.

"Yes, sweetie, Mummy's a little sad." Nasha reached down, picked her daughter up and landed Miriam on her knee. "I'll be okay now you're here to make it better."

"Is it because I yelled at the man?"

Nasha's nerves, tight as piano strings, escalated to near panic. "What man, Sweetie?" She could scarcely get the words out—her Glock sat in some police evidence locker.

"The man at the door...while you were in the shower...he told me to get my mommy. I told him to go away. Lucia said I shouldn't have yelled so loud. I'm sorry." Miriam collapsed in Nasha's arms, sobbing.

Miriam took minutes to soothe, during which every disastrous possibility streamed through an overheated imagination. Was it paranoia last night, asked the voice in her head, when you shot a British agent to save your brother the terrorist?

In the family room, Nasha asked Lucia. "Miriam said a scary man came to the door?"

Lucia glanced into the kitchen with obvious affection. "Big, gruff...not too experienced with little ones. Not scary, more like imposing. Came in one of those big, black SUVs. Gave me a card and wrote his number on the back."

Just a name: Zachary Mannheim. No company. No details. Nasha saw a cell phone prefix before the number. Not a Fairfax cop.

The house phone rang. Nasha watched Lucia answer and say Mrs. Poynter was unavailable.

"Who was it, Lucia?"

"Some woman claiming to be from the Post. She wanted to talk to you about the murder of some CIA big shot." Lucia's eyes conveyed no special interest.

Nasha established a firm grip on things she cared about—let the chaff fade into neglect. Being on-scene at Fulton Bennett's murder wasn't the worst of what would come, if the Media caught the scent of big-time scandal. Bennett's throat, sawn in half, qualified in every way.

***

Melissa Nichols stood in her kitchen screaming at the walls. "Holy shit. Holy shit. I can't believe this." She grabbed her phone.

When her husband answered, it took half a minute to figure out her scrambled demands. "Calm down, sweetheart. What do I need to see?"

"Raissa…on YouTube. Tom, you won't believe it. It's absolutely incredible."

Five minutes later, Lt. Tom Nichols listened as Agent Martin Haslett screamed epithets. "What the fuck, Nichols. What's she trying to do? You knew about this?"

Nichols waited for the rant to wind down. "I saw the video one minute before calling you. My wife says it's already viral…three million hits since it went on-line at six this morning. Who are they?"

Nichols meant: Who are the people shown as hooded demons, celebrating while Raissa burns?

"Working on it. What've you heard from Ribeiro, where is she?"

"Nada. Ask her friend Bennett."

Haslett ignored Nichols disingenuous reference. "I'm asking you. You're her go-to-guy."

"Ask Bennett…I'm in the middle of a seventeen car crash on the Mid-Cape."

"Is Cape Cod on another planet?"

"Come on, Haslett. What else?"

"Bennett was murdered last night…in his living room. D'you pay any attention at all? CIA's upside down."

***

Aaron Frankel pinpointed one of the demonic faces in Raissa's startling video: His own.

First, Khalid ends our relationship, setting in motion the closing of dozens of accounts and decimating my volume of business. Second, Fulton Bennett is murdered. Why do I think there's a connection to Khalid's conceited smile as we drank tea? Third, Raissa puts a bullseye on me, just as I tried to rebuild our relationship.

Aaron Frankel knew considerably more, but was unprepared to confront unpleasant probabilities. Absorbed with the bullseye superimposed on his face, self-preservation consumed him as he sought shelter in contingency plans.

***

Sir Edward Poynter's irritation knew no boundary.

Morning tea, one of his few reprieves from disagreeable events, went cold when the Home Secretary phoned with a word of warning.

Minutes later, the nasty little prig masquerading as the PM's chief deputy yanked Sir Edward's family jewels with undisguised pleasure. "Why is Caroline's face front and center among ghastly demons in the latest ugly piece of business on the Internet? It won't do to have a Chairman of the JIC making a family mess in public."

Edward watched Raissa's video a dozen times. Instructed analysts to ply their trade over every pixel, looking for data not apparent to the naked eye. Although difficult, he allowed himself to thank fate for delaying Ian McAlister's identification. Better tomorrow, or never, than right now.

After a discussion with McAlister's Chief at Six, he entered his club rather early for lunch. In the library, four senior Cabinet officials, dressed in variations on an identical pinstripe theme, gave the outward appearance of men off their feed. Drinks in hand, Sir Edward Poynter began a complex rebuttal which, if adequate dexterity could be applied, wouldn't deteriorate into outright prevarication. What Edward needed was a fixer. Regrettable though it might be, a fixer could be arranged. When finished speaking, he flicked away a stray piece of lint from his lapel.

***

Khalid bin Rahman appreciated the woman's audacity. Fashion and fashion models were none of his concern, and this self promotional enterprise would never have been brought to his attention absent Caroline's prominent presence. But the video itself was a brilliant stroke.

At first glance the video put PaneroGlobal in an undesirable position; Caroline was known to be the company's Vice Chairman.

Unwelcome irony intruded—pathetic Marco or brilliant Marco, Khalid's five hundred million Euro payday rested on which Marco showed up in Rio.

There was a silver lining; Billy Ray Balfour's appearance, in a video seen by most of the world, would end his career as spy and executioner. Khalid would sleep better in the bosom of such knowledge.

Caroline disappeared into reminiscence; Khalid wouldn't allow himself more than a momentary dalliance with regret.

Marco would, or would not, succeed in Brazil; Marco's best efforts were insured by an illogical, incomprehensible devotion to Caroline, a woman whose notoriety was now noxious.

Either way, Khalid could afford no further interest in, or desire for, a woman whose private qualities were eclipsed by this dazzling exposure as a deranged British bitch.

***

Kill her here, now, today—or send her to Beirut where a woman's disappearance attracted minor attention. Those were the two practical alternatives for dealing with Fathima Laniado. Nabil Hanna, Acting Lebanese Ambassador to the United States and Hezbollah apparatchik, gave himself less than a day before the decision must be made and carried-out.

Hanna believed Raissa the most desirable female he'd seen in the nude. What could've been the connection between Fathima and Raissa, one blonde and one raven-haired? Had they once been lovers? Enemies? Fathima certainly was more than she appeared. Nabil's curiosity and lust aroused, he was uncertain how to appease either.

***

Amazed and pleased were the primary emotions of David Nazarian—amazed at Raissa's willingness to make herself a target and pleased to be able to play offense after being so long on the defensive.

Nazarian ranked among very few who understood what Raissa intended to accomplish. A definitive identification of Gunther Probst's murderer, even if not in a court of American Juris Prudence, would end a nightmare brought by ill-conceived notions held by the Agency's establishment politicians.

***

Tiago the Lunatic counted ten thousand American dollars in well used banknotes no larger than a twenty. He suffered misgivings, if not outright mistrust. Cash acted as a superficial balm. Deeper foreboding persisted.

CIA Bastard Number 3 hadn't created the smallest fuss. When approached by an eleven year old in a blue and yellow pinafore which, in a past reincarnation had been a bedroom curtain, he passed the envelope, took the scrap of paper in return, and re-entered the Consulate without a word. Such trusting behavior was enough to make a man born in the favelas chary about future transactions. For now, Tiago pledged to keep all CIA Bastards, regardless of their numeral, tightly under his gang's thumb.

***

Bryson Sewell and Yusef Schwartz, complete strangers, shared information critical to anyone associated with Gunther Probst or Fulton Bennett, both now deceased. While the twosome had never met, on one occasion they shared a meal at different tables. Between them all four demons in Paolo Zabban's creation were familiar.

Sewell couldn't know his face had been omitted by no more substantial thread than Raissa's instinct. Even so, Bryson was grateful to be unidentified, in possession of his mental faculties and alive. Bryson had, on the fateful day, been invited to lunch in Boston by Fathima Laniado of the Lebanese Embassy's intelligence staff. In offhanded fashion he'd commented on Aaron Frankel's appearance at a neighboring table. More important to Bryson, at Fathima's urging he was delighted to discuss Frankel's position as banker to Khalid bin Rahman—and how Sewell's employer, Grover Norris, under a certain set of circumstances, could replace Frankel.

Laniado probed the upper limit of Sewell's appetite to manage money from bin Rahman's interests in the Middle East. Statistical results and investment strategies were reviewed. Altogether, Bryson Sewell left the luncheon on the edge of elation. Money was apolitical, he believed. Vast sums held no political views and were unconcerned with the national interests of any sovereign nation.

This morning Fathima was a Lebanese demon connected to a former super-model and three associate-demons. Her association with Frankel and Sheikh bin Rahman branded Fathima a terrorist in today's bright lights.

Today the media trumpeted the identity of a British demon, Caroline Poynter Panero, without identifying her as Frankel's luncheon companion and likely lover.

Sewell remembered the demon who escorted Fathima Laniado from the restaurant. The man in the sensational video and the man from Legal Seafoods were one and the same—a man Bryson Sewell would prefer not to meet in a close encounter. Bryson examined what action he might take as it concerned Frankel, Panero, Laniado aka demon 3, Laniado's associate aka demon 4 and himself—all dependent upon Khalid bin Rahman for economic prosperity.

CHAPTER 29

Pink strands of light pushed into the sky, harbinger of an early winter sunrise.

Right from wrong was no longer a significant distinction; differentiating among moral certitudes was a job for simpletons and patriots. Whether a batter adjusted from pitch to pitch, prepared to hit the breaking ball or high cheese, was his lasting measure as a ballplayer not a man. Amidst analysis of earned distinction versus moral imperative, a simpler question ground away at Mannheim's conscience: Can events change the valence of a man's past?

He walked past the Reflecting Pool towards the Lincoln Memorial, calm exterior a poor indicator of emotional turmoil. Neither the location nor the time of his choosing, Mannheim took note of a homeless man tightly curled on a bench. Shrugged his shoulders to free his mind of irrelevancies and turned up the collar of an ancient overcoat. Footsteps advanced on him. Only an exercise of will prevented him turning to meet fate. Passed by a man and dog, Zachary couldn't hear her approach.

"Mr. Mannheim?"

"Mrs. Poynter, good morning."

Nasha saw nothing good in any of this. "How would I know you're Zachary Mannheim? I've never seen a photograph."

"I'm responsible for counter-intelligence at Langley. We don't do class photos."

"You don't like women. Is it why you're unpleasant?"

Guilty as charged, Mannheim found it harder to push past personal history.

"If I'm unpleasant, Mrs. Poynter, it could be because you were firing your pistol like Annie Oakley moments after the Deputy Director of the National Clandestine Service was garroted. Reason enough, don't you think?"

Nasha stopped in her tracks.

Mannheim did the same, but stared off towards the Vietnam Memorial, refusing to meet her eye to eye.

"So you don't think much of me. You're not the first. I'm not a mind reader, what do you want?"

After a further pause, he turned and forced eye contact. "Do you consider yourself to be cooperating with the Agency?" Her face never changed expression. "In the matter of Aaron Frankel?"

Nasha showed her anger. "Get off your high horse. Ask something less accusatory."

Chastised, he said with a dollop more equanimity, "I'll try. Perhaps you'd tell me what you think of the video."

Brittle patience near fracture, exasperation colored her words. "What video?"

Startled, Zachary reverted to predictable form. "You must be the only female in existence who isn't glued to YouTube."

There was no hope with this man. She turned to walk towards the Metro.

At no other point in Mannheim's existence would he have run after a woman. Although he paid a steep price for letting a wife walk away, running after Marta might've brought her back, could've altered his pattern of emotional wreckage. In ten steps he caught Nasha, reaching out to touch the sleeve of her coat.

"Would you consider helping me?" He held out his phone with Raissa's video queued and waiting.

Nasha watched. Asked to see it a second time. Examined Mannheim in expectation of his next question.

"The demons...your husband's sister Caroline? And, of course, Mr. Frankel."

"Not at their best, but it's them."

"Are you aware Caroline and Fulton Bennett intended to marry, when she was twenty?"

"No."

"To the crux, Mrs. Poynter...would you describe Caroline as emotionally stable?"

"Such a loaded suggestion, Mr. Mannheim. Are you, or Sarah Gullickson, emotionally stable? You're the only Agency people I've spoken to outside social occasions. What's your working definition?"

"Would Caroline Poynter be capable of seeking the violent end of a man with whom she carried on a long-term, troubled, sexual relationship?"

Mannheim's question tore at an issue Nasha had long debated: Caroline's mental stability. "Caroline was promiscuous as a teen. She is unfaithful to her husband now. She loves her children for the most part. Caroline knows who she is and what she needs...and takes those things if she must. Those are Andrew's words, when we talk about Caroline. Does she care enough about her lovers to kill? No, I don't think so."

"How about Sir Edward, Mrs. Poynter? Does he care enough about his daughter to kill?"

Pictures from the British Embassy party flooded her mind: Sir Edward Bloody Poynter; an unknown, blandly handsome man in a tuxedo, whose face she just saw on Raissa's stunning video; and a gun in the British Embassy library.

"You're a senior member of a powerful security service. Tell me, how amoral are men of your ilk?"

***

Disinfectant, bandages and money from Gavriel brought Yusef only so far.

In the middle of the night, he went to the mosque where Ahmed and Fakhir prayed. Met at the front door, the Imam stood behind glass and wire mesh until satisfied Yusef was alone. At the point of collapse, Yusef allowed the Imam to assist him to the living quarters where a fearful, middle-aged man—had he truly been a doctor in Syria—examined the wound and surrounding joint structure. Absent anaesthetic, entrance and exit wounds were probed.

"You need blood..." the Syrian physician said "...and I haven't got blood. Bones are damaged where the bullet passed. How bad is it? I can't say without films. No sutures...let it weep. If it begins to bleed again, go to a hospital. Drink lots of water. No food or you'll be sick.

I can give you eight pills for pain…they're all I have."

***

Four pills stared back at Yusef. Could he gamble on buying more from the neighborhood drug dealers? None of this was good, he knew, not good at all. Involvement with unpredictable cretins would be the weakest among several moronic choices. Standing in the bathroom, the mirror pronounced its verdict: Death warmed over.

Call Gavriel a second time?

Papa had doctors at his beck and call: Doctors whose research funding, hospital expansion or a dozen other points of leverage would prevent them from seeing or hearing evil.

If Gavriel never told Papa.

Yusef called in sick. He prayed Billy Ray was incapacitated, because Billy Ray knew where he lived. Billy Ray possessed resources unavailable to a man whose existence was based in solitude.

The fact Billy Ray, in the throes of a life or death struggle, referred to Yusef as Bennett's Boy Wonder, hadn't yet registered.

***

Raissa attached the best of Gunther's photos, addressed the e-mail to Lt. Nichols in his capacity with the State Police and pressed *Send*. Her short note told Tom what most of the world surmised: Caroline Poynter Panero either had been, was or was about to be Aaron Frankel's lover. Without question Caroline was Frankel's luncheon companion. Without direct, personal, knowledge, Raissa accepted the second woman demon as Fathima Laniado. Laniado's luncheon partner caused Raissa to draw a blank. Raissa could provide no definitive information regarding the identity of the blonde man seated in the vicinity of Frankel's table.

***

Phyllis Martell agreed to the meeting on her own, accepting the risks of leaving Mannheim in the dark. By her logic, the meeting was a follow-up to Bennett's instructions.

Watch checked a final time, Haslett recognized time's passage as his worst enemy. If he delayed, his immediate bosses would roast him. If he failed to provide a heads-up to FBI executives, who expected advanced notice of politically sensitive events, higher-ups would post him to the Bureau's lush office in Islamabad.

Haslett answered Martell's unasked question. "Why did I let the entire Federal bureaucracy know what's happening inside the Probst inquiry...after Bennett warned me not to? Misplaced sense of duty, I guess. Now I'm street-meat for the vultures."

Martell's sympathy barely existed. "Exactly which vultures?"

Haslett moved on to more important items. "Bryson Sewell's the offspring of Congressman Jedediah Sewell. Jedediah will no more allow his first born to be skewered by association, than give up the House seat he's held for three decades. Jed Sewell's a politician's politician, a patriot...unafraid to bend Washington DC to his will."

"Back up, Haslett. What's Sewell got to do with Probst?" Phyllis was fully inoculated with Mannheim's manic focus on Probst's death, and any involvement by Bennett in his death. From Phyllis' vantage point, Sewell was outside her brief.

"Once Raissa's photos hit Senator Sewell's office, I'll have less than an hour."

"Come on Haslett, slow down a second. What photos?"

"I just forwarded the entire world an e-mail I got from Tom Nichols...photos attached. One shows Bryson Sewell at a table with Fatima Laniado...very near Frankel. Bryson Sewell works at Grover Norris's investment bank...connect the dots. Figure it out, Phyllis...they'll take me off this case and toss me overboard. Wish I'd listened to Bennett. How any of this identifies Probst's killer eludes me." Haslett's mind wandered. "Maybe you should interview Raissa Ribeiro."

Despite each having been hung out to dry, Phyllis laughed. "More than half the world's lining up to interview Raissa."

***

Anne Linton suffered from being thrice abandoned by Fulton Bennett. Too aware of the third's finality, it was the second which left her examining a way forward.

She'd met Fulton in mundane circumstances: He wanted to restore his rundown colonial; she was a restoration artist. He checked her references and walked through homes where her work spoke for itself. More than three months passed before he approached, opaquely at first, hinting at his occupation. At the six-month mark, they reached the point in recruitment where the conscript enrolled or walked away forever.

Anne hadn't been lured with false promises: Serving her country was a sufficient reward. Unrequited though it was, falling in love one day at a time was pleasant in the peaches-and-cream freshness of the experience. But after she spirited Fulton and the hard drives away from the Agency's grasp, a bitter aftertaste overpowered her. The final straw was bringing Greg Riley into Bennett's long-running, fruitless conspiracy.

Now Fulton was dead.

Did an old-fashioned concept—obligation to country—exist any longer? Was walking away without consequences possible? Only two others knew what she'd done. Like an Ostrich, her primal reaction was to stick her head in the sand.

***

Telephone in hand, Greg Riley hesitated. To discount ethics was a slippery slope. What's my responsibility? Are scientists a fraternity of loosely knit conspirators, or independent contractors with an inferiority complex?

Am I so angry at Bennett's passing, so disturbed by the wondrous simpleton occupying his office, and so pissed at the world I've allowed woods and trees to merge into sodden masses of pulp?

Screw it, he thought, waiting for Jonas to answer his cell. Jonas Olesen, nuclear physicist for hire, was the only person Greg knew at a high scientific level in Brazil.

"Jonas…Greg Riley in Virginia, how are you?" Olesen believed Riley a computer scientist at the University of Virginia.

"Greg, I'm very busy just now. Could I phone another time, please?"

"Hang on Jonas, it's important. Do you know anyone senior in submarine command?"

"Odd question, but yes?" Even with the poor connection, suspicion came across loud and clear.

"Look Jonas…I've no one else to tell. Brazil's navy is buying sophisticated data and software related to anti-submarine warfare. I believe the software is flawed. I'd like to warn someone in authority."

"I'll think it over. Goodbye, Greg." Icicles wouldn't have been colder than Jonas' inflection.

Greg's e-mail pinged with notice of Fulton Bennett's funeral.

***

Premonitions were tricky for field operatives, easily as tricky as initiative. After twenty years reading faces and learning the difference between spending money or blood, one truth stood out: There's no limit to a human's ability to rationalize the truth.

David Nazarian watched Raissa's original video a hundred times in a hundred places. Now he watched its successor. Arms outstretched, hands nailed by grotesque spikes, feet positioned one on top of the other, Raissa looked down on a muscled figure nailing her feet to a cross, highlighted by blood-red toenails. Beside her executioner lay a man's body, wrapped in white burial cloth, surrounded by three helpers holding hammers.

The cadaver's face turned to the camera, revealing itself: Fulton Bennett.

David's premonition wasn't pretty.

He'd received a coded text putting Raissa's kill-order on hold.

It was the nature of a spy's life: Send an incomprehensible message to a Field Officer, then blame the poor bastard for failing to understand. In the world of executions, terminations or eliminations, there was no such thing as a *Hold*. What the message really meant was: Success has many fathers; failure is an orphan.

***

Grover Norris glanced at his phone's screen: Mannheim for the third time.

Appended to e-mail from an ally in the Justice Department, Grover scrutinized its attachments a fourth time.

"Hello Zach, what can I do for you?"

"Are you concerned with Raissa's second video, Grover? Your

kill-order on Raissa might have been hasty."

"Fuck you, Zach, she's as likely as anyone to have murdered Gunther Probst."

"Do you think it likely Sewell's name becomes enmeshed with Aaron Frankel's reputation, or god forbid, Sheikh bin Rahman's money?"

"What would you suggest, Zach?"

Any backlash would end Grover's influence within POTUS's administration and carte blanche at Langley. Grover, Mannheim decided, had no idea Jamie's Hold had been issued.

"The outcome might be out of your hands. Raissa's termination order was an error of commission. Bennett, you'll remember, preached caution, urging us all to let events unfold before jumping over cliffs."

"Damn Bennett to hell."

"Yes, Grover, where we'll join him in the executive washroom one fine day."

***

More people were crowded into the small suite of offices than ever intended by the builders of Almirante Castro e Silva, Mocangue Island, Rio de Janeiro, where the Brazilian Navy operated a flotilla of five Tupi-class diesel submarines.

Admiral Eduardo de Almeida Jobim presided.

"Even pretenders, like Venezuela, believe submarines provide parity between navies. Brazil's Scorpènes will not be radically different from their sister-ships in other countries. One day soon, our nuclear attack boats will equal, but are unlikely to exceed, the capabilities of super-powers. What we begin today will enable us to defend our natural resources, our coast...Brazil's navy will be no whipping boy."

Cheers greeted this last sentence.

Admiral Jobim turned for the photographers, extending his right hand to Marco Panero and Andrew Poynter.

"PaneroGlobal, today, begins the software installation on our servers. While we celebrate this occasion, the configuration will be finalized followed by a short demonstration. Open the champagne."

Andrew began to type a lengthy string of code.

Dressed for the occasion in a tailored summer suit of featherweight wool, he dared not remove the jacket to reveal the trail of flop sweat from under his arms. These next few moments would be the culmination of his efforts since leaving Nasha and his children.

Home with Nasha and the children was the Holy Grail. Secondary was the pending betrayal of Marco.

Of no concern whatsoever was cheating the Brazilian Navy.

Success—getting away with the deception—was everything; a disinformation plan forced upon him by duty, family and country.

Sir Edward's computer boffins modified the PaneroGlobal code buried deep inside the software's architecture. As Andrew's demonstration of the software initialized, the server at PaneroGlobal would route the software package to Brazil via an unremarkable building at Britain's principle nuclear submarine base. Within the tolerances of Brazil's receiving network, a version of the Synovian Worm would be added to lie dormant until such time as Brazil installed the ASW system and connected it to active sonar. When asked to compare a signal from a potential enemy submarine, to the acoustic profile of *Astute Class* submarines, the stolen data from *Astute* would be corrupted by the worm and forever return a negative response to Brazil's on-board operators.

Brazil would never detect British nuclear submarines using stolen acoustics.

Data stolen by Marco Panero and Andrew Poynter, indeed the theft itself, would be rendered moot—as if it never happened.

Despite the detail required in preparing for initialization, his father's demands were a heavy weight: *For the family and Britain, Andrew, make me proud.*

Exactly what result would qualify a son for a father's pride?

Sir Edward certainly believed the theft of *Astute's* data was the result of his daughter's perfidy. Why, then, was Caroline's safety of primary importance? What character defect prevented Sir Edward seeing Caroline as others saw her.

Without a viable alternative, Andrew held tight to his father's faith: Gray skies would turn blue in the end.

Marco and Admiral Jobim took up a position behind Andrew, who heard the Admiral say, sotto voce, "Not everyone is so thrilled as I, Marco my good friend. A very unpleasant rumor is being spread by a scientist in our nuclear program...a Swede or a Dane hired for his work on the reactor." Jobim discretely watched Panero for a reaction.

Andrew went stiff as a board. For a moment he lost track of where he was in the code's sequence and only recovered as Marco spoke.

"So tell me, my soon to be very rich Admiral, what rumor could be any concern?" Admiral Jobim would be the beneficiary of ten million Euros upon payment by Brazil to PaneroGlobal.

"It's a rumor...a claim the software is flawed. I must make a response to the highest authority."

Marco responded like a brilliant negotiator. "Hold back a hundred million Euros until your people complete whatever tests they wish. Test for six months as you like. Satisfactory?"

Jobim closed the trapdoor. "Of course, my friend. We'll keep Mr. Poynter and his passport to assist with the testing. With your blessing of course."

Marco held up his glass without batting an eyelash. "To the defeat of Brazil's enemies."

Andrew held himself together. With hands whose tremors must be visible to every Naval officer in the room, he hit the Enter key and the screen filled with a download bar indicating zero percent complete. Seconds later, as the crowd gathered around Andrew, a solid blue bar crept towards one hundred percent.

Brazil's senior submariners exalted.

In a smaller adjacent office, Admiral Jobim signed a payment voucher for four hundred million Euros and watched as Admiral Bernardes, Director of Finance, added his attestation. A clerk entered the appropriate commands and a wire transfer was credited to PaneroGlobal LLC at the Washington DC branch of Michani Bank.

Marco shook hands a second time with everyone wearing a uniform. Nothing in his demeanor gave Admiral Jobim cause for anguish. He lingered twenty minutes at the buffet table answering questions about the system. As he checked the screen, forty minutes remained until the download, and the formal reception, would come to an end. With a hand draped over Andrew's shoulder, he waited in apparent contentment.

With Marco's other hand, sheltered as it was between Andrew's back and Marco's waist, he texted Marie Truchet on the chartered yacht: *911 get us out.* In the full flight of distress, Marco gave no thought to Caroline's disbursement of funds.

***

Caroline's phone received confirmation of the wire transfer. Four hundred million left PaneroGlobal a hundred million short.

Distracted, she tapped glossy fingernails on a linen covered table left by room service in her suite at the Copacabana Palace. On the beach of the same name, sun worshippers frolicked while Caroline Panero allowed herself to be consumed by demented rage.

Finished with Khalid and Marco, she called up the App written by her husband as a single-use method to distribute Brazil's payment. She could've given the shortfall's implications thoughtful consideration, but did no such thing. Raissa took first, second and third on Caroline's list of priorities. Disbursement dealt with, she tossed the phone in the direction of her handbag.

Mathematics was always demanding and fickle to those who took its majestic capabilities for granted. Percentages were the basis used by Marco when programming the app on Caroline's phone. Percentages would always produce an accurate result, unless the law of unintended consequences interceded.

Two percent of five hundred million Euros would have equaled ten million Euros. Admiral Eduardo de Almeida Jobim's bank in the Cayman Islands credited eight million Euros to his account.

Andrew's bank in Campione D'Italia received four hundred thousand Euros in the same manner.

Marie Truchet's Swiss bank received two million Euros.

Khalid bin Rahman received three hundred sixty million Euros via accounts in a number of institutions.

PaneroGlobal received the balance of twenty-nine million six hundred thousand Euros in its British, German and Swiss corporate accounts.

***

Illegal weapons, in the hands of gangs, ruled the streets of Rio.

Caroline had no difficulty purchasing a machine pistol. Pleased with instructions from the teenage salesman, she listened to him say,

"Point, pull the trigger and hold on tight. Don't kill your own damn self." She walked away with the machine pistol hidden in a cheap, woven, carryall.

***

Marie met Andrew, minus his passport, in a parking lot half a mile from the marina.

Exfiltration of a client from a country with a hostile military was dependent more on speed than guile. She grabbed Andrew's arm and pulled him uphill into the favela.

Andrew protested. "All my gear's on the boat."

"Military police were here fifteen minutes after Marco's text. Everything's gone. I had to pretend to be a drunk hooker, or they'd have kept me too."

Andrew's mind blanked. Jesus Christ, he asked himself, how will we get out of here?

As if a mind reader, Marie told him, "This favela by the waterfront…it's too small. We'll climb to the top and go down the other side…grab a bus or taxi to a bigger one. Then call for help."

"Call who?"

"Your daddy. Who else gives a shit?" Truchet cared about keeping Andrew moving forward. In a crisis only one thing at a time mattered. Amateurs never grasped these small truths.

Already winded, his new shoes hurt. Andrew ripped off the jacket and tie and left them in the street.

Marie stopped. "Carry them," was a demand not a request.

"Where's Marco?"

"Marco's not a hostage with no passport. You are."

Ten minutes further and Andrew limped noticeably.

In an alley shop, they traded Andrew's three thousand dollar suit for ragged pants, a shirt and well-worn sandals. On the downside of the steep grade, Truchet's phone rang.

She listened, hung up and spoke a single word. "Merde."

With a hard look at Andrew, she wondered how he'd respond to a worse disaster.

"Marco's hiding in Favela Providencia. Some screw-up with the money…the Admiral didn't get his full share and wants Marco to pay up. He got out of the hotel through the kitchen, leaving a trail of bribes a mile long. Marco's not exactly a prime time player."

Deep in thought, she wouldn't admit the adrenaline high was a kick. "Okay, I'm gonna get the police to rescue Marco, but it won't happen till after dark. Before anything else can happen, I need a pile of cash."

All Andrew could manage was a dull stare as she dialed Marco's phone.

"Listen Marco, I'll be hours getting something arranged. Give the woman all your money and your best goddam smile. Ask her to find Alberto da Silva. If Alberto shows up, have him call me. If not, sit in a corner until she throws you out."

They were walking faster than before, when Andrew's curiosity gained the upper hand. "Who's Alberto da Silva?"

"Kid...around twenty. Mean...hates cops. Father used to head the gang which controls Providencia. Marco's hiding with a prostitute, who can send word to Alberto. The favelas...people share joy and pain. Everyone knows everyone. Alberto can keep Marco from getting killed until I figure a way to get us out. If Alberto chooses to let Marco live."

Marie assumed her payment from Marco was short, like the Admiral's. It was the other payment—the one she extorted from Sir Edward for rescuing his two children—which interested her. Fixers never worked cheap.

***

Since the macabre happenings at Fulton Bennett's home, Nasha ventured outside only to meet Zachary Mannheim, an encounter which left a sour taste.

Leftover leaves blew across the road in slow motion, weighed down by light rain. Brad was bundled and more asleep than awake. They ambled several blocks and reached the entrance to Windy Run Park, where a single man jogged in black pants, a bright red jacket and matching knit hat pulled over his ears.

On the far edge of the park a truck backfired.

Overhanging limbs off a hundred foot oak dripped a deluge, so she pushed Brad faster. So much water under the bridge since her first encounter with a light green pickup. The lettering on this truck was white over light green. Did it claim *Coelho Grows Everything*?

Hand on her cell, memories of humiliation by Arlington police caused her to break into a jog. A mile passed but anoesis failed to banish insane fear.

When the red jacket and hat caught her, Frankel begged, "Slow down, Miss America, I can't keep up." Nasha looked across at Aaron Frankel, then back towards the park. From whom should she run faster—an Egyptian in a pickup truck or Sheikh bin Rahman's banker?

Dead serious she asked, "Where are your security people?"

Encumbered by worry for Brad, her pace increased. Wheels of the stroller spat water on her legs.

Frankel measured her stride and matched it. He'd found Nasha for a reason and wouldn't be put off. "The man with the gun in the Embassy…in the microdot…he's in those crazy videos. Who is he?"

"The videos and the Embassy's cameras show the same man. He's MI-6." Did driving away with Grace and Caroline constitute proof?

Frankel hadn't expected a definitive identification. "How would you know?"

Nasha stayed silent.

Sense of humor strained, Frankel insisted, "How do you know? Tell me."

"Why should I tell you anything?"

Frankel's mask slipped. Nasha didn't like what it revealed.

Frankel grabbed the handle of Brad's stroller with one hand, then steadied it to prevent Brad tipping over.

Nasha stopped. "Let go. I won't say it again."

On this day he needed her more than the reverse. Hands by his side, he said in a whisper, "If that guy's official, the British government has decided to eliminate me. If he's unofficial, then only your father-in-law wants me dead. Khalid bin Rahman came to the US in person and without security…told me I'd be killed before the week is out."

Aaron edged closer.

"Fulton Bennett approached me recently. Offered me a trade…Khalid's money for freedom and protected status. Now Bennett's been eliminated…bin Rahman won their war…now he'll retrench and go in another direction. I wish I'd made Bennett's deal. Will you make it for me?"

"Don't be absurd. I was bait...a fancier bobblehead in the Agency's game. They wouldn't listen to me. Who would I go to? Sarah? Jamie Norris? Grover? Who?" She stood tight-lipped, shaking her head in disbelief at his self-absorption.

"They'll listen...any of those you mentioned will listen, if they knew you had sole control over bin Rahman's accounts."

Like being wrapped in a shroud for burial; Nasha's ears refused to hear. She studied his face. Frankel wasn't kidding.

"I've lost. Against just Khalid survival might be feasible. Add Edward Poynter and the odds against become too long. Khalid's going to move his money...any time now I'll get a written directive with new banks, accounts, account owners and amounts. Before that happens...I've made alternative arrangements. Accounts all over the world. All the tricks. Under the control of one person—one person with the authorization codes. All legal or close enough not to matter. If I go to Langley directly, Grover'll screw me over...accuse me of collaborating in Bennett's death. Throw me in a hole in Berzerkistan."

He added a doleful petition. " You could be an honest broker. My life won't look like the past, but I'd like to keep it."

Nasha was amazed and surprised: She was considering how a negotiation might transpire. *Am I a politician after all?*

"How much are we talking about?"

"Over three billion US."

"How much will you pillage?"

"Nothing. Not a dime. Forensic accountants...bring'em on. Khalid's accounts are in perfect order." He threw her a mortified look. "I'm shocked at your suggestion."

Nasha didn't answer but returned his look with one which meant: *So you've stolen your share.* What she said out loud was, "How soon?"

"Now. This afternoon. When I move the money, my advantage disappears, so you make the deal without having the funds. I move the money on your say-so. Get the deal in writing, needless to say. If Langley won't go for it, I'll move the accounts another way and try a harder route."

The harder route would be negotiating with Sir Edward Poynter; Nasha appreciated how it wasn't an attractive option. Nasha floated one final, nagging, question. "If you were me, why would the answer be yes?"

An ominous stillness settled over Aaron Frankel.

Nasha detected reluctance and malevolence in equal measure. Nothing good would come next.

Had she not asked, he still would have told her—for love and desperation were the best motivators.

"Because a man like me hears things. Gets bizarre requests from an assortment of players in a deceitful world. Your husband's in deep shit, Nasha. He needs cash…the kind of cash not provided by a bank. Without it, he and Marco Panero will be dead by morning."

Overmatched—I don't belong in his world. Nasha nodded with a face showing immediate, intense strain. "You've got a way to get Andrew the money."

It wasn't a question. Frankel had found the best leverage short of kidnapping her children. "Say yes and it's done…a gesture of good faith."

Staring at the gold band around her finger, a disagreeable reflection crept forward uninvited. How could this be? Who is this Andrew Poynter in deep shit—and what have they done to my loving husband?

"Do you know Greek mythology, Aaron?"

He offered disinterest to soothe his panic.

With a look which crossed several mental states, she gave in. "I'm like Odysseus…caught between Scylla and Charybdis. Yes, I'll be your negotiator. Make your call."

In this instant of submission, Frankel's lie shone as bright as neon on the Vegas strip. Nasha Poynter would, from this moment onwards, be required to follow several tenets of the infamous Moscow Rules. Every spy knew these long-in-the-tooth bits of wisdom: *Adapt, go with the flow, keep all your options open.*

***

In the time it took Zachary Mannheim to meet Phyllis Martell, he'd heard about Gunther Probst's photographs from both expected and unexpected sources.

Mannheim had just come from a seventh floor powwow where it had been decided to say and do nothing about a domestic criminal matter being handled by the Bureau. As with Raissa's videos, the leak spiraled out of the FBI and the Senate Office Building like an insider's wet dream. In a frenzy of this magnitude, some version of a story would be media froth by tomorrow morning.

Once settled in her front passenger seat, Zachary asked, "Are you familiar with James Reston, Phyllis?" Without waiting for her reply, he continued. "Reston once said, *A government is the only vessel that leaks from the top*. Why should this situation be any different? What in these photos involves CIC?"

Mannheim was baiting Martell, albeit without malice. Could she separate perception from reality?

"Strictly from CIC's perspective, we focus on whether the order to terminate Raissa Ribeiro, by Grover Norris, was the product of a conflict of interest. Such a conflict would exist, if Grover's investment bank has ever sought to manage, or currently manages funds belonging to organizations linked to, or controlled by, Khalid bin Rahman. Pictured in the photos, Bryson Sewell is an employee of Grover's bank. Why, CIC should ask, was an employee of Grover's bank having lunch with Fathima Laniado, a Lebanese National..." Martell ran out of steam.

"Just so, Phyllis. Grover walks like a duck. Bryson may be a smoking gun. But only if Laniado is demonstrably the creature of bin Rahman. Can you, Agent Martin Haslett or Lt. Nichols prove such a thesis?"

"No, sir. I can do better than that."

Mannheim's student had studied her lessons. She pulled off at the next exit into a gas station. Turned and handed Mannheim a sheaf of papers.

"This is quite serious," Mannheim understated. "Are the copies genuine? Who's the source?"

"I met with Gavriel Rabin, head of security for Jean-Louis Michani. Rabin has been granted diplomatic immunity and is assumed to be Mossad. He handed me the documents without explanation. I suppose, alternatively, they could've come from Michani's people as a result of inter-bank espionage. Does it matter? The Agency will never use them...will we?"

Martell's meaning was clear enough: Would Mannheim use the documents in some less than straightforward manner.

"What if these came from Bryson Sewell, Phyllis? It's the kind of thing Bryson's daddy would recommend. Ever think of Sewell as a guy to let his son be flayed in the public square?"

CHAPTER 30

Vaporize a career—what this appalling escapade could accomplish. A lengthy train of thought complete, Grover Norris's Bentley stopped at the gate where the chauffeur announced his employer's arrival through the electronic interface.

"Ask Mr. Norris to exit the vehicle, please, so the system can identify him." Stripped of personality by the same interface, the voice belonged to Gavriel Rabin.

In a snit over this lack of deference, Grover considered abandoning the meeting, but thought better of an amateur's error. Compliance would allow an opportunity to influence events. As he stepped from a cocoon of privilege, an Agency SUV pulled-in behind carrying Jamie, Sarah and Zachary Mannheim.

So the die is cast, Grover reckoned, re-entering the Bentley.

When the gate swung open, minutes separated him from a first meeting of substance with Jean-Louis Michani, a man with a long shadow in the banking community. Satisfied with his preparedness, he sat in expectation, restless fingers massaging cashmere folds of his scarf.

Nasha met the two vehicles. Social norms observed, she led them up granite steps while they followed in procession. At the front entrance, Gavriel stood with his hands clasped behind his back. With a minor nod to Nasha, he stated the obvious.

"Principles only, gentlemen. If those of you in the security detail would follow me, there's coffee or tea in the garage facilities."

Once again Grover's abraded ego bled from perceived slights. "Senior Agency officers are entitled to a security detail, Mrs. Poynter."

"Can you imagine a threat to your life in my father's home, Mr. Norris?" She entered the house and held the door open for Papa's guests.

Mannheim followed straightaway, offering Nasha a perplexed expression. Jamie and Sarah came next. Grover lasered Gavriel while bringing up the rear.

＊

"Can we expect Mr. Lattimore?"

Jean-Louis played the perfect host while his visitors were served coffee, tea and sandwiches. Now he would discover whether these visitors were serious.

Grover assuaged his host. "All in good time, Jean-Louis. When we're convinced there's something to commit to writing."

Michani let his eyes wander from one to the other of the Agency's representatives. Grover Norris was a man without scruples, although such a trait wasn't unexpected or unusual. Mannheim looked vaguely unwell, suffering perhaps from an excess of what Norris lacked. Norris the Younger was blonde where his father was dark, dressed suitably for his part in this drama and infused with doubt. Finally Michani's dark brown eyes fixed on his daughter. This was Nasha's life. What she'd told him on the phone brought this group together. Jean-Louis could do no more without breaking his own canons, although his day wouldn't end with this meeting.

Nasha waded in. "Sarah recruited me to get close to Aaron Frankel, to find a way inside his operation hoping to freeze or strip Khalid bin Rahman's assets. I've done what we agreed."

She let a claim of success sink in.

"Control of the Sheikh's assets rests with me. We're here to discuss terms for transfer of those assets to the United States government. Agreement will be reached today, within the hour. Delay will be treated as abandonment...there will be no further attempt to reach agreement." She settled her eyes on Mannheim to emphasize this deadline wasn't a hollow condition born of vanity.

"Bullshit. You're not capable of such a…"

Nasha wouldn't allow Grover Norris to finish. Absent agitation or vehemence, she said, "Were you going to say coup, Grover?" If Norris could address Papa as Jean-Louis, then fair was fair. "There's nothing more for me to say. You've heard my offer. You need to arrive at a decision, if we're to negotiate terms and conditions."

"We don't negotiate with terrorists." Grover fumed in a stew whose ingredients were, in equal portions, uncertainty and exhilaration.

Reproachful, Nasha said, "I'd have thought congratulations more appropriate, Grover. Surely Sarah's expectations never included an immediate transfer of bin Rahman's assets. I've done the Agency's bidding. Acted as your unofficial agent…assuming all the risks in the bargain."

Jamie's voice quavered, giving away the stress he felt. "What would you offer as a proffer, Mrs. Poynter?"

"My word. The Agency came to me, if you remember. But the next step…what to do with the assets…was never discussed or agreed upon." Nasha turned to Sarah. "I can play the recording of our meeting, if you like, but the hour is ticking away."

Michani interrupted. "If Mr. Lattimore is to join us, he should be notified. Should he not?"

Grover said, "What's your role in this fiasco, Jean-Louis? Your daughter is teetering on the edge of arrest or detention. Whatever she knows, or whatever control she thinks she possesses, won't survive interrogation."

Michani responded in less than a whisper. "You and I, Grover, are yesterday's news. Promise me you'll never threaten Nasha again and there'll be no need for your personal and corporate indiscretions to be exposed to daylight."

Pompous and arrogant—these were traits Grover Norris understood could be applied to his persona—even indiscreet—but an easy mark? Michani might be from another century, but was infamously ruthless. What does the old bastard have?

"Impetuous of me, Nasha, and I do apologize. Civility will prevail."

Mannheim had seen steel under Nasha's comely exterior. The woman was offering a lot for a little, it would seem. "Grover, we might listen to Mrs. Poynter's proposed terms. There may be opportunity brewing where nonsense appears to grow."

Again Michani reminded them. "Not without the Agency's General Counsel present."

Grover switched wavelengths, his concern aimed at Michani's ability to do him harm. He nodded consent at Jamie.

***

Determined not to show unease, Nasha refrained from looking at the antique grandfather clock, whose pendulum's arc reduced her own with each completed cycle.

Two men entered as if they'd traveled together.

Owen Lattimore found a stuffed chair nearby Grover Norris, opened a briefcase, observed the room and recognized a stacked deck. Outmaneuvered, he would fight a delaying battle until Grover settled on a course of action.

Wesley Jackson was the kind of huge man who took a room by storm. "Look at all this gloom and doom. Jean-Louis...goodness gracious, you don't look more'n half dead despite the rumors. Grover...I was sure the President had seen through your act. Sheesh...gotta find me a double bourbon fore we get to carving up the terrorist bastard's ill gotten gains."

Jackson had been brokering deals in DC before any of the three youngest in the room were born. A Mississippian by birth, his accent varied in intensity with circumstance. Jackson shared the trait with Mannheim. With what looked more like three fingers of Michani's finest in hand, Jackson continued smoothly.

"Nasha, you're looking fetching this afternoon. What do you want these nice fellas to do in return for all the Sheikh's cash?"

Rehearsals behind her, Nasha spoke without hesitation.

"Frankel receives blanket immunity for any and all crimes, from the beginning of time to the date of the agreement, regardless of where the crimes are alleged to have taken place. The United States shall refuse to extradite Frankel to any sovereign State, regardless of claims made or justification provided. The United States will make it known through any and all channels, formal and informal, that Aaron Frankel enjoys its protection and should be left to pursue his freedom without tortuous interference of any kind, provided Frankel remains uninvolved in finance or banking in any way. Frankel's personal net worth shall remain free of claim by the United States for taxes, interest, penalties or the like and Frankel's personal net worth shall not be frozen, confiscated or otherwise usurped or taken by the United States. Those are the terms applicable to Frankel, subject without limitation to Mr. Jackson's review and approval."

Lattimore interjected, "Are there terms applicable to other parties?"

Nasha nodded yes. "I'd like to ask a few questions first…one in particular could present operational issues for Mr. Jamie Norris. May I?"

Jamie was ready to leap at a deal for bin Rahman's assets. His response mirrored enthusiasm. "Sure. We'd like to make this agreement."

"Do you have an officer on the ground in Rio? Can he access half a million dollars in two hours? Those are our conditions to finish this negotiation."

Grover stepped-in, waving Jamie into silence. "For what purpose…half a million, that's real money? Brazil isn't our closest ally, but we'll be buying a shitload of their offshore oil. We can't fund an international incident."

Mannheim injected a lighter touch. "Except when we do, of course."

Jackson laughed heartily, having extracted a couple of Presidents from a similar sort of thing. He was, seemingly, the only one immune from the instability of the moment.

Nasha faced telling the truth or inventing a lie. She thought the truth sounded completely unbelievable. "A Brazilian Admiral is holding my husband, Andrew Poynter, hostage for a larger bribe than the Admiral has already received. The money is to acquire Andrew's release."

Jackson winked at her in a way which meant: *Just right, my dear. Not a lie—not the entire, messy, truth.*

Grover, Jamie, Sarah and Lattimore left the room for consultation. In twenty minutes they returned. Grover and Lattimore spoke at the same time with Grover instantly deferring to the attorney.

"Are you seeking similar immunity from prosecution and extradition for yourself and Andrew Poynter?"

Jackson interceded. "Damned right, Owen. You think Nasha will let herself or her husband rotate slowly over a hot spit? Don't be an ass."

Grover would have enjoyed seeing Jean-Louis lose his daughter to Federal detention, but not enough to refuse. "Agreed. Jamie...do what you have to." He looked at Jackson. "How long for the paper?"

"Comin' out the printer in the next room this very minute."

When Michani spoke, his prior, taught, tone had relaxed. "Grover, assuming this all goes well, would you be kind enough to join me for dinner?"

Last on Grover Norris's wish list was being polite over dinner with Michani. But refusing would compound his troubles. "I'd love to, Jean-Louis. How kind of you."

"Say eight o'clock. Here at the house."

"Just us two then?"

"Four...there'll be four of us."

***

With all operations on hold—Jamie's own goddam order—how can he think I'll answer an unsecured call? David Nazarian stared at the phone like it was a poisonous snake.

In less than five minutes the screen showed Phyllis Martell's text from her personal phone: 911.

Nazarian allowed the possibilities to order themselves: Jamie's call is unrelated to Phyllis' purpose; or I didn't answer Jamie's call, so Mannheim pressured Phyllis to reach out. Which suggests Mannheim is briefed on Jamie's agenda. Of two choices, the latter was the obvious winner. So what does Jamie want?

Nazarian abandoned his surveillance of Paolo Zabban's studio and walked quickly until he caught a taxi. Gave the driver Avenue Presidente Wilson 147 as his destination: The U.S. Consulate would provide a secure line. This kind of craziness is how things go sideways, Nazarian thought, while swearing to himself.

Would Michael da Silva wait or head for his favorite watering hole?

Goddam Jamie better have something important to say.

***

This was a different side to her Papa, one she was never permitted to witness.

No sooner had Wesley Jackson produced copies of the agreement for all to review, than Jean-Louis excused himself and signaled Nasha to accompany him. In a small conference room, they joined Aaron Frankel and eight senior analysts from Michani's bank.

Projected on a screen was a chart of accounts and locations, colored either red or green. Some of the colored accounts blinked. Others glowed steady.

Frankel twitched near fatal hysteria.

Her father examined the information, asking a series of rapid-fire questions in finance-speak which, to Nasha, might've been the language of an alien planet. While the minutia was dense, an overarching interpretation was clear enough. Accounts in steady green held funds transferred by Frankel as per his agreement with Nasha; Michani's staff had vetted these accounts. Accounts in steady red supposedly held the agreed upon funds, but hadn't been vetted. Any account, whether red or green, whose legend was blinking should hold funds, but didn't. Funds intended for transfer to the blinking accounts had dematerialized without warning.

After a deep breath, Nasha asked, "How much is gone?"

Jean-Louis awaited his senior analyst, who said, "Two billion…give or take."

She tried to remain stern and failed. "Someone other than bin Rahman, and other than Frankel, swiped a couple of billion dollars owned by the Sheikh. Funds which were in your custody, Aaron. Am I correct?" She covered her mouth to stifle a belly laugh. "Sorry to laugh. You, all of you, are the best in the business. Is anyone embarrassed? Do we have the first idea where to look for the money? Do stolen funds leave some particular odor or a unique trail?"

To herself she asked a different sort of question: Can I finesse Jamie Norris long enough to save Andrew?

***

"What's the emergency, Phyllis?" Nazarian sat, looking unsavory at best, in an alcove off the Consul General's quarters, watched by an armed U.S. Marine.

Phyllis had been instructed in the part she was expected to play. Under the watchful eyes and ears of Zachary Mannheim and Jamie Norris, she sketched-out what was needed from David.

"We've got a NOC who's blown. You've been given a case with five hundred thousand dollars...confirm?"

David would not comply, if jail awaited a fool's acquiescence. "Confirmed. Phyllis...this smells. There's a hold order on all Ops...straight from Jamie Norris. How'd whatever this is get an exception and why is CIC issuing my orders?"

They all agreed beforehand—if Nazarian pressed for details, Phyllis would ignore him. Field Officers understood mixed signals; it was in their nature to work through such things.

"There's an intermediary to whom you'll deliver the case. Her name is Marie Truchet. I'm sending you photo and location as we speak. Confirm when you have the data."

With a tired, exasperated response he made a further attempt. "Got it. Truchet's an independent, maybe you shouldn't be okay with her?"

David wanted to know everything was SOP; telling him was a different thing altogether, because Phyllis hadn't been given a single detail to relay. "Truchet is a cutout. Treat her as such. Drop location is very public. Drop time is thirty-seven minutes from now. Make the drop and get out. Confirm."

A blind drop left a field agent deaf, dumb, and quite literally blind. Headache about to burst his eardrums, Nazarian capitulated. "Confirmed."

CHAPTER 31

Lunchtime brought crowds into the street as Marie, wearing a drab wig, no makeup, huge sunglasses and flat shoes, perused a newspaper ten meters across from the main staircase of the Biblioteca Nacional do Brasil near Cinelândia Square. By her side, a college kid played a game on his phone in a successful attempt to appear cool.

Halfway up the library's staircase his girlfriend was another fresh-faced Brazilian girl holding a clutch of magazines with a large shopping bag by her side. Nothing was out of place, when a male in his forties, perhaps the girl's relative, greeted her. Unhurried words and smiles exchanged, he put down his bag. They chatted a few moments. He kissed both her cheeks and walked on with her bag, the one holding old newspapers.

After a few minutes, the girl rejoined Marie and the boy having earned five hundred dollars in ten minutes.

Marie enjoyed the wistful innocence of their shared adventure, took the bag with bricks of cash totaling four hundred thousand dollars and hailed a taxi on Rio Branco.

***

An inexpensive hotel on Rua Aurea, not far from Favela Francisco de Castro, offered broadband and a quiet back room facing an alley.

Polícia Civil do Estado do Rio de Janeiro was responsible for criminal investigations in Rio and directed by a Chief of Police chosen by the Governor. Coordenadoria de Recursos Especiais, known better by CORE, served the Policia as its Seção de Operações Táticas.

Colonel João Bosque occupied a cargo de confiança (post of confidence) as CORE's commander and, as a media darling, was a widely known supporter of reducing police corruption and criminality.

Bosque confidently began to disrobe in anticipation of Marie's arrival.

The good Colonel's idea of foreplay made short work of her obligatory ego massage. He lasted less than half a minute on his back while she rode him to satisfaction. Like a flaccid donkey, he lay beside her, when she halfheartedly attempted to raise him a second time. Yes, she told herself, behind the affectation of sexual arousal—nothing is more dehumanizing than this.

They spoke English, Marie's Portuguese unsuitable for complex arrangements. "João...you dirty dog...do me again. Then I'll make you considerably wealthier for nothing more than your normal duties." Her nipples rolled between his thumb and forefinger, greed ballooned before his ignoble manhood.

"Reals or Euros?" Attentive, alert and commanding, he bore no resemblance to his drowsy alter ego of seconds earlier.

"Dollars, my Colonel, two hundred thousand of them. I need two men taken safely from Favela Providencia to Montevideo. Preferably by air. Definitely not over the roads."

"Who are these jackals, Marie?"

They'd arrived at the tricky bit. João's id needed the sex. His wallet preferred cash. Survival depended upon whom among his political opposition was abused, and in what manner he might antagonize his bureaucratic and legislative rabbis.

"An Italian who lives in Germany and a Brit who lives in the States. Consultants to your navy. An Admiral feels he was underpaid for opening doors. An honest mistake."

"Which Admiral?"

"Is it truly important for you to know, Mon Cheri?"

He touched her hair lightly. "Only if you want my cooperation."

Petulance a specialty in Marie's act, she pouted. "Jobim."

"How much was the good Admiral screwed out of?"

"I don't know." She wouldn't have been told those kinds of details and João understood as much.

"Who is paying?"

"The wife of the Brit." This was an acceptable lie. Wives sometimes paid to retrieve a spouse.

"So this is a charity job for you, Marie?" João Bosque was transparent as plastic wrap.

"My fee is fifty thousand. I was in Brazil on another project."

"So if I refuse at two hundred thousand?"

"We could stay here in bed…or you can take my fee. I need your help. I gave my word to his wife."

"How touching," he said, beginning to pull-on fatigue pants. "You'll be canonized a saint. Two hundred fifty it is. I'll use the helicopter, an armored personnel carrier and two squads. Another in my tireless efforts to clean out the gangs. Where are they hiding? Details, please."

***

Langley using him like this made no sense. Twice now he'd accessed the Consulate for cash: Fifty thousand to pay Tiago and da Silva, and now half a million to rescue a lost dog. Basic prudence told Nazarian to keep a hundred grand for a rainy day.

In the rag-ass bar where Michael da Silva was reputed to drink himself to a stupor each afternoon, Nazarian could've dressed as Uncle Sam wearing his July 4th outfit. Even the bartender addressed him as CIA Bastard.

Guarana Antarctica with no ice tasted like panther piss.

When a walking skeleton, holding a bottle of cachaça, sat down before he fell down, throttling Tiago till he puked became David's life's ambition. When the carcass spoke coherently, without a trace of inebriation, a decision couldn't be avoided.

Emaciated and shopworn, da Silva's first words showed him endowed with the objectivity of a professional. "Killing a woman. Killing a man. The difference is only price."

Nazarian wouldn't negotiate against himself, so he said, "How much?"

"Five thousand for a man."

"For the woman in Paolo Zabban's videos?"

The reaction was instantaneous. "Raissa is different." Da Silva's eyes rolled upwards as if some drug was, at this moment, seizing his nervous system. "She's from here...and has many friends."

Nazarian had overstayed his welcome. With or without an arrangement it was time to get out.

"Ten thousand for Raissa's death by crucifixion...like in the video. Two thousand now...eight thousand in the morning, when you bring me a video of her answer to one simple question: *Did you kill Gunther?*"

David counted out twenty hundred dollar bills. Put the bills and a tiny voice recorder on the table between them.

Double the expected payday, the hunger in da Silva's face was real. A hand flashed towards the money, and a grin widened when Nazarian was too slow to prevent the bills being grabbed up. Da Silva never asked where to collect the balance of his payment. Never hesitated over torturing Raissa to get the answer Nazarian paid for.

"In the favelas no one notices the corpses of CIA Bastards, not even starving dogs."

David left the bar contemplating whether da Silva actually might succeed, and, with no allies and nothing but money as a weapon, CIA Bastard 3 was over his head and likely to drown. In the lessening breeze of late afternoon, with the temperature holding firm in the high seventies, dimples erupted on his bare arms. They were the by-product of a spy's long experience and cold dread.

*****

Caroline Panero was all too familiar with the narrow streets and narrower alleyways of Favela Providencia. Unchanged with passing years, the favela appeared as today's inheritance from fifteen thousand yesterdays. Ignored and x-rayed by every set of eyes hanging out a window, lingering in a doorway or peddling from a pushcart, was the collective memory of Providencia accurate in regards to Caroline? Or was she another in a string of beautiful women who had reason, be it profit or perdition, to trod the cobblestones and broken pavement in impractical shoes?

The machine pistol was cold comfort, of no use other than ridding herself of Raissa Ribeiro.

Neither the hour nor day troubled Caroline. Paolo always claimed time lost its meaning while creating his photographs. So it would be today as it had been then, when Caroline Poynter was young and striking enough, but too drugged, sexed and unstable to supplant Raissa in Paolo's professional estimation.

Rebellious was how Sir Edward had described her behavior to upper-crust friends and colleagues. Unsuitable was the word father attached to Fulton Bennett. Sir Edward hadn't been capable of connecting the dots of cause and effect—rebellious and unsuitable led to rebellion as high tide ebbed to low.

Or had he been unwilling to see what was plain to others?

Sir Edward would always have things his own way.

Have things your own way—a life lesson learned from her myopic father.

***

Marie would subjugate herself as warranted by circumstance and alternatives.

"Alberto, thanks for helping. Is my client safe?"

Marco would be safe enough unless Alberto wanted more than Marie could pay.

"He whimpers like a coward."

Marie heard his pleasure from using a new word—*whimper* must be the latest addition to his English vocabulary.

"Older men frighten easily. They've forgotten what it was like to be young and strong. Can we meet, Alberto, I have important Intel...and a way to make a good payday."

Truchet walked behind decayed buildings separated by little more than the width of her shoulders. With nowhere to turn or retreat, the back alley made a perfect killing ground. Deeper in from the street, the air was heavy with dampness as hundreds of rivulets from illegal air conditioners, operating on stolen current, combined to turn portions of the surface to mud. She looked up when she heard Alberto speak. Tone diffident, he hung over the railing from the waist. A large gold bauble dangled from a heavy chain.

"What do you want?"

Adrenaline boosted readiness. Remember who's the buyer and whom the seller, Marie told herself. "In minutes the Policia will come. Armored vehicles and a helicopter to pick up two of my clients. Keep the peace, Alberto. Peace would be profitable for both sides."

Alberto stared impassively, waiting: Truchet had mentioned profit.

"My deal is with Bosque. We both know I may need a better one. Keep your eyes on my clients. If things go wrong, get them out of the country. I have fifty thousand US dollars." She'd been tempted to ask whether he understood, but it was she down in the alley and him on high ground. Inclined to offer all her remaining cash, apprehension shouted a clear warning, enough to make her skin tingle.

"Toss me the backpack," he said, disinterested in an exchange of views.

"You know where they are, my clients, don't you?"

"I know who you are. I know where you dirty yourself with Bosque. I know everything."

Was his attitude some form of crude verdict on her morality? Jesus, how tiresome. She used both hands to do as he demanded; the fanny pack with the diminishing balance from four hundred thousand dollars chafed her backside as she did.

Whatever was eating at Alberto da Silva still wasn't apparent. "Whimper was a good word to learn, Alberto. How about contemptuous? Look it up in your dictionary...maybe you'll understand how things sometime work."

Marie was no longer optimistic about the next thirty minutes. The holster, strapped to her right calf under loose fitting pants, weighed more than a burden and less than a blessing.

***

Nasha sat in her father's office chair, phone cradled between shoulder and ear. She could see Aaron Frankel and Papa through the door to the conference room. Neither man agreed with what she was about to do, although for different reasons.

She was without a husband to turn to, without a God to pray to.

"Mr. Mannheim, this is Nasha Poynter. Could we talk again, please?"

"If the mountain will not come to Mohammed, Mohammed will go to the mountain." Too late he wished away distasteful language. "I've again proven insensitive, Mrs. Poynter. I'd be pleased to speak with you again...when and where?"

"Where we met before...if I leave my father's house now, thirty minutes should work."

"It's full dark, Mrs. Poynter. Does that concern you?"

Mannheim's expression of concern was a step forward. In a softened voice, she said, "I'll wear a coat, Mr. Mannheim."

Out of the blue Mannheim shocked her. "May I assume the topic is time sensitive?"

Nasha wondered whether Zachary Mannheim knew two billion dollars was unaccounted for.

***

Raissa Ribeiro received constant updates on Caroline's progress. No Internet could be more thorough than a thousand wary eyes. Still Raissa was surprised, if not unprepared.

Is it credible? Could Caroline have followed Gunther from downtown Boston to Cape Cod? Yes, in theory, but visualizing the scenario called into question what Raissa remembered of Caroline, a self-absorbed, jet setting, queen in her own mind. Could Caroline have possessed the skill to let Gunther become aware of her, increase the pressure so he'd recognize the danger, and, finally, herd him to a lonely road on the Cotuit shoreline to be corralled, then executed?

No, beyond belief.

Is it credible to think Caroline noticed Gunther and his camera, outing her syrupy lunch with Aaron Frankel?

Getting warmer.

Is Caroline involved with people who could hunt and kill Gunther?

Yes, without doubt or question.

How about the likelihood Caroline caught a glimpse of Raissa staring through the wall of glass at Legal Seafood?

Too hot to handle.

Is it credible to believe Caroline paranoid enough to regard Raissa a serious risk—after all the years I've left her safe, sound and alive?

Positively.

Reality was simpler and more cruel than hypotheticals. Caroline saw Gunther. Saw me. Allowed her shrewd mind to justify stoking old fires of hatred for Raissa, who'd refused to die on a pyre of envy and loathing. Caroline's inclusion represented the least challenging of the demons. Unless Caroline managed to enlist a sovereign security service to support her.

In which case Raissa would run. Running would damage pride. Pride was the first thing abandoned after being burned alive.

***

Cash procured Nazarian a decent view of Zabban's studio. On a nearby rooftop he sat against a parapet wall, accepting restrictions to his vision of the street below. A sense of the bizarre descended, when it became clear there were watchers watching the watcher. On three sides, he identified at least four onlookers showing consistent interest.

David analyzed the geometry and assessed the risk from a heretofore-unseen rifle. *What I wouldn't give for support—someone to watch the roof's rusted steel entrance door.* Across the street Zabban's studio appeared the same: Blacked-out windows would let no light in or out.

Brain and body settled-in, David unwrapped an energy bar as the street came alive.

Air bristled with electricity.

Assumptions made earlier were stripped of logic.

Chaos was on the way and would exact a terrible price from those who couldn't keep their wits about them.

***

Colonel Bosque made a command decision. As a show for the media, and to justify his payment from Marie Truchet, the 14.5mm heavy gun would litter the favela in body parts. Constantly communicating with the chopper and lead APC, his vehicle carried half a squad, armed to the teeth.

Truchet's rescued clients would join troops in the lead vehicle. No interaction between those rescued, and media scoundrels, would be permitted.

As the small convoy entered Providencia, tilted under the influence of its steep slope, Bosque spoke over the radio. "Command to all units: First stop in five to seven minutes. Air 1, Cav 1…gunners in place?" Bosque was a politician first and a policeman, who loved to mimic the patois of a combat soldier, second.

***

Andrew paced in agitation.

Inside Hotel Santa Teresa events conspired against him. Wallowing in flights of fancy irrelevant to his immediate future, never would he admit: Andrew Poynter was singularly responsible for this mess.

Blaring from a loudspeaker, God called his name. "Andrew Poynter...this is the Policia Civil, come out of the hotel."

Dejected, with no hope of rescue, nowhere to run, no influential father to protect him, he trudged through the doorway. Two soldiers grabbed his arms, shoving him into their vehicle.

When they gave him a radio headset, it seemed peculiar.

The convoy began to move.

***

Caroline pulled open the studio's door, expecting frantic energy and the piercing lights which surrounded models, photographers and their flatterers. As the door swung closed she stood still, pausing for pupils to dilate. Darkness interrupted by a veiled shaft of light from the street, and the spectral glow of a green-screen, her brain struggled to re-acclimate to an altered reality.

Whether she heard compressed air propel the dart, or imagined something clawing its way towards her neck, mattered not at all. She slumped to the wood floor with Quelicin coursing through her bloodstream. Began to feel like horses immobilized or euthanized with different doses of the identical drug. Quelicin's effects would cause psychological distress while making it impossible for Caroline to communicate—the ideal drug for Raissa's purpose.

 Raissa removed Caroline's clothes, applied products producing glossy-red lips and toes, chopped dark hair so a platinum wig appeared professional, attached a microphone and fastened Caroline's arms and legs to the rig which would emulate crucifixion. Caroline's head lolled on her chest as pulleys raised her into position.

Javier's special effects computers would stream Caroline as faux-Raissa, live across the net, with one additional keystroke.

***

A solitary figure, he walked towards the World War II Memorial, hands in pockets, wariness obvious in body language. Mannheim stopped and turned.

Nasha gave him a small wave.

Within conversational range, she said, "The legend claims, when the founder of Islam was asked to give proofs of his teaching, he ordered Mount Safa to come to him. When the mountain didn't comply, Mohammed raised his hands toward heaven: *God is merciful. Had the mountain obeyed my words, it would have destroyed me. I will go to the mountain and thank God for his mercy on a stiff-necked generation.* The translation probably has everything wrong, as it traces to English philosopher Frances Bacon...what could an Englishman know of Mohammed?"

Mannheim enjoyed her light-hearted warmth, despite the exigency of their circumstances. "I have much to learn from you, Mrs. Poynter." He let words, and their multiple meanings, hang as a pointed warning in a small breeze.

Nasha said her piece before backbone broke. "With the ink barely dry on our agreement, I cannot deliver as promised. Give or take a hundred million, a billion of bin Rahman's money has been transferred to accounts I control. Nearly two billion is missing, diverted somehow during the transfer from Frankel's accounts to those established under my authority. The hack occurred while the funds were in transit. My father's top analysts are hopeful there's a trail of electrons to follow. No one will hazard a probability of recovery. I can only say...I'm sorry. Should the Agency wish to void the agreement, I'll not raise an objection."

"You shouldn't feel guilt for delaying this disclosure, Mrs. Poynter. By now the cash to ransom your husband has been delivered. We can hope for his safe return to you and your children. Were the shoe on the other foot, I would have done nothing different."

"So kind of you, Mr. Mannheim. My family's fate is in the hands of people I don't know and will never meet. It's been an adjustment...this business of being an unofficial spy."

"You've no particular allegiance to, or affection for, Mr. Frankel...do you?"

Nasha tilted her head to admire Jupiter shining in the moon's reflection. "Aaron Frankel is a complicated man. Like you, Mr. Mannheim, he's clever and smart and I've come to an enhanced appreciation of the difference. He's a charlatan, but not dishonest...a gambler with an admirable track record in his investments. I think worse men and women would be quite easily found in Washington. But no, Mr. Mannheim, my allegiance is to my country and my affections belong to my family. Our deal was three billion in return for the concessions given. I'll renegotiate for whatever one billion will buy."

"Let me walk you to your car, Mrs. Poynter. You can tell me about your children."

As Nasha Poynter's taillights receded, Mannheim dialed Phyllis Martell. "Have you located Anne Linton?"

"I'm at her home, sir. Not here."

"Found a list of her current jobs?"

"Made the calls, Mr. Mannheim...all private homes. No one's seen her."

Who had Fulton Bennett been close to? Who exhibited enthusiasm for Bennett's peculiar way of doing things?

"Do you know Dr. Gregory Riley, Phyllis?"

"By reputation, sir."

"Find him. Tell him Anne Linton has Fulton Bennett's legacy...and ask Dr. Riley to accompany you. He'll know what to do. Bring a stout shopping bag, Phyllis."

***

Nazarian watched Michael da Silva cross the street, hair blowing from the chopper's downdraft, furtive glances to the left and right unproductive. Never changing pace, a final step took da Silva inside the studio.

Dropped into a crouch, half expecting to be shot, he shuffled two steps to his right and listened hard. A distinct sound marked the spring action of his switchblade. Thirty feet from his position an attractive platinum blonde hung naked, head lolling like a drunk.

Dry mouth made da Silva crave a beer.

Raissa was taken completely by surprise, when the helicopter arrived. Were the helicopter and Caroline connected?

When the door opened and a malnourished man entered, she caught a glimpse. Not Policia. Hearing the knife spring open, and mentally drawing an equilateral triangle, she was ten steps from either Caroline or the intruder. She would wait—let the man establish his intent, because the machine pistol Raissa took from Caroline's drugged hands wasn't reliable or accurate.

***

Nazarian left his perch at the parapet for a prone position underneath several clotheslines holding children's' underwear. Only when the chopper's searchlight rotated away could he scurry forward to surveil the studio.

He monitored the inexorable ascension of the Policia's caravan. Took note of Marie, who couldn't possibly be a casual bystander, and like himself wasn't a combatant. Wondered about Tiago's current location; Tiago was a wild card.

***

Booze affected Michael da Silva's sense of artistic value. In the platinum blonde's case, hanging on the cross her beauty approached perfection. He flicked an inch long cut above the line of Caroline's pubic hair.

She jolted, every muscle and tendon shown in relief, like the sculpture she believed herself to be. Mute, her eyes spoke with eloquence. Blood trickled into a matted mass of dark curls.

Recorder thrust towards Caroline, da Silva's yell was too loud. "Who killed Gunther?"

Gunther's name shook Raissa to the core. Her finger hit *Enter* on Javier's computer, before she glided silently over the floor. Please, she implored, let the router stay connected.

Thirst drove impatience. Da Silva yelled louder. "Who killed Gunther?" Silence persisted. He slashed a longer, deeper cut above the first. "CIA Bastard wants to know who killed Gunther, before I cut out your heart."

Caroline's gasp was an involuntary spasm.
Michael da Silva knew she could speak.

***

Head on a swivel the lead APC's gunner would die first, if the gangs decided on war. Straight ahead, at a range the gunner estimated at sixty meters, an RPG was slung over the shoulder of an angelic boy.

Alberto da Silva's second-in-command launched the missile at precisely the moment the mounted machine gun fired. His teenage comrade died without seeing the RPG surge off-course.

Mesmerized by the fiery trail, hundreds of bystanders witnessed the front wall of Zabban's studio erupt in flame and smoke. Stone and stucco fragments became secondary projectiles.

Alberto launched a second RPG from the protection of the alley. Reaction time slowed by smoke and mayhem, the machine gun's death rattle pocked buildings near where Alberto no longer stood. The top of the APC lifted from the machine's frame in a fireball soaring above surrounding rooftops.

Debris rained.

Small-arms fire, from both Policia and Alberto's gang, continued as Bosque's APC retreated downhill.

Zigzagged through half a dozen alleys, Marie sprinted to confront a retreating Alberto. "You killed one of my clients."

Alberto's mouth curled into a confluence of defiance and arrogance.

Marie shot him in the groin.

"It's a matter of principle, you little prick." Grabbing her backpack from Alberto's shoulder, she began to run towards the prostitute's house where Marco would, by now, be numb with fear. Stopped short, she looked back. "Sorry...you can't be a prick any longer."

Nazarian, trying to cross the street, looked both ways like an old woman. Stayed low. Made it to the rubble pile before a ricochet went through his thigh. Lifting his head, he could see into the studio where the green-screen was still lit. Unable to stand or walk, he hoped an American tourist, like himself, would survive.

Furthest from the blast's epicenter, Raissa saw the scrawny, knife wielding, man twisted into a pretzel of torn flesh. Caroline's adrenaline driven, blood-soaked shape staggered over him, gaining adequate balance to plunge the slim blade into his unseeing eye.

"Motherfucker," she screamed, white skin pitted in a hundred locations by the storm of shrapnel. Looking intently at the knife in his eye, she said matter-of-factly, "Sir Edward Poynter...Khalid bin Rahman...Aaron Frankel...they all killed Gunther. They're all fucking bastards."

Holding the machine pistol, Raissa took five steps forward into Caroline's line of sight.

Caroline, adrenaline momentarily overriding Quelicin, arched her back in defiance. Neither apology nor forgiveness was on a menu spiced with fate's twisted humor.

Raissa ejected the clip into her left hand, dropped the weapon and disappeared into the rear of the wrecked studio.

In slow motion, as if directed by Zabban for a viral video of her own, Caroline slumped to the floor.

***

Marie Truchet climbed two flights of stairs in a sprint. Burst into the room where Marco watched the aftermath of a ten second blitzkrieg.

"Let's get out of here, Marco. We'll figure everything out as we go." Seeing his eyes widen, the cause was apparent: Caroline Panero, crawling in the road, naked as a jaybird, her torso running in blood.

Marco turned to Marie. "You've made a bollocks of everything. I'm going to help my wife. We'll go to the British Consulate...where you damn well should've taken me. Get out of my way."

"You know Andrew's dead?"

Marco's face belonged to a different man. "For the best, really. Jobim will be appeased."

Marie stuffed cash in his hand and stepped aside. "Client's always right, Marco. Scream *British Consulate*...keep screaming until the television crews arrive."

She went to the window, watching him waddle towards a private purgatory. Used the prostitute's shower. Found a stretchy skirt, t-shirt and sandals in the bedroom. Left a hundred dollars from her backpack on the bed. As she passed Zabban's studio on the far side of the street, a gang-banger observed the scene with an amused expression.

"Quite something," said Marie, tossing him the weapon she used to shoot Alberto da Silva.

Tiago caught the gun, light without its clip. Smiled at an attractive woman, and, watching CIA Bastard 3 struggle to stand, crossed the street to where Nazarian resembled a warmed-over cadaver. Tiago patted him on the shoulder, feigning wisdom beyond his years.

"Quite something, huh?"

CHAPTER 32

In a richly paneled library, in a winged armchair whose upholstery matched the chairs of his host and fellow guests, Mannheim scrutinized Grover Norris.

Grover would be thinking Poynter the prototypical Englishman of a certain age: Educated without intellectual accomplishment; alcoholic absent signs of inebriation; sloppily tailored in perfect fabrics; superior to one and all.

Between clouds of pipe smoke, Sir Edward gulped whiskey from a tumbler.

Offended at being press-ganged, apprehensive of Michani's purpose, Grover lost his poise.

"How do you manage, Edward? Andrew was a huckster peddling vacuum cleaners…married to an Arab whose own people think her a whore. Caroline's a shrew…selling herself to keep mortar in the crenellations. Look at you…an antique no longer holding its value."

Mannheim examined Sir Edward as the British spymaster focused on a grouping of family photos on Jean-Louis's piano. Had he picked out the silver frame showing Nasha holding Bradford?

Edward's eyes welled without expelling a tear.

Jean-Louis cut to the chase. "Gentlemen, Zachary wishes to discuss how Khalid bin Rahman has compromised each of us. You'll each find a folder at your elbow…perhaps you'd like to browse."

Grover Norris turned pages one at a time, each bearing his investment bank's logo. Seething, he spit at Mannheim. "I'll hang you by the balls."

Jean-Louis responded, "Which won't alter the evidence, Grover. Or save your bacon."

Edward Poynter hoped for a reprieve. "I tell you Jean-Louis...the bastard's forty million quid was promptly paid-back to the Exchequer. I won't be blackmailed by this...this functionary." Finger pointed at Mannheim, he insisted, "The PM and the JIC are fully informed."

Zachary's distaste for Sir Edward was hidden behind an unknown future.

"Sir Edward, your planned assassination of Aaron Frankel failed, but your assassin was complicit in the murder of Gunther Probst. An officer in MI-6, your man operated from bin Rahmin's inner circle with your knowledge and affirmation. Your daughter was, until very recently, bin Rahman's lover. Your son was sought by the Brazilian Navy for fraud and corruption. Your daughter-in-law risked life, limb and her future to attempt Andrew's rescue from an operation you ordered.

Mannheim turned to Grover.

"Grover, your bank holds deposits directly traceable to bin Rahman, proven by the documents you hold. Whether you directed Bryson Sewell to further the bank's relationship with the Sheikh can be debated. Were I you Grover, I'd take affirmative action to protect your reputation. It seems clear Khalid bin Rahmin is more than a worthy adversary."

Michani was Mannheim's final target.

"Jean-Louis, you've made inappropriate loans to Sir Edward. PaneroGlobal's fees, from the Brazilian fraud, were paid into an account at your bank, from which bribes were paid to Brazilian officials. And there's the strange incident where two billion dollars of the Sheikh's previously vaporized money suddenly appeared in an account, established in favor of the U. S. Treasury, at your bank."

Leverage considered, Zachary issued demands.

"There will be no public accusations of criminal activity or misconduct. However, repercussions will be unavoidable. Suffer them in silence, gentlemen. Should you do further harm, consider the consequences of being identified as Raissa's truest and most malevolent demons."

***

The very idea of Zachary Mannheim waiting in her office, first thing in the morning, gave CIA's Personnel Resources Manager heartburn. She went to greet him with no enthusiasm. Fraught with needless concern for her career, she heard only half his request. Data scrolling across her screen, she was openly nervous.

"How long ago did you say?"

"Between three and four years." Mannheim, by now, was certain what he sought would be found. What to do then, was another knot to unravel?

"Terminated for cause?"

Mannheim's mental machinations halted. Terminated was one of those words with vastly different definitions, dependent upon who used it and where. Based on reports filtering in from Rio, termination and fuckup might soon be listed together as synonyms for CIA Operations ordered by Presidential advisor Grover Norris.

"Correct. Drugs. Alcohol. Theft. Something along those lines."

"Terminated by Deputy Director Bennett himself?"

"No, definitely not by Bennett."

Ten minutes passed in reflection; Mannheim found himself approving of Bennett's dogged persistence. Noise from the printer told him the candidate list was forthcoming. When she handed it to him, he scanned the sheet, nodded what seemed vague approval and told the terrified woman, "Thank you for your assistance. You may log my inquiry by date and time, but no details please. Do you understand?"

"Yes sir, we follow protocol to the letter."

***

Morning had come and gone without anything to eat. In a bakery not far from Nasha Poynter's home, Mannheim sat on a high stool savoring a civilized cup of coffee and a decadent, cheese filled, croissant. Pre-Holiday orders of pies and other goodies made for a steady stream of cash and good-cheer at the registers.

Sadly, things wouldn't be so upbeat at the Poynter household.

She'd be in shock trying to deal with the news about her husband—with a strong dollop of denial added to her morning tea.

Riley entered, toting a large reusable shopping sack and dragging behind a man, whose file put his age at twenty-four, although his appearance shouted younger. Neither of two men took a stool, but stood close to form a ring of three conspirators.

Mannheim lowered his reading glasses and openly assessed the narrow face, suspicious eyes, scruffy beard and Cal Tech sweatshirt in need of a wash. "Randall Carter?"

The kid's Adam's Apple bobbed as a form of acknowledgment.

"Are you pleased with your results?"

"Not really." Clearly, when talking about his work, he was in his element.

"What went wrong?"

"We planned to empty the accounts on Bennett's schedule...over a year ago. I couldn't get it done. Not the way Bennett said I had to. So Anne and I, we started over. Took the funds as Frankel tried to move them. Not as elegant, but still pretty cool."

"But not the total amount, correct?"

"Frankel...or his IT guys...they're not bad. We did get two thirds of everything."

"All this done in your apartment...after Director Bennett was murdered?"

"Yeah. Mrs. Linton...Anne...told me to keep at it. I was a little frustrated. A lot pissed." Whether Carter was bored or awaiting arrest, his attitude was ambivalent.

"Would you like to come back to work, Randall?"

"Dunno."

"Would you prefer prison?"

Carter's eyes became bowling balls bulging in disbelief. "I did it for Bennett. Under his orders. This isn't fair...you can't just..." Suddenly quiet, he showed resolve by breaking his slouch and standing with a straight spine.

"The Agency would like you to come back to work, Mr. Carter. We admire what you accomplished. Perhaps you'd come to my office in CIC tomorrow?"

"Yuh. I suppose."

"By the way, Randall, tell me how you selected the depository bank for two billion dollars."

For the first time in months Randall Carter broke into a wide grin.

***

Assembled for the final time in the matter of Fulton Bennett, now deceased, Grover Norris couldn't help bitching.

"Nothing more to discuss, is there? Why have you insisted on a formal debrief, Zach?"

Owen Lattimore felt the need to interject. "Let's hear what there is to hear. Then we can all advise D/CIA Granholm of his options." Lattimore had sat in more than one meeting where Mannheim's reports upset the apple cart. By now he knew better than to let Granholm get ahead of the process.

Mannheim began, speaking in anemic monotone.

"Fulton Bennett was duped by persons unknown at the Ritz-Carlton. CIC, as well as the FBI, believe a Lebanese national by the name of Fathima Laniado carried out the ruse and committed the associated murder. Ms. Laniado may have left the United States and is believed to be in Lebanon."

Mannheim paused to closely examine the face of DD/CIA, who provided the next piece of the report.

"There is, in addition, a credible source who informed us Ms. Laniado may be deceased. Deputy Director Bennett's death, together with Ms. Laniado's status, closes the direct portion of our investigation into Bennett's actions."

Grover said, "Happy days. Are we done?"

Mannheim cleared his throat and raised the volume. "There are several areas of the investigation into Bennett's integrity which touch directly on operations within the National Clandestine Service."

Lattimore became concerned and said, "Bennett's integrity was never called into question."

"When CIC is asked to be involved, Owen, integrity, honesty and fealty are always involved. May I proceed?"

The attorney lapsed into silence. He might once have served Grover Norris; it wasn't true today.

"Three billion dollars of terrorist money has been recovered and deposited wherever Treasury determines recovered funds go. The

President offered congratulations to Grover and D/CIA Granholm. Our congressional oversight committees are content for a fleeting moment. There are, however, flies in the soup. Fly number one: During this operation, fifty million dollars were deposited in your bank Grover. Deposited from a Cayman Islands corporation with direct, well established and demonstrable ties to Khalid bin Rahman. While your tenure as D/CIA is over, it's an open secret around town…you, not Jamie, have been in charge of NCS since the Ritz-Carlton murder. You'll be asked for the standard disclosures: Like the ones you insisted upon when Fulton Bennett was in the dock. Fly number two: During this operation, Grover issued a kill order on a retired Agency officer named Raissa Ribeiro. The kill order…"

Lattimore interrupted. "Must we use that word, Zachary?"

Mannheim was in no mood to mollify Owen Lattimore's semantic queasiness. "The kill order was issued, according to several direct accounts, on the probability Ribeiro may have murdered an Agency officer named Gunther Probst. Probst, CIC learned, photographed Frankel in the company of several bin Rahman associates…in Boston…and was murdered to prevent NCS from acquiring specific Intel. Two attempts to carry out the kill on Ribeiro failed; the latter ended with the widely viewed Internet video of Caroline Poynter Panero claiming Gunther Probst's death can be attributed to Edward Poynter, Khalid bin Rahman and Aaron Frankel. Besides gross disloyalty to an injured former officer, Grover's kill order was illegal unless initiated by D/CIA Granholm. CIC found no evidence of D/CIA's involvement."

Grover deflated. He'd signed up for a celebration and come to his own hanging.

Lattimore began to think Zachary Mannheim would settle for a single scalp.

"Fly number three: Under the terms of the Agency's agreement with Mrs. Nasha Poynter, neither the Agency, its agents and employees, nor Mrs. Poynter, are permitted to profit from the activities covered by the agreement. Approximately two billion dollars, of the three billion recovered, were, when recovered from Mr. Frankel, deposited in accounts at Grover Norris's investment bank. Fees and account maintenance charges during the period in question totaled more or less eight million dollars. It will be your job, Mr. Lattimore, to determine whether Grover may be held in civil or criminal violation of the Agency agreement with Mrs. Poynter. You all may remember, at General Counsel's insistence, Mr. Wesley Jackson concurred with the premise Mrs. Poynter could be held criminally liable for any violation of those terms…provided Agency employees were reciprocally liable. It seems our hands are soiled."

Grover Norris snorted, then addressed himself to Owen Lattimore.

"Bullshit. Complete bullshit, in fact. Make it go away, Owen."

Lattimore said dryly, "There's no concern unless Mrs. Poynter were to file suit. Which she won't. Suing the Agency would be foolish…she's got fragments of a husband to bury and children to concern herself with." Lattimore instantly regretted bad taste used in furtherance of a trivial point.

DD/CIA had been silent until now. "Or she could hold a press conference. I've seen her on television…not bad at all."

Grover again defended himself in a room he well might not visit again. "Two edged sword, gentlemen. The Brazil thing was a fiasco. Her husband was dirty. Caroline Poynter is a terrorist. Edward Poynter can't find his asshole with his thumb. We'll never hear a peep from the Poynter woman."

D/CIA Granholm had the last word. "Not Zach's point, Grover. Not at all. It'll be the stink everyone smells. Whose shoes have shit on them won't matter. We appreciate your overview, Zach. Be sure and polish the written report to a Marine Corps shine before you submit it."

What D/CIA's facial expression conveyed was Washington politics at its cynical finest.

***

If it was to be a kindness as intended, Islam's traditions regarding death must be observed. Yet Andrew wasn't Muslim and his remains, mere bits and pieces, could never be washed and shrouded. The brouhaha over his behavior in Brazil was a matter for lawyers and diplomats, not the Intelligence community—Mannheim had assured the proper outcome.

Andrew could be, and would be mourned with respect.

Dressed in a suit reserved for funerals, he knocked.

Nasha, wearing black from head to toe, answered the door

carrying her son on a hip. Grief deserved notice; it was still fresh.

Her features were not marked by worry lines or her posture bent from carrying unexpected burdens.

"I'm here to express my deepest sympathies, Mrs. Poynter...and to invade your mourning for less than five minutes, if you'll permit."

"Sorry for the mess." A mixture of weariness and conjecture waited in expectation.

"Please accept my apology for this intrusion. If there was any alternative..." Mannheim stopped as she fought the inevitable flood of tears. "All bin Rahman's funds are accounted for. Quite early this morning I provided your father with electronic data governing the transfers and authorizations completing your agreement with the Agency."

"Why help me...?" She couldn't help but notice a freshly polished gold wedding band on Mannheim's finger.

Disappointment in the Agency he cared about would be one reason. Because he could, was another. Would either explanation be true? What could he say to lessen her pain?

"Because good intentions pave the road to Hell. Because good people can be reckless. Reckless people occasionally need reminders." Intentionally obtuse, this topic was best left for another day. Zachary found himself looking forward to tea in her kitchen, in the company of innocent children.

She took his hand, fingering the ring. "I keep waiting to feel something...how long has it been?"

"I used to walk with her. Her hand in mine..."

Nasha saw him tally the reckoning. Heard the sound a heart makes when memories are covered with malice. Saw the future.

"Learn to say goodbye, Mrs. Poynter."

Her world upside down and unraveling, she walked him to the door. Across the street the ubiquitous green pickup sat, windows frosted over as if parked there for hours.

A stretch limo pulled to the curb. Seconds passed before imminent danger registered. When the limo door opened, Nasha saw Fathima Laniado in the rear seat. Nabil Hanna's smarmy, burlesque smirk greeted her. From the front seat came the chauffeur and another burly thug from Nabil's closet of horrors.

Voice hoarse, she said, "They're here to take my children." Looking to where Mannheim had stood, he was nowhere in view.

In the battered pickup, Nasha's imaginary Egyptian stirred from hours of torpor, showing marginal interest in the limo or its occupants. He popped a quartered orange into his mouth.

Nasha's silent scream was overtaken by Colonel Hanna's violent promise. "No more husband to hide behind. You're a street whore whose half-breed whelps will be left in the Lebanese desert to be cleansed."

She slammed the door, running to retrieve a Glock which wasn't there.

Their feet stomped up the stairs to the porch.

Nasha felt her life coming apart. She reached to grip an impotent carving knife.

Moving with alacrity, Yusef yanked open the limo's door, observing plastic ties binding Fatima's hands and feet. Slit her throat in one efficient motion. "I'll send your regards to Fakhir."

Nabil Hanna's cruelty unleashed, he demanded, "Come quietly or I'll break the boy child's neck in his crib. Soon Lebanon will repay your loyal service."

Every inch the regal Ambassador in voluptuous vicuña, Nabil's gloved hands held no weapon. Behind him, Mahbeer's replacement appeared too willing to shoot her.

A hand grabbed her arm, twisting it behind her. Clattered to the floor, the knife never would have saved her family. For seconds extending to the end of Nasha's life, Nabil Hanna glorified in victory.

Nasha's eyes glazed over. History will repeat itself; machine-gunned like my mother, blood seeping into endless sands.

"Allah save my children," she cried.

Consecutive coughing sounds gave her back her arm as the Lebanese security man collapsed in a heap. Nabil's chauffeur stepped to his left, raising his arm to fire his weapon. From the powder room's doorway an additional two coughing sounds fragmented the chauffer's forehead.

"Don't." One peremptory word from Mannheim ended Nabil's intentions. "I've only recently met Sir Edward Poynter, but he cares deeply about his grandchildren and their mother. Resignation from your post as Acting Ambassador will be demeaning, but survival is a difficult trick to master."

Unable to resist, Mannheim spoke a final time to Nabil Hanna.

"You knew we were listening. Did you never think at all?"

Unable to apply civil standards, unwilling to leave justice undone, from point blank range Zachary shot Hanna twice through the bridge of his nose.

Mannheim made three telephone calls. With the necessary arrangements completed, he witnessed a sea change in Nasha Poynter. Standing tall, son cradled in her arms, it was clear: She was made of strong stuff.

"I'm terribly sorry you went through this, Mrs. Poynter, but I must go."

"Four months and ten days, Mr. Mannheim...the length of my formal mourning period. Come for tea. As our friend."

Coelho Grows Everything—so the truck's sign read. An Egyptian terrorist Nasha thought the driver to be, Yusef stood by the driver's door as Mannheim approached.

"Thank you for your assistance, Yusef."

Mannheim shook his head in sadness. Brother and sister—tragedy altered one's perspective.

"Walk the tightrope at your peril, young man. To whom does Yusef Schwartz belong? Not the terrorists...choose the terrorists, you become every man's enemy. Mossad sees doubles around every corner. CIA is paranoid and Yusef is Arab first, Jew second. Choose family, Yusef. Find a way to shine light into your shadows.

***

"Hey, Jew boy can't jump. Chop chop. Gotta win'em all to make the playoffs."

Ears still twitched. Brows failed to furrow. Some faces were clever enough to hide their amusement. The laws of self-preservation still trumped the laws of physics, but kowtowing to a figure of ridicule was never going to happen.

Still spewed without forethought, intended malice was more habitual than meaningful, more a comment on the speaker than those listening. Jamie Norris was too familiar, if still unknown. His irritated expression lingered long after his words were heeded.

The lead Suburban held four men and a woman, the exact gender makeup it held the last time Yusef Schwartz played basketball—but not the same players. Robby Turcott's second SUV carried an identical mix of three men and two women. Deputy Director Reggie

Crenshaw, fifty-one years old and feeling his way through his first week replacing Fulton Bennett, was a former Air Force one-star handpicked by D/CIA for the position. No one at Langley knew him well enough to describe him as a prick.

Sarah Gullickson appreciated the writing on the wall. She asked Jamie Norris under her breath, "Has he told you whether you're staying?" Sarah had three interviews lined up with lobbying firms.

Yusef Schwartz dozed. Three weeks passed since he was shot and Andrew died. His shoulder better but not good, he hid behind a claim of rotator cuff surgery. Bore the pain as the stoic he worked at being. Today he'd play with his left hand. Repeatedly, Yusef found himself in Nasha's neighborhood. Sometimes he saw her with the children.

There'd been no coded messages from the Sheikh. No visits from Billy Ray, intent on vengeance. He'd begun frequenting a new mosque. Visits with Papa were something he wanted very badly.

Nasha must hate him.

Yusef was, for the very first time, willing to recognize loneliness.

"I love this game." Deputy Director Crenshaw stood beside Yusef as he shot short-range jump shots one-handed. "Whatever happened to JET? Kid could do it all."

Yusef tossed Crenshaw the ball and watched the older man lift off the floor and bury a ten-footer. "No idea," he responded.

"Heard he got a shot with the Knicks."

"Mmm." Yusef heard other things.

"Shoulder surgery go well?"

"Mmm."

"Also heard your ego's large enough to handicap the occasional shooting competition."

"Yup."

"Those damn chocolates I found in Bennett's office...unbelievably good. How many shots you give an old man like me?" Yusef observed the new guy's athleticism and pride. Maybe one shot would be fair.

"Give you sweat off my balls. Even up. You man enough?"

"Coward. You were All-America. I'm a desk jockey. Gimme three."

"You can have two." Nothing was different after all. Nothing in the life of an improbable spy ever would be.

EPILOGUE

Summer came to Cape Cod.

The Raissa Ribeiro furor settled to a simmer—meaning full color ads were in all the women's magazines, but not so much on television. There'd been no interviews, because she refused them all.

She texted a get-well to David Nazarian. He'd done more than a little. More than he should've, if truth was told. Which was a rarity in the grinding expectations faced by a spy.

Melissa and Tom Nichols pushed open Raissa's unlocked front door and found her on the porch drinking beer from the bottle. Raissa stopped scratching Angela's ear long enough to turn and say, "Hey guys, pull up a chair. Beers in the tub."

"Wow..." said Melissa checking out the unobstructed view over the bay and out to Nantucket Sound "...what a life."

Tom remained standing, half his first beer drained. He said in a good-natured way, "Give the lady a break, Mel."

Raissa laughed. She knew what Melissa Nichols wanted. It was the same thing everyone wanted, but couldn't have. Maybe it'll be cathartic, she thought.

"Men...what the hell do they know. Twenty questions, Melissa, ask away. Then it'll be my turn. Fair enough?"

"I couldn't."

"Sure you can. It's okay. I'll tell you the unvarnished truth...this one time."

Her final three words edged in stainless steel, only Tom noticed the difference.

Melissa Nichols was no slouch in the looks department. Her first question wasn't a surprise. "In the video...you're so unbelievably gorgeous...was it hard?"

"Not so much. I needed to lure a killer."

"So what everyone says...?"

"Nope, none of it was made up for my comeback as a fashion model. Too damned real."

Melissa was embarrassed, but enthralled. "Which demon was the killer?"

"All of them...none of them. Turned out not to matter."

"So revenge...?"

"Pretty much what they say...not very satisfying. And I'll save you a question...I didn't harm a hair on their heads. Life's never fair."

Tom couldn't help himself. "Gunther's case still open?"

"There'll never be an arrest, Tom. Poor Haslett." She reflected a moment and added, "Most of all...poor Gunther."

Melissa made a face at her husband and asked, "So did you make a zillion from all the photo-shoots?"

"Nope. They didn't exist. Everything was done one afternoon in Rio. All the ads you see in the magazines...came from one set of pictures. Everything else photo-shopped. Computers are magic. Paolo Zabban got all the proceeds. I didn't do it for the money."

"The last video...where the man cuts the female demon...then she stabs him in the eye...?"

"Real. No computers needed."

"Were you there?"

"Yes."

"What happened after...?"

"It was pretty funny. She staggered out into the street naked. Her husband showed up screaming for a taxi. Imagine what the ride was like. Me...I came home to Cape Cod...got my dog back."

"Is it true..."

Raissa wouldn't make it easy. "Is what true?"

"You've killed people."

"It's my job."

Tom noticed Raissa's use of the present tense.

Melissa had one final thing she wanted to know. "Why do you look so...?"

"Ordinary? Cause it's who I am. Raissa...the one the public

knows…is an illusion."

Melissa went silent, still finding it amazing to be in this woman's presence.

Raissa said, "My turn. Do you love your husband?"

"Very much."

"Best part of the day when he comes home?"

"For sure."

"Could you imagine cheating…either one of you?"

She said, "No." Tom said, "Understand how lucky I am."

"Tom's just a cop, right?" Raissa said it unpleasantly.

Melissa fumed, too polite to answer.

"How about you, Melissa? When you got here just now…you thought trading places with Raissa Ribeiro sounded good. Well…my life doesn't include any of the things you think are normal. In my world, there's no love…just constant calculation: How to stay alive; how to stay sane; who to believe and why would God ever save me. Don't envy me. In my line of work…do a good job and you get to keep it."

She lifted the t-shirt printed with Agatha's face. Watched the kaleidoscope of reaction. "See…just the scars are real."

ABOUT THE AUTHOR

John Hayden has spent a career in engineering and construction, advising politicians and high ranking government officials across the USA, Europe and the Middle East.

John earned a Ph.D. in engineering from the University of Pennsylvania. He is married with three adult children. John and his wife Janet reside on Cape Cod.

Thank you for reading!

I loved creating the characters and their circumstances in **No Man's Mercy…No God's Forgiveness**. Stay tuned—their world of spies and politicians will be the subject of three new books to be published over the next year.

Reader reviews have the ultimate power to influence a book's acceptance and sales. Whether you loved my story or found it a disappointment, please take a few minutes to give me and other readers your opinion.

Here's a link to my author page on Amazon, where you can find all my books:

https://www.amazon.com/JohnHayden/e/B002MN7358%3Fref=dbs_a_mng_rwt_scns_share

Select the book you've read and its format. Scroll down to the Customer Reviews section and then click on the "Write a customer review" button.

Thanks again,

John

INVITATION TO SAMPLE:

The second book in the Zachary Mannheim Series is titled
PHOTOGRAPHS OF EMILY.
The first two chapters begin below.
I hope you'll enjoy the sample and continue to read Zachary Mannheim's stories of a life in
Counter Intelligence.

CHAPTER 1

"What can you see?"

Intestines strangled by fear, larynx near paralyzed by dust, blind to the happenings outside a rattle-trap panel van, Iraj Rashidi needed his question to be treated as important. To be alone, in every meaning of the word, diminished the slender scientist's confidence. He'd jumped off a proverbial cliff without benefit of the ability to fly.

"I see everything." answered the van's driver.

Hasil Sabir spoke Baluchi, the language of the Baloch people who inhabited a forgotten region encompassing portions of eastern Iran, southwestern Afghanistan and western Pakistan. Common borders were a plague to all three countries.

"I see Zähedin where the Revolutionary Guard recruits my brothers for their nefarious purposes, Chahar Burjak where Russians died from arrogance and stupidity, and Zaranj where a sheep like yourself will be sheared, if not slaughtered, before becoming another day older."

Sabir possessed no specific knowledge of his passenger's familiarity with Baluchi, but guessed a duck out of water, who might be an intellectual, wouldn't understand ironical musings. Long the epicenter of smuggling and migration into and out of Afghanistan, Pakistan and Iran, Zaranj counted for less than nothing in the world outside those countries.

Rashidi's curiosity curbed, he added, "We must be near the border. Will there be difficulty entering Zaranj?"

Among divergent views held by Iranians on every topic, Persian versus Farsi marked a symptom more than a disease in cultural or religious debates. Iraj spoke Azeri as well as Kurdish and a smattering of Sabir's Baluchi. Dari, a byproduct of Iranian Persian common to Afghanis, presented Rashidi with no difficulty. Dari and Pashtu, another common Afghani language, bastard cousins as they might be, fit the same mold of familiarity. Rashidi's fluency in English and French would be irrelevant to his immediate survival.

Sabir ceased making fun at Rashidi's expense. "We are near the border, but not near Zaranj. In an hour we meet my cousin who'll drive south and east through Mirabad, east near to Chahar Burjak, north and west not so near Laskar Gah then west nearby nothing for three hundred klicks to a place close by Zaranj. Another cousin will take you into the city."

Mind clogged with the grandiose nature of his intentions, as well as hundreds of minutiae required to convert intention to reality, what had seemed obvious to Rashidi on a map failed Sabir's transition to Dari.

"Why not cross on a direct route?" Extortionist payment demands never mentioned a ten-hour tour of Afghanistan's geographic colon. Accusations against the smuggler's integrity unwise, he restrained protest. "In what way would we be prevented from entering Zaranj?"

"How could you ask such a thing?" Hasil Sabir glanced at his passenger in disbelief. Then cast a quick look at the beardless man occupying the passenger seat. Shook his head in wonderment at the passenger's innocence.

Focused on the GPS watch on his right wrist, its data was more alchemy than physics while the van travelled an un-mapped road. provided a higher-level trust in his location. Interpretation of those GPS coordinates meant the difference between success or failure—and life or death.

Rashidi persisted. "Why not the shorter route? Thirty klicks instead of six hundred...in this wasteland a smuggler could save fuel and time." Where he would be robbed and left for dead formed his only priority, since Rashidi hoped to control not the instance of his death, but its exact location. Back resting against the van's cooler sidewall, away from the sun, death lost philosophical flavor in favor of its practical peculiarities.

***

Output from the Counter Terrorism Center's ("CTC") operational drones could be monitored in real time on a wall of flat screen monitors. Past midnight Freddy Medina, CTC's Director, yawned.

"Are we boring you, Freddy?"

Deputy Director of the National Clandestine Service ("NCS"), General Reginald Crenshaw (Ret.) couldn't enjoy the early hours of his fifty-second birthday and preferred not to reminisce about eight months as Fulton Bennett's replacement. A former Air Force one-star, handpicked by the Director of Central Intelligence ("D/CIA"), very little in a succession of desk jobs prepared him for life as America's Top Spy.

"Your words, not mine, Reggie. Three hours and not a damn thing worth my attention."

Heat from CTC's spotlight would, on occasion, burn an officer on whose authority biblical reckoning would rain on guilty and innocent alike.

"Our UAVs are killing terrorists in six countries while NCS obsesses over an un-vetted asset in a godforsaken province within a country where not a thing can be verified. I can't imagine a worse place to get caught with my dick in your hand."

Medina's work habits ran to twelve-hour days and hundred hour weeks—a load increased when CIA's primary tasking of drones had been hamstrung with a stroke of POTUS's pen. An opinionated chain smoker, who survived years of internecine battles at Fulton Bennett's side, CTC's Chief hated Crenshaw's inexperience in covert operations. Hated how Bennett's death colored his every response to Reggie Crenshaw.

"What would you suggest, Freddy?" Spit at Medina like shells from an F-15's Gatling gun, Crenshaw's words reflected anxiety and internal Agency politics.

Freddy was prone to suspicion absent black and white proof of theories adopted by spies. "So…you want me to believe Dr. Iraj Rashidi dragged his ass out of his professorial bed at Amirkabir University… and gave CIA a ringy-dingy through an intermediary…offered critical insight into Iran's nuclear development program, complete with supporting data, but submitted nothing to our experts for review. NCS believes Rashidi's messenger who, because God ordains him, the professor can't or won't identify. So we wait, expecting a squirt on a frequency we never use, so this bird..." Medina pointed at the orbiting *Reaper's* visual display "...can put a missile on a group of smugglers, or Revolutionary Guards, to keep Rashidi's testicles being fed to nomadic goats. There are no NCS operatives on the ground who speak Baluchi, and given all the above you seem not to appreciate the holes in this operation. Why should my birds remain on-call for as long as it takes? Why should I go blind watching hundreds of square miles of Balochestani sand? How could I be bored?"

***

Rashidi felt his throat tighten as he asked a second time, "What do you see? You must see something."

Their failure to respond revealed as much as the pulsating *thump...thump...thump* of the smuggler's carotid artery.

Populated with regret, Sabir's eventual answer amounted to a whispered prayer. "Nothing. I see nothing, but feel everything." Unnerved by the passenger's persistence, Sabir grunted. "You're carrying nothing to identify you as a city dweller?"

Filled with purposeful calm, Iraj unrolled his left sleeve's cuff to examine its white cloth for a hint of discoloration. The American device, polar opposite to integrated circuits designed for long-term stability, consisted of integrated magnesium and silicon on a thin film, enclosed in silk protein. Whether dissimilar materials dissolved with high reliability, within a proscribed interval, remained an unsolved challenge. Such technical nits, beyond any ability of Rashidi to influence, qualified as trivial. His misgiving, metaphysical as some might see it, formed a more mountainous obstacle: How many of Dr. Gregory Riley's promises were lies?

A dissolvable medical diagnostic tool? To be swallowed by a human? More like science fiction, thought Rashidi, a man who believed in science more than he believed in Muhammad, God's prophet.

He found the device with his tongue. Swallowed it with a gulp from a half empty plastic bottle.

***

At CTC, a voice erupted through speakers. "BusStop...Sentinel. Weak signal acquired...transmitting now."

Sentinel, the designation for Air Force intelligence analysts attached to the Ground Command Station ("GCS") operating a flight of two Reapers, numbered several analysts, a pilot and a camera/sensor operator. Communications with the UAV occurred via encrypted satellite signals. CIA, with limited exceptions, depended on final policy decisions made by the Air Force under strict Pentagon guidance.

BusStop, an off-the-wall reference to failures during the 1980 rescue of American hostages kidnapped by Ayatollah Khomeini's Iran in 1979, was the code name selected by D/CIA Theodore Granholm for the exfiltration of Iraj Rashidi.

Much of what could or would happen to Rashidi was out of Medina's hands—unless authorization to fire a Hellfire missile was rejected, or withdrawn, after an earlier approval. Then Freddy's voice could argue for green-lighting a Hellfire onto a target illuminated by the drone's laser.

Medina pointed at Billy Goodman. "Check with BusStop Alpha 3...Nazarian should've acquired Homeboy's signal."

"BusStop Alpha 3...BusStop."

Most BusStop participants doubted Riley's futuristic toy, floating around Homeboy's hostile digestive tract waiting to dissolve.

Riley voiced a request. "Full screen on signal from Sentinel."

Blurry graphics clarified into an EKG. Line after line of medical data refined into a series of graphs.

"Put up Homeboy's baseline data."

Acquired in a dangerous operation involving Agency personnel in several countries, and an Iranian physician who administered the EKG, Homeboy's baseline data blossomed on-screen.

"BusStop...BusStop Alpha 3." Nazarian's voice seemed to originate at the bottom of a well.

Medina grabbed an unused microphone. "BusStop Alpha 3; have you acquired a signal?"

"BusStop Alpha 3; negative on acquisition."

For Medina one definitive fact stood out: Nazarian and his sniper were close to Zaranj—so Rashidi must be lost.

"BusStop Alpha 3...hold position."

Goodman exchanged glances with Medina. "Sentinel...BusStop; distance from new signal to Target Zone 1?"

"BusStop...Sentinel; thirty-three klicks from TZ 1...repeat thirty-three klicks."

Medina did the math: Reaper at thirty thousand feet; Rashidi's van thirty-three klicks from Zaranj's central market; Nazarian a single kilometer from the bazaar. Why was the van so far away?

"Greg, why would Rashidi be so far from the primary destination?"

Ph.D. in almost everything, and the only scientist at the Agency who held Medina's confidence, Greg Riley rolled his eyes.

Medina questioned the data. "EKGs match...agreed?"

Riley superimposed the field EKG over its baseline. "EKGs match."

Reluctant to involve himself further, Medina looked across at Crenshaw. "Make the call, Reggie."

Crenshaw, whose career left him unprepared for such a moment, found himself wracked with indecision. With a choice between a bad decision and Medina's hyena laugh, Crenshaw pronounced, "Homeboy's extraction is authorized and confirmed."

Medina nodded again at Billy Goodman.

"Sentinel...BusStop; recommend BusStop Alpha 1 and 2 be declared *Go* to *Rifle* any threat to Homeboy. Targeting decisions are transferred to you, Sentinel."

"BusStop...Sentinel; roger your 'go' to rifle threats." Sentinel's communication shifted. "Pilot...Sentinel; proceed with target acquisition and pre-attack checklist."

"Sensors...Pilot; Go to initiate target acquisition."

Lt. Col. Peter S. Finch (USAF), known at Creech AFB drone operations as Dragon, felt war's realities rumble his intestines. Joystick manipulating drone course and altitude, the deaths of Homeboy's pursuers were guaranteed. Irony not a factor, Dragon knew not one detail about an Iranian under his protection.

"Pilot...Sensors; target's co-ordinates acquired. Target acquired. Weapon spun-up. Laser selected and locked."

***

Rashidi heard the missile impact, felt the explosion shake the ground and watched the fireball erupt in Sabir's rear-view mirror. Brakes squealed, the van swerved and slid three hundred feet before Sabir regained control.

Sabir directed a semi-automatic at Rashidi. "How did you signal the Americans?" With great respect, he turned to the beardless man, addressing him for the first time. "Sardar Dawoud, would you, please, search our passenger again?"

Elevated by Sabir's use of the honorific *Sardar*, Dawoud forced Iraj to stick out his tongue, take off his shoes and stand naked in the heat while blowing sand insulted his body as its cavities were invaded.

Dawoud removed a latex glove. "There is nothing."

Rashidi stood erect.

The fact nothing could be found was inarguable, unless a trained surgeon dissected and examined my entrails with a microscope. The dissolved device would, according to Riley, the American spy, protect him for an interval between an hour and three hours—nowhere near enough time to drive the route intended by Sabir.

Rashidi offered a non-explanation. "They told me nothing...only they would find me. Cameras in their drones show both ordinary pictures and heat-based outlines. They know our individual infrared signatures. If you abandon, or shoot me, they will incinerate you...like those poor fools behind your van." Rashidi pointed at the Iranian armored vehicle, its machine gun exploding amongst burning flesh. He watched as the odor assaulted the nostrils of a Balochi-Iranian smuggler and his Afghani companion.

"Take me direct to Zaranj. With the one patrol eliminated, no Iranians will prevent us crossing into the city."

Expression impenetrable, Dawoud stepped away from the van and raised a Sat phone to his ear.

***

Medina's skin tingled watching Dawoud separate himself fifty yards from Rashidi.

At GCS they shared Medina's concerns. "BusStop...Sentinel; are we intercepting the call?"

Billy Goodman shook his head in the negative.
"Sentinel...BusStop; negative on intercept. Recommend you maintain BusStop Alpha 1's protocol and vectors. BusStop Alpha 2 to acquire eyes on a direct route from Homeboy to BusStop Alpha 3's position."

Reggie Crenshaw believed there could be no stupid questions in matters of this importance. "Freddy, what's happening out there?"

Medina bit the end off a cigar. "This thing will turn to liquid shit pretty damn soon."

***

Sand blasted the left side of the van as it pushed to the north. Still more blind than not, Sabir navigated by maintaining a fixed position relative to the wind and monitoring his GPS. Because no phone call could be justified following the attack on an Iranian military vehicle, he watched Dawoud with more frequency than he observed Rashidi,

Seven thousand miles separated Hasil Sabir and Freddy Medina, but their instincts pulsed on the same frequency.

Dawoud's conversational command broke the threesome's silence. "Stop here."

Sabir complied, beginning to pierce the future's veil and his role in it.

***

"Sentinel...Pilot; Oncoming vehicle two klicks from Homeboy."
"Pilot...Sentinel; confirm one vehicle approaching."
"Sentinel...Pilot; one vehicle confirmed.
"Pilot...Sentinel; confirm remaining ordnance.
"Sentinel...Pilot; seven missiles and two bombs on Alpha 1 and 2.
"Pilot...Sentinel; engage at your discretion."

***

Dawoud's autocratic instruction would be obeyed. "Drive towards the flames."

Sabir increased the van's speed, fascinated by gushing smoke and an intense fireball. *Which of my competitors, or Dawoud's personal enemies, are dead? Who else might be exterminated in this game of blind cat and frenetic mouse*—where the Americans treat any vehicle as a voracious cat and Iraj Rashidi the perfect bait?

Four corpses lay in twisted testimony to their horrible end alongside what, moments ago, was a sand-colored van. A fifth lifted an arm in supplication. Dawoud held the gun close, firing twice into a face burned to bone.

With slouched posture and narrow eyes, Dawoud didn't so much speak to Hasil Sabir as issue a whispered peroration.

"You'll be troubled no more by this thief's moral degradation. We'll deliver the Iranian professor to Zaranj, as he paid you to do."

Rashidi watched Sabir turn towards the van where he'd vomited into the sand. Half expecting Dawoud to shoot them both, the Balochi handed him a bottle of water.

"My grandfather would say about such things... *The mud of one country is the medicine of another.*"

***

Freddy Medina stared in minor disbelief. For the videotape, he said, "Sentinel...BusStop; what just happened?"

"BusStop...Sentinel; the white image is, literally, a hot gun...just been fired. It appears a member of Rashidi's group shot a survivor of Alpha 1's missile strike."

Reggie Crenshaw gazed in disbelief as Sabir's van reversed course, resuming its three hundred mile trek to Zaranj.

From the rear, where she sat as an observer, Beverly Lawson spoke to Crenshaw, her boss. "One group of Balochi smugglers used CTC to wipe out another. Not a big deal...we've been used worse than this."

Lawson's bone fides as an NCS analyst included two years in Islamabad and months in Afghanistan.

"A few years ago, Iran designated its border with Nimruz

Province...where Zaranj is located...a no-go area for foreigners. Erected a fifteen-foot wall over half the border's hundred fifty-mile length. Iranian guard towers began to shoot the same refugees who once would've been waved into Iran with a smile. Now the van will travel three legs: These Iranian-Balochis will take them part way. Pakistani-Balochis will take Rashidi onward. Different Iranian-Balochi smugglers will finish the job. Needless to say, this assumes Rashidi isn't disemboweled somewhere along the way."

Wary of certainty, Medina inquired, "Can you tell us the identity of either the shooter or the dead guy?"

Lawson's answer was blunt. "No, sir, I cannot."

"How do you know the route they'll take?"

"No mystery. Even the *Times* published an article about smuggling in this region...and Iran's efforts to reduce the flow of Afghan refugees."

"Who can identify the smugglers we're dealing with? Does Nazarian know the locals?" Medina disliked being coy, unless coy served a purpose.

Lawson wouldn't miss a chance to pontificate without repercussion. "Nazarian's got a wealth of field experience, but hasn't been in Afghanistan, Pakistan or Iran in over a decade. Our military, even at full strength, never operated in Baloch territory. I can't answer your question, sir."

"So nobody knows?"

Lawson glanced at Crenshaw for help, receiving a blank expression for her trouble. "Nobody active within NCS."

Empty of senior officers, Billy Goodman and Beverly Lawson kept their thoughts to themselves.

***

A different voice at *Sentinel* indicated a mandatory shift change for pilots, sensor operators and analysts.

"BusStop...Sentinel; vehicle stopped two klicks in front of Homeboy."

With a glance at the elapsed-time clock, Goodman wished Crenshaw and Medina would exhibit equal concern for his state of readiness.

Lawson asked Goodman, "Will Sentinel engage on their own?"

Goodman understood a gentle prod. "Sentinel...BusStop; Recommend BusStop Alpha 1 and 2 be declared no-Go...I repeat no-Go. Confirm."

Goodman swore in silence at the added layer of bullshit needed to implement command decisions.

"BusStop...Sentinel; Sentinel concurs new vehicle is undeclared. BusStop Alpha 1 and 2 are no-Go. Pilot, confirm."

Goodman didn't recognize the fresh voice at Sentinel, but smiled at the sound of Colonel Oliver Pawluk, a pilot with boots-on-the-ground experience at CIA.

"Sentinel...BusStop; acknowledge Ollie Pawluk at the stick."

Two occupants exited Homeboy's vehicle and transferred to the waiting truck. With four aboard, the new truck resumed a gentle, curved track leading to Zaranj. Homeboy's original vehicle maintained position three car-lengths behind.

Beverly yawned. "Well, that's it for the next six hours. Homeboy will make it as far as Zaranj."

Squawk from the speakers announced a different possibility. "BusStop...Sentinel; no vital signs from Homeboy. Repeat, no signal from Homeboy."

Goodman picked up the phone to wake Reggie Crenshaw. Homeboy was either dead, ending Crenshaw's operation, or Greg Riley's device ran out of juice.

"All BusStop personnel...BusStop; Homeboy is home alone. Repeat...Homeboy is home alone. Sentinel...request you maintain contact with Homeboy's convoy and direct communication with BusStop Alpha 3."

CHAPTER 2

Someone banging on the door invaded Ellen Pawluk's semi-conscious state. Coffee mug in hand, Ellen stared without purpose over a small balcony. A familiar voice boomed, replacing the pounding.

"Ellen...it's Connie. UPS. Gotta couple packages for you. Gotta sign, honey. Open up."

Born Ellen Aileen Gallagher, she dragged herself back to the present from another time and, some who knew her would say, another world. A University of Wisconsin t-shirt, stained from yesterday's soft-boiled egg, hung limp on a thin frame. No underwear, no pants or shorts, she wore nothing else. Habits of a lifetime and the goddam world in general contributed to an obsessive need for a weapon. Ellen knelt behind the kitchen island, and hoped her voice sounded firm.

"Come on in, Connie, door's open."

"Hey, girl, don't shoot me. Okay? Gotta date with a new guy tonight."

On the wrong side of forty-five, Connie was a triathlete and single, as in divorced, like Ellen. Single, as in looking for a new relationship all day every day, unlike Ellen. Sober, again unlike Ellen. Sympathetic and open to expressing kindness, not in the same universe as Ellen Pawluk.

"Jesus Christ, I'm sorry Connie. You know me...paranoia queen of the unemployed, middle-aged spy community."

Ellen placed the semi-automatic within easy reach, holding out a mug to a woman who still held two small packages and her breath.

One of these days, Connie admitted, Ellen won't wait to see who's at the door, or offer coffee. One of these mornings she'll shoot till the clip's empty. Unsure staying for coffee was a smart idea, nerves kept Connie's mouth running.

"Got any sugar, honey?"

"How long before they ping you? Wanna sit for a minute?" Ellen tore open the smaller of two packages.

"Yuh, sitting sounds good...girl's gotta take a dump, after all, for all my dispatcher knows. What'cha got there, kiddo."

Ellen emptied the envelope, certain enough and irrational enough to ignore the idea of a letter bomb. The first 3x5 print was blurry. A second showed a birthday party at a neighborhood park. Ellen shuffled through two rolls, thirty-six shots to a roll. Or six rolls of twelve. Or who gives a damn how many rolls. She arranged her face so not to let Connie see how the pictures pole-axed her. Raised her eyes. A sudden conclusion embellished by a lonely and sick heart, Connie the UPS driver counted as one of only three remaining friends.

"Pictures of kids...nothing to bother with." Ellen shoved the pile across the kitchen table. Looked at the writing on the package without recognition. "Just kids at a park."

The tall, muscular woman in brown shorts handed the electronic pen to Ellen and watched her scribble. Connie delivered this package from CIA each second Tuesday--a quick calculation suggested six or seven years of deliveries. Checked the tablet controlling her routes, deliveries and expected timetable. Gulped hot coffee, glanced at the photos, and screwed-up her face in surprise.

"Jesus Ellen...these photos are four freaking years old. Where'd they come from?"

Face set in indifference, Ellen raised her coffee in slow motion.

Like she's in a trance, thought Connie--weirder than usual. "Back to the salt-mine, girl. Maybe you could try and get out for some air."

Ellen heard, but never moved to watch the brown truck roar up the street of a semi-urban Virginia suburb. Listless, she spread out the prints across a teak table which needed to be oiled and hadn't been cleaned in forever. Inevitable emotions washed over her. She padded to a drawer for the magnifying attachment of a Swiss Army knife. In a grid pattern, she examined the snapshots for the expected, then focused only on anomalies. Defeated and frightened after three prints, she considered utilizing cheap Bourbon for real, not as the prop it still was and had always been.

Ellen wouldn't ever permit herself the luxury of dreaming about Emily: Her precious child dead and buried years ago.

Booze bypassed, she twisted her head underneath the tap's flow of cold water. Hair wet, eyes tearing, she slow-walked to the Master Bedroom, entered the closet and sat on its carpeted floor. To sit was important, because balance could no longer be trusted. Her path forward would appear safe to the uninitiated, but peril lurked underneath. In the closet's hush, doubts could be shoved aside and ugly scars, from other times, could go unseen. Walls closed-in, seeking entrance to her private place. She threw her shoulder, arm and hand backwards in mindless violence. Plunged through drywall and ended in a collision with brick, the blow's vibration rattled her teeth. Rivulets of blood drained from battered knuckles. Darkness hid Ellen from all but the worst of intruders—herself.

***

UPS's tracking system could never have presented an obstacle. Mounted in every delivery vehicle, the system laid out a map from which the heavy, elderly woman could select an intersection suitable to her purpose. Fewer keystrokes than she expected granted illicit entrance to the console in Connie's truck. She spoke to a subordinate without introduction in an accent peppered with several languages.

"Where is the video?"

An angst ridden male voice responded. "My wireless is down."

"Did you see?"

Hesitation whispered a tantalizing possibility; he could lie and she wouldn't catch him. "No."

"ETA?"

He checked the time on his phone. His English was natural and idiomatic. "Four minutes at the outside."

Four minutes is too long; exposure made fools of any covert operative. Turned away from the intersection's traffic, she faded into a pharmacy's anonymity along with a cashier wearing a Sikh's turban, a white kid huffing glue from a paper bag and a yuppie mother ignoring a baby in a two thousand dollar stroller. Face towards the street at the ATM machine, no meaningful description would be extracted from these three. Still her hands quivered.

One stoplight west, the brown truck approached.

She raised the phone. "Next intersection."

To her subordinate, it seemed some additional instruction had been intended. After a moment, he concentrated on the accident to be caused; little risk would accrue to himself, only to her. His SUV cut into the right lane, then turned hard left in front of the UPS truck. To an onlooker, this obvious stupidity prompted a question: Was the driver texting? Regardless of causation, the driver's negligence led to a predictable evasive maneuver by the UPS truck, and a collision at thirty miles per hour. Two vehicles slewed into and over the curb, where the heavy woman stood leaning on her cane, hands covering her face in abject terror.

Injured wasn't the correct description; Connie Meyers felt woozy, off her game. She contemplated her safety record and the accident's impact upon her performance review. Connie saw compassion, when the heavy woman appeared in the open door. When the woman's cane came flying in her direction, in a losing battle with a nasty fall, Connie didn't feel the bee sting. Injected with Succinylcholine, Connie's motor skills disappeared, but she didn't lose consciousness as a separate chemical agent quickened the pace of death. Settled in her lower leg's musculature, a pellet awaited discovery.

***

The House Subcommittee on Terrorism, HUMINT, Analysis, and Counterintelligence awaited the gavel of its Chair, Congressman Rupert Jones Perry of the Great State of Alabama, who, seated with his notes arranged just so, observed an untimely milling about by today's witnesses.

Smug smile fixed in place, he observed to no one in particular, "These dicks look like they'd rather be elsewhere." Perry chuckled to himself as General Theodore P. Granholm (Ret.), D/CIA less than a year, wriggled round to speak with a woman behind him. "Anywhere else by the look of it." Perry's voice conversational, he inquired, "Y'all ready to go to work, Mr. Director..." Granholm wouldn't be given the satisfaction of being addressed as *General* "...any opening statement you wish to make?"

Theodore Prentice Granholm arrived at the Agency, after a quick Senate confirmation, from an uncelebrated career in the military, highlighted by the affection in which the President of the United States held him. Political from the get-go, his appointment received few rave reviews at an Agency with different values and customs than the military.

Nancy Pettigrew, the Agency's Deputy General Counsel, observed D/CIA's cheeks color in pique. Her job, in this situation, was to protect D/CIA and the reputation of the Agency. She neither liked nor admired her absent superior, Owen Lattimore, CIA's General Counsel, who should've been present in her place.

Pettigrew whispered in D/CIA's ear, "How could you prepare a statement, when we've no idea why you're here." She hurled an accusatory look at Zachary Mannheim, seated one chair to D/CIA's right.

Mannheim, the former Chief of CIA's Counter Intelligence Center ("CIC") and it's current ranking officer, refused to acknowledge her.

D/CIA's face recovered its normal pallor. "No, Mr. Chairman."

"Danny..." Congressman Perry's eyes sought the attention of Lead Counsel. "...let's get this show on the road."

Daniel Santamaria examined a sheaf of scripted questions. "Good morning, Mr. Director."

From a hundred additive accusations, he hoped to build a gallows from which the body of Granholm would swing in slow motion, creating a teachable moment for future spies: Black-ops might be a euphemism for withholding information from voters, reporters, and non-members of the Subcommittee, but not from Rupert Jones Perry.

"Mr. Director, in the months since Fulton Bennett's death has his assassin been identified, captured or eliminated?"

"No." Granholm's jaw strained under this undeniable fact.

"When you last appeared before the Subcommittee, you asked for leeway in determining whether Fulton Bennett, former Deputy Director of NCS, committed breaches of Agency policy, and/or crimes, in his efforts to seize the assets of the terrorist, Khalid bin Rahman. Are you prepared to deliver a final determination?"

"CIC's final report stated Bennett's efforts, in the matter of bin Rahman's funds, existed in a gray area of Agency policy. CIC concluded Bennett committed no crime."

Santamaria, thin to the point of appearing malnourished, high cheekbones emphasizing an angular face and, with eyebrows raised, his was the piercing expression found in raptors. "Do you endorse the CIC report?"

Granholm listened as Pettigrew whispered, then answered. "The Subcommittee should interpret my suspension of Mr. Mannheim, former Chief/CIC, as an expression of my dissatisfaction with the subject report."

"Does Mr. Mannheim's appearance today suggest his suspension is no longer in effect?"

"Mr. Mannheim is, as of today, a counter-intelligence officer serving within CIC."

"Who have you appointed to head CIC?"

"Colonel Ike Stanton, U.S. Air Force (Ret.) is the current Chief/CIC." Granholm wouldn't concede an inch regarding qualifications of Air Force officers he recruited to the Agency. This sharp beaked, scumbag congressional lawyer could jump up a fat lady's ass.

Congressman Rupert Perry reached for his microphone, sick of the folderol. "Mr. Director, the Subcommittee is pretty relaxed in closed session. Go ahead and refer to Mr. Crenshaw as Reggie and Mr. Stanton as Ike...it's all-good" The Chair nodded at Santamaria. "Continue, Daniel."

"Mr. Director, what counter-intelligence experience does Mr. Stanton bring to the Agency?"

"No explicit counter-intelligence experience. Mr. Stanton, Ike, managed large organizations in the Air Force and is, in my judgment, well suited to manage CIC."

"Has Mr. Stanton authored a critique of Mr. Mannheim's performance in L'affair Bennett?" Santamaria glanced at his boss—had his snark overstepped?

"Ike wasn't on-board for any of it. He's read the CIC report and agrees with my re-organization of CIC."

Preliminaries dealt with, Santamaria bore in. "What were the mistakes or misjudgments committed by Mr. Mannheim in regards to Bennett and the successful recovery of three billion dollars from the world's best-known financier of terrorism?"

Well, it's out in the open. Mannheim—the old buzzard—found a Congressman to play the part of poodle-in-heat.

"He lied to protect his old friend, Bennett. Interfered with a kill-order authorized against a prime suspect in the heinous murder of an Agency Field Director. Negotiated against the Government's interests in obtaining the cooperation of a Lebanese Muslim who infiltrated bin Rahman's money management schemes. Refused my order to limit his investigation of former senior Agency officers. Obstructed the operation to recover the funds you referred to. Add Mannheim's routine failure to behave as a team player...I re-assigned him in the best interests of the Agency."

***

"Can't leave the Land Rover behind, not an option." Nazarian responded to Gulam 'Gul' Zadrai's opinion the SUV marked them as American or Iranian spies intent on harming the smuggling trade. "You think we can walk into Zaranj with you carrying a bag of sniper's gear?"

Gul endorsed cynicism, when it came to David Nazarian in particular and Americans in general. "Rifle, ammunition and rangefinder are in the backpack. We'll walk. No more than an hour we'll be on the rooftop. Unless the building and this Iranian scientist don't exist."

Nazarian ignored this minor rebellion. Gul wasn't twenty-five but had used all his nine lives. Still and all, he was Nazarian's sniper and single ally, an educated Afghani with years of experience fighting the Taliban, Al Qaeda and the Pakistani Army. If I allow myself a moment of introspection—no, he cut off the thought—introspection will see us both dead.

David noticed people huddled against a long, low wooden fence. "Where are we? Why are they all here?"

"Bus stop." Gul paused, waiting to see whether Nazarian would laugh. "Migrants...trying to reach Iran. For a few months now, they've gathered here."

Gul examined hundreds of hopefuls: Hazaras, Tajiks, Pashtuns, Uzbeks and Balochis watching smugglers prepping dozens of pickup trucks.

"A few hope to continue on to Turkey or Greece. Most think they'll be okay living as illegals in Iran. Most won't find a better life."

Men waiting waved to compatriots as a weighted-down pickup

accelerated towards Iran, sixteen klicks distant. Two minutes later a tremendous explosion hurled body and truck parts like mulch from a wood chipper. Smoke rose straight as a string until a zephyr of wind overcame heat.

"Will survivors get to hospital?" Nazarian regretted a dumb question.

"Zaranj is isolated. Only in Heraat would help be available. You're the only Western man in Nimruz today. When you're gone, there won't be anyone promising great promises."

Nazarian admitted—violence and mistrust overhung Zaranj like overripe fruit. Knowing-glances followed the immediacy of suspicion. Every man a traitor. Every woman an exotic temptress. No one immune.

"How many are employed by Iran?"

"All or none…it's why Iran built the wall." Gul made no attempt at elucidation. "It's why Chinese, Romans, Israelis and Americans built walls."

***

As he looked down on tents and stalls in the bazaar, Nazarian's nerves pinged tighter than piano wire.

Gul's radio, tuned to the local police frequency, erupted when fresh explosions gave birth to black smoke half a mile across the town. Rifle, scope and rangefinder unpacked, Gul explained. "Likely the police station. A police vehicle and three officers...blown to bits."

"Yes, Iranians looking for Rashidi." Nazarian swept the bazaar with field glasses, seeing the best and worst of a covert operation share a moment. "Gul....by the money-changers, there's a boy weeping. See his chest?"

Gul's scope swiveled, then steadied.

"Across the bazaar...sixty yards to your right by the beggars and the kids selling fruit...there's Rashidi with four smugglers."

Field glasses fixed, Nazarian again studied the weeping boy with a too chubby chest. Too young, David thought, to be sacrificed.

"They sent the boy to die." Gul controlled his breathing. "He believed dying for his country would make him worthy. Now being blown into rat food is real. He weeps for himself, for the man he'll never be. For the life he'll never live."

One of the hardened men with Rashidi identified the boy-bomber, raising a handgun for an unlikely shot. The other three pushed Rashidi towards an alley.

With no time to compute the kill radius, Nazarian couldn't use his cell phone or radio; Sentinel couldn't help. "Gul...take the three around Homeboy."

Gul's rifle fired and recoiled three times.

In his pocket, Nazarian triggered a high-speed device to search and block every active cell phone frequency. No philanthropy intended towards the boy, he predicated the action on requirements established at Langley, just not by men whose motives mixed politics and ladder climbing in a nasty stew. Cynicism pushed into shadow, he waited for the boy's destiny. The tortured face of a mother, running towards the boy, became the last thing seen in the bazaar.

Semtex sucked all oxygen from the market; smoke and flames filled the vacuum. The blast alone would've ripped apart the dense mass of shoppers, merchants and children. Added devastation came from iron shavings, like needles, sewn with meticulous care into the fabric of the boy's explosive vest.

Gul stripped his rifle for storage in the backpack. Cursed the Iranians who sent the boy, Balochi smugglers who brought Iraj Rashidi here in return for money, and David Nazarian for America's endless, mindless arrogance. Temptation leapt from his eyes as Gul tilted towards mindless retribution.

An electrical line fell, arcing as a random reminder of its instability. Thick smoke masked merciless destruction.

Nazarian hurried through side alleys filled with people unconcerned with heritage, status or future prospects. Another bomb blasted in the direction Rashidi had taken. Sat-phone shoved against his ear, he spoke, formality dropped in heat spawned by desperation. "Sentinel...you see anything?"

"Negative."

"I'm on foot, hoping Homeboy's still breathing. Keep one eye on my sniper...he's gone squirrelly."

A quarter mile from the bazaar, around a corner where laundry hung between buildings, three young women brewed tea over a brazier. Nazarian's briefing contained a description of teenage boys, educated as Jihadists in a Zähedin mosque, who infiltrated Zaranj disguised as women wearing blue burqas. Two of three burqas blue, the third was black as the semi-automatic firing at Nazarian.

Too few months after a leg wound, Nazarian's reactions were too slow. A bullet ripped through his right chest. He fell, the hissing of Gul's suppressed handgun interspersed with gunfire from black and blue burqas. Twisted onto his uninjured side, David drew his weapon. Greeted by unadulterated silence, pain crawled through his mind's objection and an insistent voice penetrated.

Gul probed for an exit wound. "Get up. You're not hurt so bad..." Gul hauled Nazarian to his feet. "...but you're too old for this sort of work."

"Why do you think they sent me?" Nazarian saw befuddlement spread across the too-soon-old Afghani's face. Complex, and very different, conclusions pleased David: Irony was lost on snipers and he needed to stop the bleeding. He grunted, concerned with how long low blood pressure would support consciousness.

"BusStop...BusStop Alpha 3; Homeboy status unknown. Advise."

Billy Goodman offered cold comfort. "BusStop Alpha 3...BusStop; retrieve Homeboy. Repeat...retrieve Homeboy. BusStop Alpha 1 and 2 will remain on-station."

As a field officer, Goodman recognized the detached voice of an injured colleague whose life would merit no consideration--not when the Op was careening sideways. As Controller, Billy phoned Freddy Medina, then Reggie Crenshaw: Operation BusStop wouldn't be abandoned.

Nazarian crumpled to his knees as disinfectant from Gul's kit contacted the wound. A gas penlet injected antibiotics and painkiller. With wads of bandage held in place with elastic wrap, Nazarian drifted towards a black hole.

Gul pushed a water bottle enhanced with electrolytes into Nazarian's hand. "Drink. I'll retrieve the SUV."

***

"Sorry to interrupt again, Danny...why don't you toss Director Granholm's grenades at Mr. Mannheim. See if the former Chief of CTC blows himself up."

Congressman Perry's every instinct drove him to dislike D/CIA Granholm; a smarmy intellectual dishonesty seemed to infuse the new D/CIA. Granholm, of course, would not be a willing participant in telling lies to power, unless lies benefitted his political allies. Lies were antithetical to governing, Perry told himself, in particular when lies emanated from those whose sole purpose was to tell the truth. *I was wrong. We made a mistake. The President is incorrect in his assessment. Americans died because we were lazy, ineffective, stupid--or all three at once.* Congressman Perry yearned to hear those sorts of truths, but spies believed themselves entitled to lie to anyone and everyone.

"Mr. Mannheim, how long did you serve as Chief of CIC?"

Zachary Mannheim's Upper-Midwest accent emphasized his parents immigration from Germany after the Second World War. "Close enough to fifteen years, Mr. Santamaria."

"Was the aforementioned Fulton Bennett, now deceased, your friend? Did you lie or dissemble, prior or subsequent to his death, to save him criminal prosecution in the former instance and embarrassment in the latter?"

"Bennett wouldn't apply the word friend to a co-worker, Mr. Santamaria. He was prickly..." Mannheim scanned Congressmen who, with one exception, had witnessed Bennett's prickliness firsthand "...and difficult. We were colleagues. I admired his intellect and courage. I neither lied nor dissembled...though your choice of words is admirable...to protect Fulton Bennett from any accusation. Neither the man nor his professional behavior needed protection from CIC."

"Was Bennett guilty in the call-girl murder which preceded his own...or is assassination the proper descriptive in Bennett's case?"

"Fulton Bennett was assassinated, killed as the CIC report details, to lessen CIA's capabilities by eliminating a most experienced senior officer. Subcommittee Members are aware...the FBI investigation of the call girl's murder remains open. For the purposes of this hearing, I assure the Subcommittee the person responsible for the call-girl's callous murder and Fulton Bennett's assassination is, herself, dead. A Lebanese national with connections to both Sheikh Khalid bin Rahman and Hezbollah, she served as bin Rahman's second in command in the US. After ascending to primacy, she died in an exchange of gunfire with members of Her Britannic Majesty's Secret Services."

Irrelevant to today's proceedings, Mannheim's expected to someday pay a price for the single lie. He would pay the piper with no qualm of conscience.

D/CIA fought to hold his tongue. Nothing of Mannheim's revelation was part or parcel of CIC's report.

Santamaria recognized gold. "What was her name, Mr. Mannheim?"

"Fathima Laniado."

"Did she die on US soil?"

Mannheim noted the invitation to mask sensitive information; a slippery slope would be avoided. "She was shot in Virginia. Where she died, I couldn't say."

"Were you present at this exchange?"

"No."

"Who shot this thorn in the Agency's side, Mr. Mannheim?"

"She was shot by an officer of MI-6."

"Whose name is unknown?"

"For security reasons, the Subcommittee doesn't require the identity of a serving officer involved in lethal use of force. You know this all too well, Mr. Santamaria."

"Do you carry a weapon, Mr. Mannheim?"

"No."

"At any time during Bennett's black-op to expropriate bin Rahman's funds, was there an opportunity to kill Sheikh Khalid bin Rahman?"

"The Sheikh's elimination was never an established priority of the Agency, the Administration or this Subcommittee. Expropriation of bin Rahman's money was the goal and the Agency's triumph...demonstrated in its aftermath by public praise heaped on D/CIA Granholm and the Agency."

"What kill-order was Director Granholm referring to?"

"Not being a mind reader, I can only assume Director Granholm referenced the proposed elimination of Ms. Raissa Ribeiro, a then retired Agency field officer."

Santamaria bit his tongue from wanting to ask: *Aren't super-models as field officers a bit of a rarity?* He stayed on-point. "Proposed elimination?"

"The order to eliminate Ms. Ribeiro was not approved under oversight guidelines. So the order was unofficial and unauthorized, although two attempts at implementation were carried-out absent success."

"Did you, Mr. Mannheim, interfere with the order to eliminate Ms. Ribeiro?"

"In the course of CIC's investigation of Mr. Bennett...an investigation ordered and authorized in writing by D/CIA Granholm, former D/CIA Grover Norris acting as POTUS's representative, and CIA General Counsel Lattimore...CIC learned of the kill-order. No action, either active or passive, was taken by CIC to influence or deter the subject kill-order. I opposed the action, believing it illegal and, worse, misguided. I expressed my opinion on several occasions to the aforementioned Agency executives."

"Was Ms. Ribeiro cleared in the death of the Agency's field director?"

"Yes...the evidence of her innocence was quite demonstrable." Mannheim allowed himself a memory of Raissa's viral Internet videos, including the last one where her guiltlessness was proven live and in full color.

Santamaria believed half the world watched the videos--a nude Raissa accusing her *demons*-- and an unclothed faux-Raissa accusing an Arab Sheikh, a New York Banker and a Knighted British aristocrat of the crime-in-question.

"In what way did you obstruct, or represent an interest other than the government's, in negotiations to recover three billion dollars of terrorist money?"

"Those funds were in the absolute control of an American citizen...a Muslim American woman. Mr. Grover Norris threatened the woman with illegal detention and rendition unless she transferred control of those funds to the Agency. She insisted on certain conditions, including a half million-dollar cash payment to ransom her husband from a complicated, illegal instance of corporate and inter-governmental espionage. The matter time sensitive, I urged Mr. Norris the Older, and Mr. Norris the Younger to accept proposed terms...to not allow three billion terrorist dollars to hover in electronic limbo, where it might go poof. They agreed."

"A half million dollar payoff, Mr. Mannheim. How could such a payment be construed as legal?"

"It represented the cost of doing business. These types of payments aren't unusual as the Subcommittee knows better than anyone in government."

"Did you refuse any order of the D/CIA as it related to

investigating, or not investigating, current or past senior Agency officers?" Santamaria's tone carried a warning: *Here is the crux of the matter.*

"I could equivocate. I could tell the Subcommittee no such order ever issued from D/CIA...not in writing and not by inference. The presence of Ms. Pettigrew is fortunate, because she can, if questioned, testify there are no records of such a written order. Mr. Lattimore, whose absence is unfortunate, would be compelled by the canon of ethics to testify no verbal order was issued by D/CIA." Mannheim's opinion, relative to either Lattimore or Pettigrew's allegiance to the canon of ethics, needed no enhancement.

"Did you then investigate past or current senior Agency executives?"

"During CIC's authorized investigation of Director Bennett, information became available relating to financial transactions by Mr. Grover Norris which might have...could have...warranted further investigation, if authorized by D/CIA. Such additional authorization never materialized."

"What were these financial transactions?"

"I'm not at liberty to say, Mr. Santamaria."

"What do you mean, Mr. Mannheim? This Subcommittee requires you answer the question as asked."

"I can't answer, with all due respect."

Congressman Perry slammed the gavel. "You'll answer, sir. Right damned now."

Mannheim sat mute.

Granholm admired the stagecraft. Mannheim's absurd refusal—answering a question anyone who mattered knew the details of already—was an effective ruse which avoided the issue of Bennett's, or Mannheim's, role in stealing two billion of the three billion. Was the theft temporary? Yes, but they stole it nevertheless. Because Bennett was an outlaw, not a proper manager—a covert cowboy, like so many in the Agency's history.

At the far left of the dais, Congressman Emile Wright pulled a microphone close. "Mr. Chairman, I don't mean to interrupt esteemed Counsel's questioning...or your own Mr. Chairman...but might I ask one question? Just one, I promise."

Granholm's mouth went dry.

Congressman Emile Wright of Texas, a decorated veteran of Iraq, a former liaison to the Agency in Afghanistan and, from Granholm's point of view a loose cannon, was in his second term.

Chairman Perry, surprised and pleased by the interruption because of Emile Wright's on-again off-again friendship with CIA, presupposed this single question as a humdinger. "Congressman Wright, the floor is yours."

"Mr. Granholm, I'm in possession of information which troubles me. Who, sir, is Iraj Rashidi? Why is the Agency killing Iranian soldiers to protect him...while we sit here thumbs up our asses?"

www.ingramcontent.com/pod-product-compliance
Lightning Source LLC
Chambersburg PA
CBHW021530250626
47154CB00006BA/2043